time of the cat

An Annotated Adventure of Time Travel, Cats & Occasional Academia, with Endnotes

Tansy Rayner Roberts

Copyright © 2024 by Tansy Rayner Roberts

Cover art © 2024 Psycat Covers

Taking History Seriously illustration © 2023 Pepper Raccoon

Proofing by Earl Grey Editing & Isabel Dallas

KICKSTARTER EDITION

All rights reserved.

No part of this book may be reproduced in any form or by any electronic or mechanical means, including information storage and retrieval systems, without written permission from the author, except for the use of brief quotations in a book review.

Ebook ISBN: 978-0-6457025-2-1

Paperback ISBN: 978-0-6457025-3-8

Created with Vellum

For the iconic Valerie Forsyte, trailblazing woman of the film industry and the first producer of **Cramberleigh**: *a TV show so thoroughly excellent that no trace of it exists in this century.*

Also for her cats: Lambert and Terrance. >^..^<

contents

part one
chronos college

1. DON'T GET LOST — 3
2. DON'T LOSE YOUR CAT — 4
3. "IT'S AMAZING YOU CAN STILL SPEAK IN FULL SENTENCES." — 6
4. LOST MEDIA — 11
5. "HAVE YOU WATCHED IT?" — 14
6. CRAMBERLEIGH — 17
7. UNAIRED PILOT EPISODE — 22
8. INTRODUCING PROFESSOR BOSWELL — 30
9. LOST PROPERTY REPORT — 36
10. ADMIN IS NOT A DIRTY WORD — 38
11. "CRAMBERLEIGH, OF ALL PLACES." — 47
12. BOSWELL AND LOVELACE — 57
13. BOSWELL AND CRESSIDA — 61
    - Nowhere, The Kingdom of the East Angles, 512 CE — 61
    - Nowhere, The Kingdom of the East Angles, 612 CE — 65
    - Kechwic, The Kingdom of the East Angles, 712 CE — 66
    - Kettwic, The Kingdom of the East Angles, 812 CE — 67
    - Fenthorp Manor, Kettlewick, Norfolk, England, 1512 — 68

part two
the cramberleigh job

14. THE TRUTH ABOUT EVENTS	73
15. "WE'LL NEED A CREW."	76
16. "I HAVE IT ON GOOD AUTHORITY THAT THIS ADVENTURE IS NOT TECHNICALLY AGAINST ANY RULES."	86
17. THE ROSE GARDEN INCIDENT	92
Incident Report CRG-511-A — formal interview with Traveller Lakshmi Tunbridge, witness to events	92
Incident Report CRG-511-B — formal interview with Traveller Ptolemy, witness to events	93
Incident Report CRG-511-C — formal interview with Control Techs Alex Quant & Mawaan Khan, witnesses to events	93
Incident Report CRG-511-C — formal interview with Traveller Nero, witness to events	93
18. RUTHVEN IS NOT IN 1964	95
19. MONTEREY IS SOMEWHERE AFTER 1788	98
20. AT LEAST SOMEONE MADE IT TO 1964	104
21. RUTHVEN COULDN'T POSSIBLY BE IN 912	110
22. LOVELACE AT CRAMBERLEIGH	116
23. FLEUR SHROPSHIRE	123
24. RUTHVEN IS WELL AND TRULY OVER 912	126
25. "YOU'RE GOING TO HAVE TO FORGET EVERYTHING YOU KNOW ABOUT TIME TRAVEL."	130
26. THE ANACHRONAUTS	138
27. SKULKING IN THE SCULLERY	140
28. CLEOPATRA CALLING	147
29. KETTLEWICK, 912	154

part three
everywhere but 912

30. **THE ANACHRONAUTS ANNUAL FESTIVE FUNCTION 1899** — 159
    always prepare for uninvited guests
31. **48 BCE** — 174
    Cleo vs Cressida
32. **1978** — 177
    keep partying until it's 1979
33. **1923** — 188
    party like it's...
34. **48 BCE** — 197
    Lovelace Smells Something Fishy
35. **1215 & 2034** — 205
    "I can't remember what I had for lunch yesterday."
36. **1526** — 216
    further back than you might think
37. **2034** — 220
    "Before Monterey. Before Cressida."
38. **24TH CENTURY PARANOIA** — 226
39. **2034** — 227
    "It's always about lost media for you, isn't it?"
40. **1969** — 232
    "Don't tell me you don't have the jade pineapple either?"
41. **THE ANSWER** — 239
42. **1664** — 240
    Party of the Delights
43. **BASIC TIME** — 249
44. **ELSEWHERE IN THE 24TH CENTURY** — 255

part four
the future

45. **THE ANNE BOLEYN INCIDENT** — 265
    Transcript from the undisclosed surveillance recording outside the Second Reading Room, Museum of Lost Things, Chronos College. — 265

46. CELLMATES	270
47. THE MATTER OF THE JADE PINEAPPLE	279
Transcript from the Trial of Nero, Banksia (in absentia) and Aesop (in absentia). Location: Theatre of Justice, 2912. Broadcast live across Mewtopia. Judicial Administrator Felicitas presiding.	279
48. THIRTIETH CENTURY CATASTROPHE	286
trial of the century	
49. THE MATTER OF THE VIOLET SUNFLOWER	294
50. THE MUSEUM OF LOST THINGS	302
51. MEET THE PROFESSORS	310
52. AESOP	321
53. THE END OF TIME TRAVEL	334
54. A CONVERSATION IN THE OFFICE OF PROFESSOR BOSWELL	337
55. HERE'S TO THE FUTURE	340
Historical Events and Those Responsible	347
Cramberleigh: Production Guide	351
Bonus Kickstarter Thank You Page	373
Isn't Everyone Obsessed with Lost Media?	381
by Tansy Rayner Roberts	
About the Author	397
Also by Tansy Rayner Roberts	399

part one
chronos college

one
don't get lost

Dear Boz

Wish you were here. Wish you were here. Wish you were here.

Wish this postcard was working. What's the point of a call for rescue that doesn't pick up?

Nothing works. My opal's not working. This stylus clearly doesn't work— this is the fourteenth message I have written you.

No rescue. No hope. No cat.

I wish that I knew you were safe. (I wish I knew I was safe.) I hope you're doing better without me than I'm doing without you.

Always your partner in crime,
Cressida

> Fragment discovered at Fenthorp Manor during minor archaeological excavation, early 30th century. Origin unknown. Materials unknown. Author unknown. Probably nothing to worry about.

two
don't lose your cat

The secret to time travel is cats. A secret so devastatingly unlikely, it's no wonder it took humanity so long to catch on. Once we did finally crack that tricky corner of theoretical chrono-physics, time was our oyster.

Or, at least, our squeaky mouse toy.

Fact the first: A human cannot travel through time (except the most dull and predictable form of time travel, 1:1 ratio moving forward) without a cat by their side.

Fact the second: Cats may travel wherever they like, including through time, regardless of human company. According to most cats.

Fact the third: in 99 out of 100 time experiments, cats travelling in time without a human at their side ended up... well, no one can say for certain where they ended up. But it wasn't back home, that's for sure.

History is silent on whether or not this was intentional; cats, of course, claim that everything they do is intentional.

On the whole, it is best to accept that the proper method for safe and efficient time travel is by means of an equal partnership: one human, one cat.

The greatest danger in time travel is not treading on a

butterfly or accidentally having sexual congress with one's grandparent. It is losing one's feline travelling companion along the way.

Bathsheba Tonkins.

The Human Time Traveller's
Almanac of Practical Advice
First Edition published 2384 CE
Second Edition published 1066 AD
Third Edition published 10,000 BCE
Fourth Edition published next Thursday

three
"it's amazing you can still speak in full sentences."

RUTHVEN HATED THIS PART: when the time travellers returned. Every brick and pane of Chronos College vibrated as the portals in the quad hummed back into life.

Students and staff gathered to watch the spectacle: giant hooped ovals brimming with oceanic light, cresting, bubbling...

Finally, the travellers appeared: humans in their shabby, travel-worn costumes, accompanied by cats looking exhausted and smug. Cats and humans, humans and cats. A little charred, perhaps, a little worse for wear. Proud as punch. Why not? They had the best job in the world, and they'd all come home alive. Together.

Ruthven knew exactly what it was like, to be one of them. But that was long ago.

Before he lost his cat.

Normally, Ruthven would concentrate on his work so as to conveniently ignore the return of the travellers until the footage from their travels cascaded into his in-tray. He had a particularly good digital recording of *Midsomer Murders* Season 85 to re-colour before he uploaded it to the media archive.[1]

He had many other excuses, lined up and ready to pull out if he needed them.

But Oxford was due back today, and while Ruthven had become a bitter and cynical recluse in recent years, he was also trying to be (where possible) a half-decent friend. That meant showing up to witness your friend's victory lap.

Reluctantly, he put his work on hold and headed out of the dank recording suite to face the blazing sunshine of the quad. It was noisy, of course, and far too bright.[2] He strolled past the statue of Cressida Church with her perfect hair and form-fitting medieval gown. He angled his head as he always did so he didn't have to look at the other, smaller marble statue nearby, of a heroic-looking calico cat, lost too soon.

If a physical description of Elliot Ruthven would be helpful at this juncture, consider the platonic ideal of a Byronic hero, wrapped in a futuristic jumpsuit and a thin layer of insecurities.[3]

If asked to describe him, the majority of Ruthven's colleagues at Chronos College would use the word 'intense,' possibly attached to the clauses 'way too' and 'don't you think?'

He wasn't popular, which did not bother him in the least. The only human he ever wanted to impress was about to step through one of the time hoops in the quad.

Humming. Cresting. Swirling. Bubbles.

As the travellers emerged from the time hoops, the crowd converged upon them. Professors, well-wishers, students who hadn't yet lost their heady enthusiasm about the coolest academic specialty ever, datemates. Ruthven might as well have not bothered. No way Oxford would think to look for him in all this chaos...

"*There* you are!" Oxford loomed over him, dusty and dishevelled but basically perfect. He was a tall man with sandy hair, blue eyes and the kind of stupid handsomeness that was especially fashionable in the early twentieth century during activities involving boating and cricket.

Oxford's partner Nero, a snooty and extremely fluffy white cat, lay sprawled over one of his broad shoulders, too busy and important to walk anywhere under his own steam.[4] Oxford, as ever, showed no objection to being treated like cat furniture. He turned his entire attention on Ruthven. It was like being caught in a spotlight made of sunshine. "You wouldn't believe how hot it gets in Egypt."

"Careful," said Ruthven, smiling up at his friend. He couldn't help it. His natural state was morose and brooding, but as soon as he stood in Oxford's presence, he found himself warm with happiness. He couldn't even be embarrassed about it because Oxford had that effect on everyone. "Don't go leaking any details before you put in your formal report. Melusine will have your head."

"Pish tosh," said Oxford airily.

Ruthven's eyes narrowed. "They haven't let you near the 1930s again, have they? Your vocabulary has gone a bit vintage."

"It will wear off. Besides, I was in the 80s this time. Hung around with some terribly English writers in Egyptian cafes."

"English writers abroad? That's worse! It's amazing you can still speak in full sentences." Ruthven paused. "The 1980s?" he added in a small, hopeful voice.

"Yesssss," said Oxford, looking like... well, the time traveller who got the cream.

His cat Nero cracked an eyelid open. "Stop flirting and get on with it," he rumbled. "Melusine hates it when we're late to report in. She might cancel my shore leave."

Oxford blushed furiously, for no reason that Ruthven

could guess at. "Sorry, Nero, were we interrupting your vital napping plans?"

"Clearly. Give the lad the tape and let's get on with our debrief."

Ruthven gave a start. It was too early in the day to have his hopes raised so suddenly. "Tape?" he mouthed.

Oxford winked, in a manner he probably thought was covert and subtle. "Good to be back," he said, and went in for the hug. Oxford's hugs were rather like being pleasantly assaulted by an armchair, if that armchair also had a swishy cat perching irritably upon it.

Ruthven felt the slight pressure of a hand on his pocket, and something slipping inside. Too light to be a VHS or Betamax tape. "Did you actually —" he said in disbelief.

"Shh," said Oxford, his lips brushing Ruthven's ear. "Don't distract me. Don't you know I have a report to make?"

He strolled off, whistling while being handsome. Several nearby undergrads sighed romantically as he went past them. Nero rode upon Oxford's shoulders like a Napoleonic soldier on horseback. His white tail swished behind them both, and a trail of soft white hairs fell like breadcrumbs in a forest.

Ruthven poked his hand into his pocket, and felt the unmistakeable circle of glass between his fingertips. A chronocle. "You unbelievable bastard," he muttered under his breath. To his annoyance, it came out sounding fond.

---

1. Season 85 of *Midsomer Murders* screened internationally in late 2084, and is generally considered by fans to be the last decent season before the show really started to run out of steam.
2. It was not real sunshine. There was no reason at all for the brightness dial to be turned up so high on a space station, but someone was a little too pleased with their environmental controls. That person was Debby. Don't worry about Debby. She has her own stuff going on.
3. Ruthven had the cheekbones of a villain, the brooding stare of a poet, and a mild allergy to sunshine, artificial or otherwise. Also, dark hair

falling into his eyes, making him look mysterious. Add to this a sort of tragic air, caused by the loss of his feline companion three years previously, and the overall effect would have been romantically devastating if one had never met him. Sadly for Ruthven, Chronos College was a closed community, and opportunities to be perceived as a mysterious stranger were few and far between.
4. Oxford could never wear dark colours, thanks to Nero's constant shedding. Luckily, he looked good in cream and white. And everything, probably.

four
lost media

As all media collectors know, the twin enemy of preserving any kind of filmed media is 1) time, and 2) format. Anyone who has, for example, spent many hours of babysitting money on precious VHS tapes in their teens, only to see that format replaced over and over by cheaper, more robust options as the decades fly past, knows that the only thing worse than having to re-buy all of your favourite shows is when your favourite shows are finally too obscure to make it over to whatever the cool new media storage widget is.[1]

Then there were the content massacres of the Streaming Wars in the mid twenty-first century, which taught a whole generation that you can't take for granted your favourite show will always be there, in its entirety, at your fingertips. Even piracy has its limits.

Time travellers obsessed with vintage media have it particularly tough.[2] Most people have one lifespan's worth of media platform updates to take on the chin, and a finite number of stories to which they might get unreasonably attached. Time travellers have access to many centuries of weird cult TV shows, old timey music, obscure arthouse films, and multi-media injectibles.

Combine a completionist personality with access to time travel, and that individual may never have a moment's peace.

Then there is the tragic fact that most media formats are incompatible with being physically transported through time. Even when multiple cats are involved.[3]

Luckily, the recent invention of the chronocle solved many of these problems. This cunning little device not only has the ability to upload store huge amounts of data from various antiquated platforms and devices, but it has the added benefit that it looks like a small circle of glass, and not an obviously clunky technological anachronism.[4]

The downside, of course, is how often these very expensive devices get accidentally broken or lost due to someone attempting humorously to wear a chronocle as a monocle. Time travellers are the worst.

> Zadie Kincaid, *A Rough Guide To Time Travel*

---

1. What do you even do with all those outdated VHS tapes and dodgy audio cassettes? Throw them away? Don't you know they were *worth something* in the 90s? No, obviously hanging on to them makes sense. Just in case there's some kind of media apocalypse wiping out all digital media and leaving a small community of survivalists with no hardware but perfectly functional VHS players. All very logical, nothing to see here.
2. Which is to say, 98% of them; vintage media is a known gateway drug for potential time travellers. If you've ever daydreamed about travelling back in time to read, view or listen to something that is not currently available in your timeline… you're a possible candidate. Have you considered applying to Chronos College? They're always looking for capable, enthusiastic young people. Though 'always' does refer to a specific couple of decades during the twenty-fourth century.
3. Yes, they tested this. The trick was finding enough cats who had strong opinions about the early seasons of *Doctor Who*, and were willing to join the experiment on the off chance of saving the lost episodes of

"Marco Polo." Sadly, the experiment only salvaged ten minutes or so of an episode of "The Space Pirates" which hadn't even been lost in the first place.

4. For a reference on why the latter is a bad idea, check out the monograph by Montague J Monterey on how he almost got arrested in Ancient Rome by dressing up as a flute girl and trying to smuggle a camcorder into a religious party hosted by Caesar's wife.

five
"have you watched it?"

BACK IN THE RECORDING SUITE, Ruthven slotted the glass disc into his retroplayer and waited for the familiar opening credits to flick up on to the screen.

To his left, the terminals of the Media Archive lit up with pings and notification sweeps as the footage from today's returning time travellers poured into the system. This was the best part of his job, usually — getting first eyes (apart from the travellers themselves, jammy bastards) on whole new vistas of history. He might not get to experience it in person any more, but he got to watch it and file it, which was almost as cool.

Today, Ruthven didn't even glance at the notifications. He could file vital snippets of Monterey and Lovelace swashbuckling their way through their aesthetically pleasing shenanigans tomorrow.[1] He was far more interested in seeing which lost episode of their favourite ancient TV show Oxford had managed to smuggle home to the twenty-fourth century.

Ruthven frowned as the janky electro sounds of the 80s revival theme tune flooded the small space. *Return to Cramberleigh*? Why on earth would Oxford think he cared about one of these dreadful late 80s reboot episodes? Unlike the original run, these had been recovered pretty much in their entirety by fans in the early years of time travel. 38 out of 39 episodes were logged and archived, and the only one missing was a clip show.[2] You could watch your *Return to Cramberleigh* episode of choice on any wall screen in the college. You could remix them, revoice them and consume the karaoke versions as jelly chewables.

The usual credit sequence played out, showcasing the main cast from 1985: Lady Cradoc, Bones the butler, Sheena Swythe, Dead Desmond. All the usual suspects glammed up with their enormous fringes and shoulder pads to make the show seem more relevant.

Then the episode's title card came up: Blast From the Past. Ruthven stilled, eyes locked on the screen. It couldn't be. Could it?

Clip show.

Ruthven didn't see Oxford again until the canteen. He had just sat down with his tray (soup of the day, bread roll, pouch of juice) when his friend appeared, changed from his stripes and boater hat into the generic Chronos College jumpsuit that most people wore around campus. The garment was comfortable, robust, and somehow both stretchy and tweedy at the same time. It looked like a librarian had been asked to design a yoga outfit for a professor of archaeology.

Naturally, Oxford transcended this generally unflattering garment, because he was incapable of looking bad in anything. He bounded across the canteen now, collected his food (somehow his smile earned him double portions even though it was a literal robot distributing the trays) and flung himself carelessly into a chair opposite Ruthven. "Well?" he demanded, glowing with enthusiasm. "Have you watched it?"

"Waited for you," Ruthven lied.

Oxford's face broke into an even wider-than-usual grin. "Liar," he said. "Is it amazing?"

"It's interesting."

"Tell me everything."

"Have *you* watched it?" Ruthven countered.

"When would I have had time?"

"If it screened live while you were there..."

"Nah, I scanned it off a VHS tape I found lying around. Does it really use footage from the unaired pilot?"

"Fragments," Ruthven admitted. "Cobbled together with a bunch of clips of a dying Lady Cradoc reminiscing with Bones the Butler about the good old days. Never mind that he wasn't even in the pilot episode..."

Oxford cheered. "Screening party, yes? Tonight!"

"I haven't checked the whole thing for grading errors," Ruthven protested.

Oxford leaned in. His eyes really were exceptionally blue. "Screening party. Tonight."

As if Ruthven could say no to that face.

---

1. For sheer entertainment value, Ruthven had learned to watch Monterey and Lovelace first. If for no other reason than to mentally prepare himself for the truly astonishing anecdotes they were likely to be relaying in the pub all week.
2. Note for those born later than the 1990s: a clip show is an artefact of twentieth century television production in the pre-internet era, when TV was largely assumed to be ephemeral. This budget-friendly episode format traditionally involved a small number of cast members reminiscing about past events, as illustrated by repeated film clips from previous episodes. The tradition died out thanks to easy access media, when viewers were assumed to be binge-watching their favourite shows on a constant digital loop, and very much up-to-date on that one time someone did something amusing with a stuffed turkey, or a cream bun.

six
cramberleigh

IN THE TWENTY-FOURTH CENTURY, if you happened to be residing at Chronos College (one of three universities featuring an active time travel operation, built on space stations orbiting the Earth), the one thing you could be certain of was everyone you met was likely to be obsessed with a twentieth century TV show called *Cramberleigh*.

All episodes had been wiped from television archives in 1989, in a terrorist attack by a group calling themselves the Anachronauts. For many fans who were not born until centuries later, this was the seed of their obsession. No one would care as much if the episodes were easy to find.

Cramberleigh began as a period piece: an Edwardian drawing room family drama airing between 1965-1971. It followed the family of Sir Victor Wildegreen, a cranky patriarch and serial widower with an assortment of creepy children, doomed wives, charming step-children, and interfering elderly aunts.

Once every possible drop of melodrama had been wrung out of the suffragettes, the sinking of the Titanic, the War Years and the Spanish flu, *Cramberleigh* was reinvented as a quirky Roaring Twenties sci-fi show from 1972-1975, which included the Season With The Carnivorous Plants, the Season with the Invasion From Mars, the Season With the Vampires, and (most beloved of twenty-fourth century operatives) the Season with the Time Travellers.

The 1975 (Time Travellers) season featured such wonders as a baking Boudicca and a rakish Rasputin. It concluded with an explosion which rocked the Wildegreen household, apparently killing everyone. When *Cramberleigh* returned in 1976, a drastic reboot saw four survivors of the explosion thrown forward in time to the present day. They set themselves to solving murders, battling foreign spies and disarming killer robots until the show was finally cancelled in 1978.

The show was briefly revived in the 1980s gothic melodrama *Tales from Cramberleigh* (1982), a single anthology season of tele-movies featuring many of the original cast, set across a variety of time periods and cramming in every supernatural and historical drama trope you might imagine: demonic possession, ghost smugglers, werewolf suffragettes, portal travel through the multiverse, and a cyborg Queen Victoria.

Finally, between 1984-1986, there was the cheaply made and critically reviled (later reclaimed and ironically adored) final reboot: *Return to Cramberleigh*. In this version of the show, the most popular fan favourite characters were all alive again, trapped alongside their own modern-day descendants (each actor playing multiple roles), in the original manor, now submerged beneath the earth's surface thanks to a freak timequake.

The budget was halved, the plots were impenetrable, and the 80s fashions were eye-watering. The whole thing came across as harshly over-lit experimental theatre done on the cheap in someone's living room. The dialogue was arch and sarcastic enough to entertain a small core fandom... who themselves were also this version of the show's worst critics.

Collecting and restoring lost episodes of *Cramberleigh* was a favourite hobby of time travellers, if their work should happen to take them to the relevant decades. (1969, 1978 and 1989 were sadly inaccessible thanks to Anachronaut-caused Events, but most of the *Cramberleigh* broadcast window of 1964-1977 and 1982-1986 were fair game.)[1]

There were still quite a few gaps left in the Chronos College collection of episodes. Every now and then, a traveller was able to smuggle a new piece of lost media back on to campus, where they found a hungry audience ready to consume the missing episode like the Ancient Romans hanging out for one more lion-eats-centurion water cooler moment.

Ruthven was a little taken aback when he first learned that nearly the entire student body at Chronos College was obsessed with the same obscure, centuries-old piece of dodgy costume drama that he had been fanboying over since he was a kid. He was used to *Cramberleigh* being his thing, shared only with the occasional fellow enthusiast on a vintage media forum.

He had not been prepared for the handsome and popular Oxford to befriend him on their first day by showering Ruthven in compliments about his Cousin Henry's Terrible Fate enamel pin like that was a normal thing to display on your jumpsuit. He had not been prepared for every other student of their intake class to nod like they knew what Oxford was talking about.

Ruthven did not know how to like things that other people also liked. The whole concept was bewildering. But he didn't know how to abandon *Cramberleigh*. So he fell into... being friends with the most popular student in his year, and having something in common with the entire student body.

Then, three years ago, Ruthven lost his cat and his ability to time travel in one terrible day. He was transferred to the Media Archives, which meant being unofficially in charge of the repository of lost-and-found episodes. It rebranded him as the resident *Cramberleigh* expert.

Without *Cramberleigh*, Ruthven might have become completely untethered from campus life, wrapping himself up in his misery while everyone else was off having adventures. But it was hard to be a complete loner when your sad little cave was constantly being interrupted by randoms who wanted to remind you how many episodes were left, to chat about whether more would ever be found, and to rant about how suspicious it was that no one had ever reclaimed even a single frame of Season 3.[2]

Once you'd watched the Season with the Carnivorous Plants for the fourteenth time, you had to embrace your identity as a true fan. A diehard Cramberry.[3] Ruthven couldn't roll his eyes in judgement at the obsessive tendencies of everyone around him, not with the number of facts he had personally memorised about long-dead British actors just because they had non-speaking roles in The Season with the Vampires.

He could, on occasion, roll his eyes in judgement at himself.

He was doing it right now.

Settle down, it's just an old TV show.

Unaired footage of your favourite old TV show.

Which Oxford just presented to you like he's a cat dropping a delicious dead mouse on your doorstep.

Maybe it's OK to get a little excited.

---

1. It was generally assumed by experts that the Event in 1969 was due to the terrorists attempting to prevent the Moon Landing, or at least attempting to hide all actual evidence that there was a Moon Landing. Others theorised that it was because the Anachronauts wanted free rein to attend Woodstock without interruption.
2. Monterey's conspiracy theory about the Mysteriously Missing Season 3 was thirty pages long in a double-spaced document. He had attempted to submit it as a chapter of his graduating thesis. At which point, the Board of Chronos College achieved their first ever unanimous vote in committee by banning *Cramberleigh* as an academic topic. When challenged by students, Professor Harpo of the Chronological History department threatened to put all classic British television under the same ban, and the protest was dropped. Pressure from the local chapter of the *Blake's 7* Appreciation Society was never proven.
3. Various alternative names for the *Cramberleigh* fandom had been mooted, adopted and discarded by fans over the years, including Cramberbitches, Cramberpeeps and Cramberlumberjacks. Ruthven would have quite liked Crambutlers, but it never caught on.

seven
unaired pilot episode

THE TROUBLE with being Oxford's friend was that Oxford was friends with *everyone*. He attracted people like time travel attracted cats.

When Oxford threw a party, there were no limits.

To be fair, he did actually take physics into account with his party planning for this particular shindig, which necessitated a last-minute venue change from the dorms to Professor Mycroft's rooms. Because of course, the professors all loved Oxford too. He and Monterey were both sons of Founders, and thus were treated by longer-serving staff members as something halfway between honorary nephews, and college mascots.

Professor Mycroft was a cheery, rotund sort of fellow, well-liked by the students. No one remembered a time when he had not been in residence in the Department of Practical History.[1]

Mycroft's comfortable suite was heaving with students, professors, travellers and cats by the time Ruthven turned up to the viewing party with the chronocle safely stored in his jumpsuit pocket.[2]

"Rrrrrreally the unaired pilot?" asked Lovelace, an

Abyssinian short-hair whose notorious time travelling exploits had made her a local icon.

Ruthven's cat, Aesop, had been good friends with Lovelace, whom she looked up to as something of a mentor. She always acted so casual in Lovelace's stately presence, then squealed afterwards with Ruthven about how cool she was.

Damn, he missed Aesop so much.

"Fragments," he said now, in response to Lovelace's question. "It's a clip show, so it's certainly not all of it, but it's the only footage of the unaired pilot that we're ever likely to see."

"Good enough for me," sniffed the cat.

The humans had gone all out with Cramberleigh cosplay, aided and abetted by Fenella from Costume.[3]

Ruthven had never spent much time with Fenella. The only thing he knew about her was that she had never been partnered with a cat. No tragic backstory: she simply had not been issued one upon graduation due to an administrative error currently in its fourth year and counting.

It wasn't that he avoided her exactly, but it irritated Ruthven that everyone assumed they must be great friends because of their mutual lack of feline companionship.

If a physical description of Fenella would be helpful at this juncture, imagine an extremely petite young woman, with dark hair in a pixie cut, and unnaturally large eyes like someone who had fallen out of the Silent Movie era. She constantly flitted back and forth in wild, quick movements, and always had several pairs of scissors and a spool of thread somewhere about her person.

Fenella's relationship to her old school sewing machine, despite the availability of far more sophisticated garment printing technology, was similar to Ruthven's own interest in vintage media players… yes, all right. He could see why everyone thought they should be friends.

In any case, Ruthven had little reason to visit the costume

department these days, so avoiding Fenella (or not avoiding her, as the case may be) was largely out of his hands. He was no longer a time traveller, and he rarely attended the sort of parties where a costume was expected.

He hadn't planned to dress up tonight, but as soon as he entered Professor Mycroft's suite, Oxford and Fenella pounced upon him. Somehow, he ended up wearing a top hat.

"Won't it block everyone's view?" Ruthven protested meekly. Fenella had already darted away with an armful of cravats and shawls for other party guests who had failed to put in the appropriate costuming effort. Somehow, she had figured out Ruthven would not say no to Oxford.

It disturbing to be known so well by someone he barely knew.

"It won't block anyone's view," said Oxford, who had done himself up in bowler hat and suit, just like the debonair Mr Knight from the Seventies Spy Hijinks era of the show (1976-1978). "You're going to sit at the back and not talk to anyone. Might as well look good doing it."

Oxford said things like that all the time. Ruthven couldn't even resent it, because he knew Oxford didn't have a bitchy bone in his body. He was being *genuine*.

What a dick.

The screening was about as chaotic as Ruthven expected. Drinking, laughing, hushing each other, making fun of the terrible 80s fashions, and commenting loudly on the differences between these scenes from the unaired pilot, awkwardly sandwiched into the episode as a series of flashbacks, and the 'canon' version from 1965.

The fact that the maid was called Gladys in the early

footage and not Gladioli had everyone so excited that Oxford paused the show for five whole minutes.

Lady Ann's slightly different hairstyle almost caused a riot.[4]

Ruthven had taken precautions against being annoyed by the distracting antics of the fannish crowd by watching the episode twice ahead of the party, and uploading a short but pithy article to the Cramberries fan forum.

He had not been paying enough attention. That became obvious very quickly.

"Wait," said Oxford loudly, spitting out a mouthful of cucumber sandwich. "Is that?"

"Pause it," gasped Lovelace, leaping up on the back of the padded couch. She arched her back in a menacing silhouette.

"No claws on the furniture, please," said Professor Mycroft in a long-suffering tone.

It was Monterey who moved first. He was wearing a replica of the same dressing gown worn by Sir Victor Wildegreen in the 1972 episode "Why Didn't The Petunias Eat Evans?" Ruthven had been coveting it all evening.

If a physical description of Montgomery J Monterey would be helpful at this juncture, imagine a bright-eyed gentleman of warm brown complexion and dark curly hair. Monterey had a taste for the finer things in life: silk dressing gowns, designer suits, and vintage port. He was a little shorter and stouter than was fashionable in the twenty-fourth century, but a perfect fit for the nineteenth century and earlier, depending on the theatricality of the relevant crowd.[5]

Monterey was vaguely senior to most of the active travellers, and liked to pretend he was decades older than the rest of them. In fact, thanks to an early start and a pinch of nepotism, he was only two years older than Ruthven and Oxford. As a traveller paired with Lovelace, Monterey was a slapdash maniac who constantly left disaster in his wake, while remaining unruffled.

He was ruffled right now. Practically wild-eyed. Monterey bent over the media player, winding it back frame by frame, then going too far, snapping irritably at Oxford when he tried to help.

For anyone to snap at Oxford wasn't just a warning sign, it was practically an emergency siren. Something was very, very wrong.

Ruthven shuffled closer to Fenella, who could usually be relied on for gossip. "Do you know what's going on?"

He was trying to remember what was in this particular scene to cause this level of commotion. It featured Lady Ann meeting her new husband's horrible Aunt Phyllida (Lady Cradoc) for the first time, outside the greenhouse. Like most of the scenes from the pilot, it was mostly interesting because it was a location shoot.[6]

Fenella turned to look at him, and oh — she looked upset. Her enormous eyes were larger than usual. Tears prickled on the edges of her long lashes. Starting a conversation with her had been a terrible mistake, but it was too late to back out now. "Ruthven," she said, her lip trembling. "You didn't do anything to that footage, did you?"

"Do anything?"

"*You* know," said Fenella. "You didn't just edit something into that episode to be an arsehole. As a prank, or something."

The thought of editing anything else into that chaotic jigsaw of an episode was beyond belief. It was a clip show from the 80s, using footage from the 60s. Hadn't it suffered enough?

One part of her accusation stood out. "Do people think I'm an arsehole?"

Fenella didn't answer him, too busy sniffling into her sleeve.

"THERE," roared Monterey, almost tackling Oxford to the floor to get him out of the way.

"Ohhh," said Ruthven, finally realising what they were all going on about. "That's shot where the sound operators are caught adjusting their boom mike. They never edited it out of the original pilot episode because they'd run out of money. Kind of hilarious that when they edited those fragments into the 80s episode, they left in. I guess at that point the only people watching were obsessive fans... like us?"[7]

Ruthven trailed off because everyone was looking at him impatiently. "What?"

"That," said Fenella, pointing a dramatic finger at the frozen black and white image of the paused video. There were two sound operators in that slightly blurry shot — a faceless man, and a blonde woman with big hair. "That's *Cressida*."

Ruthven felt his whole body go very cold. "It can't be," he said weakly. "The resolution isn't that good — are you sure?"

Cressida Church. He knew what she looked like, of course. He used to see her at a distance, in his early student days, before her tragic disappearance. He'd watched plenty of vid footage of her travels since then, and he was used to walking past that honking great statue of her in the quad. He hadn't been looking for her when he previewed this grainy black and white film footage. He had been paying more attention to the boom mike itself, trying to figure out what make and model it was.

One didn't turn on an episode of centuries-old television expecting to spot a lost time traveller. Now Ruthven came to think of it, he was surprised it didn't happen more often.

Monterey stood up to his full height, somewhere around Oxford's shoulder, looking murderous. "1964," he growled. "She's in fucking 1964."

"How is that even possible?" hissed Lovelace. "It's not even the right century."

Fenella did burst into tears then, heaving noisily into her hands. Tunbridge went to her side to comfort her. Ruthven tried to step discreetly away.

Oxford stood up slowly, looking grave. Nero, sensing a speech was about to happen, leaped dramatically on to his human's shoulder. "I hate to say it," Oxford said. "But we need to speak to Admin."

Everyone in the room was shocked. Speaking to Admin was the absolute last resort for most problems, but for Oxford it was practically against his religion.

"Worse than that, old man," said Monterey, folding his arms. "We need to speak to Professor Boswell."

Lovelace sighed. "You mean I need to," she corrected him.

"Yes," Monterey agreed firmly. "People who are not me need to speak to Professor Boswell."

---

1. Practical History focused on social traditions, etiquette and how to figure out the safest possible conversation topic in any given century. The discipline, developed mostly by Professor Mycroft himself, was largely concerned with how to bluff your way through short visits to a century without giving away the fact that you were a time traveller. Mycroft's tests were legendary, designed to build what he liked to call 'robust historical reflexes.' He had been known to leap out of bushes shouting questions like "Fourteenth century France, snuff or no snuff?" and "It's 1794, have you read the latest Jane Austen?"
2. Ruthven could not pull off the tweedy jumpsuit look nearly as well as Oxford, but people looked askance at you if you walked around the fake sunshiney quad of Chronos College wearing all black, and of all things Ruthven most preferred to be unobtrusive.
3. Cats, of course, are too dignified for cosplay.
4. Fleur Shropshire, the iconic actress who played Lady Ann Wildegreen from 1964-1968 until her character died during the sinking of the Titanic, actually inspired three hairstyle related riots during her short but epic life. This was not one of them.
5. Monterey was a man of many talents. Always somehow managing to find a theatrical crowd who appreciated his charm was one of them. His other top talents included: poaching a perfect egg every time, tying knots, choosing flattering outfits for himself and others, close-up magic

tricks, pick-pocketing, and French kissing. He also had excellent handwriting, though this was not quite as good as his poached eggs.
6. Most early 1960s television drama was shot on video, in long single takes as if they were running a play. *Cramberleigh* tried to do things a little differently. The original pilot was almost filmed on location at a genuine historic manor instead of in the cheaper studio set versions of the same house to which they reluctantly moved the following year. The unaired pilot retained something of a mythical status among the more devout Cramberries.
7. For decades it was believed that using footage from the 1964 unaired pilot instead of the 1965 broadcast pilot in "Blast From The Past" (1985) was an error, or an ill-advised attempt to avoid paying an extra Equity fee for using so many flashback scenes in one episode. However, the later-published production diary of Jay T. Dee, the executive producer of *Return to Cramberleigh,* made it clear that this had been a deliberate creative choice "to f**k with the nerds."

eight
introducing professor boswell

THE MARMALADE TABBY glared into the lecture hall of undergrads from his position on the tilted lectern. First years. They didn't know enough to be intimidated by him yet. Some of them probably thought he was adorable.

There was nothing more frustrating to a grumpy old professor than being stuck in the body of a glossy-coated cat with big eyes and soft fur just crying out to be petted.

Petting him would be a mistake many students would regret. He might be in a position of authority over them, but that didn't mean he would hesitate to bite.

"Future travellers!" the tabby boomed, using nothing but natural projection with a hint of ominous vibrato for good measure.[1] "This year, we will delve into the inner mysteries of time itself. Please keep your questions to the end. Over the next hour, I will provide you with an exhaustive timeline of the Chronomancial Sciences, and the development of rudimentary mechanics, engineering and natural philosophy in relation to time travel. You will take notes. There will be an exam. I shall not inform you ahead of time when your exam will take place, so I do not recommend that you absent yourself from class without prior notice and an exceedingly good excuse."

That had them wide awake and scribbling on their tablets. Nothing like a little student terror to make one feel alive.

"I am Professor Boswell," pronounced the marmalade tabby, twitching his whiskers in a self-satisfied manner. "I am your worst nightmare. Let us begin."

After the first lecture of the new semester, Professor Boswell had plans. Very important plans involving the staff room, a saucer of tea, and a short nap in an extremely time-specific sunbeam.

He was, therefore, not the least bit pleased to be waylaid by a disreputable assortment of former students.

He recognised them all, of course. Nero, that fluffy white buffoon who thought himself the intellectual superior to literally everyone. Clement Oxford, Nero's human. Eliot Ruthven, a rather gloomy figure whom Boswell remembered as an enthusiastic essay writer with a solid knack for comprehensive citation. Fenella Church, whom Boswell had taken great pains to avoid for years. He saw no reason to break that habit now... even looking at her gave him a headache. Perhaps it was the particularly virulent shade of green eyeshadow she wore, or her matching boots.

"Excuse me," Boswell rumbled in a purr intended to rattle the nerves of his unwanted visitors. "I don't believe you have an appointment. Perhaps you could return after semester is over and I am on holiday, somewhere far from here."

The humans all looked appropriately intimidated. This usually gave Boswell a glow of satisfaction. Right now, with his favourite sunbeam slowly disgorging its peak warmth into an ungrateful piece of carpet, he felt nothing but irritated.

Fenella stepped aside, and *Lovelace* of all cats wound around the girl's ankles before stalking directly up to Boswell. Her deep amber eyes glowed with utter contempt.

"Stop fucking around, Boswell," she snarled. "This is important. Believe it or not, you care about what we're about to tell you. So let's go somewhere private."

Even Boswell at his grumpiest knew better than to cross Lovelace.[2]

They did not go to the staffroom. Too many opportunities to be interrupted, and Boswell knew that once he caught sight of the dying light of his favourite sunbeam, he would not be able to listen to a word they had to say.

Since it was Lovelace asking, he broke another ingrained habit and allowed this rabble into his inner sanctum: his office. It was a point of pride to Boswell that not one student had ever been allowed over the threshold.

These weren't students. They were graduates, which was worse.

"No Monterey?" Boswell asked, leaping up on to his desk as the two cats and three humans squashed themselves inside his office. It might be considered roomy quarters for a cat-sized professor were it not for the towering piles of books which filled most of the floor and air space.

"It conflicted with his inability to get out of bed before noon," said Lovelace, leaping to a higher position thanks to a teetering stack of the Loeb Classical Library. She left a slightly damp paw print on Herodotus without shame, glaring haughtily at Boswell as if *he* was the one at fault.

The only way Boswell could move to a higher position than Lovelace now was by climbing the bookshelves, and that would be a little too obvious. Instead, he licked his paw to convey abject boredom.

"You mean he's still hiding from me?" he said mildly. Monterey was, like most humans, entirely predictable.

Lovelace glared down at him. "I couldn't possibly comment." Her loyalty to her ridiculous human was one of the things Boswell respected most about her, though he could never let her know that.

He had once had his own ridiculous human; he knew how attached one could get.

"We found something of interest," blurted Oxford, the alarmingly tall human who was the only reason that Nero had the second highest position in the room.[3] That white long-haired bastard was getting hair *everywhere*. It drifted off him like dust motes in a sunbeam.

Damn. Now Boswell was thinking about that sunbeam again.

"I doubt that, young man," he said grumpily. If he had a pair of spectacles (the lack of which was a constant disappointment in Boswell's life) he would have chosen this moment to peer over them in a disapproving manner. Humans got all the best props.

"We've found a trace of Cressida Church," said Lovelace. "A genuine lead, Boswell. In the twentieth century, of all places."

Church.

Professor Boswell remained very still. It was too much to hope that by freezing to the spot, the annoyances in his office might assume he was a statue and leave him alone. This was a technique he often resorted to when under great shock, or strain.

He did not like to be surprised. One of the best things about being a cranky professor specialising in Time Mechanics at a secret university in space was that surprises were few and far between. They lived in a bubble, protected by the Global Official Secrets Act. Most staff rarely left campus except those who disappeared through time hoops on a regular basis.

Why would you bother to go anywhere, if you could not travel in time?

Students were always the same. Once they graduated, the best of them became travellers. The teaching staff around Boswell rarely changed — except when a student transitioned into a professor, and he was expected to learn their first name.

Nothing ever changed around here. Not since he lost Church.

That was years ago. He was over it. Humans were hardly an endangered species. Getting attached to them was the height of foolishness.

(He had almost torn time apart, looking for her. He couldn't do that again.)

"Well?" Professor Boswell said irritably, once he had recovered from the first wash of shock. "What do you expect me to do about this? I have essays to mark."

"It's the first day of semester," protested Oxford.

Boswell hissed, his hackles rising quite literally. "I have to decide which students I shall take up an irrational dislike against for the rest of the year," he snapped. "Demanding essays is part of my process. I don't have time for this kind of frivolous nonsense."

He had almost lost himself in his agonised hunt for that wretched human when she first disappeared. Whole tracts of the tenth century were now inaccessible due to his obsession with getting her back.

Seven years. Church had been gone seven years. She was *lost*. He had done everything in his power to find her, and he had failed.

He was not going to allow hope back in, not again.

The only possible thing for Professor Boswell to do now

was to glare at this group of intruders and give them the silent treatment until they awkwardly left his office.

And damn it, he was going to have to dust Nero's fallen hair off all the books.

Today's sunbeam was gone forever. Professor Boswell would allow himself a brief moment of mourning, and then he would move on.

He was good at that.

---

1. Learning that cats could speak at all was something of a social adjustment for humanity; learning that they did it extremely well was, however, a shock to no one.
2. It was not that Lovelace was more popular or likeable than other cats, or even more terrifying (she was a little more terrifying). It was mostly that she knew where the bodies were buried. She had dirt on everyone, and she *never* used it. Anyone who spent any amount of time on campus owed Lovelace far more favours than they cared to count, and Boswell had been around long enough that his was not so much a list of favours as a hoard.
3. Humans often win the higher ground game by accident, which is why they are not allowed to play in any formal manner. This is also why so many of them have, over the years, been felled by one of the most useful tools in the cat's arsenal: the seemingly random weaving around the ankles. Cats like to look down on their enemies and their friends alike... but that doesn't mean they want anyone to know how much they care about doing so.

nine
lost property report

NAME: Boswell

PURPOSE OF TRAVEL: That's rather a sticky philosophical question for this early in the morning, don't you think?

LOCATION OF LOST PROPERTY: I really don't think I can wait until the comments section at the end to complain about what a bloody stupid form this is. Not to mention how downright insulting it is to have to use an automated lost property form for a somewhat more significant loss, actually. If we knew where our lost property was, why would we need to fill in this form in the first place???

Caution: failure to answer question appropriately and accurately will make it difficult to progress with the automations built into this essential form.

LOCATION OF LOST PROPERTY: England. The village of Kettlewick. 912. Only not there, clearly, because we looked there. We looked all over the tenth century. The only reason we stopped looking was because we caused a significant Event that blocked off the most relevant years. And when I say 'we,' yes, I do mostly mean 'I.' I've already filled in *that* form.

ESTIMATED VALUE OF LOST PROPERTY: Ask her family.

ten
admin is not a dirty word

ADMIN IN A WORKPLACE like Chronos College might refer to a variety of places and people. It might mean Sara from accounting and payroll, who always remembered everyone's birthdays and tax file numbers.

It might mean Ethel from the front desk, who took vindictive pleasure in telling students their essays were due in three days before the actual due dates, just to make them sweat.

It could mean the Admin Office, the central hub around which all travellers, students and professors revolved, even (especially) when closed.

For Ruthven, most of the time, Admin meant the "helpful" AI that constantly told him he was making errors on his requisition forms and other Media Archive related paperwork. At least, he hoped it was an AI. If there was a real person out there who devoted so much of their energy to making his life more difficult, he didn't want to know about it.

Most days of the week, any administrative problem that could not be solved by a paper clip, access to the photocopier or an industrial strength Band-Aid, inevitably ended up on the desk of Melusine.

Melusine from Admin was a beautiful woman. It was the

kind of beauty that people described as 'striking' or if they were really being truthful, 'intimidating.' She was hovering around fifty years old, and carrying a few more kilos than she had in her own glamorous undergrad days (she had studied Performance and Theatre Design, not that anyone ever asked), and yet her beauty was more luminous than in her youth.

'Intimidating' was a good word for Melusine. 'Scary' wasn't inaccurate. On a good day, she made Professor Boswell look like (forgive the comparison) a pussy cat.

She wore shoulder pads. *Shoulder pads*. No one had worn shoulder pads in the workplace for two hundred years, and even then it was a recycled fashion that everyone agreed was a terrible idea.

Her desk was so tidy it hurt the eyes. The only thing in the entire room that smacked of anything other than 100% business was a black stoneware mug shaped like an Egyptian sphinx. It had the words 'wish you were here' written jauntily in the side in DIY silver sharpie.

She was also, as if this was not daunting enough, a Founder of Chronos College, and Oxford's mother. One of his mothers, at least. Ruthven had never met the apparently even more glamorous and efficient Celeste Oxford, who worked on another campus.

"Let me get this straight," Melusine said now, leaning back in her comfortable, ergonomic chair. Behind her, the complex and colour-coded web of The Schedule unrolled as digital wallpaper in a slow but pointed loop to remind anyone who visited her office that Melusine was responsible for deciding everything that happened here at Chronos College.

Pertinent to the scene about to unfold, it reminded them that The Schedule was planned out meticulously weeks or even months in advance. Wiggle room was a mythical construct that Melusine refused to acknowledge. Personal requests were almost always met with an icy stare... and yet she was capable to responding to an actual crisis faster than most people could draw breath.[1]

Today, Melusine glared at Oxford and Ruthven. The latter felt his face grow hot as embarrassment poured over him. That was the Melusine Effect. Somehow, it didn't seem to bother Oxford at all.

Professor Boswell had failed to be convinced to join their ragtag crew. Monterey was still either napping or in hiding from Boswell for some reason Ruthven did not quite understand. Lovelace was so furious about Boswell's rejection of the call of adventure that she was doing angry laps of the roof of this building. No one knew where Nero had vanished to, though at the rate he had been shedding lately it was entirely possible that he was now spread thinly across every surface of the campus. Fenella, still horrifyingly emotional about this whole business, had gone to the toilet at one point and not returned.

Ruthven couldn't blame her. He wished he'd thought of that. He did not like being the centre of attention. Being part of a reckless group of troublemakers with a wild idea was one thing, but now there were only two of them left. He couldn't exactly drift to the back of the group to avoid notice. He didn't like being thought of as difficult — not when his department was widely regarded as the most disposable whenever budget time rolled around. He preferred for most people at Chronos College to forget that Ruthven existed at all.

He hadn't known Cressida all that well outside the footage in the Media Archives; she certainly would not remember him. He didn't have a stake in this. Even now, he was fighting the urge to dive under the antique rug and scuttle out of this office on his elbows.

Being friends with someone who was determined to do the Right Thing was the worst.

Melusine from Admin glowered at them both. "Clement,"

she said, adding to the bizarreness of the situation. No one ever used Oxford's first name. "You wish to add some kind of dramatic personal rescue mission to my schedule. Using Chronos College resources. Based on a brief burst of pixels spotted on a lost television artefact…"

Ruthven stared sideways at Oxford, expecting him to launch into the 'call to action' speech he'd been practicing since they first spotted Cressida in 1964. But faced with Melusine and her dramatically tidy desk, Oxford looked like a wallaby caught in the glare of headlights. He said nothing, merely gaping a little.

"Wait," said Ruthven. Oh, no. What was he doing? Speaking up? That wasn't like him at all. "What do you mean personal? Cressida was lost during an official mission."

Oxford only offered Ruthven an alarmed widening of the eyes which either meant 'keep going, you got this' or 'please shut up this instant.'

"Indeed she was," said Melusine after the tiniest of pauses. "Considerable resources were poured into her rescue effort. The budget for that semester never recovered, and neither did the tenth century."

"They were looking in the *wrong* century!" Ruthven argued.

He was getting fired up now. What was happening? Oxford's sidelong glance now appeared to give off mildly impressed vibes, which only made things worse. Feedback like that would only encourage Ruthven. Why was no one stopping him?

"And," Melusine continued sharply, unhappy about being interrupted. "Which of our current missions do you think we should reschedule for this little outing? Oxford here is supposed to be in the Court of George II with Nero next Thursday. Monterey and Lovelace — who I see didn't bother to get out of bed for this meeting — are due in Caligula's

Rome. Don't get me started on Tunbridge and Ptolemy's intense British Raj schedule for the next four weeks. Do you know how badly it would affect our funding reconciliation if we started adding extra missions based on spurious evidence? Do you know how much grant money we could lose? The Founders are not an inexhaustible resource."

"What if we didn't use a scheduled operative?" broke in Oxford, finally locating his bottle. "We have a qualified, experienced and entirely available traveller right here. His schedule is wide open."

"*What*?" Ruthven said explosively.

"*What*?" said Melusine at the same time. She managed to simultaneously convey her outrage at Oxford's suggestion and her deep annoyance that Ruthven agreed with her. A master scheduler at work.

Humiliation burned the tips Ruthven's ears. "Was this your plan all along?" he demanded of Oxford, who looked only a fraction as ashamed of himself as he should be. "I don't have a cat."

"He doesn't have a cat," Melusine insisted at the same time, and looked even more frustrated at being on the same wavelength as Ruthven.

"We have a spare cat," Oxford said, on the verge of actually smiling in triumph, the bastard. "A cat without a human partner. We just have to convince him…"

"You are not taking my Professor of Time Mechanics out of this college in the first week of semester," roared Melusine. "There is a *schedule*."

"You want to pair me with Boswell?" Ruthven said quietly. "Why didn't you mention this before?"

He felt ambushed. And stupid. He'd thought that Oxford wanted him here for moral support, not shark chum.

Oxford didn't seem bothered by Ruthven's distress. Thoroughly warmed up now, as if he finally remembered he should be wheedling instead of standing around like a decorative lamp, he leaned over his mother's desk. "Don't you think it would be good for the students to see that the college prioritises the safety and wellbeing of our travellers?" Oxford wheedled at Melusine. "I'm sure it's the sort of thing the rest Board would approve. Optics and all that.." He gave her an earnest, pointed look.

Melusine looked furious. "Did Celeste put you up to this?"

"Of course not," Oxford said, a little too quickly. "All my own idea."

His mother gave him an entirely scornful look. "Since when do you have ideas, Clement?"

"It's *Cressida Church*," Oxford said, putting on a plaintive voice that made Ruthven (and Melusine too, probably) want to punch him. "The Lost Traveller. Cressida and Boswell were *icons*. They're legendary. Imagine the story if we finally bring her home. Imagine the prestige. Imagine all the alumni donations."

Melusine hesitated. "I'm listening."

Oxford widened his pretty blue eyes and leaned in with a smoothness that might be charming if Ruthven wasn't extremely pissed off at him right now. "If Professor Boswell agrees to do this, will you at least think about adding a new team to the schedule? For one glorious, reasonably priced rescue mission?"

Melusine tapped her long red nails on her desk. Of course, she had long red fingernails. She had probably murdered someone with them earlier today during her fifteen-minute compulsory recreation break. "Come back to me with Professor Boswell's enthusiastic consent, a completed leave of absence form, a pre-arranged substitute lecturer, and a comprehensive budget for this little outing you have in mind. And I will *consider* passing it up to the Dean in time for next quarter. That's our Dean," she added crisply. "Not any other Deans of other Colleges we might mention."

Ruthven was confused, but that seemed to mean something to the other two people in the room.

"Thank you," said Oxford, looking both over and underwhelmed. "Uh, is that really the best you can do?"

Next quarter was eight weeks away. Academia did not like to be rushed.

"Leave my office immediately," said Melusine.

"Right you are, Mum."

"Thank you," added Ruthven, who felt like he was about to be sick.

Melusine softened for a moment. "If you're not up to travelling again, don't let him push you into it, Elliot."

Now he was offended coming and going. "It's not that I'm not up to it," Ruthven said hotly. "I didn't know it was on the table."

Oh, hell. He wasn't up to it, though, was he?

Melusine was already looking away, typing quickly to demonstrate just how disinterested she was in this meeting. "No, that's it, that's all the empathy you get from me this year. Consider it your Secret Santa gift. Get lost, both of you."

Ruthven was left feeling unsettled, which was standard after any kind of interaction with Melusine from Admin.

Being furious with Oxford, though, that was a new and entirely unwelcome feeling.

"I can't believe you did that," Ruthven said as he strode away from Admin, trying to keep up with Oxford's long legs. It was so frustrating when the person you were annoyed at could easily walk faster than you. It made flouncing away so much harder.

"But this is perfect," Oxford said earnestly. "It's a good start, at least. That gives us weeks to work on Professor Boswell."

"What about me?"

"What about you?"

"I don't want another cat," Ruthven raged, letting his bubbling fury overspill. "You don't know what it's like to lose your partner. To nearly not make it home at all. I don't want to travel again. Why would I?"

The thought of it was revolting. Aesop was his partner. She was the best cat in the world, and she was *gone*. Nothing was bringing her back. No one had spotted *her* in a lost piece of film footage.

Oxford looked taken aback, and a little upset. As if he had offered Ruthven flowers and chocolates, and Ruthven had kicked him in the knee. "But I thought..."

"Just because I make the occasional sad face while thinking about the past does not mean you can pity me!" Ruthven roared. And now he was the person yelling on the quad, in full view of curious students and co-workers. A full circuit of embarrassment. "I'm not convinced it was Cressida, anyway. I think you all had a collective hallucination about some long-dead sound engineer with a blonde bob."

"Her hair was more of a..."

"Why are you so set on this?" Ruthven challenged. "What's in it for you?" He hadn't realised Oxford even knew Cressida that well. He certainly hadn't. They were only in their second year of undergrad when she was lost, and they hadn't exactly run in the same circles.

(Except, of course, that as the son of a Founder, Oxford always seemed to know everyone on campus).

"It's important," said Oxford, looking bemused.

"So important that you didn't even ask me if I was ready to travel in time again?"

"I didn't think."

"Clearly." Ruthven was calming down now, which only meant that the humiliation of having made a scene was beginning to fold around him like a blanket of mortification. "Don't follow me," he warned. "I'm done with this." He turned on his heel and walked quickly in the direction of the Media Archive. There, at least, he could be alone.

Forever, hopefully.

---

1. When Ruthven suffered the devastating loss of his cat and fellow traveller Aesop, Melusine re-assigned him to the Media Archives before he had even trudged his way up from the quad to report to her office. Efficiency matched with a near-psychic ability to predict outcomes made for a terrifying combination, even if Melusine herself at least had the common courtesy to pretend she did not know everyone's exact birthday.

eleven
"cramberleigh, of all places."

BEING ALONE WAS NOT on the cards for Ruthven. His dark, safe cave with its terminals, chronometers and vintage media screens had been infiltrated.

Ruthven's office was in the basement floor of the Media Archives building, most of which consisted of storage. It just about summed up the relative importance of his role at Chronos College that storage got windows and views over the artificial landscape of the campus, and he did not.

He hovered on the threshold of his office. Inside, he saw a petite woman wearing a two-horned Viking helmet over her pixie-cut. Fenella's luminous eyes were illuminated by the flickering lights of Season 8 of *Cramberleigh*, displayed on the small screen of the retroplayer.

Season 8 was one of Ruthven's favourites. The Season With The Carnivorous Plants (1972) was the third season in colour, and the first to be affected by the show's supernatural soft reboot. It must have been a shock to the viewers at the time, used to nothing more surprising happening at *Cramberleigh* than the occasional wedding, sinking of the Titanic, or visit from a historically appropriate celebrity such as Agatha Christie or Winston Churchill.

Suddenly the widowed and heartbroken Sir Victor was doing mysterious experiments in the greenhouse, Mrs Merryday the cook was hosting seances in the scullery, and a footman got eaten.[1]

Fenella, scrunched up in Ruthven's favourite chair with her chin on her knees, was currently watching episode 8B — A Potting Shed With A View, in which Gladioli the maid fell in love with the new gardener only to discover he was a homicidal collection of enchanted grass clippings in overalls and wellies.

God, Ruthven loved this show. It was the bedrock of his childhood, his adulthood, his entire life to date. He recalled his mother telling him about a very old and popular television program from centuries ago which had most of its episodes erased. Some had since been found, but many were lost forever.

He was seven years old at the time, had not even watched a frame of *Cramberleigh* yet, but a part of his brain instantly committed himself to the project. *I can probably find them*, he swore to himself.

When Ruthven was recruited to Chronos College, and learned the extraordinary fact (covered up from the general public by the Global Official Secrets Act) that time travel was a scientific reality, one of the first things that passed through his mind was: *That's all the lost episodes of* Cramberleigh *sorted, then.*

He was instantly embarrassed by his own shallowness, only for another recruit (Lakshmi Tunbridge, bless her cotton socks) to put up her hand and ask their orientation supervisor if it was possible to use time travel to reclaim lost media "like Season 3 of *Cramberleigh*."

The supervisor, a recent graduate who lounged over the lectern with laughing eyes, a halo of curly black hair and a bright orange silk shirt, looked delighted at her question. "What makes you think we haven't already *found* Season 3 of

Cramberleigh?" Monterey teased, even as Lovelace swished her tail in disgust.

That was it. Ruthven was sold. Time travel was his future.

Ruthven dropped into the chair next to Fenella. The trick to awkward situations was to lean into it. Accept that it's going to be a little stilted and uncomfortable. Carry on regardless.

On the screen, Rosamund Radcliffe paused outside the Round Library, having just overheard Lady Cradoc having a conversation with a china doll, voiced by the same creepy child actor who played Rosamund's half sister Abigail.

Ruthven meant to say something reassuring to Fenella in this time of confusing emotions, but instead he found himself saying: "You know there's very little historical evidence that Vikings ever wore horned helmets."

Fenella lifted her chin to give him an absolutely filthy look. "This happens to be a historically accurate reproduction of a helmet designed by Carl Emil Doepler for the 1876 production of Wagner's opera *Der Ring des Nibelungen*."

"Oh." Ruthven reassessed the situation. "It's nice."

"Thank you. It's my sister's security opera helmet. I wear it when I'm under extreme stress."

A slight memory stirred Ruthven. "Didn't you wear it to Oxford's 21st?"

"Parties are stressful," mumbled Fenella. She paused the retro player. "Did you want something?"

"This is my office," he protested.

Another filthy look, which he didn't think he deserved. He also hadn't deserved the accusation that he might have edited Cressida's face into lost media footage as some sort of cruel joke.

Fenella was the first person in a very long time to assume

Ruthven even had a sense of humour, let alone a warped one. If she was looking for emotional comfort, she had come to the wrong place.

That was what Aesop was for, an unbidden thought rose up inside him. Ruthven stifled it quickly. It was no wonder his lost partner was on his mind today, but he didn't need to indulge such thoughts.

"How are you doing?" he managed.

Fenella sighed, looking slightly like she planned to cheer herself up by murdering him. "Either we've just found the first clue in seven years about my missing sister, or we haven't. So, that's a thing."

Oh, hell. He hadn't realised she was Cressida's sister. Did everyone else know that? Ruthven knew he was a bit useless about people, but this was a glaring piece of tragic backstory he had missed.

Fenella didn't care about his panicked internal thoughts. She was staring at the frozen image of actress Joan Buckingham (Lady Cradoc), pulling her iconic "I just sucked a lemon" expression.[2]

"It can't be true," Fenella muttered. "I mean, it's ridiculous, isn't it? Cress and Boswell were nowhere near the twentieth century when they got separated. How did she get there? On the set of *Cramberleigh*, of all places."

"That part's quite logical," noted Ruthven. "If I was stranded in the mid-twentieth century: no cat, no opal, no postcards, I'd head directly for Fenthorp and wait for a time traveller to notice me."

"Fenthorp?" Cressida frowned.

"Fenthorp Manor. The stately home where they filmed most of the location shots of *Cramberleigh* in 1964 and then later after they started shooting on film in 1969," said Ruthven. "I thought you were a fan," he added before remembering that was a terrible thing to say to anyone, and this was why he had trouble making friends.[3]

There Fenella went with another of those patented filthy looks of hers. "Don't gatekeep me. I'm having a hard week."

"Sorry. But uh, yes. The only place better to wait for rescue would be a rubbish tip within twenty miles of the television studios, where a whole bunch of film canisters were accidentally thrown away in the Seventies. Travellers are always bunking off there at the first opportunity, especially the big purge of 1974 — I'm surprised that year hasn't been walled off as an Event already."

Fenella screwed up her remarkably small nose in thought. "You think she was trying to be found? My sister was a bigger *Cramberleigh* nerd than anyone. Maybe even a bigger nerd than you."

"Thank you?" Ruthven tried. It didn't sound like she meant it as a compliment.

"So," said Fenella. "Why would Cress deliberately show herself in an episode that she knew would never go to air, and no one had even found yet in our century?"

"Because," said Ruthven, who had actually been thinking about this quite hard since last night's party. "Time is a bastard, and paradoxes don't exist."[4]

This was true. Since time travel was invented, there had not been a single recorded paradox. There were many theories for this: time healing all rifts as she went, time forking into alternate realities too efficiently for humans to notice, and Time Is God, All Things Are Meant To Be.

But it was the Time is a Bastard theory that was largely accepted by most practical time travellers. How else could you explain the number of coincidences and accidents that regularly occurred to prevent the changing of history?

Video, sound recordings and other ephemeral data could

(often, not always) be brought through to the present day; objects, living creatures and people could not, unless their purpose in the timeline was irrelevant or complete. Some success had been achieved through the rescuing of endangered wildlife from forest fires,[5] works of art from cathedrals on the verge of obliteration, and film canisters which had been dumped by the TV network and somehow not reclaimed by fans in their own timeline.

Never guaranteed success, though. Never enough to be certain that yes, this was the Rule of Time, and if you followed that rule you would get predictable, replicable results.

The lack of rules around time travel was something that Ruthven, for one, often found rather unsettling.

Monterey and Lovelace had, for example, devoted at least six hops to trying to save the Library of Alexandria, and had only managed to recover one slightly dented book bucket and one very surprised librarian who died of a heart attack after three hours exposure to the twenty-fourth century.[6] The final conclusion of their report was that a) someone else must have saved it already b) maybe it was never destroyed in the first place, or if it was destroyed, definitely not in 48 BCE[7] or c) clearly the burned fragments of parchments and pottery still had a part to play in the timeline.

It was now the official policy that travellers wishing to save precious relics and works of art from history should do so using chronocles and other data recording devices, rather than wasting everyone's time and energy lugging vases from century to century.[8]

Did this mean no one had free will? This was a controversial topic amongst those who knew about the existence of time travel. Most arguments usually resulted in a reluctant agreement that most people in the known history of the world felt like they had free will, most of the time. So it shouldn't be keeping anyone up and staring at the ceiling with existential dread at 3AM. Those who knew how time travel worked, meanwhile, had at least as much free will as anyone working for a difficult boss.

When Ruthven said: "Time is a bastard, and paradoxes don't exist," what he meant was: Cressida could not have appeared in any episode of *Cramberleigh* that she or anyone who might recognise her might have watched before she was lost in time. Which ruled out every episode available for viewing at Chronos College up until seven years ago.

There was no point in Cressida trying to get caught on camera in, for example, 1C: Governess In the Attic (1965) because Monterey and Lovelace had rescued it eight years ago to great fanfare, on their first postgraduate mission. Ruthven remembered it well: he and Oxford were first year students at the time, and had sneaked into Monterey's Governess in the Attic Restoration Party for a glorious twelve minutes before being spotted and unceremoniously thrown out.

Everyone at Chronos College had seen 1C: Governess in the Attic multiple times, including the remixes, memes, and the digital stills that Monterey had printed on a particularly tight-fitting pair of trousers. If Cressida's face appeared in that episode, she and her fellow graduates would have spotted it long before she and Boswell left on that fateful mission to 912.

As long as no one at Chronos College had ever seen it, the possibility of Cressida's face being caught on film and recovered centuries later was still that: a theoretical possibility.

It had always been that way, before she made the decision to do it (assuming she indeed did it deliberately). Her face was on that frame of film long before she was born. There had never been a timeline in which Cressida was not caught on camera in 1964, in the Unaired Pilot of *Cramberleigh*.[9]

Ruthven was impressed by Cressida's strategy. She had obviously taken the very first chance she could to arrange her own appearance on the iconic TV show — and she must have known that if her plan didn't work, she would have more than half a year before she could try again, with episode 1F: "Where Butlers Fear To Tread."

No production company in the 1960s was likely to allow the same sound engineer to keep accidentally getting caught on camera during a live recording session. If her pilot episode gambit didn't work, Cressida would have to go further. She'd have to *become an actress*, or at least an extra.

She'd have to accept or reject work with obsessive precision, refusing to be involved with any episode of a TV show that she herself had ever watched in the twenty-fourth century. This, given her interest in vintage TV (a common satellite hobby of *Cramberleigh* fans) would be trickier than you might imagine.

Ruthven was about to fire up his media wiki forums and search engines to do a deep dive into obscure British TV performers (non-speaking roles) of the late 1960s whose headshot was lost to the twenty-fourth century, before realising he was an idiot.

Cressida didn't need to keep trying, because her first attempt *worked*. Against all the odds, Oxford had found the episode.

They now knew where she was, and that meant they could go and get her. Seven years too late, perhaps — but for Cressida it might only have been a matter of days. Weeks. Months. Years. There was no way of knowing.

So as long as they could retrieve her efficiently enough not to get the whole year walled off as an Event, Cressida would not have to hang around to see what 1965 had to offer her in the way of a brand-new acting career.

"Don't worry," Ruthven told Fenella with more confidence than he could usually muster. "We'll find her, and bring her home."

"I'm sorry," said Fenella. "We? I don't know if you've noticed, but you and I are not time travellers."

"Speak for yourself," said Ruthven, feeling oddly buoyed at the thought of getting to see 1964 for himself. "All I need is a cat."

---

1. In Season 7 of *Cramberleigh*, the third Lady Wildegreen died of the Spanish flu. No explanation was given as to why third time was the charm as far dead wives leading to mad science experiments, but everyone had agreed the show was looking a bit stale until this surprising turn of events began to unspool. Barbara Hill, the actress who played Lady Sophia (wife no. 3) famously said that the reason she never married because she didn't want to risk inspiring a real-life *Invasion of the Triffids*. She lived to be 97, so the issue never came up.
2. Actress Joan Buckingham was famous for playing archetypes such as 'the tall, plain spinster who's a demon in the sack once she takes her glasses off' in British sex comedies of the 1960s and 70s, including one famous role as a leopard print bikini-clad Jungle Queen in *Here We Go Round The Jungle Again* (1967) and another as Nurse Birdie in *Dirty Laughs at St Al's* (1974). The fact that she concurrently played the tartarish, judgemental Lady Phyllida Cradoc (a character at least 20 years older than herself) on a long-running historical television show was a constant surprise to fans. Joan came and went from *Cramberleigh*, but despite her success in other creative fields (she was also an award-winning ballroom dancer) she always returned to her iconic role with gusto, even in the show's waning years during the 80's. Joan Buckingham went on to win the Best Actress Oscar in 1999 for her gripping, nuanced performance as a homicidal grandmother with a brain tumour in the popular bleak comedy *Mrs Hollywood Is Watching You*. Two years after that, at the age of 72, she raised 50,000 pounds for Comic Relief by sitting in a bathtub full of creme patissiere. What a legend.
3. Ruthven didn't need to make an effort to collect friends thanks to Oxford, who towed people in his wake like the Pied Piper. When Oxford wasn't around, Ruthven pretty much forgot people existed, hiding out in the Media Archives like some kind of brooding bat creature with a collection of antique remote controls. If his life ever depended on him being charming and likeable, he was screwed.
4. "Time is a bastard, and paradoxes don't exist" is a direct quote from a lecture regularly given to first year students by Professor Boswell, entitled *Let's Just Debunk All Your Stupid Paradox Theories At Once, Shall We?*
5. Rescuing endangered wildlife was the primary focus of travel missions co-ordinated by Banksia College, which had the net effect of making most of their alumni insufferable at parties. It's hard to compete in a

"What cool stuff have you done lately" conversation when the other person has "saved the koala from extinction, actually" in their back pocket.

6. Monterey and Lovelace had better luck with saving the complete works of Sappho (a little too effective, as they realised when they came across a specific poem discussing how strange it was that her first drafts kept disappearing), the autobiography of Agrippina Minor (actually a collection of recipes, a few of her mother's letters and a highly annotated version of her shit list, on which the names of relatives and senators were listed in the order she wanted them to die horribly), and most of the Mona Lisa, which otherwise would have been lost to the twenty-second century event known colloquially as the Louvresplosion.

7. It was a surprise to no one that the attempts of Monterey and Lovelace led directly to 48 BCE becoming an Event, ensuring that the mission could never be officially completed. Not long afterwards, the entire lifetime of Cleopatra VII likewise became an Event, making it doubly unlikely that the Library of Alexandria incident would ever be resolved to anyone's satisfaction.

8. Data recording itself was not a foolproof system. Recorded media had only a 66.6% chance of making it through to the twenty-fourth century intact, and that was without counting the various incidents that often occurred between the recording of said media and the return journey home. Not every traveller took the hint, especially in the early days of time exploration. 431 BCE became an Event thanks to Boswell and Cressida's over-enthusiastic attempts to record the first live performance of Euripides' *Medea* from three different angles.

9. This of course is based on the assumption it actually was Cressida on the screen and not, for example, an ancestor who happened to have exactly the same facial structure, a possibility that was more believable to *Cramberleigh* fans than to any other human people on the planet. This was a popular trope recurring frequently in later seasons, almost as often as "this character now has a completely different face, due to an emergency recast," something that happens in real life with far less frequency.

twelve
boswell and lovelace

LOVELACE KNEW where Boswell would be. He might be a cranky old tabby, but he was also a creature of habit.

The Museum of Lost Things was a love letter to Chronos College's history of mildly unethical looting from the past.

When the Founders first commissioned the three colleges of time travel, they based the campus design on antique universities past. With Chronos College, they were so awash with nostalgia that they got halfway through building a replica chapel before remembering that public religion had fallen massively out of fashion in the mid twenty-third century.

They then attempted to turn it into a library, before remembering that Chronos College already had three libraries, despite the fact that all anyone actually needed for a library these days was access to the Global Digital Reading Archive, and a comfy armchair.[1]

Abandoned and neglected, the Not A Chapel Or A Library building eventually filled up with the various marvellous and chronologically obsolete objects brought back by travellers despite the unforgiving time hop process. Mostly these were small items that had been forgotten in pockets.[2]

There were a few highlights among the collection: half of a

statue of Venus, whisked from the dying minutes of an earthquake; various drafts and fragments of Sappho's poetry including charred medieval manuscript fragments (painstakingly copied out by one group of monks, and then nearly burnt to ashes by a slightly different group of monks); a cosmetic pot snatched from the Bonfire of the Vanities in 1497 Florence.[3]

Salvaged items from the past tended to be innocuous, mundane, the sort of scraps left behind (deliberately or metaphorically) in a deep-pocketed coat. One glass cabinet lovingly displayed a series of chewing gum wrappers. A mosaic constructed of coffee shop receipts was mounted on cork board. The shrine of dramatic cigarette warning labels was considered a major highlight. Best of all, there was the Pens Nicked From Famous Authors display, with Cressida's trophies arranged on blue felt and Monterey's on red felt.[4]

Lovelace found Boswell sulking underneath the Never Again exhibit, a glass case full of objects reclaimed from years that were no longer accessible due to Events.

"I see you're handling this well," she said gravely, crawling in beside him and curling up so that her warm fur rested against his own.

Boswell sighed loudly, or at least gave her a pained expression which implied a sigh; quite against his will, her proximity had started the purr reflex. "I'm too old for this, Lovelace."

"Nonsense," she said, butting him with her head. "We're outside time, you and I."

"Says the cat who didn't have to read fifteen first-year essays last semester about why time hoops are *round*."

"What you need is an adventure, my dear."

"I don't do that anymore. I can't."

"I know Cressida was special to you..."

"She was a maniac in trainers," he said scornfully.

"Yes, yes," soothed Lovelace. "They're all very silly, these humans of ours. But they keep us young. And we keep them alive."

She had never imagined she would become particularly fond of Monterey when they were first partnered together: she thought him a deranged scoundrel who was constantly distracted by shiny things, and pretty people. But over the years, she got attached. Even when she wanted to scratch his eyes out because his had paused in the middle of a mission to try on a set of bishop's robes, shag Casanova (and/or steal his pen) or taste every dish at a Roman banquet so he could blog about it afterwards.[5]

Boswell scowled at her, an expression that looked faintly adorable when whiskers came into play. "Low blow, Lovelace."

She butted him with her head again, harder this time. "We've found her, Boz. Finally, after all this time. Are you really going to leave the humans in charge of retrieving her?"

Boswell huffed. "I wouldn't leave that lot in charge of a paper bag."[6]

"Well, then," said Lovelace. "It looks like you and I are going to 1964."

Boswell paused long enough to make her worry, then leaned in and butted her face with his. "You're smug when you're right," he complained.

"How dare you," said Lovelace. "I'm always smug."

---

1. Libraries attempted to fall out of fashion in the mid twenty-second century, but no one would allow them to do so. The protest marches were extremely well organised and documented.
2. Time travellers do, of course, brazenly attempt to steal, rescue, retrieve or transport items of interest from the time periods they visit. Time tends to allow a higher percentage of objects through the hoops if they have been forgotten in a pocket rather than deliberately stolen. See: the recent published monograph of Montgomery J Monterey "On the Subject of Whether It Is Feasible To Cheat Time's Cruel Whims by Actively Forgetting Precious Antiquities in Large Pockets Designed Especially For This Purpose." The mono-

graph itself is substantially shorter than the title, comprising merely of the sentence: "Demonstrably, it is not, but trying is rather fun," and several appendices detailing his experiments in this direction, along with a patented pattern for the Coat of Extremely Large Pockets.

3. Cressida and Boswell were sent to 1497 Florence on an experimental mission to rescue artworks from the Bonfire of the Vanities. The mission was designed and approved by Professor Valadon, then Professor of Time Mechanics at Chronos College, whose obsession with Botticelli had begun to have a detrimental effect on her life and work. When asked why they only brought back a small cosmetics pot and not one of the many Botticelli artworks famously destroyed in those fires, Traveller Boswell was heard to say: "We did rescue one, but Botticelli himself threw it back on the flames. I thought, if he wants to burn it that badly, I'm not going to fight him."

    "I was perfectly prepared to fight Botticelli," Cressida added, in their official report. "But I didn't think the sketch was much to write home about, so I didn't bother."

    Professor Valadon put in her resignation shortly afterwards.

4. Early in their careers, Monterey and Cressida challenged each other to steal the most writing implements from famous writers of history. Cressida's collection comprised fourteen pens, pencils and broken nibs that she claimed had passed through the possession of such notaries as Jane Austen, Sappho, Pliny the Younger, William Goldman and David Bowie. Monterey's hoard, including writing implements associated with Pliny the Elder, Casanova, all three of the Bronte Sisters, William Shakespeare and Nick Cave, comprised over ninety pieces. When asked if he considered it fair to continue the challenge after Cressida's tragic disappearance, Monterey was heard to reply: "Just because she's probably dead is no reason not to beat her into the ground, darling."

5. Due to the Official Secrets Act, Monterey's food blog Anywhere But This Century And Twice As Tasty could only be read on the Chronos College intranet: exclusively accessible to staff, students and official visitors. He had a higher readership than any other publication on campus at a peak of 93%, to the point that Melusine from Admin once asked if he would publish urgent campus announcements. It was an embarrassing conversation for both of them.

6. The paper bag collection was three tables away, between the display of Lost Umbrellas and the display of These Keys Probably Aren't Necessary To The Timeline, Right?

thirteen
boswell and cressida

Nowhere, The Kingdom of the East Angles, 512 CE

"DAMN," said Cressida, tripping over a rock and splashing mud up her woollen stockings. "This air's a bit fresher than Victorian London, Boz. Take a whiff. I feel giddy."

Boswell, as always, refused to acknowledge the sudden change of environment. He didn't love the feeling of sixth century mud squishing beneath him, but Hogarth from Costume was experimenting with a new spray-on sealant which would hopefully protect his dainty paws. He could do without cracks and callouses like the ones he had developed that time he spent three weeks running around Ancient Rome.

(The Caesars really did get far too much credit for their roads.)

"Did you have to wear that hat?" Boswell remarked. "You look entirely foolish."

It was quite the feat for Cressida to have smuggled in her double-horned Viking helmet (based on Wagner's opera, not genuine Vikings) past the reliable Hogarth.

Cressida's ability to talk people into just about anything was one of her great skills as a traveller. Since their partnership began, she had talked herself and Boswell out of so many outrageous scrapes, disasters and on one notable occasion, the guillotine.

Boswell had learned not to underestimate her when she opened her mouth.

"It's my own experiment," Cressida said, patting the helmet fondly. "Is it possible to start a fashion in Britain several centuries early?"

"Two horns on Viking helmets has only ever been in fashion for opera, cartoons and costume parties. The Vikings haven't invaded Britain yet!"

"But," said Cressida, waggling her eyebrows in a manner that humans probably found humorous. It made Boswell want to swipe her in the face. "Imagine if the Viking horde rolls into the harbour, and all of Great Britain is already wearing these helmets. Two horns and all."

"We wouldn't have been able to make this hop at all if that was a possibility," Boswell replied.

"Ugh, you're such a Time apologist, Boz. Stop sucking up to her. She's done us no favours."

"Speaking of which," Boswell said. "We have duties to complete, Church."

"Fine," she muttered. "Activate your opal."

He gave her a disbelieving look. "I've already activated my opal. Why would I not have activated my opal? Have you *not* activated your opal?"

The tiny, essential beacon hung from Boswell's collar, as was standard for cat travellers. It drew attention in earlier time periods where the idea of putting a collar on a cat was unheard of (speaking of starting fashions! There was one Ancient Egyptian statue that Boswell swore was inspired by his own natty ensemble) but their union stood by the cat travellers when they refused *en masse* to agree to implants.

A cat reserved the right to leave a party at any time, without leaving a forwarding address.

"Activating my opal," said Cressida, tapping that awkward spot behind her shoulder where her opal implant was embedded. Her skin glowed briefly. "Writing a postcard," she added, unstrapping the small pack she carried on her hip, disguised in this instance as some sort of generic sackcloth satchel.

The 'postcard' was a digital pad that worked as a tablet, connected back to twenty-fourth century Chronos College. Boswell thought it was a fascinating, devious and horrifically not-thought-through piece of tech. That, of course, was true of most inventions by humans that did not involve chairs or food.

It looked like a vintage postcard from the early twentieth century — image on one side, sometimes of the location they were visiting; blank back for travellers to scribble on with an over-designed stylus that could take on the appearance of a variety of period-appropriate writing implements.

The postcard was soft, the pad's digital parts woven of natural fibres, which meant it could also be used as an emergency field dressing. There was a rumour that if you found the right setting, it might inflate to create the world's most comfortable camping pillow, but no traveller had ever proved it despite a great deal of experimentation.

The postcard always looked like a literal postcard, which meant that its useful camouflage waned the further back in time you went.[1]

It didn't matter what you wrote. There was little anyone needed to convey in the first 5 minutes of a journey other than 'arrived safe' or 'instant catastrophe, bring us home right the fuck now,' and the latter could be activated by the Urgent Return setting on the opal beacon.

Today's postcard wasn't even trying to look like the right time and place; it displayed a giant pineapple, which was certainly not authentic to sixth century Britain, let alone this particular patch of mud.

Cressida did what all travellers did upon a safe landing: she wrote the words

Wish You Were Here

in her familiar, looping script, and then shoved the pineapple postcard back into her satchel so that any witnesses would not see a small rectangle of illustrated 'card' glow brightly before delivering its message.[2]

"Right," she said when she was done. "Eight minutes. Let's have a poke around."

"I really don't see the point of these short hops," complained Boswell.

"Literally the goal of today's mission is to practice short hops," said Cressida. "You're just mad because you missed out on Versailles."

"Aren't you? I just know Monterey and Lovelace are going to fuck something up, and the entire reign of the Sun King will be an Event before I get to see it."

"Louis Fourteen ruled for seventy-two years, they're not going to turn all of that into an Event with one visit. Just probably the most interesting years with like, the ballet and the poisons and the burnings."

"Harrumph," said Boswell. "It will be the Tudors all over again, mark my words."

"You haven't noticed yet," said Cressida in a sing-song voice.

"Noticed what?"

"Where we are."

Boswell turned his head this way and that, his nose twitching. The air might be less polluted than in most places they visited, but the mud wasn't filling him with inspiration. In his immediate vicinity, he could see sloping hills, green grass, a mass of dark forest, and precisely nothing else. "I think I can safely say we are in the middle of nowhere."

"For now," Cressida teased, pulling out her chronocorder, disguised to look like a small wooden loom. Boswell did not remark on how pointless the device was. Their opals already recorded everything they heard and saw, footage to be uploaded later to the Media Archives databank. He had lost that argument many missions ago. "You'll figure it out," she added in a sing-song voice. "Let's see how many hops it takes you."

Nowhere, The Kingdom of the East Angles, 612 CE

"Exactly the same middle of nowhere," pronounced Boswell, forty-five minutes and one century later.

"I see a sheep, that's different," said Cressida, rummaging in her pack to pull out another postcard to write on.

Wish you were here.

"Is that a sheep, or a particularly grubby hedge?" he remarked.

"Bit of both, I reckon."

Kechwic, The Kingdom of the East Angles, 712 CE

"There's a settlement now!" exclaimed Cressida, pulling out the next postcard for the journey. This one displayed the image of a purple sunflower. Supply weren't even trying for authenticity anymore. That's what came of wearing helmets with two horns. Colleagues stopped taking you seriously.

Wish you were here.

"That means actual people might see your hat," said Boswell, awash with second-hand embarrassment.

Cressida gave him a cheeky grin. "We can only hope. Legend in my own lifetime!"

"This isn't your lifetime."

The village was a tiny gathering of shabby wooden buildings further down the muddy slope. Boswell could see a stone well, and several thatched roofs.

Now he paid attention, he noticed slightly fewer trees than in the previous century. That was human progress for you.

"They're going to love my opera helmet," said Cressida happily. "Come on, let's see how many turnips we can trade for it." She set out for the village with great strides of enthusiasm.

"This is why humans used to burn witches," Boswell muttered into his whiskers.

Kettwic, The Kingdom of the East Angles, 812 CE

"They've been going at this forest again," remarked Boswell while Cressida wrote on the back of a postcard featuring an Egyptian sphinx carved from black basalt.

Wish you were here.

"Some of it looks a little scorched around the edges," Cressida agreed. Was that the Mercians, do you reckon?"

"Hmm."

"I can't believe the Dean confiscated my helmet between hops," Cressida added, now wearing a very dull looking headscarf with no horns attached. "We hadn't even got to the Vikings."

"I rather think that was the point," said Boswell. "You were clearly trying to anachronise."

She rolled her eyes at him. "Testing Time's ability to prevent paradox is not anachronising, Boz. It's our job, more or less."

"All I know is that the hoop home didn't open for us last time until after you went back to re-trade those turnips and get your helmet back. You're lucky we made it home at all."

"I can't believe Time is such a sour old crone she won't even let us prank archaeologists. Ooh look, Boz." Cressida bounced up on her toes. "They've built a whopping great hall up on the cleared bit of forest over there. Exactly there. Isn't that awesome?"

"I suppose it will come in handy when the Vikings invade," Boswell said dubiously. "They can use it for their council meetings, the Allthing."

"Ugh! You are sadly lacking in observation skills," Cressida said in frustration. "I swear you're doing this deliberately!"

Fenthorp Manor, Kettlewick, Norfolk, England, 1512

"Where the fuck did that wall come from?" yowled Boswell as he hopped through the time hoop, finding a tall brick edifice only a metre or so from his face.

"What the hell?" exclaimed Cressida. "This isn't the tenth century. We missed the Vikings!" She pulled out the next postcard (Alaskan mountain goats) and wrote carefully on it: *WTF. Amateurs. We skipped half a millennium.*

"This is rather more civilised," Boswell noted. He prowled around the corner of the new building to peer down the road that now wound in the direction of the village — still the same village, by the looks of things, though the cottages were all stone now, and the thatching technology had come a long way. "Early fifteen hundreds, do you think?"

"Six centuries off target, that's embarrassing for Control," complained Cressida. "Can you at least see where we are now, Boz? This has been the most dragged out surprise since I filled Monterey's coat pockets with fake spiders just before he retired his winter wardrobe."

Boswell went for a long, slow walk away from the building so as to turn and examine it with dignity. He did not like encouraging Cressida in these games, but neither did he like to lose.

It looked like a very fancy manor house — or at least as fancy as you could get in an era before flushing toilets had been invented.

"You have to imagine the gardens," Cressida called after

him. "They're getting started on the planting over there. Squint up at the house and imagine all that red brick covered up with mathematical tile. Corinthian pillars added to the front there, they won't do that for another two centuries. And the Long Library, of course. That wing won't be added for…"

Boswell looked, and then he saw, and then he rolled his eyes so hard that his opal registered a bleep of medical distress. "Cressida Spanish Armada Church. We could have done this exercise anywhere. Did Control ask you to pick the site?"

"I mean, they didn't ask," she said. "I might have made a teeny suggestion. As a treat."

"You have been bouncing around like a maniac all afternoon because you tricked our bosses into doing a deep dive into the secret origin of the location of your favourite TV show?"

It was quite obvious once you knew what to look for. It was — or at least, it was the skeleton of a building that would one day be — Cramberleigh.

It was not Cramberleigh yet. This was a sixteenth century manor that would eventually be called Fenthorp: a stately home dripping in wealth, privilege and hot and cold running butlers, until the post-war slump of the twentieth century when the estate would be hired out to film crews so that the Hepple family's descendants could afford to pay the heating bill.

"If you two are quite finished," called an impatient voice through the time hoop that, Boswell realised belatedly, had been sparkling actively for several minutes now. "I figured out the glitch with the tenth century," reported their Control tech. "I reckon we can manage a couple more hops before we knock off for the day."

Cressida dragged her feet. "But I wanted to wander the grounds a little," she whined. "Maybe convince one of the lords of the manor to fall in love with me and paint my portrait so that I end up hanging mysteriously on a wall they just happen to use for a background shot in Season 3..."

"Church," said Boswell, feeling both grumpy and old. "If you come with me right now to finish this mission, you might get to meet a Viking."

His human partner hesitated, and then her face broke into a wide grin. Humans really were so easily distracted. "You had me at Vikings," she decided. "Let's go, Boz! 912, here we come!" She scampered through the hoop at top speed.

Boswell proceeded behind her at a more leisurely gait. Cressida must never know that he himself was genuinely excited to meet a Viking. He would never hear the end of it.

---

1. The under-funded Props arm of the Costume Department tried developing sleeves to make the postcards look more appropriate to the relevant century, with options including leather-bound journals, wax tablets, clay potsherds and illuminated manuscripts, but the project stalled when it turned out that most travellers were deeply committed to the writing of ironic twentieth century style postcards regardless of which century they were in.
2. There were never any witnesses. Time would not allow it. The hoops would not activate unless there was zero possibility of the travellers being seen during the two minutes it took for the hoops to deliver them to their destination, with all the associated bright swirling lights and sound effects. Control referred to setting up a new hop as 'fishing' because of how many tries it took to 'catch' an unoccupied piece of ground. It is for this reason that no active time traveller has ever managed to visit Tokyo or New York in the twentieth century, except by hopping a great distance from the city in question and commuting by train.

part two
the cramberleigh job

fourteen
the truth about events

You know the term. Everyone knows the term. It's usually said in ominous tones.

Event.

It means extreme time fuckery has occurred over a specific time period to such a degree that the Powers That Be cannot condone further visits to that zone.

Time travel access to that year has been retracted. Denied. Cut off. Forbidden. Further visits to that year are now *impossible*, regardless of geography.

If, for example, the wild, erratic and increasingly desperate search for a lost time traveller causes time stress points in and around East Anglia on the second day of Skerpla in the year 912, the triggered Event would seal off the entire year.

If that wild, erratic and highly irresponsible search continues to badger at the surrounding years, you might end up with an Event that fractures outwards, encompassing multiple years or even decades.

Why, yes, the mass Event covering the entire lifespan of Cleopatra did have quite a brutal effect on my ability to complete my PhD thesis on Mariamne I of Judea. Thanks, Anachronauts.[1]

The big question is: who presses the button to declare an Event? Is it Melusine from Admin, or Time herself? Bureaucratic intent, or natural disaster? Is it possible that humans and cats have done so much damage to the chronosphere that history cauterises its own wounds? Is it possible that someone, somewhere, is sitting at a desk making these decisions on a case by case basis?

We usually know who claims responsibility for causing the massive damage to the time stream necessary to create an Event, but we don't know how it happens.[2]

The Colleges claim that the policing of Time is within their administrative control, but that can't be true, can it? How could they physically wall off years and even decades from access by all time travellers?

If the Colleges can do that... what can't they do?

The trouble with time travel, is that we don't know the limits. We sure as hell don't have any form of appeal to a higher power. For those of us who believe the meta-process of time travel is a topic worthy of its own academic discipline... it's important to acknowledge how much we don't know.

How many travellers to a single year does it take before that year is taken away from us forever? How many visits is the magic number? How much damage has to be done before the wound gets a whacking great gatekeeping Band-Aid stretched across it?

One strike, or twelve strikes, and you're out?

Who can say?

Why don't we know?

Will we ever see those lost years again, or have they slipped through our fingers forever?

Zadie Kincaid, *Yes, I'm Rather Bitter About Time, Actually* - blog post deleted seven days after first publication

---

1. The credit for the Cleopatra Lifespan Event (69-30 BCE) was claimed by the anarchist organisation known as the Anachronauts, and has never been conclusively proven that this was from any specific intent to sabotage the postgraduate thesis of one Z. Kincaid.
2. Causes of Events are generally ascribed to the Anachronauts, whether or not they have personally claimed a specific Event as their own work (though they usually do claim credit). Travellers from Chronos College have also caused quite a few by returning to a particular year or series of years too many times. See, for example: Boswell and Cressida (the Medea incident of 431 BCE), Monterey and Lovelace (the Burning of the Library of Alexandria 48 BCE), Boswell and Chronos College (the rescue attempt of Cressida 911-915 CE). Banksia College has only claimed responsibility for two Events: 1936 CE, thanks to several failed attempts to rescue the last thylacine to die in captivity, and 2012 CE, thanks to a successful attempt to rescue Lonesome George, the last Pinta Giant Tortoise in the Galapagos. George now lives happily in an artificial recreation of his original habitat in what used to be the Banksia College Rec Centre, along with his genetically engineered queen consort and fourteen children.

fifteen
"we'll need a crew."

THE NEWS that Melusine from Admin had technically approved the Cressida Church retrieval mission was met with great scepticism from the unofficial rescue committee.

"Bullshit," Monterey said immediately. "Six weeks? She's trying to bury it."

"I agree," said Professor Boswell, to everyone's surprise.

Ruthven didn't know either Monterey or Boswell all that well, but even he had heard on the campus grapevine that something 'went down' between the two of them sometime between Cressida's disappearance, and the erection of her statue. Everyone knew that Monterey and Boswell had barely spoken to each other since.

The fact that they both agreed that rescuing Cressida had to happen immediately, with or without the assistance of the college authorities, was significant.

Then again, they were time travellers. Given the choice between doing something irresponsible, or waiting until the proper paperwork was completed, they were always going to choose the former.

Ruthven had expected Oxford, at least, to put up an argument for doing things by the book, but Oxford had been in a weird mood lately, and was rather enthusiastic about defying his mother.

They all met in Monterey's rooms, which featured a distracting number of satin throw cushions strewn across the room. At least it was comfortable.

Ruthven was not comfortable. Every mote of his body resisted joining groups of people that required in-person gatherings. He was wildly out of his depth.

Monterey provided drinks, a folding card table, a charcuterie board and a powerful sense of melodrama. "We'll need a crew," he announced, spreading his arms wide so that his invited guests could admire his vintage smoking jacket with the peacock lining and, like all of Monterey's custom-made clothes, enormous pockets.

"Why is he talking like he's in a heist movie?" asked Tunbridge, picking the greenest stuffed olives off the board with sharp-nailed fingers.

"There was a late night vintage movie binge session I was unable to prevent," admitted Lovelace with a sniff.

Professor Boswell was present, perched on top of an antique bookcase, and glaring down at them all, but especially at Monterey. Hopefully he wanted Cressida found more than he wanted to murder everyone in this room, but you certainly could not tell that from his face.

"Keep it simple," said Oxford, sprawling all over one of Monterey's chairs. He was fidgeting more than usual. "In and out. Jab jab. Anything too complicated and we'll make waves. Cause ripples. Incite anarchy."

Oxford did not say the word 'Event' aloud, but they were all thinking it.

"We may only get one chance at this," said Monterey. "Cressida is already disrupting the timeline just by existing in 1964. Us clodhopping in to pull her out could cause as many problems as it solves."

"I think you will find Traveller Church is not disrupting the timeline at all," said Nero. The fluffy white cat had not exactly voiced his disapproval of this endeavour, but he had heartily implied it through a great deal of dramatic flouncing, scratching and shedding in Oxford's general direction. "She would not be there at all if she posed a threat to the timeline."

"Yes, yes, Time is an all-knowing control freak, we bow to her whims," said Monterey impatiently. "Moving on. We need three teams of two to hop on to the grounds simultaneously, from different positions. From there, each group will attempt *discreetly* to find out Cressida's location."

"That's ambitious," said Tunbridge, chin on hands. "Discretion isn't our strong point."

"It's risky," agreed Lovelace. Her eyes were bright, and her tail swished. "Three teams at once. Could get complicated." Swish, swish.

That was when Ruthven realised that no one was going to be the voice of reason. No one was going to stand up and say: this is ridiculous, let's pack it in now before someone gets hurt.

Not even him.

Ruthven had hidden himself away for years, pretending that it didn't matter that he'd lost the best job in the world. Thanks to the Global Official Secrets Act, he was pretty much guaranteed some kind of time travel adjacent job for life. He didn't have to be on the front line to feel special. He was lucky.

And, yet. If Ruthven was given free rein to choose One Last Time Hop before hanging up his spats, then 1964 and the filming of the Unaired Pilot Episode of *Cramberleigh* would have been high on his wishlist.

A few days ago he had been furious at the idea of being handed over to Professor Boswell as his new partner. But he had warmed up to the idea. It was actually pretty exciting...

"Ruthven," said Oxford with a brilliant smile.

Ruthven jolted in his seat. He found himself captured by

Oxford's amused gaze. "Yes?" he ventured, without knowing to what he was agreeing.

"You've done the research, haven't you?" said Oxford with confidence. "About when the pilot episode was filmed. To narrow down the possibilities for us."

"Oh, yes." Ruthven scrabbled for his tablet. "I've cross-referenced all known data about the *Cramberleigh* filming schedule for the pilot episode in 1964. There was a two-week block in late April which included five days with the actors in the grounds at Fenthorp Manor, one day in the nearby village for that scene in the post office, two days for the shots of the house and hedgerows and general scenery. Then a couple of days at Nottingham for a scene they didn't end up including in the pilot at all."

'Not bad," said Fenella, sounding impressed. "Which days in April were they filming at the manor?"

This was where things got rather less impressive. "No idea."

"Which day did they film the greenhouse scene? The one with Cressida?"

Ruthven gave a helpless shrug. "Not recorded anywhere that I could find."

Fenella batted those long eyelashes of hers, turning scornful. "So we could turn up on site and find that the whole crew have finished the job and sodded off to Nottingham?"

"It's worse than that," remarked a cheerful, round-faced person who sat on a stack of Monterey's shiniest throw cushions. "It's tricky to lock on to specific dates. The potential for witnesses futzes with the controls. Our best chance of successfully targeting the filming period exactly is to aim the time hoop at a point where we know they're definitely *not* filming."

Nero gave the newcomer a steely gaze. "I'm sorry, who are you?" he demanded.

"They're Quant, I'm Khan," volunteered another, similarly cheerful (but bearded) face. "We're from Control."

"You invited techies to this secret meeting?" Nero demanded of Monterey. He curled his lip. "Can they be trusted?"

"Don't be such a snob," said Oxford, dragging Nero into his lap and stroking his head. "We trust Control all the time. They're the ones who get us where we're going. We like Control."

Nero sniffed, and allowed the petting. It stopped him snarking at everyone for five minutes.

"We're not going to go around hopping through time hoops without a Control team," said Monterey. "Anyway, it's not a problem. We'll hop into the first day of the location shoot and stay the full two weeks if we have to. Lie in wait."

"I'm sorry, what?" said Tunbridge in alarm. "Stay in the past for two weeks straight? Are you insane?"

Most hops lasted four hours or less. Even when travellers were sent on long-haul missions, that meant no more than two days at a time. Missions requiring the development of relationships, connections and data-collection were staged over a series of connected time hops without spending unnecessary time wandering around the French Quarter trying to find accommodation, or figuring out the money.

"Will we be sleeping in hedgerows?" Lovelace said in distaste, staring at her partner. "Or worse, camping?" Her entire body shuddered.

"There will be a pub," said Monterey airily. "It's the twentieth century, there's always a pub."

"That's not a bad idea," said Ruthven, not realising he was agreeing with the most erratic person in the room until he said it out loud. "This is a television location shoot, pre-1990s," he said as all eyes in the room went to him. "Drinking is a huge part of the culture. The local pub is our best chance to meet the cast and crew, that's probably where they're all staying. The only problem will be if they've booked up all the rooms."

Professor Boswell cleared his throat. "Meeting the cast and crew of *Cramberleigh* is a priority, is it, young man?" he questioned in his low, rumbling voice.

Ruthven felt his cheeks grow hot. "I'm not hunting autographs, professor. Cressida is *among* the crew. If we don't find her straight away, we need to figure out what name she's using, so we can track her down. The pub is a better plan than hiding in the Fenthorp greenhouse for a fortnight and hoping the cameras eventually roll past."

"Right," said Monterey, moving swiftly on. "Let's talk clothes — Fenella, I assume you have a plan for us."

She arched her long neck at him. "Don't you think you'd better select your teams first? Before we arrange fittings."

Oxford and Monterey glanced at each other. They'd clearly discussed this between themselves already.

"Lovelace and I are the senior travelling team of the group," Monterey began.

"Senior? Is that what we're calling you?" drawled Nero.

Monterey pressed on. "We worked alongside Cressida. She's our friend, and she trusts us. Speaking of which," and Monterey glanced up at Professor Boswell, expecting him to chime in.

The marmalade tabby continued to glare down from atop the antique bookcase.

"Uh," said Monterey. It was rare to see him lost for words. "Right. Boswell will partner with Ruthven."

"Jolly good," said Oxford, warming the room with his smile as he met Ruthven's gaze. "As it should be. Nero and I will be the third pair. Tunbridge…"

"Ptolemy and I will handle things here," said Tunbridge, looking relieved at being left out of the adventure. "Someone will need to play interference with Melusine and the campus staff. Everyone knows *you* can't lie to your mother."

There was a brief pause in which everyone tried and failed to imagine Tunbridge lying to Melusine of Admin.

"I'll help with that," put in Ptolemy. The Russian Blue was draped across Tunbridge's shoulders, absently kneading her with his claws.

"I should go," blurted Fenella suddenly.

The room got a shade bit more awkward.

"Do you really think that's a good..." Oxford started.

"I'm just as qualified as any of you. I might not have done as many hops, but I'm not lacking in practical experience."[1] Fenella turned her fierce expression on Monterey, and then up at Professor Boswell. "Cressida is my sister. I should be on this mission. I know her better than any of you. All I need is a cat."

Crushing disappointment swept over Ruthven. This meant more to Fenella than it did to him. She was Cressida's sister. Of course she should go.

No 1964 pub full of gaffers and key grips and British TV actors for him after all.

"No," Monterey said flatly. "You're too close to this, Fen. Ruthven has the research and production history in his head. That's going to be more useful on the ground than your costume know-how."

Before today, Ruthven hadn't been 100% sure that Monterey knew his name.

"We're all fans of *Cramberleigh*," Fenella snapped, throwing her hands up. "He's not special."

"None taken," muttered Ruthven.

Fenella glared at him. "I didn't say no offence."

"I noticed!"

Professor Boswell cleared his throat. Everyone stopped what they were doing to look up obediently.

Everyone in this room (apart from Monterey and

Lovelace) had been students under Professor Boswell. They all had emotional scars from his Time Mechanics lectures and his strict marking protocol. The professor's disapproving expression had a power over them that was hard to shake.

"What is the name of the makeup supervisor credited for the unaired pilot?" Boswell asked thoughtfully. "Head cameraman on locations? What was the name of the script editor's wife and children?"

Fenella frowned. "Anyone can look those things up."

Boswell peered at Ruthven. He had his most professorial face on, which gave the strong impression he was peering over vintage spectacles.

"Daphne Gold was the makeup supervisor," said Ruthven, mildly embarrassed that he did not have to pause to think about the answers. He might have become some sort of doctor!lawyer!genius if he didn't have a head full of *Cramberleigh* production notes. "Sidney Barrat — there were three cameramen working on the pilot, actually, no one was credited 'head,' but Sidney's the one who wrote an autobiography with extensive reference to his *Cramberleigh* work, so he's the best known, and he claimed he was working in a leadership position. And, um. There wasn't a script editor until 1968, but Anthony Spooner was the story editor for the unaired pilot. Left due to creative differences, and he was replaced by Aldis Whitby the following year. Spooner's wife's name was Carol. No children. Whitby wasn't married."

There was a long, mildly horrified pause.

"Yep," said Monterey, snapping his fingers. "That's who I want in the pub with me when I try to meet these people. Good job, Ruthven. Sorry, Fencakes."

After the meeting broke up, Ruthven sidled over to Fenella, who was being a surprisingly good sport about her rejection from the team.

"Sorry for taking your spot," he muttered.

Fenella rolled her eyes at him. "Don't be such a doormat, Ruthven. I was trying to steal *your* spot. It's probably for the best. The first thing I'm going to do when I see Cressida is yell at her for two months straight. I'm the first to admit that might not be helpful to the mission."

"Bold of you to assume Monterey won't do exactly the same thing," Ruthven said dryly.

Fenella gave him a small smile. "Now, turn around so I can get your measurements. I can't believe I've never had a chance to dress you before!"

"Bags I a bowler hat," Monterey called from across the room.

Fenella groaned. "No bowler hats, Monterey, certainly not in the country. I don't care how many episodes of *The Avengers* you've seen."

"Meet at the assignation spot at midnight," Lovelace informed everyone. "Strict secrecy. Tell no one. Any advice for these youngsters from the elderly and wise, Boz?"

Professor Boswell gazed imperiously down from his high position, meeting the eyes of each of his former students, one after the other. This process took a while, and made everyone deeply uncomfortable. "What's the most important thing to remember when you set off on a mission?" he demanded finally.

"Don't be an Event," Tunbridge, Ruthven and Oxford all chorused.

"Be fabulous wherever you are," said Monterey at the same time. He laughed at Boswell's disapproving glare. "Don't pout, old man. You're not the professor of *me*."

---

1. All students were required to complete several short but comprehensive time hops with assorted feline supervisors before graduation. Fenella Church's practical marks were in the top 10% of her year. It really was quite mysterious that she had missed out on being officially assigned a cat.

sixteen
"i have it on good authority that this adventure is not technically against any rules."

"ALL THIS RULE breaking brings me out in hives," admitted Tunbridge as they approached the rose garden. She, Ruthven and Ptolemy had come along early to help carry the gear required by Quant and Khan, the two rogue Control staff who were joining them for their secret mission.[1] "What are we, Anachronauts?"

"You're not even going," said Ruthven. How dare Tunbridge speak aloud the very thoughts that had been rattling around in his head for the last few hours.

"That's not the point," said Tunbridge. "I'm aiding and abetting. Malice aforethought. I'm an accomplice."

"My dear Lakshmi, you do worry so," said Ptolemy. It was adorable that such a bundle-of-nerves human had been matched with a cat who was all chill, all the time. "I have it on good authority that this adventure is not technically against any rules. Chronos College does not have any rules. Nor does time travel."

"You always say that, Ptol, and we always get into trouble."
"Not real trouble."
"Being glared at by Melusine of Admin counts as real trouble. Her eyebrows are stabby!"

"You worry too much about what people think of you," Ptolemy sighed.

"You don't worry enough," retorted Tunbridge.

"I always thought it was strange, the whole 'no rules' thing," said Ruthven, still caught on the 'no rules' bomb that Ptolemy had dropped on them. "Considering how many human resources workshops on the subject of responsibility that we've all been forced to attend."

Now he came to think of it, the human resources workshops were often rather soft in their language. Words were thrown around like 'preferred behaviour' and 'optimum outcomes.' Ruthven usually tuned out in the first ten minutes, so as to spend the time updating cast and crew bios on the Cramberpedia he'd been working on.

"That's what I've been saying for years," muttered Tunbridge.

"As the only person in this conversation who has read the entire Chronos College charter back to front, and a witness to many, many admin meetings on this exact topic," said Ptolemy in a self-satisfied purr. "I can assure you, it is trrrue."[2]

Tunbridge looked annoyed. Clearly this had been a bone of contention between them for some time. "Melusine made me fill in three different written reports last time I came back from the Middle Ages, because I couldn't account for one of my socks. Are you saying I didn't have to do that?"

"I mean," said Ptolemy lightly. "It's polite to do something when another person asks. Unless you don't want to. In which case, don't do it."

"That's so cat of you," she sighed. "Humans *like* rules."

"Do they really?" said Ptolemy, licking his paws. "That statement does not bear much examination, my dear."

"I like rules," Tunbridge muttered.

"We don't have rules in Control," volunteered Quant. "But we're close to finalising some official guidelines."

"We learned a lot about what not to do with time hoops during the Summer of Experimentation," agreed Khan gravely. "Learning experiences all around. Especially for that one bloke whose leg ended up permanently lodged in last Tuesday."

"Which last Tuesday?" asked Tunbridge.

"Good question. No matter where you are, there's always a last Tuesday, and that bloke's leg seems to be in all of them. Not at the same time, of course. That would be weird."

"It's weird regardless," said Ruthven.

"We thought so, too. But after we'd all visited it and poked at it and written elaborate journal articles about it, we accepted it as normal."

"Anyway," said Quant, interrupting their partner. "I double-checked our contracts. There is literally nothing to say we shouldn't help you lot stage an unsanctioned multi-team time drop without filling in the required paperwork first."

"Told you so," sang Ptolemy.

"I'm not mad, I'm disappointed," said Tunbridge.

Quant grinned at her. "I'm not saying we won't get into trouble. Just that, *technically*, we're doing nothing wrong."

"So many good decisions have started out with a sentence much like that one," said a deep, sarcastic voice as Professor Boswell padded gently out of the darkness. "Laddie," he greeted Ruthven politely, as they headed through the archway into the Staff Only rose garden, where the team had agreed to meet at midnight.

"I am twenty-six years old," Ruthven muttered.

Boswell ignored his complaint. "Ready for the trip, young man? Nice threads," he added.

Ruthven glanced down at himself. He was still considering how he felt about Fenella deciding that he was a grey turtle-neck jumper under a blazer sort of chap.[3]

The rose garden was not the largest of spaces on campus,

but it was in the open air, and a reasonable distance from any security camera coverage, which made it the ideal spot.

Quant and Khan worked away, setting up the hoops. Tunbridge and Ptolemy continued to bicker comfortably with each other. Ruthven stood at an awkward distance from Professor Boswell, trying not to think about Aesop, his own cat. His real cat.

He could imagine her up there on that wall, swishing her tail at Boswell and yawning. "What a stick in the mud. Let's ditch these nerds, Ruthven. I've got a taste for the sardine markets in Pompeii."

Time travel used to be so much *fun*. Tonight, he felt a sick sort of dread lodged low in his stomach.

The rest of the crew for the secret mission drifted along while Control worked on the set up: Monterey, still in his shirt sleeves, talking a mile a minute. Lovelace, perfectly groomed as always. Nero, already shedding bucketloads over Oxford's brand new outfit.

Fenella rolled in last, still working on the swinging coat for Monterey that was apparently essential to his look. She sat on a decorative boulder to finish up the last buttonhole while the hoops were checked and double checked by Control.

Oxford strolled over to Ruthven. He wore a turtleneck too, but in a light olive green colour, and without the blazer, which was probably for the best. Put too many tailored garments on Oxford, and people started swooning. Inconvenient.

"All ready, are we?" he asked Ruthven, looking unusually jittery. "No stage fright? It's just like riding a bicycle, I imagine."[4]

"I'm fine," said Ruthven, studying Oxford. He'd never seen him nervous before a hop before. "Are you all right?"

"Ah, well." Oxford gave him a pained smile. "Rebellion.

Not really my bag. More of a Monterey thing." His long fingers flicked back and forth, like he was trying to physically shake out his nerves.

"And there's nothing else bothering you?" Ruthven pressed. He still felt a bit guilty about yelling at Oxford after the meeting with Melusine. Oxford had been avoiding him since then.

"You still miss Aesop, don't you?" Oxford blurted. "Sorry. Obviously you do. I shouldn't have pushed you into this. I didn't realise it was all still so…"

"It's fine," Ruthven said quickly. "I mean, it's not fine. But it will be. I think."

They stared at each other, utterly sunk in mutual awkwardness. Then Oxford's face broke into a beautiful smile. "Better than fine," he proclaimed. "You and Boswell. Dream team. What could possibly go wrong?"

"Ugh," said Tunbridge, making a face at them both from across the rose garden. "Now you've done it. Everything that goes wrong with this mission is officially your fault, Oxford."

"As ever," said Oxford, and his smile no longer met his eyes. "Come on, you lot. We have a fair damsel to rescue!"

"Young man," said Professor Boswell gruffly. "If Cressida Church heard you referring to her as a fair damsel, she would bite your face off."

---

1. As is generally the case with cats, Ptolemy's contribution to the heavy lifting was merely that of moral support.
2. The lack of formal rules for the practice of time travel continues to be a matter of grave concern to the Chronos College administration, and has been an agenda item on every staff meeting since the college first came into being. However, the argument that Time basically regulates herself is hard to beat. Banksia College, who had a similar concern under discussion for many years, eventually resolved the issue by banning staff meetings.

3. The grey turtleneck jumper under a blazer was the most comfortable outfit Ruthven had ever worn. This could have life-changing consequences for him, if he survived this mission.
4. Bicycles were globally banned in the twenty-second century but continued to be used as if they were a relevant metaphor until the extinction of humanity.

seventeen
the rose garden incident

Incident Report CRG-511-A — formal interview with Traveller Lakshmi Tunbridge, witness to events

MELUSINE: What happened in the rose garden, Tunbridge?
TUNBRIDGE: I don't know what you're talking about!
TUNBRIDGE: I get so confused.
TUNBRIDGE: Ptolemy said that it wasn't against the rules! Is it true that Chronos College has no rules? I find that very upsetting.
MELUSINE: Does it seem likely to you that Chronos College has no rules?
TUNBRIDGE: Have I mentioned how confused I get sometimes? I think I've fallen in with a bad crowd.
MELUSINE: So, Ptolemy was in the rose garden with you.
TUNBRIDGE: I didn't say that. I don't think I said that?

Incident Report CRG-511-B — formal interview with Traveller Ptolemy, witness to events

MELUSINE: What happened in the rose garden, Ptolemy?
PTOLEMY: What rose garden?

Incident Report CRG-511-C — formal interview with Control Techs Alex Quant & Mawaan Khan, witnesses to events

MELUSINE: What happened in the rose garden, Quant?
QUANT: So, the fractals of the hoops started to de-click just as we locked on to the successful hop, and normally you can just wind back the chronoverticals, but having three hoops in close proximity to each other set off a Belovnikan chain, and the pre-sets interfered with the time circuits, and one of the hoops started making a sort of *bzzz-wheeee* sound, and that's when the central hoop burst into flames, and started to topple on to...
KHAN: What they meant to say was, no comment.
QUANT: Oh, yes. No comment. Sorry.

Incident Report CRG-511-C — formal interview with Traveller Nero, witness to events

MELUSINE: What happened in the rose garden, Nero?
NERO: I can't imagine. I suppose it's going to end up filed as some kind of unsolved mystery. Ah, well. These things happen.
MELUSINE: Where's Oxford, Nero?
NERO: I haven't the least idea. Gadding about, I imagine. That's humans for you.

MELUSINE: What about Monterey and Lovelace? Professor Boswell? Elliot Ruthven? Fenella Church? They're all missing.
Nero: Goodness, somewhere else must be having quite the party.
MELUSINE: Why aren't you with them, Nero?
Nero: If you'll excuse me, I have a long overdue nap awaiting me in my quarters.
MELUSINE: Nero? Nero! Come back here. How can we rescue them if we don't know where they went?
NERO: Pardon my old-fashioned vernacular, madam, but this seems like a 'you problem'.

eighteen
ruthven is not in 1964

RUTHVEN LANDED IN MUD.

This wasn't how it was supposed to go. Sure, it was a while since he had made a time hop, but there weren't supposed to be flames…

He and Boswell had been standing calmly on one of the platforms, ready to hop through. Oxford and Nero were stationed at the middle hoop, with Monterey and Lovelace on the far right.

Had they already hopped when it all went wrong? He remembered cries of warning, and he tried to turn back, but there was a steady paw on the back of his ankle, pushing him through…

And then he was here. In the mud. Without Professor Boswell in sight. He was alone.

Slowly, Ruthven picked himself up, peering around hopefully for feline paw prints in the mud. There was a routine for these things, even if everything went to shit. Even if you had hopped from a slightly illicit operation in a rose garden, and not the usual wide open courtyard of Chronos College.

Even if, for the second time in his history as a traveller, he had lost his cat.

(Don't panic, don't panic, don't panic.)

> First, you activate your opal.

Ruthven's opal had never been removed. *We might need you in the field again, one day*, Melusine of Admin suggested at the time.

Still aching from the loss of Aesop, Ruthven had nodded and agreed that maybe, someday, he would return. He was pretty sure they both knew he never would.

But there it was, still implanted in the back of his neck, ready for action. Activating his opal took a second, and Ruthven heard a small confirmation beep. As it should be.

> Second, you write your postcard.

Ruthven rummaged in the satchel that Quant had pushed into his arms before he approached the time hoop. Standard travelling satchel. His hand closed over the soft, spongy mass of the postcard — it felt like the opposite of paper, its digital surface too busy looking like a postcard to bother with a realistic texture.

As he pulled out the postcard, Ruthven glanced around. He knew what you were supposed to do. You were supposed to write *Wish You Were Here* and get on with things. Khan had told him to behave like this was a normal hop.

Nothing about this felt normal.

Had Boswell gone on ahead deliberately? Or had they been separated in the time stream? Was Boswell like Cressida, doomed to be trapped in 1964 until a team came to rescue him?

(Would Oxford be seven years older when they saw each other again?)

Ruthven sighed, his stylus hovering near the postcard

while he thought about it. There was a hill nearby. If he climbed to the crest he would at least be able to see if Fenthorp Manor was within walking distance. He could write his postcard once he knew where he was.

He took a deep breath, reminded himself that being a valiant adventurer had been his No. 2 ambition as a small child, and set off up the hill.[1]

Five minutes later, he wrote his postcard. It went a bit like this:

> Oh shit, oh shit, this is not 1964, that's a fucking medieval village, oh fuck, I think I just saw a Viking, oh god, I'm lost, Boswell's off fuck knows where, oh shit fuck what do I do now???

---

1. Ruthven's No. 1 ambition as a small child, as previously discussed, was to rescue and restore all the missing episodes of *Cramberleigh*. His No. 3 ambition was to become a professional cricketer, though in his teens he revised this to 'make out with a professional cricketer.'

nineteen
monterey is somewhere after 1788

MONTEREY WAS good at his job.

Monterey was a lot of things: melodramatic, stylish as hell, obstinate and utterly charming[1].

Most of all, he was good at his job. Even he knew that he would be insufferable without that particular mitigating quality.

If Monterey had any qualms about the supreme success he had made of being a time traveller, they were confined to the tiny voice in the back of his head.

Luckily, he was excellent at not listening to tiny voices.

Mostly, he listened to Lovelace. His partner was one of the smartest, most capable individuals he had ever met. She was his favourite, and his best. He wouldn't be who he was without her.

(She couldn't be dead. She couldn't be. But he had seen the hoops fall, had seen Lovelace leap out of the way of one only to fall under another...)

Lovelace was going to be fine. He had to believe that.

But Lovelace was not here.

More to the point, Monterey did not know where 'here' was. So far his only clues were that it was dark, and he had landed on something soft. In the dark. When he reached out, he could feel wood panelling. Was he on a ship?

"No, it's not a bloody ship," said the body lying beneath him.

"Hello," Monterey said, making a few experimental prods. "Who's this? Did I save your life?"

"Get off me, you arse," said a voice that, disappointingly, turned out to be Oxford. "I saved yours, actually."

"Sounds fake." Monterey climbed off his well-built fellow traveller and got to his feet. "Thanks for breaking my fall. What's the situation?"

"We're fucked," said Oxford.

"Oh, thanks for reminding me." Monterey activated his opal, pulled out his postcard from the satchel that still hung across his chest, and wrote the words:

We're Fucked.

The words glowed for a moment, and then disappeared. "Where are we?" asked Monterey, not really expecting an answer.

Oxford stood up, and didn't bump his head on the ceiling despite basically being a giant. "Secret passage?"

"Be sensible."

There was a squeaking, creaking sound. A whole length of wood panelling slid to one side. Light streamed into the space where they were standing, proving that it was indeed a secret passage.

"Lucky guess," muttered Monterey. He should not resent Oxford for being here instead of Lovelace, but he did. He wanted his cat. Two humans and no cat was the worst possible time travelling combination.

Oxford strode out ahead of him into a Victorian gentleman's study, or possibly a smoking room given the thick, tobacco-heavy air. Every inch of wall that was not covered in more wood panelling was covered in well-appointed book shelves. Nicotine fumes aside, this was kind of decor Monterey had always hoped to set up in his own digs at the college, if it wasn't for the criminal costs of leather-bound books in the twenty-fourth century.

"Never mind *Cramberleigh*," Monterey said, strolling to the window to peer down at the formal gardens. Pretty as a picture. "They should have filmed Sherlock Holmes here. Maybe a touch of Evelyn Waugh."

"Um," said Oxford, who had been fidgeting more than usual since this whole rescue mission began. Monterey suspected he was in the middle of an emotional crisis, and rather hoped to not be around when it came to a head.

Luckily, Oxford was a master at repressing his emotions, so they should have a few hours or even days left before anything exploded.

Still, he was looking rather wild about the eyes, and was pointing at something through the window... oh.

Monterey looked. And then he swore a few times. That was a horse drawn carriage sweeping up the driveway, wasn't it? Even whacking great poshos wouldn't have a horse-drawn carriage on hand in 1964, unless it was a wedding or a coronation.

"Are we even in the right stately manor?" he demanded.

"Think so," said Oxford, leaning half out the window. "Never seen it from this angle before. But it's got to be the right house. Doesn't it?"

"Doesn't got to be anything," said Monterey. "If it's the wrong year, it could as easily be the wrong spot. Could be bloody Scotland for all we know. Poland. Japan. Prague! Do you know how many fancy old houses there are in Prague?"

"It's England, at least," said Oxford, pulling his head back in from the window.

"How can you tell?"

"It's raining."

"Something that never happens in Prague."

"Then, there's that," said Oxford, pointing back across the library.

Ah, yes. Well. That portrait with Lord George Hepple neatly engraved across the frame was a bit of a giveaway. The Hepple family had owned Fenthorp for centuries. Didn't narrow down when this was, exactly.

"Red brick or cream tile?" Monterey asked, remembering a whole Cressida rant he had sat through once, about the history of the house where *Cramberleigh* was filmed. He'd always been good at remembering dates. "Hang on a minute. 1688 for red brick, that's when they built the big house. 1788 for mathematical tile. They started the Long Library wing... is this the Long Library?"

"It's not very long," Oxford said dubiously.

"Right. It's not the Round Library. So this is just an everyday cigar-smoke-themed tiny library. How many libraries would one family need?"

"The internet hasn't been invented yet, so all of them?"

Monterey leaned out the window to examine what he could of the house exterior. "I see marble columns! That puts us some time after 1788."

"After 1810," corrected Oxford, examining the portrait of Lord George Hepple. "That's when this one died, apparently. But also there's a copy of *The Old Curiosity Shop* on that shelf, so I think we're well into mid-Victorian."

Victorian times. That was promising. Monterey had always liked Victorian times, theoretically. He'd never got to stay very long, which was why 'kiss a butler' and 'taste kedgeree' were still on his bucket list.[2]

Still, he'd read a lot of Dickens and that counted as deep research. Enough to know this was a tea-drinking era of history, at least.

Monterey did not enjoy the feeling of not knowing exactly when he was. He usually had Lovelace to rely on, with her excellent nose for history.[3] "What year was *The Old Curiosity Shop* written?" he asked.

Oxford reached out and took hold of a small green volume off the shelf. He consulted the early pages. "1841," he said. "But this edition was published in 1854."

"Right," said Monterey. "So that means we're in…"

"1899, you turnips," said a voice behind them.

Both men spun around.

A secret door had opened out from one of the many bookcases. A woman stood before them wearing a most extraordinary outfit — it featured leg-of-mutton sleeves, corsetry, and a bustle that could go head to head with an aggressive hippopotamus. It was entirely constructed from tie-dyed pink, yellow and orange poly-cotton, with a matching bonnet of embroidered denim.

Monterey had taken the Intro to Costume elective.[4] He knew that nineteenth century tie-dye wasn't a thing. Not in England, anyway. Come to think of it, if this was 1899, that bustle was nearly ten years out of fashion.

"What the hellfire are you wearing?" he blurted.

That was easier. Easier by far to freak out about the dress than to wrap his head around the presence of *Cressida*. He hadn't set eyes on his friend in seven years. But it was her. Sharp eyes, bright blonde hair, and turning up at the wrong place at the wrong time. Who else could it be?

They'd been colleagues. Rivals. They'd met their cats together, gone for their first time hops on the same day. They'd once made out in a cupboard at a party and then pretended it never happened.

Monterey had felt he was going mad ever since he first saw that glimpse of Cressida in the footage from the unaired *Cramberleigh* pilot of 1964.

Why was she here, and not there? Why were any of them in 1899? What on earth was going on?

Cressida Church stared at him like he was the problem. "Montgomery Jolyon Monterey. What the hell took you so long?"

---

1. As long as there was a strong cup of tea in his immediate past, or immediate future. Once tea was taken off the table, his charm had a tendency to wane.
2. Monterey's bucket list was extensive. He had managed to cross many decadent items off it in his eight years as a fully qualified time traveller, but it was a great personal tragedy to him that many were now impossible thanks to Events. Items still remaining on his bucket list at this time included: kissing a butler, tasting kedgeree, attending Woodstock, nicking a pen from the signing of the Magna Carta, dancing at the Last Met Gala, tasting Andrew Jackson's cheese, and swapping fashion tips with Cleopatra. Monterey was particularly salty about the last one, because the lifespan of Cleopatra was so thoroughly sealed up by Events that he had missed his window.
3. Lovelace claimed to be able to tell what year it was by the scent of the air. Monterey was convinced this was some form of elaborate long con, but if it was fake he had never been able to figure out how she pulled it off every time.
4. The final assignment of the Intro to Costume elective was to be locked in a barn with nothing but a blanket, five pillow cases, a cardboard box and a basic sewing kit, with eight hours to produce a non-anachronistic outfit for a nominated year of history. Monterey had created a credible recreation of Queen Victoria's wedding dress, and got a B+.

twenty
at least someone made it to 1964

FENELLA WAS TRYING NOT to panic. She had wanted to come along on this mission, after all. She longed to prove she was every bit as capable a traveller as the rest of them, if not for the admin issue that had somehow prevented her from the career she was meant to have.

Why couldn't she have a cat? Why should she, a graduate with excellent marks, have been prevented from travelling in time? Sometimes Fenella wondered if she had been too much of a doormat in accepting it. She was sure that, deep down, she was the sort of person who railed against injustice. Protests and barricades and all that sort of thing.

In another life, perhaps.

Even the bravest of souls found it hard to raise complaints when faced with the unstoppable force that was Melusine from Admin, who said things like "the matter will be resolved in six to ten weeks. I'm sure you will enjoy this temporary assignment to Costume while you wait" with all the confidence of the person assigning lifeboats on the Titanic.)

Anyway. Fenella had wanted this. But she was not supposed to be here. Something had gone terribly wrong. Had she wanted it so much that somehow she manifested this outcome?

Surely not.

In Fenella's dream of swooping into the Swinging Sixties, locating her sister and saving the day, she had not been wearing a grey Chronos College jumpsuit under a hand-knitted cardigan. She had planned her ideal outfit in her head — a lovely yellow jersey knee-length dress that was comfortable enough to run around in, paired with an adorable beret.

And here she was, a time traveller for the first time since her student pracs, basically in her pyjamas.

Fenella could weep. Wrong clothes, wrong cat.

At least they were in the right place. It was hard to mistake that particular house for any other. Fenthorp Manor. *Cramberleigh.*

"Are you all right?" Fenella asked Lovelace. The cat had been thrown a few metres from her, into a tall green hedge.

Lovelace rose to her paws with grace. She was a long-limbed, tawny Abyssinian short-hair with a ticked coat and large pointed ears. Fenella had always been slightly in awe of her, one of the most legendary travellers in Chronos College history.

Here they were, partnered, if only by accident. There was no sign of any of the others. The success of the mission was down to them.

Lovelace gave Fenella a hard stare with her intense, light green eyes. "Did you do this deliberately?"

"No!" Fenella made a wild gesture down at her inappropriate outfit. "Don't you think I'd have been better prepared?"

"I suppose so," sniffed the cat, peering around the corner of the hedge. "I don't smell the others anywhere nearby."

"Perhaps they're elsewhere on the grounds." This was the famed Fenthorp hedge maze. Quant from Control had thought it was one of their best options to set up a discreet hop while the estate was crawling with people.

"Perhaps," said Lovelace, striding onwards. "I suggest you keep up," she added. "I won't wait."

"Oh, but," said Fenella. "I need to —" She made a short, strangled sound. No satchel. *No postcard.* She had an opal, at least, from her time as a student. She activated it now with a quick touch of her finger. "Do you think Control will be able to rescue us?"

Lovelace gave her an expression that was two parts exasperation to one part pity. "Let's start by finding your sister. Then we can worry about being stranded in time forever."

Fenthorp Manor, 1964.

Once they found their way out of the maze, the human and the cat circled around the enormous building, heading for the greenhouse. Filming was already well underway, with trucks parked nearby and a mess that could only have been caused by wheeling cameras about on soft ground not adequate for their weight.

No wonder the production team behind *Cramberleigh* gave up on location shooting soon after this![1]

Fenella found a stray run-sheet which showed they had the right year. It was marked Day 4, which was something of a concern, as they'd been hoping to get here earlier. Even more of a concern was the lack of people anywhere on site.

"Perhaps the carnivorous plants got them?" Lovelace suggested, leaping up on to a bench covered in abandoned tea mugs.

"That's not until Season 8," Fenella said absently. She might not be a complete *Cramberleigh* nerd like some people, but she had the basics down.

"I wouldn't know," sniffed Lovelace.

"You're not a fan of the show?"

"I prefer the one with the baking."[2]

"Oi, can I help you?" The voice sounded vaguely threatening.

Fenella spun around in surprise, trying not to look guilty. Unfortunately, guilty surprise was her default expression. "Hello!"

A sturdy-looking young chap in overalls and a flat cap stood there holding a cardboard box, with the burning end of a cigarette expertly balanced between two of his nicotine-stained fingers. "Was that a cat?" he asked, as Lovelace slunk behind some flower pots.

"I don't know," said Fenella quickly. "We're not together. She must belong to the house."

"Right," said the young man, starting to pile the empty cups into his box. "I'm Sid, production assistant. You are?"

"Fenella," she blurted, not having had the wherewith-all to come up with a period-appropriate name. Fenella was sort of old fashioned no matter where you were. "I'm assisting Costume, but I'm not sure where to go."

"Crikey, there's a lot of you birds in Wardrobe," said Sid. "Reckon it needs three of you to carry some of those dresses around?"

"Oh, yes," said Fenella with a little laugh. "Crinolines. What a hoot. So very heavy. And flammable." She felt she was doing brilliantly at talking to a real historical person. She even managed to stop before rattling off all the facts she knew about flammable crinolines, which was good *because this was an Edwardian costume show, Fenella.* "Where is everyone?"

"The pub, of course," said Sid. "Something bollocksed up the camera cables this morning, and the director was so browned off, he called an early lunch. Not that Barry needs an excuse for his long lunches, eh?"

"That's Barry for you," said Fenella brightly.

"Worked with him before, have you?" said Sid, looking more closely at her. "You look familiar."

People always said that Cress and Fenella looked alike, which neither sister thought was remotely true. Cressida was tall, blonde, and had all the curves in the family. Fenella was tiny and twitchy and had eyes too big for her face. If she had a tenth of her sister's confidence, life would have been a lot easier for Fenella Church.

Cressida would not have meekly gone along with an administrative error that meant she could not be partnered with a cat... not that such a thing would ever have happened to Cressida in the first place. Cressida sailed effortlessly through life with all the luck and success in the world... until her tragic disappearance, of course.

At least Fenella's pixie-cut was not massively unfashionable for this decade, if was a little daring for 1964. She'd be the cutting edge of fashion, if she was in London instead of East Anglia!

"Are the sound crew down at the pub?" she asked Sid. "I had a message for one of them."

"Nah," said Sid. "Back in the van to London, ain't they?"

"What?" Fenella gasped. Had they missed Cressida? What kind of stunt was her sister pulling, leaving a clue for future time travellers and then leaving the county in a van? That was like setting off a rescue flare at sea and promptly jet-skiing on to another location.

"Funny story," said Sid. "Sound aren't even supposed to be here on site! We always record mute on location, pick up the voice track back in the studio. Don't know what they were thinking, turning up in the first place. You look upset, miss. Fancy a cup of tea?"

Tea was unlikely to fix this disaster. However, given a

choice between being miserable with or without a cup of tea, Fenella knew the right answer.

"Oh, yes *please*."

---

1. The unaired pilot of *Cramberleigh* was a disaster from beginning to end, the entire production rife with drama and problems. Still, the final product caught the eye of one TV executive, Melvyn Davenport, who insisted the show continue. Exterior shots of the house from that original shoot were later used and re-used in the opening credits. Long-shots of the grounds and the village were used as scene transitions for many years to come. Seasons 1-4 were filmed on sound stages using a house design based on Fenthorp Manor. When in 1969 the production moved to film instead of video, and embraced location shoots once again, the producers contacted the Hepple family, offering a respectable stipend for further use of their house. This financial arrangement continued on and off for the next two decades. After the death of Emmett Hepple in 1983, his heir Phillip George Hepple demanded a much higher location fee, which was rejected. *Return to Cramberleigh* (1984-1986) therefore included no footage of Fenthorp Manor, except for the episode Blast From the Past, which included previously unseen scenes shot for the Unaired Pilot (1964).
2. In 2028, Fenthorp Manor became a filming location once again thanks to popular reality show Stately Baking: celebrity chefs and amateur home bakers teaming up to recreate historical recipes in the large, old-fashioned and deeply under-resourced kitchens of stately homes across Britain. The show ran for twenty-five years, and was famous for the catchphrases: "Hand whisking isn't for everyone," "Who needs electricity?" and "It's Suet Week!"

twenty-one
ruthven couldn't possibly be in 912

RUTHVEN HAD WRITTEN a dissertation on Viking Britain society in his final year of study at Chronos College. He knew what to expect from a village like this.

Thick-walled longhouses, small and rectangular, made from wood and mud. Mostly mud, though there were probably animal droppings wedged in there for good measure. Roofs cut from thick wedges of turf — or thatched, with sticks and straw. The distinctive smell of animals and people living in close proximity, in a culture that wasn't big on sewage systems.

Hand-woven clothes: bright coloured embroidery used to brighten simple garments that were mostly made of basic brown wool. So much brown wool. Braided hair. Beards. Damp linen. Leather. Fur. Brown.

It was market day. The streets were filled with tables and benches covered in all manner of food and wares, as the local farmers did their best to feed the villages while eking out a living for themselves.

Not a double-horned helmet in sight. Not even any helmets with a single horn.

Ruthven knew a reasonable amount about village-dwelling

Viking settlers in Britain. More to the point, he knew a great deal about this specific village. The first file he had researched in depth when he was assigned to Media Archives was that of Boswell and Cressida's legendary visit to Kettlewick, 912. The last time anyone had seen Cressida Church alive.

Kettlewick had never made the history books in a general sense. Nothing important ever happened here, in the grand scale of human endeavour. Not over centuries. Not over millennia. Not a single recorded battle of significance. No perspective-changing archeological finds. No one born here had ever gone on to become a celebrity, serial killer or Nobel Prize winning scientist.

This village only had one moderate claim to fame, of interest only to those who studied at Chronos College during the twenty-fourth century. This was the first time and place where a time traveller was lost.[1]

The frenetic search for Cressida Church had been so destructive to the timeline that the years 911-915 were walled off by Events before Ruthven graduated.

When Ruthven opened the files to review the footage from the Matter of Kettlewick 912, he was aware that this was the only way that any traveller would ever again experience this specific year of history.

So, he paid attention.

Kettlewick belonged to the Kingdom known as the East Angles (a name it kept after it was invaded by Mercia, and then again after it was invaded by the Vikings).

But that was just history. Geography. Ruthven knew more than that. As he approached the market, he recognised *faces*. That turnip seller with the rude-shaped vegetable stall, those two dirt-smeared children in braids playing knucklebones in the street (with actual knuckles, oh that was a historical detail he could have lived without witnessing in person)... he'd seen them before, in the vid footage. Cressida had bought turnips off that fellow and chattered to his kids, who happily ignored her. If not this actual market day, she and Boswell had visited a market day very like this one, at a time very close to what Ruthven was seeing now.

That meant he was in trouble.

912 was inside an Event. Inaccessible. For Ruthven to be here, now, meant he was also inside an Event. No one had ever managed to hop inside an Event before.

Also, he continued to lack a cat.

Though, that might not be entirely true. Standing in the muddy streets of this tiny East Anglian Viking village, the one thing Ruthven could hear above the general bustle of market day was cats. A great many cats.[2]

Things only got stranger when he moved through the market. Every smallholder had at least one cat — in many cases, several, crowding around them. Sitting on tables, rubbing against ankles, staring down from rooftops. So many cats that Ruthven gave himself whiplash, constantly checking whether any of them were marmalade tabbies.

He could hear music, above the yowling of the cats. Lute music, which was unusual for Vikings. The lutist was playing a Britney Spears cover from the early twenty-first century.

The villagers were oddly polite to Ruthven, despite the fact that this must be their first encounter with a beardless man wearing a turtleneck jumper under a blazer.

Oh, he realised as he rounded a corner and found three Viking children squabbling over what an open packet of Tim Tams. *This isn't 912 at all. It's some kind of gonzo college training module.* Clearly, he had fallen into a VR projection designed to unsettle the unwary student and test them on how to spot anachronisms.

Like the fact that the woman with braided hair selling wooden carvings over there was wearing a Grateful Dead t-shirt. Ten points to Ruthven for spotting that deliberate mistake.

He crossed the street between thatched houses and was almost run over by two kids in some form of go-kart pulled by cats. He blinked, staring after them.

Was that a *My Other Cart Is A Longship* vinyl bumper sticker?

Above his head, someone snickered.

Ruthven looked up, and spotted a twitching orange tail and a familiar grumpy face nestled into the mossy thatch. "Boswell?"

He dropped the professor title. Cats who ran away from their partners during time hops did not deserve honorifics.

"Shhh," said the grumpy cat, scrunching down further in the roof so that Ruthven could only see the tips of his marmalade ears. "Go find your own observation spot, laddie. You're making too much racket."

Ruthven's eyes narrowed. "I thought you were dead! Or scattered. Or in a completely different time zone — we're not supposed to be in 912."

"This isn't 912," muttered Boswell. "I've put in my time in and around 912. This isn't it."

Ruthven glanced around. No one was paying attention to them. Probably because there were a couple of large bearded Vikings nearby, fighting over whose turn it was to use a purple skateboard.

"I'm coming up," he informed Boswell.

"Your contribution will be invaluable," sighed the cat.

Ruthven found a barrel nearby. He stood on it to boost himself up into the thick, rough thatch of the cottage roof. It was more dried moss than straw, and smelled better than whatever was going on at ground level in this village.

He crawled on his elbows until he was level with the

marmalade tabby who was now officially the bane of his existence. "How many anachronisms have you spotted?" he asked.

Boswell gave him a baleful glare. "This isn't a puzzle."

"Isn't it? Because I think I just saw a woman in tube socks."

"That's Vikings for you. They're fashion forward." The sarcasm rolled off Boswell's tongue.

"If this isn't 912," said Ruthven. "Where is it? I was thinking some sort of VR training exercise..."

Boswell rolled his eyes so hard, it was amazing they stayed in their sockets. "Obviously not. No one has ever managed to convey this level of pungency in a digital landscape. Good enough to convince human noses, perhaps. Cats? Never."

"Who's to say what level of technology is possible," said Ruthven. "In a culture that has managed to develop both the yo-yo and the throwing axe."

They might have gone on like this all day, if Boswell had not suddenly stiffened, his hackles spiking along his spine. He hissed, poised to leap off the roof like a cat half his age, spoiling for a fight.

"Keep the high ground," Ruthven said in alarm. He had just got up here and didn't fancy scrambling down quite so soon. "What is it?"

Hard to see which of the many confusing and upsetting sights of Not!Kettlewick in Not!912 might have stirred this reaction... and then Ruthven saw exactly what had upset Boswell.

Yep. That would do it.

A woman stood on the far side of the market street, between a mead stall and all the enthusiastic customers for the mead stall. She wore all the standard Viking gear for women — dull brown linen apron dress decorated with a wide band of bright embroidery, light brown under-gown, long blond braids. Topped off by a helmet with two horns on it.

"Really?" said Ruthven. "We're two anachronisms short of a zeppelin, and the one you're going to get pissy about is the two-horned helmet? They're historically accurate for opera, you know!"

Boswell leaped.

Ruthven spent the next several minutes shuffling backwards, hanging backwards off a moss roof. He landed awkwardly on both feet, nearly tripping into a horse trough. Debonair as always.

"Aesop would have waited for me," he grumbled to no one.

By the time Ruthven made it out to the market street, Professor Boswell and the mysterious woman in the non-standard Viking helmet had disappeared. Of course they had.

---

1. To be fair, Kettlewick had three claims to fame, two of which involved filming locations of popular TV shows up at 'the big house' known as Fenthorp Manor. But even the most rabid, lifelong fans of *Stately Baking* and *Cramberleigh* had to admit that Cressida's disappearance was slightly more significant.
2. There are many collective nouns for cats: a clowder, a litter, a cluster, a nuisance, and a destruction. When it comes to talking cats, there is only one collective noun: a judgement.

twenty-two
lovelace at cramberleigh

AT CHRONOS COLLEGE, you couldn't avoid *Cramberleigh* if you tried. Lovelace had tried.

She held out for the first three years of her partnership with Monterey with nothing more than a mild disinterest in "that show with the hats". She sneered when Monterey and his friends whooped over a newly salvaged episode. She deliberately fell asleep when he pawed drunkenly at his retroplayer in the middle of the night, looking for a fix of nostalgia to send him back to sleep. She ignored all invitations to costume parties. She learned to leave the canteen in a hurry when that dratted theme music started up on the large holo-screens. (It wasn't only her partner who loved the ridiculous adventures of the privileged Wildegreen family and their vassals, it was literally everyone on campus.)

Lovelace rose above it all. She remained aloof.

Then, Monterey got sick.

Humans were such fragile, messy creatures. Medical science was supposed to compensate for that, but the human body would insist on finding new vulnerabilities in every generation. Even in the twenty-fourth century.

Monterey went down with a nasty strain of an especially

messy virus only two days after he and Lovelace returned from a hop to 1919. Obviously, with all of the artificial antigens pumped into the travellers, and the rigorous research on what could and could not be transmitted via time hoop, they knew it wasn't the Spanish flu. There was absolutely no way it could be the Spanish flu.

Melusine of Admin decided that it was a good idea to isolate both of them, just in case.

Lovelace was locked up with Monterey in a medical wing at the far end of the campus, with him all sniffly and feeling sorry for himself. Both of them were aware, though they never discussed it, that there was a minute fraction of a possibility that he might be about to die. (Of boredom, if nothing else.)

Lovelace weakened.

It started with Season 6, set in 1919 and featuring a plotline where Lady Sophia Wildegreen did indeed die of the Spanish flu. Then Season 7, because you couldn't just stop your marathon there, apparently you had to at least watch as far as the Agatha Christie episode.[1]

Things got rather out of hand after that. Lovelace couldn't stop watching the awful humans in their starchy costumes. The whole thing was ridiculous and terrible and somehow she was inhaling old black and white episodes even when Monterey was asleep. Once she found out there was a whole era of the show involving spies jumping in and out of vintage sports cars, she was sunk.

Stupid humans with their comfy blankets and TV shows.

Stupid manor houses that gave you a warm tingly feeling just because it was the location of a stupid human TV show.

Monterey must never know how excited Lovelace actually was to visit the location of the real *Cramberleigh*. No one must know her shame.

Monterey wasn't here to know her shame. Lovelace would

(almost) sacrifice her dignity to have him back. Fenella was no substitute.

Lovelace lingered under the table for a few moments while Fenella conversed with the Sid person. It wasn't like she could aid the human conversation by revealing she was a talking cat in 1964.[2]

A little explore would hardly hurt anyone.

She set off for the house. Greenhouses were all very well (Lovelace enjoyed the Season with the Carnivorous Plants as much as the next feline), but inside was what it was all about.

In quick succession, Lovelace visited the butler's pantry where Gladioli discovered Mr Bones was a vampire, the staircase that Lucy Wildegreen walked down in her wedding dress, and the pineapple parlour where Sir Victor was standing shortly before the house exploded in Season 11.

Cramberleigh exploded, that is, not Fenthorp Manor. Some sort of clever arrangement involving dollhouses and firecrackers, Lovelace imagined. Twentieth century media technology was so primitive.

A loud ringing sound from downstairs reverberated through the carpets. Lovelace leaped into the air in alarm, then quickly behaved as if that hadn't happened before remembering that she was alone in the room, so no one had witnessed her startlement.

What was that noise?

As she trotted back down the stairs, she heard the ringing stop with a clatter. "Hello? Yes, Gordon, it's Bunty."

It bloody wasn't Bunty, whatever a Bunty was. Lovelace knew that voice. She poked her head through the banisters and peered down. She could see a puffy blonde hairstyle — was it a beehive? Half a beehive? — and a fringed blouse. Glossy pale pink fingernails. Could it be?

"No," said that very familiar voice. "Joan Buckingham can't have high tea in the Long Library like she's Lady Muck, that wing is off limits to the likes of us. She can have a cup of tea in a tin mug at Craft Services, or come down to the pub like everyone else. This isn't a hotel. We're barely supposed to be filming inside the house. There's no one on site to make finger sandwiches. And we're not allowed to touch the good china, it's in the contracts... I could tell her, Gordon, but you're the floor manager."

A long pause. "Yes, I see it's not in your job description, but do you think it's in mine? I'm on production assistant wages. All right, do your best, love."

There was a loud click, as the woman hung up what was clearly a rotary telephone. Lovelace didn't have time to stop and marvel at the revolutionary concept of a telephone having its own distinct table. Next time Monterey had something to apologise for, she was demanding a telephone table of her very own.[3]

Lovelace scampered down the stairs and was confronted by a shocked blonde production assistant with high blonde hair and a knee-length dress, who promptly screamed.

"Oh my giddy aunt. Who let that cat in here?"

"Don't piss about, Cressida," Lovelace said impatiently. "It's me, Lovelace. We've come to rescue you."

Cressida Church, one of the most daring, adventurous and downright irresponsible time travellers that Chronos College had ever produced, stared at the talking cat in horror. Her eyes rolled up and she crumpled to the floor in a dead faint.

Lovelace leaned over her body, frowning. It was Boswell's Church. It had to be. But something was very, very wrong. Cressida Church would never be caught dead in kitten heels.

A door banged, and Fenella rushed in. "Lovelace, there you are! The sound crew have... oh." She stared down at the body of her fallen sister. "What did you do to her?"

Usually Lovelace appreciated the fearsome reputation she

had cultivated among the younger graduates, but this was just silly.

"Your sister is afraid of cats," she said scornfully. "And she's a production assistant called Bunty." Not a sound engineer after all. Considering the gender restrictions of this decade, that wasn't a surprise.

Fenella blinked rapidly. "Scattered?"

"Scattered," Lovelace agreed.

That must be why Cressida had not activated her opal to let anyone know she was here. Mind you, it also suggested that the whole business about appearing on screen during the Unaired Pilot was a lucky accident, instead of a devilishly clever master plan. Lovelace did not believe in lucky accidents.

"We need to get her out of here," she said. "Before 1964 becomes an Event."

"Do you think that's likely?" Fenella asked in alarm.

"Depends on how many of our fellow travellers come crashing in here — or how much mess we make on our way out."

Lovelace had caused a few Events in her time — or as she preferred to describe it, she had been present when Monterey caused Events. The trick to survival was to get out ahead of the catastrophe.

They had to drag Cressida somewhere quiet — at least somewhere less busy than a main hall of a stately home crawling with film crew. Hopefully Quant and Khan would have sorted out whatever disaster occurred on their way through, so Lovelace and Fenella could hop Cressida home before the rest of the *Cramberleigh* cast and crew returned from the pub.

Unfortunately, Fenella was basically four twigs in a jumpsuit. Her older sister was a solid piece, and inconveniently unconscious. Lovelace was a cat. Minimal lifting ability.

"You get her arms," Lovelace advised. "And also her legs.

I'm here for moral support. Do you think we might find some sort of transport dolly?"

A door slammed somewhere in the enormous house.

"Cupboard under the stairs!" hissed Lovelace. "Quickly."

Fenella half-dragged Cressida across the floor. Her sister chose this moment to moan as if about to wake up.

"Goodness," said a voice from behind them, so effortlessly posh that it probably had its own Hampstead postcode. "What *do* we have here?"

Fenella dropped Cressida with a squeak. "Lovelace!" she hissed.

"I know," Lovelace gasped back. "I know."

Neither of them could move, too busy staring wildly at the newcomer.

Lovelace had met all manner of historical celebrities over the last decade. Catherine De Medici. Rasputin. Andy Warhol. Sting. She had been present at the execution of Marie Antoinette, and two of Henry VIII's weddings. She was one of the tiny number of travellers who would ever meet Cleopatra (and wasn't Monterey disgruntled he had missed his chance).

This was different. Right now, staring across the hallway at a tiny, elegant woman in an Edwardian tea gown and giant Chanel sunglasses, Lovelace the time travelling Abyssinian cat was utterly captivated. Starstruck.

This was Fleur fucking Shropshire.

They should probably curtsey.

---

1. 7F - A Mysterious Affair At Cramberleigh featured the surprise appearance of Agatha Christie as a house guest and family friend of Lady Cradoc. Agatha was played by Purr Templeton, who went on to great success as the romantic lead in the *Whoops Britannia* series of comedy films about life on board an English holiday cruise ship. This version of Agatha Christie was a young woman at the very beginning of her writing career, with a deep and morbid interest in poisons. Templeton was never available to reprise her role, despite

being asked back every year. Eventually during the 'Seventies Spy' era of the show in 1976, a script was approved to bring a now-elderly Agatha Christie back to *Cramberleigh* in the episode 12F - M is For Mousetrap. The real Agatha Christie's lawyers got wind of it and issued a Cease and Desist. The episode was eventually filmed featuring a different famous lady crime author named Tabitha Gristie. Played by Margaret Sims-Justice, the elderly Gristie was revealed to be a sinister mob boss using Russian espionage connections to fund theatrical adaptations of her popular whodunnit novels.

2. The ability of cats to communicate directly with humans was a comparatively recent twenty-fourth century social development, coinciding with the invention of time travel. Someone should probably look into that. Seems like it might be a significant detail.

3. The enduring professional relationship between Monterey and Lovelace was a matter of wide speculation among the residents of Chronos College. How were they still such an effective team given their mutually strong personalities? The secret was out-and-out bribery. Monterey had access to family funds, and exquisite taste in historical reproduction furnishings. He regularly indulged in extravagant gifts for his partner whenever he had annoyed her beyond the bounds of all reason. Lovelace's apartment on campus was furnished with, to name but a few items: a Louis XIV chair, a Victorian hat rack, a grand piano and a mosaic bath.

twenty-three
fleur shropshire

FLEUR FUCKING SHROPSHIRE.

If you weren't there, you had no idea.

Fleur Shropshire was the girl next door, the wide-eyed ingenue, the cheeky Britminx of the Swinging Sixties.

No one understood why her agent kept signing new contracts for the same boring old TV costume drama when she was so sought-after, but Shropshire served four years as the trapped, bewildered and slightly Gothic heroine Lady Ann Wildegreen on *Cramberleigh*, in between big budget film projects where she kissed, cried, giggled and swooned her way across global cinema screens.

When she did finally leave, Shropshire insisted Lady Ann die on the Titanic, so she couldn't be dragged back to the show ever again. "Drown the poor thing and put her out of her misery" was the quote famously printed in the *Radio Times* that year. The actress laughed when she repeated that story in interviews, so compelling and kooky and genuine that even devoted *Cramberleigh* fans couldn't hold it against her.

Freed from the small screen at last, Fleur Shropshire transitioned from sweet romantic roles to sultry seductive ones just as the trends in cinema changed with her. She was London's It Girl for nearly two decades.

The most famous photograph of Fleur Shropshire is that magazine cover with the crocheted bikini. Yes, that one. The one with a lot less crochet yarn than you might expect.

She was technically a Bond Girl, though only for five minutes before she was fired from the set for pranking the lead actor. Infamously, she raided the costume trailer on her way out, then turned up at the BAFTAS the following year wearing a certain deconstructed tuxedo as a mini-dress.

Fleur Shropshire kissed every leading man who was anyone in 1969. Yes, him. And him. All at the same party.

In 1974 she married a millionaire and retired to the country to "raise ducklings and babies in my Wellies." In one of her many interviews, Shropshire smiled her glorious smile at the cameras and said: "I've done everything, darling. I've made every film I wanted to, and none that I didn't. I've kissed so many lovely men along the way, and I've worn the best clothes in the business. I've played Juliet, Cleopatra and Queen Victoria. I even died on the bloody *Titanic*. Quit while you're ahead, that's what I say!"

Within eighteen months she was back in London, divorced and pretending her rich ex-husband never existed, all hemp blouses and golden mascara: modelling for Vivienne Westwood and partying with the Sex Pistols. She returned to TV in three glorious Technicolour episodes of *Silver Sails*, a glam sci-fi drama in the US in which she played Farrah X, an android woman looking for love.

In another timeline, Fleur Shropshire would have aged like a good whiskey. She would have shifted from movies to glamour soaps in the 80s, fitted in a sitcom or two in the 90s, turned up on panel shows for decades. She would have finished out her career as some lovely posh old lady detective in a long-running cozy crime series, or the naughty grandmother in a quirky small town comedy-drama.

Maybe she would have reinvented herself in her later years, as a judge on a TV show about ballroom dancing, or as the presenter of Most Stylish Canal Journeys of the Cotswolds.

None of that happened because in 1978, two days before her 40th birthday, Fleur Shropshire was killed during an accident on set. The entertainment world was thrown into shock and grief by her horrifying, unforeseen death during a film shoot for what would have been her most iconic movie yet.

She drowned on a replica of the Titanic.

twenty-four
ruthven is well and truly over 912

RUTHVEN WANTED to scream and swear. He wanted to go back in time and remove every single lecture on bloody Time Mechanics he'd ever attended under Professor Boswell. Clearly the cat had no respect for anything to do with time travel.

> Rule 1: don't separate from your partner.

Ruthven spun around, searching the street, but all he saw were Vikings. And a mead stall.

Mead sounded pretty good about now, actually. It was the first thing in this time period that smelled appealing.

"Can I help you?" asked a burly man in furs, ladling out wooden cups of sweet-smelling fermented honey. "You seem lost, stranger."[1]

"I'm looking for an orange and white cat," said Ruthven.

"Lots of cats in town today. It's the Time of the Cat!"

"Is that a local festival?" Ruthven stepped hastily out of the way as another child-laden sleigh pulled by cats went past.

"Yes, indeed! Cats are sacred to the goddess Freya. They are mighty warriors and strong sailors."

"I'm also looking for a woman," said Ruthven. "She had a helmet with two horns on it." Hopefully that was still an unusual thing to see around here and not the latest trend along with distressed denim and Pokemon cards.

"Oh," said the mead guy. "You mean Cressida. I saw her a minute ago wearing that hat of hers." He chuckled. "Two horns. What a character."

Of course it was Cressida. Of course they had turned up in the wrong century and stumbled across her anyway.[2] One more cinnamon stick in the surreal mead cup of Ruthven's life.

"You know what," he said. "I will have a drink. I don't have anything to trade for it..." He reached into his pockets, considered the historical ramifications, and straight up handed over a ballpoint pen.

Suck on that, Time.

"Excellent!" roared the Viking in delight. "My brother-in-law collects these."

"Of course he does." Ruthven accepted the brimming mead cup, and was about to take a mouthful when an arm hooked into his, pulling him along the street.

"Leave the mead, no time," said a breathless woman in braids.

Ruthven did not drop the cup. He did let himself be propelled along by a living legend, because it seemed the quickest route to having everything explained to him. "You're Cressida! You're really her, aren't you?"

Close up, it was obviously her. The hours of footage he had reviewed of Cressida and Boswell's travels through this particular time and place were not entirely conclusive: Cressida's footage had been recorded from her perspective, and the angle of the camera on Boswell's opal meant that Ruthven was a lot more familiar with the shape of Cressida's ankles than the shape of her jawline.

Still, he passed a statue of her on a daily basis. He was confident in his identification.

As Cressida hustled him along through the market, Ruthven realised that her 'helmet' wasn't a helmet at all, not like Fenella's. It was a sturdy felt hat — the horns stuck on the side were attached with large, ugly stitches. The whole aesthetic, matched with the blonde braids and the Viking apron, was a bit more Last Minute DIY Ren Fair than Approved by Costume. But no one seemed to care. Not with this many designer trainers and crop tops floating around 912.

"Top marks," said Cressida, setting a brisk pace. "Have we met?"

"You kicked me and my friend out of a party once. Also, you're sort of famous where I come from."

She was unsurprised. "Tragic moral lesson, am I?"

"Something like that. We thought you were in 1964."

"I wouldn't rule it out. Walk faster, kid."

Ruthven gripped his cup of mead as they hurried through the town, trying to prevent spillage. He was pretty sure he was going to need it when they got to wherever they were going. "Where's Professor Boswell?"

"Professor. That kills me." Cressida barked a laugh. "He's waiting for us. Somewhere safe."

"Oh, good." Ruthven considered everything he had seen of Kettlewick thus far. The happy, laughing children. The entertaining anecdotes. The friendly mead seller. The humorous vegetables. "Are we not safe now?"

Cressida gave him an impatient look, not halting her stride. "This is 912, Rudolf."

"Ruthven," he corrected her. "Why is 912 not safe? Apart from the obvious — casual violence and lack of antibiotics."

They reached a longhouse at the edge of the village, which was full of goats. Cressida tugged him inside. The smell of goat closed in around them like a fog made of, well. Goat. "I could explain," she said. "But that might give the Anachronauts time to catch up with us. I'm trying to avoid that."

"Good call." Ruthven had no idea how wading through the world's largest goat shed would keep them safe from Anachronauts, but he was sure he wouldn't like the answer. "Where is this safe place we're going?"

Cressida unbarred a large door to what looked like a store cupboard. "You'll find it easier to believe if I show you."

"I almost never get into cupboards with strange women!" he protested.

"Go on. It will do you the world of good."

Boswell trusted Cressida. Ruthven wasn't sure he trusted Boswell, but what was the worst that could happen?

(Somewhere in the deep recesses of his mind, Ruthven heard the voice of Lakshmi Tunbridge calling him out for thinking such a thing: "Now you've done it, Ruthven. Everything that goes wrong with this mission is officially your fault.")

He stepped into the cupboard.

---

1. The translator unit built into every opal implant was fairly decent when it came to nuance over content, but you could never be certain that what you heard was exactly what had been said. The translation defaulted to making locals sound more polite than they might have intended. They grew politer with every software update. This was cited as the reason for fewer reported cases of travellers getting into fights with locals, but did create an uptick in travellers assuming that everyone they spoke to was flirting with them.
2. Technically if this was 912 then it was not the 'wrong' century as it was exactly where Boswell had lost Cressida in the first place. But when you're aiming for 1964, 912 CE is wrong no matter which way your scone is buttered.

twenty-five
"you're going to have to forget everything you know about time travel."

LOVELACE DID NOT KNOW whether to scream or ask for an autograph as she stared at the beautiful actress who had disturbed their conversation.

She had spent so many hours watching Lady Ann Wildegreen in the early black and white episodes of *Cramberleigh* — those that had been recovered, at least. She had also watched a variety of films and other pieces of media ephemera featuring Fleur Shropshire, mostly at Monterey's behest.

(The two of them once spent an entire day eating tiny salmon sandwiches while watching half a season of *Silver Sails*. They'd only meant to watch the Fleur Shropshire episodes but somehow ended up consuming eight episodes in one sitting.)

Even now, it didn't feel real to see her in person — a small woman, even daintier than Fenella (if that was possible). Miss Shropshire was costumed as Lady Ann: a long Edwardian tea gown and enormous Gibson Girl hat. The only modern touches were her sunglasses and handbag. She was young, so painfully young, like a ghost stepping out of a movie screen.

Lovelace rarely paid attention to the age of humans. But there was something about knowing this one would die fourteen years from now. Seeing her here, in her mid-twenties, was discombobulating.

"Fleur Shropshire," Fenella said wildly. "I loved you in *A Scandal to Remember*."[1]

Fleur Shropshire, tiny wide-eyed silver screen goddess, smiled sweetly and opened her enormous, bright green Hermes handbag. "You're a darling," she said, and pulled out a very small pearl-handled revolver. "But I'm afraid I haven't made that one yet."

"Ohh," said Lovelace slowly. "*Damn it.*"

It was never a good thing when the locals knew about time travel. It usually meant you were getting close to an...

The wallpaper changed colour, sage green stripes to orange polka dots. For a moment, every portrait on every wall displayed an image of a jewelled pineapple, then Marilyn Monroe, then the Mona Lisa, then a large mug shaped like a sphinx.

"Event!" screeched Lovelace. "Fenella, we have to go."

"Don't rush on my account," said Fleur Shropshire, still somehow appearing sweet and harmless despite the gun. "I want to hear all about which BAFTA Awards ceremonies of the next decade are worth bothering with."

"I can't leave Cress," Fenella said, panicking. "She's still unconscious."

The wallpaper now had aeroplanes printed all over it, and the floor was covered in houndstooth black and white carpet instead of the parquet from two minutes ago.

All the fur on Lovelace's back spiked straight up in the air, as if she needed the physical confirmation that they were in grave danger.

The door under the staircase burst open, and an entirely different Cressida appeared. This one was dressed in the full Victorian nightmare, all corsetry and ruffles, though the colours were unbelievably garish and the sleeves belonged to a later century. "You absolutely can leave her," she yelled. "Trust me, Fen, she's the wrong one. Let's go!"

Lovelace didn't wait to see what choice Fenella made. She scampered directly at the ankles of this other Cressida, the one that was talking sense.

As Lovelace took shelter underneath the largest and most virulently tie-dyed chartreuse bustle known to history, Fenella flung herself into the cupboard after them.

The door closed.

"This way," said New Cressida, managing somehow to turn around and make room for the rest of them to follow, despite her enormous behind.

They followed. For some time. The storage space in this manor house was really quite exceptional.

"Cress," said Fenella in a shaky voice. "Is it really you?"

"It's me, Fen. Look at you. I can't believe you graduated already."

"I can't believe my favourite twentieth century actress tried to kill us."

"She wasn't trying very hard," Lovelace remarked. "Her handbag to gun ratio was distinctly unimpressive."

"You weren't her target," said Cressida grimly. "She was after 1964 — and she got it."

Another cupboard door opened, letting them out in a room that seemed like a parody of a Victorian parlour if the only Victorian history you knew was from Sherlock Holmes novels. All it required for the full effect was some chap in a deerstalker, puffing on a pipe. (It smelled like one had been here recently. It also smelled like 1899.)

It took Lovelace, Fenella and Cressida some time to squeeze out of the cupboard, largely because Cressida's gravity-defying bustle took up the same space as several people.

"Is this still 1964?" asked Fenella.

Lovelace didn't bother to tell her what year it was, or why

they now appeared to be several floors higher in the same house despite having only walked a short distance through a cupboard. She didn't care about any of that.

She did not care because *her human was here*.

Montgomery J Monterey, wearing his high necked jumper, lounged in a green leather chair like he was waiting for a butler to bring him his deerstalker hat and pipe.

Oxford was here too, but whatever.

Lovelace leaped. She landed claws out, as was only right and proper, directly on to Monterey's lap, and biffed him aggressively in the face with her own face, several times.

He let out a low laugh, and scratched her behind the ears. "Hello, darling. Were you worried?"

"You're not allowed to travel without me," she informed him. "You get into the most terrible trouble."

"I've been here the whole time, and haven't caused the least amount of trouble," he informed her. "How about you, sweetheart?"

This was awkward. "We may have caused an Event in 1964," she admitted.

Monterey laughed, long and loud. Lovelace didn't care. He was here, and she was never letting him out of her sight again. She pressed her head to his ribs, and purred.

"A good thing too," remarked Tie-Dyed Victorian Cressida, who was a lot more useful to have around than her screaming, fainting 1960s Production Assistant Bunty persona. "Or I'd never have been able to get to you."

"That makes no sense!" Oxford said, sounding baffled. Lovelace peered over her shoulder at him, allowing Monterey the appropriate amount of scritching access to her ears. "Events don't make time travel easier," Oxford went on. "That's what makes them Events."

"You're going to have to forget everything you know about time travel," Cressida informed him. She popped back into the cupboard, closing the door behind her bustle.

"Wait!" yelped Fenella, flinging the door open immediately. "Huh," she added, tapping on the back of the clearly empty cupboard. "Where did she go? Is this a secret passage?"

"We should pretend it's a secret passage for the sake of our sanity," Monterey said, shifting his scritching of Lovelace's ears to that tricky spot on the arch of her spine.

Oxford looked more rattled than usual. He was probably missing his cat. "If it was possible to get inside Events," he muttered to himself. "Why would no one tell me?"

"Perhaps no one knows," Lovelace said coldly.

She'd never been a fan of Oxford. She knew Monterey considered him as some sort of honorary sibling, but she could never fully trust a person who had been chosen by Nero, the most slippery and self-involved of cats.

Fenella perched on the arm of Oxford's chair, patting his arm as if he was a cat needing to be soothed. "Are we the only ones who made it through the hop?" she asked.

"Hard to be sure," said Monterey. "There was a bit of a mess, obviously. Remember the flames and the screaming? Nero was supposed to be here with Oxford. Lovelace and I were supposed to be together. And you, Fen-my-love, were not supposed to be here at all."

"Thanks," Fenella said sourly. "I didn't do it on purpose."

"Hmm," said Monterey. "The fact that you said that out loud makes me wonder if you are in fact the devious mastermind behind it all. It's the quiet ones you have to watch."

"Ruthven and Boswell," Oxford said in a low voice. "They were already through the hoop when everything went wrong. We haven't seen them."

"We didn't spot them in 1964 either," said Lovelace. "I suppose we have to wait for Cressida to tell us what's going on. Assuming she is Cressida."

"That is most definitely Cressida," said Monterey. "I've never met someone so Cressida as that woman in that cupboard."

They all stared at the closed cupboard door.

"Was she always this annoying?" Oxford wondered.

"I'd forgotten that side of her, what with being so upset about her being tragically lost for seven years," remarked Fenella. "But she hasn't changed much. Except for the bustle. That is an extraordinarily anachronistic bustle. I find it personally insulting to the Costume Department."

The cupboard door opened again.

"Right," said Cressida, squeezing through in her obnoxious bustle. "It's going to save time if you trust that I know more than you about what's going on around here."

"Where's here?" asked Monterey. "Apart from the smoking room that murdered Sherlock Holmes."

"Fenthorp Manor, 1899," Cressida informed him.

"But 1899 is an Event..." Monterey paused. "No, I've got the hang of it now. We're inside an Event. Everything we know is wrong." He scratched Lovelace behind her ears again, showing the proper priority. "Carry on."

"Good," said Cressida. "Please save your questions to the end. I need to collect something very important that I left in 912."

"Let's just stroll there, shall we," Oxford muttered under his breath.

Monterey patted his arm. "I'll explain it to you later."

"Can you do it without being insufferably smug?"

"You'd find that even more confusing." Monterey continued to scratch Lovelace's ears, proving himself to be the best of all possible humans.

"What about the version of you that we left in 1964?" Lovelace asked, pushing down the purr that threatened to take over her whole being.

Cressida didn't seem bothered. "Useless. Scattered."[2]

"Why are there two of you?" complained Fenella.

"Questions at the *end*, Fen."

"Later meaning after we've visited 912," said Monterey, carefully formatting it as a statement, not a question.

"Yes." Cressida looked relieved. "912 should be safe for a while."

"And we *can* just stroll there, can we?" He gave Oxford a look that was almost apologetic.

"Absolutely," said Cressida. "Hope you're all wearing comfortable shoes."

"You're going have to explain things in more depth soon," Oxford said sternly. "And by more depth, I mean, at all."

"I will, I promise," said Cressida. "But I need to get you all out of this house before dinner time. I just checked the date on the downstairs calendar and it turns out this particular day in Fenthorp Manor, 1899, is about to become rather busy. I was aiming for April, but got a bit turned around in the time aisle."

"Why?" said Oxford. "What happens at dinner time?"

"What's a time aisle?" Fenella interrupted.

Lovelace dug her claws into Monterey's leg. He pressed his hand firmly against her spine. *Don't freak out. At least we're together.*

The sound of a loud bronze gong reverberated through the house.

"Damn it," said Cressida. "Okay. The house is about to fill up with Anachronauts. Don't lose your heads."

---

1. *A Scandal To Remember* (1970) is a farce comedy in which a hapless British Prime Minister (Ronnie Connor) is haunted by the sexy ghosts of Cleopatra (Fleur Shropshire), Lucretia Borgia (Valerie Windsor) and Marie Antoinette (Sheila Troughton) who all gleefully interfere with his humorous attempts to settle down with a nice respectable bride. He

ends up married to Doris, also played by Fleur Shropshire: a secretary with an uncanny resemblance to a certain dead Pharaoh.
2. Scattered: a term also known as time-blinded, or chronologically discombobulated. Can result in memory loss, identity crisis and a little light swooning. If your travel partner is afflicted, all you can do is return them to the twenty-fourth century, fill in a Lost Memory form on their behalf, and hope for the best.

twenty-six
the anachronauts

What about the Anachronauts? How do they fit into the popular Time is a Bastard theory of the single, unbreakable, 'everything that happened was always happening and was always meant to happen, just accept it or so help me Time will screw with you until you get it right' timeline?

The Anachronauts make things awkward. We don't know nearly enough about them to be certain of anything, thanks to the Global Official Secrets Act, and the corruption of university administration bodies. They know how to cover up scandals.

Here's what we do know: there were three colleges established in the twenty-fourth century more than a decade ago, for the purpose of studying, practicing and formalising the procedures for time travel. The funding was 100% private, provided by nine individuals known as the Founders.

Only those connected to one of the three colleges, or in a select number of high positions in the world government, even know that time travel technology exists.

One of the three colleges went... well, *evil*. They went to the bad. Descended into villainous monologues and dastardly deeds. How else to explain it?

We know that their leaders are named Zephyr, Abydos and Professor Shelley.

We know that one of their early mission statements was to 'save' key historical people who died untimely deaths.

We know that the Anachronauts have caused irreparable damage to Time, including (at least) twenty separate Events, walling huge portions of history off to legit travellers forever. We suspect that the majority of these activities were deliberate acts of sabotage, rather than accidental (as with the Events caused by the reckless behaviour of Chronos College travellers).

We know that large numbers of the Anachronauts were captured and exposed during the Medici Raid, though we don't know what punishment (if any) they received.

(One of those captured Anachronauts was my sibling, so I'd QUITE like to know more.)

We know there are still plenty of Anachronauts out there, and that their movement continues to grow.

We haven't heard much from them for a while. That means they're probably up to something so diabolical that we won't see it coming until it's too late.

> Zadie Kincaid, *Getting More And More Worried About Time Travel, Actually* — self published pamphlet, exclusively distributed to trusted friends and allies on campus

twenty-seven
skulking in the scullery

MONTEREY WAS NOT PANICKING. Why would he panic? He had Lovelace back. They'd found Cressida, after all these years — or she had found them. They were about to be overrun by Anachronauts.

No reason to make a flap. Right?

Cressida dragged them out of the smoking room and down to the ground floor via a set of back stairs that existed because houses run by servants liked to make sure everyone had their own staircases.[1] The whole gang were currently squashed into a room called a scullery, which contained large boxy sinks and a wild assortment of clean pots and kettles, showing no sign of having been recently used.

Despite the surfeit of kettles, there was no evidence that tea was on the cards. Distressing, but one had to endure.

The plan was for Monterey, Oxford, Lovelace, Cressida and Fenella to move discreetly through a house full of dangerous time saboteurs in order to step into yet another cupboard which may or may not lead them directly to 912 CE. Monterey was not loving this plan. He'd had enough of surprise cupboards.

At least Fenella and Oxford were asking the stupid questions so Monterey could pretend to be aloof and above it all.[2]

"*Why* are the Anachronauts coming here today?" asked Fenella.

"1899 is one of their favourite years to use for meetings and social functions," said Cressida, sounding annoyed with herself. "I should have known better than to bring you all here, but Fenthorp is such a useful conjunction."

"What's a conjunction?" Oxford asked.

"Will you be upset if I use words like 'magic door'?"

"Let's leave magic out of it," sighed Lovelace. "We're not *kittens*."

"Okay," said Cressida. "We're currently inside an Event. Once years are sealed off by Events, they start going very odd. Separated from the proper timeline, they can... get a bit wild. Paradoxy. After a while, they drift from the path of all known Time Mechanics." She gestured at her bustle as if this should explain the fabric. "Spend enough time in here, you can even find ways to encourage some of those anachronisms. Usually that just adds more chaos. It's handy, though, in a jam."

"So, the Anachronauts hang out in these years having committee meetings?" Oxford demanded, his voice getting a bit too loud.

"Committee meetings, cocktail parties, you name it. Event Space is their territory. That's why they damaged the timeline in the first place. I'm not sure if they're delighted or frustrated that they can indulge all of their anachronistic impulses without making a dent in Basic Time. Basic Time is the term they use for everything that isn't Event Space, by the way."

"Patronising," Oxford noted.

"That's how they roll," said Cressida.

"I still don't understand how we're inside an Event," Fenella frowned. "And how we crawled from 1963 to 1899 through a secret passage in a cupboard."

"It's called a time aisle," said Cressida.

Monterey was finally unable to hold back from joining in. "I know that phrase. Wasn't it in a *Cramberleigh* episode?"

Cressida looked weary. "Tell me you're not surprised that the Anachronauts named a time concept after something in a *Cramberleigh* episode. Anyway, the more anachronisms filter in, the more Event Space gets — oh, soft, I suppose. Pliable. Spongy. The Anachronauts have connected up the soft spots. They've done a lot of work here, at Fenthorp Manor — again, time travellers who are obsessed with *Cramberleigh*, not a shock. Some of their aisles travel in time and space. Some are just in time. The softest spots of conjunction are usually at ground zero of what created the Event in the first place. This particular house is the squishiest hot spot you can imagine."

"How do we get back to Basic Time?" asked Oxford abruptly. He really didn't look well, poor fellow. That was what came from putting your trust in institutions. Oxford had always been a bit too willing to go along with whatever the Founders wanted — a parent pleaser, if ever there was one.

There was a long pause after Oxford asked his question. Monterey didn't love that long pause.

"We *can* get back, can't we?" he pressed.

"I'm still figuring that out," Cressida admitted. "I hadn't rescued myself yet when you all crashed in here. I have no idea how you even got here. I had a theory about me, but it doesn't fit this." She made a sweeping gesture to encompass them all under the umbrella of 'this.'

"Cressida," said Monterey as a thought woke up inside him and started to dress for the occasion. "Are you saying that we can access *all* the years that have been walled off by Events?"

Lovelace patted him with a paw. "Just catching up, are you, darling?"

"Don't mind me. Thinking through the ramifications, *darling*." His mind was ablaze with the possibilities.

"Technically it's possible," said Cressida. "I only know a fraction of the available aisles, though."

Monterey waved off the details. "Can I finally meet Cleopatra?"

Lovelace groaned loudly. "What has that poor Pharaoh done to deserve your flailing attempts at conversation, Monterey?"

"Easy for you to say, met-her-three-times," he retorted.

Cressida took the question seriously. "I recommend against it. Cleopatra's not a fan of travellers these days. She's met too many Anachronauts."

"Does this mean I can attend Freddie Mercury's legendary 1978 Halloween party?" Monterey pressed, getting more excited. "1978 has been an Event *forever*."

Cressida looked sceptical. "It wasn't that great."

"How dare you."

"The year, not the party. I haven't been to the party."

"What a waste!"

"Monterey," Lovelace said huffily. "There is more at stake here than ticking items off your precious bucket list."

"I know," he said, fluttering his eyelashes at his partner. "But wouldn't it be a lovely reward for all our hard work?"

"Roll it back a bit," Oxford said in one of his stuffier tones of voice. "The Anachronauts are here, in this house, right now? How many are we talking about?"

"Filling the dining room as we speak," Cressida sighed. "It's their Annual Festive Function. The aisle that leads to 912 is in the small ballroom leading off the dining room, which is why I wanted to get there ahead of the crowd. We'll have to wait them out."

"How many of them?" Oxford demanded.

Cressida gave him an awkward shrug. "Enough for a

festive dinner. They've been recruiting since the Medici Raid — and honestly I don't think they suffered as many losses from that as we were told. I'd say they're back up to full strength."

Monterey saw which way the wind was going. "Dear fellow, you had better not be thinking what I think you're thinking."

Oxford straightened his shoulders. "I know you don't have a sense of loyalty, Monterey, but those people are traitors. It's our responsibility to…"

"To what, arrest them?"

"At least identify them. Detain them if needs be. We can take them back to Chronos College to face their crimes."

"Excellent plan," said Cressida cheerfully. "How exactly were you planning on doing that?"

"That's not the point," said Oxford, floundering only a little. "You're proposing we skulk around and save our skins without taking any responsibility for the house full of time terrorists."

"Skulking around and saving my skin is most of what I've been doing since I found myself in Event Space," Cressida snapped. "You don't know what you've stumbled across, and you are not ready to start making decisions on behalf of this group, let alone Time herself. You didn't even have the sense to bring your cat!"

Oxford reared back, as if it was the height of rudeness to point out his lack of Nero.

Monterey brushed his hand against the back of Lovelace's spine, to reassure him that she, at least, was still here.

"You lost your cat seven years ago, Cressida," Oxford grumbled back. "You're hardly in a position to…"

Cressida looked like she had been slapped. "Seven *years*? Is that how long it's been?"

"I thought you knew," Fenella said in a small voice.

Stricken, Cressida turned and gave her sister a hug. "I knew it had to be years," she muttered. "But that's... wow. Seven. Big number."

"You wouldn't believe how many pens I've stolen since you ditched us," said Monterey, to break the tension.

Cressida, teetering on the brink of tears, laughed instead. "Fiend. Not Shakespeare?"

"Shakespeare was easy," he told her gravely. "The Bronte sisters were the ones that put up a fight."

"So what are we to do?" Oxford demanded. "About these Anachronauts. Our duty."

"We're going to avoid them, Oxford," Cressida said, the smile wiping off her face. "Like sensible people. You can write as many reports for your mothers as you want, once we're safely out of here."

"Actually," said another voice, breaking into their conversation. "It's a little late for that."

They all looked up to see the pantry door wide, and two Anachronauts standing there.

Monterey recognised them. Zephyr Kincaid — a tall, gracefully androgynous human with long, braided silver hair. Abydos — a black cat with shining golden eyes and a single tuft of white fur over one eyebrow. They had once both been trainees at Chronos College, before being lured over to Aleister College by generous scholarship and funding grants.[3]

Monterey had kissed Zephyr at a party once. Their parents were friends, just like Oxford's, they'd known each other since they were kids. He hadn't seen Zeph in years. The Kincaid family didn't like to advertise that one of the scions of a Founding Family had run off with the Anachronauts.

Today, Zephyr was dressed in some kind of toga over deep silk sleeves. Abydos sat on their left shoulder, poised to attack.

"This is awkward," Monterey drawled. "Looks like you don't have to worry about arresting anyone, Oxford."

"If anyone's under arrest," said Zephyr calmly. "It's you clowns. Consider yourself under the protection of the Liberated Anachronance." Their eyes flicked to Cressida, and they frowned. "What are *you* doing here, Church?"

"Getting arrested, apparently," she said brightly. "Let's get on with it, shall we?"

---

1. Monterey had once spent an enlightening weekend in a country home rented by Lord Byron, which featured six completely different sets of staircases, so that entire categories of servants could avoid not only the gentry, but each other.
2. Thus far, no one had asked the burning question that Monterey was most interested in, namely: where *were* the servants and indeed all the other people who should be swanning around a fancy old manor in 1899? Monterey wasn't willing to ask the question himself because he had a horrible feeling Cressida would tell him, and he'd already taken on a great deal of upsetting information today.
3. The downfall of Aleister College, which went from being a respectable time travel facility to a centre for illicit Anachronaut activity in less than a year, was largely put down to over-funding, an issue that universities are rarely equipped to handle.

twenty-eight
cleopatra calling

"TIME AISLES," Ruthven repeated, absorbing the new vocabulary. Familiar vocabulary, for anyone who had watched Season 11 of *Cramberleigh*. "Why do they call them time aisles?"

"Why hoops?" Viking Cressida replied. "Why hops? I'm not in charge of naming things, Rupert. I'm sure there's a committee for that. Someone came up with 'Anachronauts,' after all. That has three hour group decision written all over it."

You never actually saw the time aisles referenced in Season 11 of *Cramberleigh*: it was deemed too expensive to build an extra set. Ruthven had always wondered what they would look like, especially considering the wildly contradictory descriptions in the novelisations.

This particular time aisle started out as a wooden passage with a visible thatched roof, like the rest of the buildings in the Viking town they came from. As they walked along its endless length, the colour bled out of the walls. Everything became white and shiny.

It was futuristic in an old-fashioned way, like other TV shows from the twentieth century, where they expected a certain bland whiteness and platinum gleam in future architecture; before the trend for badly-lit grunge kicked in.

"I know you know that my name is Ruthven," he said.

"Sorry," said Cressida. She did look slightly sorry. "I've been alone a long time. No one to calibrate my sense of humour against, except imaginary Boswell. That cat is even grumpier than the real one."

"Sounds fake," said Ruthven, refusing to admit that he had an imaginary Aesop in his head most of the time.

Cressida's burst of laughter made the null corridor feel like a friendly place, for about five seconds.

The time aisle began to narrow ahead of them. Ruthven remembered all over again to be worried.

"Where are we going?" he asked Cressida.

"48 BCE."

"Now I know you're bullshitting. 48 BCE is an Event."

She rolled her eyes at him, and walked faster. "You remember that 912 is also an Event, right?"

Ruthven scrambled after her. "But 48 BCE is... *double* an Event, if that even is a thing."

"It isn't."

"Monterey and Lovelace triggered an Event trying to save the Library of Alexandria too many times, and then the Anachronauts triggered a massive event covering Cleopatra's lifetime..."

"Time aisles, Rumpole," said Cressida impatiently. "They connect Events. We're in Event Space. The problem is not that those years are inaccessible. Ask me how much I wish that was the problem."

Ruthven knew when a person was hinting he should ask a different question. "What is the problem, exactly?"

The corridor tapered into an alarmingly narrow point. Cressida shoved at the point with her hands, cracking open a door that hadn't been there a minute ago. It opened out, scraping and juddering along a stone floor.

Scent wafted through the doorway: incense and oils, dried roses and salt. Smellwise, it was a distinct improvement on 912. They must be about to step into a century where baths were in fashion.

"Two problems," said Cressida, shoving the door open further. "The first is that the Anachronauts flit back and forth between Basic Time and Event Space... but I don't know how they do it. I've been stuck in here since I got lost."

Ruthven had follow up questions, particularly about who decided on the phrase 'Basic Time.' He shelved them for now. "What's the other problem?"

Cressida waved a dramatic if tired arm. "You saw 912. College policy has always been so smug about how Time regulates herself. She doesn't allow paradoxes. Within Event Space? Time is all about paradoxes. It's a paradoxapaloosa."

"So the skateboards and the Pokemon cards..."

"*Exactly*. 912 is the worst example, but you see it all over. It can't be sustainable. The Events are supposed to be rock solid, protecting Basic Time from damage. But who's to say that's a constant, when... well, see for yourself."

One last shove and the white door swung open. Cressida went ahead, with Ruthven trailing behind.

He'd been here before. Not *here*, exactly, because 48 BCE was already an Event when Ruthven first qualified as a traveller. He and Aesop had, however, visited this specific palace during the early reign of Ptolemy XII, father of the most famous of the Cleopatras.

Trips to Egypt were highly sought after. Aesop was so chuffed to finally score one. "Taste everything," she commanded as she and Ruthven took their places at the banquet table (so low in the pecking order that they barely ranked above foreign scribes and mathematicians). "If the locals wish to worship me, instruct them to add their names to my dance card."

They weren't supposed to be there, in the palace or at that dinner. But that was Aesop for you — easy and charming. Somehow when she was around, Ruthven had been easy and charming too.

It was the same palace. Its red granite pillars and sturdy walls stood upon the island of Antirhodos, in the harbour of Alexandria.

It would sink underwater in around five centuries after a terrible earthquake, along with a temple of Isis, two sphinxes, and the unfinished palace of Mark Antony.[1]

Ruthven remembered the vivid red and gold decor, the marble statues, the sumptuous silks and shining statues (and the food, oh the food — he could practically taste the deep, melting flavours on his tongue).[2]

What he did not recall was the introduction of the telephone.

Cleopatra, Pharaoh of Egypt, sat cross-legged on a futon. Her strong-featured face was familiar enough from coins and statues, but also from the footage Ruthven had watched of Monterey and Lovelace's disastrous Alexandria campaign. A great deal of that footage was transformed over the years into hilarious memes, music vids and other forms of mixed media, making Cleopatra a favourite historical celebrity among Chronos College students.[3]

She wore a long white silk gown, tied by ribbons under her breasts, and draped in a beaded belt. She also wore silver sandals poking out from underneath the gown. Her face, made up with the traditional kohl and bright colours, wasn't what anyone would call beautiful if it wasn't the face of a queen, but would stand out as 'interesting' at any given dinner party.

Cleopatra was speaking into the receiver of a classic bright green rotary-dial telephone, the curly cord tangled around her limbs and disappearing around behind a basalt statue of Osiris.

Ruthven stared at it for a moment, wondering where (and how) it was plugged in.

"Hang on, she's here," Cleopatra was saying into the phone. "Yes, bring the parcel. See you later, alligator." She hung up, letting the phone drop carelessly to the floor. "Cress! You made it back."

"Cleo!" replied Cressida with rather less enthusiasm. "You kidnapped my cat."

The Pharaoh of Egypt shrugged a graceful shoulder. "A little kidnap between friends, who's to mind?"

Ruthven gave Cressida a slightly betrayed look. "You said Boswell was safe."

"Depends on your definition of safe," she said with a shrug. "He was kidnapped by two guards wearing the mark of the Pharaoh painted on their tasers. I knew they wouldn't do too much damage."

"Ancient Egyptian guards have tasers now?" Ruthven was distracted enough by that revelation to not worry about the possible diplomatic impact of referring to Egyptians as 'ancient' while they were still current.

"Also skateboards," Cressida said with a sigh. "Whatever experiments the Anachronauts have been running in these Events... somehow there are always skateboards."

Cleopatra cleared her throat. "I'm no friend of the Anachronauts, Cressida. You know that. If any of those worms show their faces around me, there will be executions all around. But I can't say I hate all of their gifts."

The double doors opened, and several bare-chested guards entered wearing white linen garments around their hips and — yes, Ruthven could see them clearly now he knew what to look for — holstered tasers alongside the curved swords that hung from their jewelled belts.

They were carrying a rolled up carpet.

"You didn't," Cressida said in a low, threatening voice.

"Never neglect a stylish entrance," said Cleopatra, standing up as the carpet was presented before her. "Elizabeth Taylor, eat your heart out."

Now she was this close to them, Ruthven realised that the Pharaoh's sandals were made of a jelly-like plastic, featuring silver glitter. She had bright Hello Kitty decals stuck to her toenails.

The guards lined themselves up symmetrically and unrolled the carpet. As the last layer flattened out, it revealed a marmalade tabby clinging by his claws to the carpet. Boswell looked more pissed off than Ruthven had ever seen him, even when marking exams.

"Hi Boz," said Cressida, her voice soft. "Rescued your new partner. He seems fine. Not as cool as me, obviously."

Boswell's eyes flared as he slowly unhooked his claws from the carpet. He locked eyes on Cressida. "Ruthven," he said in a low, rumbling voice. "Step away from that person."

It was rather nice to be called by his real name. "Professor, what's going on?" Ruthven asked.

"Professor?" Cressida laughed hollowly. "So it's true. Don't tell me academia swallowed you whole, Boz. You were always such a rebel."

Boswell approached in a slow stalk. "You, young lady, are not Cressida Church. What happened to her?"

Cressida's face hardened. She removed the felt Viking helmet with its two horns. "You tell me, Boswell," she replied in an icy tone of voice. "You're the one who lost her."

---

1. It was Cleopatra's idea to build Mark Antony his own palace. A Pharaoh can't be expected to share her palace with her boyfriend. It's important in a relationship for all parties to have their own space.

2. It was a matter of great confusion to historians that the Egyptians, who had a massive fishing industry, ate a largely vegetarian diet. Why did they catch so many fish they did not eat? Surely they didn't all get sacrificed to the gods... The answer, as Ruthven and Aesop discovered firsthand in the court of Ptolemy XII, was a population of extremely happy cats. Ruthven cherished the memory of Aesop with her small mouth wrapped around a fried perch almost as large as she was: the personification (or cattification) of pure joy.
3. Monterey could often be heard lamenting that he never got to meet Cleopatra despite the many (one might say far too many) hops he and Lovelace had completed in order to save the contents of that library. Lovelace met Cleopatra three times during those same trips. It was amazing that their partnership survived his overwhelming jealousy.

twenty-nine
kettlewick, 912

"I'M CALLING IT NOW," complained Cressida. "912 is the worst year of all time."

"That's quite the statement," said Boswell. "Can you back it up with citations?"

"It's raining, it's muddy, and there are Vikings everywhere."

Cressida had decided on reflection that Vikings up close were less fun than she had imagined.

Except that one turnip seller. She'd liked him, if only because he appreciated the value of a good humorous vegetable. His kids had been rather sweet, too, before they tried to make off with her satchel and learned a very quick lesson in why you don't piss off a marmalade tabby.

Now Cressida and Boswell were back at the site of their hop. There was no sign of a glowing time hoop anywhere.

"Where are they," Cressida muttered, jogging on the spot to keep warm, something she was only capable of keeping up for about three minutes. "I'm cold and damp."

"Serves you right for not being a cat," remarked her charming partner.

Finally the hoop appeared: a glorious circle of shining light cutting through the grey and muck of Kettlewick, 912.

Cressida let out a "Woo hoo!" as she scooped up Boswell in the hand that was not carrying her souvenir turnip.

"Please refrain from treating me like a handbag," he said with maximum dignity.

"Wouldn't want to lose you, Boz."

They hopped through, as they had a hundred times before.

Cressida knew what to expect: the warm cobblestones of the quad, the artificial sun on her face and the happy babble of returning travellers. The satisfaction of another mission complete, even if this one gave her no opportunity to nick pens from historical celebrities.

Instead, she stumbled into a dusty museum, with empty arms.

Not the Museum of Lost Things at Chronos College. Not anywhere familiar. There were real antiquities in the cases: valuable items, properly labelled. A private collection?

"What the fuck?" Cressida spun around, frantic. "Boswell! Where are you?" She'd lost her cat.

"You're wasting your breath," said a low, purring voice.

At first, she could not see anything but glass cabinets of curiosities. Then she followed the gleam of orange light to a burning fireplace, where a black cat warmed himself on the hearth rug.

"What have you done to me?" Cressida demanded. "Where is my cat?"

The black cat glanced at her, conveying maximum disdain. He had a tick of white above one of his eyes.

"You should worry about yourself," the black cat purred. "Everyone knows that humans are the ones who shouldn't travel through time on their own. So many rules to time travel. How could anyone possibly keep them all straight?"

"There are no rules," said Cressida. "I've read the charter. There's just things that work and things that don't. Trial and error. Basic facts we'd be idiots to ignore. Everything else is experimentation." She scowled. "I know you, don't I? Abydos. We trained together for a while."

"A short while," said the black cat, Abydos. "I found something more interesting. You will, too."

Cressida's eyes narrowed. "Is this a kidnapping, or a job offer?"

The black cat preened, swiping a paw against her ear. "Can't it be both?"

Cressida frowned. "How much of a choice do I get?"

There was something odd about Abydos' eyes. One of them was rather more purple than the other, and shiny as if... well, if Cressida didn't know better, she'd think the cat was wearing a monocle.

"Let's find out," said Abydos.

part three
everywhere but 912

thirty
the anachronauts annual festive function 1899

always prepare for uninvited guests

SHORTLY AFTER BEING DISCOVERED by the Anachronauts, Monterey and Oxford were shoved and locked into a pantry.

It was full of polished silverware, because this house was fancy enough to have a whole pantry set aside for shiny things only. Still no prospect of a nice cup of tea on the horizon.

Monterey did not like to think about why he and Oxford might have been separated from their colleagues. Being apart from Lovelace *again* made him want to punch dents into every punchbowl on the third shelf.

As usual, when under pressure, he reacted by being as annoying as possible to people in his near vicinity. This was bad news for Oxford.

Monterey flopped dramatically against a wall. "I wonder how the Anachronauts dispose of their inconvenient prisoners. Guillotine, do you think? Or, since this is the nineteenth bloody century, will they pull out some delicious green wallpaper for us to lick?"

"Can you just," said Oxford tiredly. "Shut up. For like, two minutes."

This felt like a win. Oxford had spent most of his life being far too friendly and genial to tell anyone to shut up. Monterey could only consider this to be a new and improved version.

"Such a waste of a hop to the Victorian era," Monterey drawled exactly two minutes later. "Cressida's running around reinventing the bustle, and I never even got a chance to snog a butler. That's on my bucket list. The Brontës didn't have one, and Lord Byron... well, his butlers had suffered enough."

"You are the worst person to be stuck with in a silverware pantry," moaned Oxford.

Monterey slid to the ground. "No one ever appreciates my attempts to keep their spirits up."

"I wonder why."

Oxford slid down to the ground on the opposite side of the silverware pantry, about two feet away. He looked drained, poor fellow. Monterey should be nicer to him. After all, Oxford had gone through this entire hop without his cat. Monterey never had much time for Nero: snobbish, sarcastic ball of constantly-shedding white fur that he was. Still, Oxford was probably missing him.

It is a peculiar fact that Monterey deciding to be nice to a person is fairly indistinguishable from Monterey being as annoying as possible.

"Oh, by all means," he drawled. "Snatch the duty of making conversation from my tragically tea-deprived hands. Why don't you fill the hours lamenting to me about your failed five-year plan to seduce that Media Archives hobgoblin who is clearly already in love with you. I promise to be attentive and sympathetic."

"I don't — Ruthven's not a hobgoblin," muttered Oxford.

"Doesn't get out much, though, does he?" teased Monterey.

"He's... lovely. And you're an arse. And I *don't* have a five-year plan."

"I know, darling," Monterey said in what he intended to be a soothing voice. "No one thinks you're planning to move that fast."

There was silence for about a minute, which was long and awkward enough for Monterey to wish he could flay his own skin off.

"You don't think we're going to be in here for hours do you?" Oxford asked plaintively.

"Who can say? I hope Lovelace is having a better time than us."

Lovelace was not having a good time. During her career as a traveller, she had been abducted, kidnapped, incarcerated and generally detained a grand total of 22 separate occasions, mostly in the company of Monterey. The two of them had invented their own rating system for prison cells. They had a series of entertaining word games to play when stuck in a room together with nothing to do but wait for the escape plan to kick in.

Being together made it easier. As long as Monterey was not deprived of tea for too long, which usually led to Lovelace wanting to scratch his ankles.

This part was familiar, at least. Having been arrested, Lovelace now found herself forced to wait about on an uncomfortable chair while her human companions changed their outfits.[1]

"What a ridiculous waste of time," Cressida huffed, leaning against the door of the dressing room in which they had been deposited by Zephyr and Abydos. "I already look dinner-party-ready. A tie-dyed crinoline isn't business casual."

"As the person who accidentally time travelled in their pyjamas," said Fenella from behind an embroidered screen.

"I'm all for a chance to freshen up. These people know you, Cress. How on earth did you get acquainted?"

"I mean," said Cressida, shrugging. "Recruitment lunches, mostly." She glanced at Lovelace. "You get recruitment lunches too, right?"

Lovelace tossed her head. "On occasion. A cat has to eat."

"So you just sit around and eat lunch with the enemy?" Fenella said amid some serious rustling. "While they pitch job offers at you?"

"They're not the enemy," said Cressida immediately. "I mean, they are, obviously. Very different time travel philosophies. But, ah. Anachronauts are just people from another college, when it comes down to it. It's hard, only being allowed to socialise with people who have signed the Official Global Secrets Act. It's not as if we have a lot in common with people who aren't time travellers."

"I wouldn't know," her sister said dryly. Fenella emerged from behind the screen wearing a Napoleonic officer's coat over a long white Ancient Greek peplos, and her own sneakers. She looked a little like a child playing dress-ups. "Do you think they're going to feed us while pitching job offers tonight?"

"Hard to say," said Cressida.

"I hope so," said Lovelace, whose tummy was beginning to protest the lack of fish suppers. If this was Ancient Egypt, she'd have been fed three times already.

They knew how to treat a cat in Ancient Egypt.

In the silverware pantry, Monterey thought to ask: "How much do you think we can trust Cressida? Seems like there's a lot she's still not telling us."

"I don't know," Oxford said bleakly. "Trust is a funny

thing, isn't it. Secrets and all that. Push enough of them down, it's hard to fish them back out."

"Are you having a nervous breakdown, old thing?"

"I don't think *one* nervous breakdown is going to cut it. Processing all this is going to take at least three."

Lovelace perched on Fenella's shoulder. She didn't like it. She was unhappy relying on any human other than her Monterey, whom she had personally trained. But she and Fenella had hopped through time together since 1964, and it was good manners to dance with the one who brought you.

Zephyr kept darting strange looks in Lovelace's direction — no, it was Fenella who had unsettled their captor. Surely it couldn't be the outfit.

A draped banner in the dining room declared this to be ***The Anachronauts Annual Festive Function 1899***. As was common for Victorian times, the dining room was dark and high-ceilinged, with wallpaper so busy you could get lost in the narrative.

Lovelace had to imagine that before 1899 became an Event, the wallpaper had not been covered in pictures of art deco cartoon dinosaurs fighting art nouveau little green aliens, but you could never quite tell with the Victorians.

A large table took up most of the room, laden with displays of flowers, along with several pineapples intended for decoration rather than snacking. At least two dozen well-dressed humans and cats were seated around the table, already tucking in.

The food was spectacular: fancy cakes, towering jellies and glistening vegetables, all those things that humans seemed to enjoy. To tick the anachronism box, there were also goldfish crackers, sushi towers, and ruby chocolate cronuts.

Then there was the good stuff, clearly prepared with cats in mind: roast meats, baked trout, and creamy savoury pastes set into amusing shapes. That was worth a visit to 1899.

Lovelace licked her lips.

There was chatter and gaiety — this was a party of humans and cats who enjoyed each other's company. There were cushions piled up so that the cats could reach the food as easily as the humans, and a few footmen hovering around with big spoons to assist if necessary.

Because the room was so over-stuffed with decor, including several busts of eighteenth century British prime ministers on plinths, the footmen kept tripping and/or banging into awkward antiquities, but that only added to the jollity of the event.

The chatter trailed off as Zephyr and Abydos brought Fenella, Cressida and Lovelace into the party.

Fleur Shropshire sat at the head of the table, wearing bright red Cardinal's robes and a Santa hat. She looked older than she had in 1964, though Lovelace struggled with human faces to tell the difference when it came to a decade or two. There were definite face crinkles around the eyes and mouth.

"Zephyr, give me strength," groaned the actress. "Can we not have one dinner party in peace without you interrupting? We're time travellers, surely it can *wait*."

Zephyr looked offended. "Professor Shelley, this is important. You said we should detain the Cressidas. Don't you want to interrogate this one about the blue invaders? The Grimalkins? Don't you want to ask her about the Jade Pineapple?"

Professor Shelley. The leader of the Anachronauts. No one had ever known what she looked like — which made sense, if what she looked like was a slightly crinklier version of a famous actress from the twentieth century.[2]

"What do you mean, Cressidas?" Fenella asked. "Why would there be more than one?"

"I'll explain later," said Cressida.

Fenella gave her sister a searching look. "Will you, though?"

"Also," said Abydos, taking over introductions from Zephyr, who was clearly losing control of the situation. "We brought Lovelace. And another person."

Fenella gave a small wave.

"No idea who this is," Zephyr added, rather quickly.

"Rude," said Fenella. "You could ask."

Lovelace ignored the humans, staring around the table. The Anachronauts. She'd met a few of them here and there at those recruiting lunches — or in some cases, before they themselves had been recruited. But there were faces she recognised for other reasons — several familiar historical personalities crammed around the table. Anne Boleyn. Christopher Marlowe. An elderly fellow with a distinctive nose who had to be one of the Caesars, though Lovelace could never tell them apart. So, this was how the Anachronauts had been recruiting — from human history.

Smart. Why hadn't they thought of that at Chronos College? It would save all that faff with the Official Global Secrets Act.

"Cressida Church has been crawling around in our private Event Space for weeks since she was so discourteous as to turn down our job offer," said Fleur Shropshire. "It's hardly an urgent revelation that some of her Chronos College friends have joined her." She gave Fenella and Lovelace a stern look. "One of my Scattered selves spotted these two in 1964. They were rather helpful in sparking off an Event we'd been working on for a while. Good show all around, but hardly worth barging in before dessert."

"You're not wondering how they got in here?" Zephyr

asked, their voice rising in inflection. "Maybe if you spent more time taking the leadership of the Liberated Anachronance seriously, and less time throwing indulgent parties, our mission would be closer to completion!"

"Congratulations, Zephyr," broke in a drawling, sarcastic and highly familiar voice. "Oh, jolly well done."

Lovelace stared wildly, her claws digging instantly into Fenella's shoulder, making the human wince. It couldn't be. Could it?

Nero. Not any of the historical Caesar Neros, but the fluffy white cat Nero. He sat on top of at least six cushions (he really did hate for anyone to take higher ground) with two paws resting on the table. He glared at Zephyr with his piercing blue eyes, then turned an even more scornful glare on Zephyr's cat.

"You had one job, Abydos," said Nero. "Detain the interlopers. Could you not find a cupboard to stash them in? By bringing them into this room you've managed to expose dozens of secret identities and allegiances directly to our enemies. Including mine."

Monterey had tried to pick the lock twelve times now. No joy.

Oxford, who had removed his jacket so as to sprawl even more pathetically on the floor, looked up at him. "Is it that you don't like being locked in, or is it that you don't like being excluded from a party?"

"Both, obviously." Monterey huffed back down beside Oxford, taking off his own jacket. It was getting rather stuffy in here. "I've been thinking."

"Bit dangerous."

"Fuck off. Why are they out there and we're in here? If Cressida is working for the Anachronauts…"

"Oh," said Oxford in surprise.

"You hadn't considered that possibility?"

"Of course I had. I didn't think you had."

"She'd want to keep Fenella close, maybe turn her to their side. If Cressida is not working for them yet... well, they probably want to hold Fenella over her head, same reason. They're recruiting, why wouldn't they want the Church sisters? And Lovelace... well, a cat is always valuable. Especially an experienced traveller. You and I are squishy disposable humans. Nothing useful here."

"We're not, though, are we?" Oxford said quietly. "Squishy disposable humans. If they want to get the attention of Chronos College, of the *Founders*, you and I are rather valuable."

Yes, there was that. Their parents were Founders of Chronos College. Nearly everyone else in the Traveller programme had been selected on merit. They were the ones who had slid in on pure nepotism.[3]

"They already have Zeph," Monterey said. "Did anyone make a fuss about that?"

"The Kincaids disowned Zephyr as soon as they and Abydos defected to the Anachronauts," Oxford reminded him.

Monterey frowned. "I'd forgotten that. Did I know that?"

"Zephyr had younger siblings," Oxford added. "There's a Kincaid over at Banksia, and there was a sister who came to Chronos College for a while. You and I are..." He swallowed, making an odd expression. "Only children."

If the Anachronauts could prove they had the heirs of the Monterey and Oxford families as hostages, the Founders would almost certainly listen to their demands before hanging up the call and writing their deaths off as a tax loss. Monterey could see why Oxford thought it was a good plan.

Unlike Oxford, Monterey had no particular illusion that his family considered him to be valuable.

"Let's hope they haven't thought about the ransom option," he said fervently.

"Hmm," said Oxford, who clearly had no other theory for why he and Monterey were in a pantry together.

"Let's hope it really hard."

If Lovelace had ever considered the possibility of being murdered by one of her fellow cats in the Travelling programme, her money would have been on Nero. Not because he ever seemed especially evil, but because he was entirely selfish.

Still, it had never occurred to her that he might see her as an *enemy*. It was oddly hurtful.

"You," said Fenella of all people, finding her voice before Lovelace or Cressida got their acts together. "Nero, you were *there* when the time hop went wrong, in the Rose Garden. Did you do this? Did you send us into Event Space?"

Professor Fleur Shropshire Shelley rolled her eyes. "Nero, you nuisance," she chided. "Have you been setting up unlicensed experiments again?"

"What kind of maniacal villain do you take me for?" said the fluffy white cat. "Of course I've been setting up unlicensed experiments. That's our whole thing." He flicked his tail. "Ruthven and Boswell?"

"Lost in time," grumbled Lovelace.

"I wasn't asking you, my dear." Nero turned to Abydos and Zephyr. "Monterey? Oxford? The Founders will be quite interested in getting those two back, I expect."

"They're in the silverware pantry," said Zephyr grudgingly.

"I suppose that's sufficient," sniffed Nero. "Next time we

arrange a dinner party, let's do it somewhere with dungeons, shall we?"

"You colossal arsehole," said Lovelace, arching her back.

No one paid any attention to her. The dinner party had split into those who wanted to complain to Nero for setting off rogue experiments in Event Space, and those who wanted to complain to Fleur Shropshire — or rather, Professor Shelley, their leader, for not thinking of it first.

Zephyr gave Fenella a particularly sharp look. "We haven't all had our memories tampered with, you know," they said pointedly.

Fenella looked startled. "I don't know what you mean."

Abydos, perching on Zephyr's shoulder, yawned and randomly clawed his human. "Don't confuse the humans, my dear. Can't have them running off."

"Where would we go?" Lovelace asked plaintively. Her eyes darted to Cressida. This strange, bustled Cressida who was so full of secrets. She hadn't twitched when Zephyr mentioned tampering with memories.

That was a horrible thought. Was it how the Anachronauts had hidden their double agents for so long?

This whole situation seemed wildly confusing. Professor Shelley knew all along that Cressida (more than one Cressida?) was here, traipsing around Event Space. *Nero* had known. For how long? The whole seven years?

Why had the Anachronauts allowed Cressida to remain here, if not to follow her, watch her, use her against their enemies?

Enemies.

Cressida inched closer and closer to a bust of William Pitt the Elder. As Lovelace stared at her, the human woman laid her bare hand on the statue quite deliberately. After a moment, the statue began to take on a deep apricot colour.[4]

Zephyr noticed, too. "What are you doing?" they demanded.

Cressida hummed under her breath. The bust of William Pitt the Elder was starting to look remarkably orange. "Who, me?" she said. "How could I be doing anything? We're in an Event, Zephyr. Random anachronisms are what you signed up for with your little club of history-eating anarchists."

"You're doing something," Zephyr insisted.

Cressida smiled. For a moment her eyes were bright orange too. "Haven't you heard? Time's a bastard, and she wants 1899 back."

A door at the far end of the dining room burst open. A snarling, shrieking monstrous creature covered in soft brown and green feathers came tearing towards the dinner party, rather like a duck had grown to the size of a velociraptor, and taken on the personality traits of...

Oh, it was actually a velociraptor. Yes, that made sense.

Even Cressida looked shocked.

Someone shouted "RUN!"

Fenella obeyed immediately, which was a relief to Lovelace, relying on her as she was for transport. Lovelace clung to Fenella's Napoleonic coat as the two of them tore away, down stairs and corridors.

There were Anachronauts all around them, fleeing for their lives. Lovelace couldn't see Zephyr and Abydos anywhere. Or Cressida, come to that. Fenella scampered towards the kitchens, where they had last seen Monterey and Oxford. Good girl.

Silverware pantry.

Fenella and Lovelace found themselves in an endless corridor full of stores cupboards. There were screams and an unholy dinosaur screech from the floor above them, best ignored.

Fenella looked up and down the corridor wildly. "Which

one is the silverware pantry? What does a silverware pantry look like?"

"Monterey!" Lovelace hollered. "Scream like the damsel you are, baby!"

A door swung suddenly open.

"HA," said Monterey, flourishing a cake fork that had been twisted beyond all recognition. "Thirteenth time lucky."

"Yes, you're very skilled," said Oxford, ducking his head so as not to hit it on the lintel as he eased all his arms and legs out of the pantry.

Lovelace leapt neatly from Fenella's shoulder to Monterey's. She only drew a little blood, and he managed not to cry out in pain.

"This way!" said Fenella, taking off at a run again. They followed her in a rush, Lovelace clinging to Monterey tightly.

"Did you miss me, dear one?" she asked him.

"Desperately," he replied, chucking her under the chin. "Where are we heading?"

"Away from the dinosaur," she informed him.

"Oh, fuck!" he laughed. "Lucky you. I've never seen a dinosaur. Were there feathers?"[5]

"I don't wish to discuss it."

"There you are!"

Cressida powered towards them in her outlandish Victorian gown. She did not look particularly savaged-by-velociraptor, though her hair was a tad rumpled. "So," she said, as if she had not recently summoned a dinosaur to interrupt a dinner party. "912 is out, the way to that aisle is currently occupied. Change of plans. There's a conjunction in the greenhouse that I've always found useful, if a bit of a wild card. Should work out fine."

"You really think we're going with you?" Lovelace demanded. "You think we're going to listen to a word you say?"

Monterey stroked her back. "Darling, you're trembling. What happened up there?"

"We can't trust her," Lovelace hissed.

Cressida looked a little forlorn. "Look, I wasn't expecting an actual velociraptor, if that's what you're freaking out about," she said. "That's Event Space for you. The anachronisms are getting out of hand. We have to stop all this before they damage Time herself. I need your help to do it. But first, we have to get out of here."

"By 'here', do you mean the nineteenth century, or Event Space?" Monterey questioned.

"One, then the other," said Cressida.

Fenella hesitated only a moment. "I'll come with you, Cress. But you have to tell us the truth. All the truth."

"I promise, Fen. Soon." Cressida looked at the others, hope in her eyes. "Oxford?"

Oxford hesitated. To Lovelace's surprise, he deferred to Monterey. "What do you think?"

Monterey reached up to scritch Lovelace under the chin. "I don't know," he said finally. "Lovelace, you decide. Do we follow her?"

There was a distant scream above them. It did not sound human.

Lovelace made up her mind. "Let's get out of 1899. And then we'll assess whether or not we can trust her."

"Thanks for that unwavering vote of support," said Cressida. "To the greenhouse!"

---

1. Naturally, there were a great many costume changes involved when travelling with Monterey, especially during their Versailles capers, though these were usually at his behest, not weirdly imposed upon them by a captor. Apart from that one time Elizabeth I put him in a neck ruff.
2. Fleur Shropshire wasn't just famous — she was famous for time travellers. Most Chronos College graduates wouldn't bat an eyelash at the

surprise appearance of Audrey Hepburn, Grace Jones or Sandra Bullock, but if Joan Buckingham or Fleur Shropshire crossed their paths, you can bet they would pay attention. How had the Anachronauts kept this a secret?

3. Thanks to the family connections, Oxford and Monterey had known each other long before Chronos College. Monterey had a clear memory of Oxford as a prissy eight-year-old who used to complain when the other children changed the rules of hide-and-seek halfway through a game. Oxford had a clear memory of Monterey as a bossy kid who liked to dress up in the curtains, while encouraging the other children to change the rules of hide-and-seek halfway through every game.

4. There was a time in Lovelace's life when she could not see orange-red hues, only the blue-violet and yellow-green spectrums. Whatever technological advancement had given her the ability to travel through time and speak twelve human languages, also brought the orange-red spectrum into her life. Which was at least helpful when explaining to Monterey which silk dressing gown made him look washed out.

5. While Chronos College did not have rules, they still considered the safety of their travellers to be of moderate importance. So far all officially sanctioned time hops had been contained to no earlier than 1000 BCE on the grounds that one should walk before one should run. There was a small group led by Lakshmi Tunbridge who had been patiently putting in requests for dinosaur related hops for years. Somehow, these never quite made it past the scheduling meetings. If Tunbridge had been told that the Anachronauts had access to Cretaceous-era time travel, her personal commitment to rule following might have been severely compromised.

thirty-one
48 bce

Cleo vs Cressida

IN SEVEN YEARS as a tenured professor of Time Mechanics, Boswell had never wanted to kill a human. Maim a little, possibly. Bite and scratch? Constantly.

Right now, facing an imperfect human replica of his lost partner, he felt homicidal.

Ruthven was at least backing away from the blonde in the fake Viking helmet. Sensible move from the lad.

"Professor Boswell," Ruthven said plaintively. "Are you sure this isn't the real Cressida? How would they even make a new one? And how do you know?"

"Her smell," said Boswell. He felt remarkably calm, under the circumstances.

Cressida, still playing along with her ruse, rolled her eyes at him exactly like his Church did, all the time. "Come on, Boz. I've been stuck in the wrong time period for seven years. Of course I smell weird. I was in 912 five minutes ago, and you just stepped out of a gross old carpet, no offence, Cleo."

"Full offence," said Cleopatra. "That carpet is *vintage*."

Boswell blinked slowly. "It's been seven years for us, Church," he thrummed in his lowest register of voice, the one that was basically 90% threatening purr, 10% vibrato.

"At Chronos College. Are you saying you've been here exactly the same amount of time? That's quite a coincidence."

"My replacement mentioned how long it had been," she said immediately. "Remington."

"Ruthven," corrected Ruthven, taking another step away from Cressida. "I don't think I did."

Cleopatra moved to Ruthven and Boswell's side, glaring up at Cressida. She might be a glamorous Pharaoh, divine ruler of Egypt, but even in jelly sandals she was nearly a foot shorter than the other woman.

"I have spent my entire life chasing Anachronauts away from the palace, because *you* told me it was important when I was nine years old," Cleopatra said, her chin high. "Now you're not who you say you are?"

"I am exactly who I say I am," Cressida insisted. "More or less."

Boswell hissed. He didn't care if her voice had that familiar 'upset' tone that he knew so well. He didn't care if she looked exactly like the partner he had lost. She didn't smell right. This had to be a trap.

"Guards," called Cleopatra. Her men stepped closer, reaching for their tasers...

"No. Wait!" Cressida fell to her knees, facing Boswell as if she only cared what he believed. "Boz. I know it's been a long time for you. And everything is different. I'm not quite your Cressida, you're right. It's complicated. But I still remember everything we did together. All our mad travels. The City Dionysia: how hard we worked to record that bloody play for posterity. Pompeii: the stolen honey cakes. That time we spent three days stalking David Bowie through the grottiest clubs in Soho. I remember all of it."

Boswell blinked, slowly. He didn't trust humans as a rule. He had trusted Church.

"We're supposed to go along with you?" he demanded. "Even though I know you're not her?"

"Yes," Cressida replied with a hiccuping gasp. "Just a little while longer."

Trusting Cressida had been easy, once. A matter of life or death. Boswell got used to running when she said run, jumping when she said jump. She did the same in return. They argued, of course. They often disagreed wildly on their methods. Not when it was important.

His confidence wavered.

"Go on," Boswell challenged Cressida. "Prove it."

"Wait, what?" said Ruthven.

"Is no one even slightly interested that I'm in charge around here?" demanded Cleopatra.

Cressida's smile lit up like a fireworks display. "One more time aisle," she whispered so that only Boswell could hear her. "This is a good one."

She leaped to her feet, and dashed across the palace floor like it was on fire.

"What are you waiting for?" Boswell ordered Ruthven. "Run!"

He took off after Cressida, without waiting to see if the other human was following. His new partner.

It was as good a time as any to find out how much Ruthven trusted him.

Run when I say run.

thirty-two
1978

keep partying until it's 1979

CRESSIDA'S wild card conjunction took them through a glass corridor that led out of 1899. They arrived in the middle of a party, which was Monterey's favourite way to arrive anywhere.

"Where is this?" he asked Lovelace. "Where are we?"

"The 1970s, I think," his cat said, digging her claws into his shoulder as she sniffed the air.

"Bellbottoms?" Monterey eyed a few dancing hippies with bright yellow clothing. Sunflowers were a common motif, not only printed in large, obnoxious patterns, but the flowers themselves — in necklaces, tucked behind ears, bursting forth from vases on every surface. The occasional rose, the occasional marigold... but mostly sunflowers.

Going by the fashions, it wasn't *not* the 1970s.

"Petrol fumes," Lovelace said primly. "Eau de fossil fuel."

No one was looking at them strangely, despite the fact that four people and a cat had just climbed out of a remarkably small shed. Oxford and Monterey were dressed for an unobtrusive stroll through the 1960s, all blazers and turtleneck jumpers with high-waisted trousers. For the 70s, they looked like terrible squares but not especially anachronistic.

Cressida and Fenella in their long historical dresses looked like attractive women who liked to wear vintage, an archetype readily available across the spectrum of every century from the twentieth onwards. Even Cressida's bustle wasn't likely to make anyone suspicious, not at a sunflower rave.

The crowd around them danced to groovy tunes played on a phonograph (this late in the century, it was probably called a record player) in the backyard of a country house (not a manor like Fenthorp, just a moderate sized house in the country). Long hair, fringe on everything, and the scent of gentle cannabis in the air. Hip and happening.

"Wait," Monterey breathed. Something wonderful had occurred to him. "There's only one Event in this decade that I know about. Is this 1978?" He scanned the garden eagerly, and then sighed. "Not Halloween *or* South Kensington."

Lovelace gently head-butted him in the side of the face. "You can't judge all parties by whether or not Freddie Mercury is throwing them."

"I thought it was impossible to ever set foot in this year," he whined. "And now it is possible. But there's bloody tulips growing over there, so it's probably not even the right month."

Cressida staggered, falling against her sister.

"Cress?" asked Fenella in concern, holding her up.

"I'm fine," Cressida muttered. "Dehydrated, I think. Time aisles do that." She looked distinctly unwell.

Monterey knew when chivalry was called for; one didn't spend time hanging around medieval tourneys without picking up a thing or two. He took Cressida's other elbow and led her to a chair to the side of the party. It was occupied by a large porcelain vase overflowing with bright yellow sunflowers. He placed the vase on the floor, and pushed Cressida into the chair. "Oxford, get the lady a drink. Apparently we all need to moisturise, so sort that out too."

Oxford huffed a bit in Monterey's direction, but couldn't resist the urge to be gallant.

"If there's any chance of a cup of tea," Monterey added in a winsome whine as Oxford strode away.

Oxford made a gesture behind him that was most ungentlemanly, no matter what decade they were in!

"I don't trust Cressida," Lovelace whispered in his ear. "If this even *is* Cressida. What kind of person summons a velociraptor to a dinner party? Even for a dinner party including Nero, it's a bit much."

"Sorry I missed it," Monterey replied, and shamelessly took the only seat next to Cressida for himself. "Fen, would you be a lamb and help Oxford with the tea? Or the G and T, if that's on offer."

Fenella looked annoyed. "I'm sure he can manage."

Monterey waggled his eyebrows at her. "Can he, though?"

She gave him what she probably thought was a dirty look — sweet — and stalked off through the crowd of sunflower children.

Lovelace, getting wind of what Monterey was up to, dug her claws in extra hard as she leaped from his shoulder to the ground. "Don't think you're getting rid of me," she said, and sat on his feet, out of sight. "Pretend I'm not here if the two of you want a moment."

Cressida gave Monterey a menacing look. She was better at it than her sister, though the slight sway of her body did rather ruin her credibility. "Oh my," she said. "What can he have to say to me now he's got me alone in a sea of hippies?"

Monterey patted Cressida's hand, and looked her over — the usual sort of casual examination that one might make when a friend returns home through the hoops. Checking that they still had the right number of fingers and ears. That their tail was the correct length.

"Monterey, you're starting to worry me," Cressida said with half a laugh.

She looked fine. Bustle aside (and the least said about her towering hair arrangement the better), she looked perfectly normal. Lovelace might have her own theory this was a creepy doppelgänger, a trap, but all Monterey saw was Cressida Church.

He'd liked her since that first day, when they turned up for orientation and he caught her pulling faces behind the back of the pompous Dean Pennyworth.

They'd never been lovers; they'd barely even been friends. Work acquaintances, sure. Their cats adored each other. It was like when the two best friends of the main characters in a movie are forced to hang out together.

Monterey liked being bitchy to Cressida, and he loved it when she insulted him in return. They *got* each other. They entertained each other. After they graduated as time travellers, the best job in the world, they became viciously competitive pen-stealing rivals.

That was even better than friends.

And then she was lost, and Boswell's heart was broken, and Monterey was so busy being grateful he hadn't lost *his* partner, he never let himself mourn the enormous Cressida shaped hole she had left behind.

Leave that to Melusine from Admin and the statue-building committee.[1]

"Let's pretend I never did this," Monterey told Cressida, and enfolded her in a warm hug.

Hopefully Oxford and Fenella were out of sight. It would do his reputation no end of damage if anyone thought he cared about anything beyond his clothes, or his cat.

"Oh," said Cressida, sounding surprised. She leaned into the hug regardless. "But, Monterey. I'm your least favourite person."

"True," he muttered into her hair. "I fucking missed you, fiend. I'm surrounded by children now. Chronos College is wall-to-wall toddlers and grumpy old cats. How dare you disappear for seven years?"

Lovelace bit his shoelace with something adjacent to fondness.

"They're not that much younger than us, the new batch of travellers," murmured Cressida.

"Speak for yourself," said Monterey, feeling weary. "I came here the long way."

She gave him a squeeze, then wriggled out of his arms. "Nice to know I was missed, you absolute sap."

"Oh, they turned you into a patron saint, back home," he informed her. "There's a marble statue, and a scholarship in your honour."

"Lies," she smiled.

Monterey's own smile felt rather less warm now. Chilly. "What aren't you telling us, Cressida?"

"You know," she said, looking away. "There's a few famous actors in this crowd once you look beyond the giant sunflowers and floppy hats. I'm starting to think I know exactly what party this is."

"Don't even try to tease me," he warned her. "If Freddie Mercury was within a ten mile radius of this quaint little farm house, I would *know*."

Someone stopped the record player. Someone else clinked two glasses together, which caught on like wildfire until there was a full chorus of clinking glassware.

A pretty woman in an ankle-length cheesecloth gown and pale yellow hair nearly as long stood up on a table, followed by a shaggy ginger-haired gentleman in denim flares. They were more than casually attractive, and ever so slightly familiar in a way that made Monterey wonder which film he knew them from.

She wore a necklace of gold sunflowers, and a fresh flower tucked behind her ear. He wore a series of sunflowers stuck into his beard.

"Hello darlings," said the woman, projecting with a clear, professional voice at odds with her delicate appearance. "Geoffrey and I wanted to share a few words about our guest of honour, who can't be with us tonight."

The mood of the crowd shifted. The well-heeled flower children fell upon each other, performatively sad. A few of them sniffled. One very drunk young lady covered in paper sunflowers started sobbing into a large cake in the corner.

"Is this a wake?" said Monterey in a mild panic.

Oxford and Fenella pushed their way through the weeping crowd, carrying a mug of water and a large jug of party punch. No tea, which Monterey took as a personal attack.

"We've figured out what party this is," announced Oxford.

"I could have told you that," remarked Lovelace, still sitting on Monterey's feet.

"Wench," said Monterey, nudging her.

"That's Britt Manning," said Fenella. "And that's Geoffrey Spoon." She gave Monterey a smug look, like she hadn't forgiven him for ruling that Ruthven knew more about vintage media.

Monterey considered this. "Britt Manning. She was in a couple of episodes of *Cramberleigh*. Not that long ago, if it's 1978 now. She was Boudicca in Season 11."[2]

"That's really not what she's famous for," Fenella sighed.[3]

"The twenty-fourth century begs to differ. Let's not pretend you recognise her from *Neighbours*."

"Shh!"

"...and you know she'd want to have a drink in her honour, and keep partying until it's 1979," said Britt Manning, full on crying now, tears pouring down her bare cheeks.

"Charge your glasses," said an equally weeping Geoffrey Spoon, whose beard must be sodden. "And join us in a celebration of the life of the one, the only, the iconic Fleur Shropshire."

"Fleur Shropshire," chorused the party guests.

"Ohh," said Monterey, finally figuring it out. "Did the Anachronauts turn 1978 into an Event on purpose, so no one in the future would be able to figure out she faked her death on the set of that Titanic movie? Is Fleur fucking Shropshire the reason I couldn't attend Freddie Mercury's most famous party of all time?"

"Almost certainly," said Cressida from her chair, where she was dutifully sipping the water provided by her sister.

Everyone else was into the punch. Monterey accepted a glass from Oxford, not admitting he would rather have a cup of tea. It tasted like raspberries and gin. There were marigold petals floating atop it.

"These are all film people then," he said, observing the crowd.

"A lot of them are cast and crew from the, uh, *Titanic* film," said Oxford. "They never got to finish it. Fleur's death wrecked the whole production."

"Did as much damage as she could on the way out, then." Monterey hadn't quite come to terms with the fact that the fabulous *Cramberleigh* actress was a diabolical mastermind, and a leader of the Anachronauts. "She was my favourite Lady Wildegreen," he added in a morose voice.

"So basic," said Cressida, smirking at him from over her glass. "She was everyone's favourite Lady Wildegreen."

"I liked Lady Sophia," said Fenella, with a hint of rebellion. "I cried when she died of the Spanish flu."

Lovelace was now perched high on a table covered in baked slices, sprout sandwiches and celery curls. Her back arched in a way that Monterey recognised as a significant crisis signal. He abandoned his glass of raspberry hooch and ambled after her.

"Spotted a Bond actor?" he suggested. "You're going to have to let your grudge against Roger Moore slide if we spend much longer in 1978."

"Do you see that?" Lovelace asked in a tense voice. "Over there, in blue."

Monterey looked. Beyond all the swaying sunflower children, he spotted a group who did not quite fit the party's general vibe.

There were half a dozen of them, standing in pairs here and there around the garden. They wore dark blue robes with hoods, and expressions that were neither mournful, nor blissed out, the two modes for most people at this gathering.

If Monterey could describe this gang's facial expressions in single word, it would be: intense.

"Looks a bit culty," he murmured to Lovelace. "Let's regroup."

Fenella and Oxford were still hovering around Cressida, who did not look much better than when she first sat down.

"Time to leave," said Monterey cheerfully. "Spotted some sinister blue space nuns. Also, this isn't much of a party."

"Blue space nuns," repeated Cressida. "Are you drunk?"

"Wouldn't that be nice," Monterey said wistfully. From the tideline on that jug of party punch, he was going to have to be the designated driver. "Can we get out of here? There's not a lot of point to hanging around the late 70s if Freddie Mercury isn't going to turn up."

"We'll head back to the time aisle separately," began Oxford. "So as not to raise suspicion... oh, you're gone."

Monterey had spun himself around the second that Oxford began his sentence. That was the trouble with working alongside someone you'd known since childhood. Everything he said was so predictable.

"Left," hissed Lovelace as they made their way through the crowd. "Go to the right of Honey Gale.[4] Between those two Led Zeppelins."

"Neither of those men is from Led Zeppelin," Monterey shot back, but his cat's descriptions were efficient. He slid apologetically between two men with long curly hair. They were nearly back at the shed.

A woman stepped directly in his path. Her deep indigo hood was pulled down low on her forehead. This close, it was clear that she was hairless apart from her eyelashes.

"You're a bit early," Monterey said breathlessly. "Dune isn't filming for at least another…"

The stern space nun in blue held up a hand, and he fell silent.

"Where is the jade pineapple?" she asked in a voice that didn't sound like it thought she was talking nonsense.

Monterey batted his own eyelashes, to check they were there. "Excuse me?"

"The jade pineapple."

"Yes, heard that part."

"Where is it?"

"I don't know," he considered. "Is it in the brownies full of drugs? This seems like that sort of party."

The space nun took a step towards him. Lovelace hissed — properly hissed, teeth bared and hackles raised.

The nun stepped back. "We will find the jade pineapple," she warned him. "The Judicial Administrator will be informed that you failed to assist us."

Monterey nodded solemnly. "Sounds fair."

Clicking her tongue with an impatient sound, the space nun pushed her way past him. Lovelace took a swipe at her robes as she went.

"Jade pineapple," Monterey murmured. "More Anachronaut bullshit?"

"They have been recruiting," said Lovelace. "But this doesn't seem like their style."

"We've got trouble," said Oxford, lurching up at them from the crowd. He and Fenella were half-carrying Cressida, who looked... well, no. Not pale.

Monterey could see through her. Cressida's hands glistened like rainwater, like air. Utterly translucent.

"Oh," she whispered. "I thought I'd have more time."

---

1. Boswell and Monterey had never agreed so fiercely on anything as they had agreed on how much they hated the Cressida Church statue in the quad. The design was awful — it barely even looked like her — and the fact of its existence was *awful*. They had both agreed to boycott the ceremony.

    Monterey meant it, too. To this day, he didn't remember what changed his mind. He had no idea what Melusine, or Dean Pennyworth (or his parents, probably) had said to get him up on that podium, making the speech on behalf of the Chronos College and the Founders.

    He could barely look Lovelace in the eye afterwards. She had been horrendously kind to him about what he had done. Boswell had never forgiven him. What followed was seven years of being stared at blankly by a furious marmalade tabby whenever their paths crossed.

    Monterey had deserved every single blank stare.
2. Season 11 of *Cramberleigh*, also known as The Season With The Time Travellers, introduced several time travelling historical personages who were later revealed to have been drawn to the house by Sir Victor Wildegreen's experiments with 'time crystals'. Characters who wandered through time aisles into this season of classic television included Rasputin of Russia, Cassandra of Troy, Sir Galahad of Camelot and Empress Sisi of Austria, along with Boudicca. A homeless man believing himself to be Guy Fawkes was then partly responsible for the explosion at the end of the season, which killed off a large number of the regular characters, setting *Cramberleigh* up for a contemporary spy reboot the following year. (Sir Victor's time crystals were also blamed for the explosion, because 1970s fictional narratives were capable of blaming literally anything on crystals.)
3. To the general public of the late twentieth and early twenty-first century, Britt Manning (1952-2043) was famous for three reasons: 1) an iconic photograph in 1976 of the actress/activist naked and hugging a tree to raise awareness for environmental concerns, 2) Manning's

arrest for defiling a police officer's helmet during the Greenham Common protest in 1982, 3) the false but beloved rumours that she was about to be cast to play the lead character in *Doctor Who* in 1996 and again in 2029. She was also briefly in *Neighbours*.

4. Honey Gale was a budget film star of the 70s, famous for the *Yes, Miss* films about a pretty school teacher who kept getting into saucy scrapes with her co-workers. Ms Gale was later famous as the inventor of the digital sandwich press.

thirty-three
1923

party like it's...

RUTHVEN WAS NOT sure why Boswell had chosen to follow this apparently-not-Cressida, but he had spent far too long in the Professor's lectures not to obey when he grumbled a command.

The three of them ran through Cleopatra's glorious red-walled palace, skidding around corners and down highly decorated hallways.

It was probably embarrassing that Boswell could run faster than Ruthven. Wasn't it? Or was that normal for cat vs. human?

Cressida flung herself into a room full of cats. So many cats. They were arranged shelf by shelf in order of height, painted in lush colours and giltwork.

In the far corner, there was an enormous human-sized sarcophagus, decorated to look like a gold cat with a disturbingly cheerful expression on its face.

"Oh no," growled Boswell. "Don't tell me that's the next cupboard."

Cressida gave him a bright, hopeful grin. "You love me, really."

"Don't push it."

She unlatched the sarcophagus and held it open. Inside, another of those long, narrow, creepily white time aisles.

"And where is this one going?" Boswell asked dangerously.

"Paris."

That threw him. "Paris."

"Home of all the best runny cheeses," Cressida said in an enticing voice.

"*Fine.*"

Neither Cressida, nor Boswell, asked Ruthven about his thoughts on runny cheeses or Paris, but he knew his place — several steps behind them both.

In the winter of 1923, on an enormous barge floating on the Seine River in Paris, something beautiful happened. In celebration of the opening night of brand new ballet *Les Noches*, the charismatic socialite couple Gerald and Sara Murphy hosted the afterparty to end all afterparties.[1]

There were no flowers to be purchased in Paris because it was a Sunday, so Sara Murphy decorated their long refreshment table with pyramids of children's toys: racing cars, fire engines, clown dolls and stuffed animals, for the adults to play with. Champagne cocktails were plentiful. The guest list included Cole Porter, Pablo Picasso and Jean Cocteau.

Igor Stravinsky, the Russian composer responsible for the ballet, was at the centre of it all; a dour man in a dark suit and spectacles who was thoroughly uninterested in the Bohemian cavorting that surrounded him.

According to history, this was an epic night which exploded into unforgettable scenes of merriment, hijinks, and champagne.

A night like this was catnip to time travellers.

Ruthven did not generally enjoy parties. Standing

awkwardly in the corner of this epic, glamorous event felt like sneaking into one of Monterey's parties back on campus. Worse — he knew fewer people than usual and couldn't even look forward to a friendly word from Oxford.

Aesop loved a party. Aesop had loved any excuse to nibble a square of cured meat off a toothpick, or lap up a saucer of champagne. Parties with Aesop had been almost fun, because she would happily lounge at Ruthven's side, entertaining him with her snarky commentary.

Missing his cat was at its worst on a night like this: Ruthven the wallflower, nursing a drink he hadn't wanted in the first place while Pablo bloody Picasso rearranged stuffed animals in 'amusing' dioramas that made sense only to him.

Boswell and Cressida were no substitute. Cressida was nervous and tense, her eyes flicking around the crowd on deck as if she was waiting for someone or something.

Hopefully not another velociraptor.

Boswell was just grumpy. Even the fresh oysters Ruthven had collected for him from the refreshment table were worthy of nothing more than a glare and a lick. "What are we waiting for, Cressida?" the marmalade tabby demanded.

Cressida put her hands behind her back. "I think I need to get changed." She was still in the Viking apron, and braids. "Back in a minute."

"Hang on," said Ruthven, reaching out to grab her arm. "You can't just…"

He stared. Her hand was pale. Too pale. He could see Pablo Picasso through it; the man was on the floor putting toy train tracks together.

"Damn it," said Cressida. Even her voice was fading out. "Thought I'd have more time. Listen, Ruthven. You need to… Boz, can you claw me, or something?"

Without hesitation, Boswell reached out and drew his paw

over her ankle. Lines of red spiked up instantly. Ruthven winced as Cressida began to bleed.

"Oh, good," she said, clapping her hands together. Not entirely solid, but they were more opaque than previously. "So, Fleur Shropshire should be at this party. She's one of the Anachronaut leaders. Very high up."

"Wait," said Ruthven, unsure whether he had heard her correctly. "Fleur Shropshire? Lady Ann from *Cramberleigh*?"

Cressida looked exasperated. "I'm dissolving before your eyes and you want me to repeat myself?"

"She won't be born for another five years. Ow!" Ruthven looked down to see that Boswell had taken a swipe at his own ankle. "What was that for? *I'm* not dissolving."

The marmalade tabby glared up at him with the heat of a thousand suns. "Ruthven. We're time travellers."

"I know we're..." Ruthven stopped and thought about it. "Really, Fleur Shropshire?"

"Shall I go on?" Cressida asked between gritted teeth.

"Please do." His mind was whirling. How many cast members of *Cramberleigh* were implicated in the Anachronaut organisation? Was it a Cramberspiracy?

"Shropshire is meeting someone. It's crucial we find out who that is."

"Crucial to whom?" Boswell asked acidly. "Who is 'we' in that sentence?"

Cressida looked somewhat hurt. "You sound like you don't trust me, Boz." She was fading again. Her long golden braids were the colour of champagne. Her green Viking apron dress was filmy and pale. "Ugh," she said. "This isn't helping. I need to recharge in the time aisle." She poked a finger into Ruthven's chest. "You. Follow Fleur Shropshire. Find out who she meets. Don't be seen."

She whirled around quickly and disappeared into the dancing, laughing, champagne-drenched crowd.

"What is happening?" Ruthven asked no one in particular.

Boswell sat on his foot. "I believe, young man, you have been charged with stalking a *Cramberleigh* actor at a party. It's the mission you've been training for all your life."

"Hilarious."

"Up, please."

Ruthven picked up Boswell, holding him carefully. He was a solid mound of warm tabby, but Ruthven wasn't quite ready to let him settle on his shoulders, not with how quick he was with his claws.

Boswell settled in his arms, as if this was what he had wanted all along. "You'd better get more champagne," he commanded. "It will help you blend in. And don't let any of those artists pet me. I don't know where they've been."

The party showed no sign of winding down.

Ruthven had to admit, these things were a lot more entertaining when you had a purpose. In this case, searching a barge full of Bohemians and ballerinas for an actress who was going to be rather popular in around four decades.

He'd absorbed the idea of Fleur Shropshire being one of the bad guys, as long as he didn't have to actually speak to her; talking to celebrities, historical or otherwise, was one of those things guaranteed to bring Ruthven out in a cold sweat.

After two hours of completely nothing, he was almost bored enough to welcome the challenge. Perhaps he should take a leaf out of Monterey's book and flirt the night away with Cole Porter instead of sitting around awkwardly.[2]

"Is *that* Fleur Shropshire?" asked Boswell with a disinterested sniff from where he was currently perched, on top of one of the three grand pianos on the barge.

"No, that's Clara Bow," said Ruthven.

"All humans basically look alike to me."

"I figured that when you asked if Charlie Chaplin was the woman we're looking for."

Boswell's paw suddenly lashed out, swiping at Ruthven with just enough claw to sting. "That," he said in a low snarl. "Is not Fleur Shropshire."

"No," said Ruthven, staring. "It's not."

He knew who Boswell was talking about. It was hard to miss her. On a ship full of ladies with hair cut fashionably short and shingled, this woman had long dark red hair all the way down her back. She wore a knee-length floaty silk coat which was not out of place here, on a 1923 party boat, but also had the unmistakeable style of a 1980s Zandra Rhodes.[3]

It was Melusine from Admin. Oxford's mum. Founder of Chronos College.

Ruthven crouched so that Boswell could climb on to his shoulders without having to jump. Neither of them spoke. This was too serious for snark and banter.

What was she doing here?

No, that was obvious. Ruthven's task was to find out who was meeting covertly with Fleur Shropshire. Unless this particular party was a hub for time travellers making assignations, this had to be the person they were looking for.[4]

Ruthven made his way through the crowd, making sure to keep at least three ballerinas between himself and Melusine at any time. This wasn't especially difficult, as the party kept sprouting more ballerinas as the night wore on. No firefighter in the world would approve of the tulle-to-human ratio on this barge.

Boswell hissed in Ruthven's ear, and Ruthven stopped still.

Melusine sat at a small table along the deck, ignoring the arrangement of porcelain clowns and glove puppets in the centre of said table. A passing server placed a brimming champagne saucer in front of her.

Melusine's back was to the party, and so she did not see the Anachronauts approach her. At least, Ruthven guessed that was who they were. A tall, androgynous person with glittery eyelashes and an Yves Saint Laurent suit strode through the party with, quite blatantly, a black cat resting on one of their shoulders. Bit of a giveaway.

"Zephyr and Abydos," Boswell whispered in his ear.

That made sense. Ruthven had never met either of them, but he heard their names whispered around campus. Anachronauts.

Beside them — well, it was Lady Ann Wildegreen. It had only been a few days, relative time, since Ruthven watched those fragments of footage from the unaired pilot: Fleur Shropshire was charming and adorable as the new Lady Wildegreen, aetherial in the small-waisted, large-hatted Edwardian fashions whether she was listening at doors, falling with a gasp upon her swooning couch, or being walled up in secret passages by the villain of the week.

Fleur Shropshire had never worn 1920s clothes in the show — her character was long dead on the Titanic by the time the Roaring 20s reached *Cramberleigh*. She was making up for it tonight, wearing a glittering blue butterfly gown with matching headdress, every inch the fashionable flapper.

Boswell clawed Ruthven gently. "Are you having a moment?"

Ruthven shook himself. "We've got what we came for. Should get back to Cressida before someone points out that there are two people wearing cats at the same party."

Boswell leaped into the air and ran lightly through the crowd, away from Melusine and her co-conspirators.

Ruthven took longer to cross the deck, because he was human-sized and incapable of bumping into people without apologising about it. He managed an awkward, uneven path towards the cupboard door which would lead him into the time aisle.

At the last moment, he almost crashed into a woman, only to startle back. "I'm so sorry," he sputtered anyway. "Excuse me..."

"Oh," said a surprised voice. "It's you."

Ruthven stared. The woman looked familiar, but her presence was incomprehensible to him, much as when you spot your class teacher at the supermarket, or your family doctor at a nightclub.

She had a pale complexion. She was in her mid-thirties. She had dark hair pulled back from a high forehead into a braided knot. If not for her hair, she looked every inch the 1920s socialite, wearing a black fringed dress, a string of pearls and a harsh, dark red lipstick.

She looked very much like a person cosplaying the 1920s with the least amount of effort. Her boots, Ruthven noticed as his gaze slid lower, were classic Doc Martens.

This woman was a traveller. She had to be, really. Not because of the boots.

He'd first met her in 1526.

Anne Boleyn looked Ruthven up and down with careful scrutiny. "Where's your cat?" she inquired in a perfectly polite voice. "I rather liked her."

"Sorry, must dash," Ruthven said idiotically. He lurched around the Tudor Queen, accidentally knocking over several champagne-sozzled ballerinas and a teetering stack of upsettingly racist soft toys.

When he looked back, Anne Boleyn was gone.

---

1. The Murphys were a popular, wealthy It couple of the social set known as Bright Young Things in the 1920s. They were later immortalised (or

as they would describe it: libelled) in the novel *Tender is the Night* by F. Scott Fitzgerald.
2. Tragically for Ruthven, sitting around awkwardly was his best party trick, and he had never flirted with anyone except by accident.
3. Ruthven had done excellently at the Intro to Costume elective. For his final exam, he assembled a trench coat out of recyclable tote bags.
4. Discretion was not taught at Chronos College, and if it *was* taught it was hard to imagine any of the current crop of travellers would have passed those exams.

thirty-four
48 bce

Lovelace Smells Something Fishy

LOVELACE LIKED to follow her nose. Her nose was excellent at many things, such as guessing what year it was, spotting the difference between seventeenth century French and Spanish footwear (when you were a cat, you spent a lot of time near human feet), and finding the last salmon-flavoured soy ball in a bowl full of party snacks.

She hated these glaring white time aisles. They smelled of nothing. Places weren't supposed to smell of nothing. They should carry the footprints of every person or animal who had ever passed through them.

There were no footprints here, literal or olfactory. Every time Lovelace set paw into a time aisle, it was as if she was doing it for the first time. This might not be the same one they had stepped out of earlier. It looked exactly the same, but Lovelace could not detect her own recent presence.

Still, the time aisle had saved Cressida's life. You couldn't see through the woman anymore; her skin was as fleshy and solid as it should be.

"Look at you," said Monterey gently. "Run out of excuses for explaining what's going on?"

He couldn't fool Lovelace; she could hear the relief under

his snark. He'd always liked Cressida more than he chose to admit.

"Why yes, I do feel better, thanks for asking," Cressida shot back.

"Probably a fit of the vapours," Monterey replied, patting her on the bustle. "Corset too tight, old thing?"

"Actually, the damaging nature of corsets has been wholly exaggerated..." Fenella started to say.

"Where now?" Lovelace interrupted. She had always felt a little unsettled about Fenella's scent. Probably because the young woman spent all day touching clothes worn by or about to be worn by other humans.

Fenella's scent hadn't bothered her too much before this adventure began, but after so much time in close proximity, Lovelace rather felt a headache coming on.

"Somewhere familiar," said Cressida. "Somewhere we won't bump into Anachronauts every five seconds. Or strangers in blue robes with a pineapple obsession," she added with a sceptical look in Monterey's direction.

"I didn't make it up!" he insisted. "Lovelace was there, weren't you, love?"

Lovelace nodded solemnly. "Blue space nuns looking for a Jade Pineapple. Or a jade pineapple, I'm not sure how proper their nouns were. I understand the scepticism. I wouldn't believe him either."

Monterey scratched her behind the ear. "I can always count on you to have my back, darling."

"You often sound entirely irrational," she informed him. "Even for a human."

Cressida pressed on through the time aisle, somehow finding room for her entire gown despite the narrow angles. "Here we go," she said, pushing on a door. "This is a good one."

Scent flooded over them as they stepped out into a wide,

airy room thick with humidity, spiced oils and the overpowering scent of large sardines being grilled to perfection.

Lovelace was going to need a swooning couch.

"I know this place," she said, sniffing the delicious air. "Are we in Egypt?"

"This is that palace," said Monterey, snapping his fingers. "The one we ended up in by accident that time, when we were trying to get a run up on the library of Alexandria." He pointed an accusing finger at Lovelace. "You met Cleopatra here."

"Yeah, we're going to do our best to avoid Cleo this time around," said Cressida. "She's not my biggest fan."

As she spoke, a small woman in jelly sandals, a bobbed black wig and a flowing gold gown stepped out from behind a red granite pillar, widening her kohl-lined eyes at them all. "Brilliant," she said, throwing up her hands in exasperation. "More time travellers, Cressida? I warn you, my guards are trained to taser Anachronauts on sight."

"We're not Anachronauts," Monterey said with hearts in his eyes. "Also, your pedicure is fabulous."

Cleopatra looked more exhausted than Lovelace had ever seen her, despite the excellent makeup job. It couldn't be easy, being a Pharaoh trapped in a lifelong time bubble that meant you were constantly assaulted by anachronisms and unwanted guests.

Lovelace stepped forward and, in the universal cat gesture of friendship, wound herself slowly around Cleopatra's ankles.

"Oh, hello, Lovelace," said Cleo, giving her a scratch behind the ears. "Are you hungry, sweetheart?"

Best. Pharaoh. Ever.

The feast was glorious. Dishes for days, and twelve different kinds of fish. Lovelace was in heaven.

Monterey was happy too, lolling around on cushions beside the Pharaoh, flirting like mad while mentally ticking 'swap fashion tips with Cleopatra' off his bucket list. Lovelace was happy for him.

"Tell me something about the future," said Cleopatra at one point, her fingers idling in a dish of honeyed figs.

"I already told you about platform shoes, the Met Gala and holographic underwear," said Monterey. "What more do you need to know?"

"I want to know about cats," said Cleopatra. "They're sacred here in Egypt, you know."

"Well aware," said Lovelace with her mouth full of eel. "Good job, Egypt."

"But ours don't talk. Except those like you and Boswell, who come from the future."

"Wait," said Oxford, rousing himself from the sullen flop he had been in since they arrived in this heavenly place. "You've seen Professor Boswell? Is he all right? Is Ruthven with him?"

"I want to know," said Cleopatra, ignoring Oxford with ruthless Pharaoh privilege. "When cats first began to speak as humans do. Have they always had this skill in secret? Are ours pretending they cannot speak? Is it something that changes a thousand years from now? Two thousand years? Surely you know."

Monterey hesitated. An odd look crossed his face, as if he did know the answer, but couldn't find the words to express it. As always, when unsettled, he looked across the table to meet Lovelace's gaze.

Cats cannot shrug. It was the only gesture she could think of that conveyed her own thoughts. She swallowed the last of the eel.

Cressida didn't have an answer either. She frowned as if trying to work it out. Fenella, beside her, ate some grapes.

"It's recent," volunteered Oxford. "In the scheme of things, I mean. A new development within our lifetimes."

"That's right," said Monterey, sounding relieved someone else had started them off. "No talking cats in twentieth century media... or even in the twenty-third, if my recent marathon of the *Coronation Street* reboot is anything to go by. Lovelace, you must know more?"

"Cats have spoken for as long as I remember," she replied, reaching out a paw to hook a promising dish closer to her. Marinated chunks of something, decorated with blobs of sea urchin pulp. She had been hoping for mullet, but now that this dish came closer to her the scent was more suggestive of crocodile.

She was going to eat it regardless.

"And you must be..." Monterey invited, then trailed off.

"Never ask a lady her age," said Cressida, amused. "Talking cats go hand in hand with the discovery of time travel. I never heard a cat speak before I came to Chronos College."

"Me neither," said Fenella.

Lovelace saw Monterey glance in Oxford's direction. "There were a lot of cats around," murmured Monterey. "When we were kids. Weren't there? Your mothers were mad for them, Celeste especially. Kittens everywhere. I don't remember holding conversations with them, though. Not until..." He frowned.

"Oh, honey," said Lovelace, batting her eyelashes at him. "Was I your first?"

"Banksia was a talking cat," Oxford blurted. "She and Professor Burbage brought the secrets of time travel to the Founders. I suppose she might have been the first." He looked down at his plate, found something wrapped in vine leaves, and put the whole parcel in his mouth.

"Fascinating," said Cleopatra in a tone that suggested she thought they were all lying through their teeth. "Don't they teach you this sort of history when you are young? Tutors and wax tablets and abacuses, and all that. Surely it's important."

Lovelace was thinking about it, really thinking about it. Had her mother spoken to her with a human voice? She wasn't sure she remembered her mother at all, except as a vaguely fuzzy figure and a sensation of warmth, like a blanket.

She felt a low hum in her ears as she concentrated on the thought. Pain spiked her head for a split second. And then, just like that, she stopped thinking about it.

The conversation moved on. Cleopatra had other questions — mostly about cinematic depictions of herself, which she had learned about from other time travellers. Monterey was delighted to answer in lavish detail thanks to his personal obsession with HBO's *Rome*, and *Xena: Warrior Princess*.

Lovelace noticed that while Cressida and Fenella joined in the conversation enthusiastically, Oxford stayed quiet. As if he had something on his mind. Eventually, the tall young man slipped away from the dining couches altogether and stood at a window overlooking the cliffs below the palace. His fingers picked away at the sleeve of his jumper.

Lovelace was not an expert on human facial expressions, but she could spot unhappiness easily enough.

Oxford had been an enthusiastic trainee as a student. They had performed a few hops together, Lovelace as the experienced traveller graciously volunteering to supervise the occasional student when Monterey was busy or hungover.

Lovelace remembered sitting on a high shelf of one of the many campus libraries, years ago. Aesop was snuggled on one side of her, and Nero on the other. Neither of them had taken a permanent human partner before, but planned to choose from this particular cohort of graduates. Lovelace, who chose her human long ago, was interested to see who her friends would pick.

Ptolemy had already selected Lakshmi Tunbridge before graduation was official, the two of them forming a close and good-humoured bond.

There were six human graduates remaining to choose from, and Aesop and Nero had been exhausting about it.[1] "I'll take that one," Nero said finally in his superior way, nodding down at Oxford. "Clearly the most suitable candidate."

Aesop exploded into a splutter of laughter. "You're choosing him because he's the tallest," she snickered. "Oh, Nero. So predictably obsessed with taking the higher ground."

Nero sniffed and trotted away, shedding copious amounts of white hair over the books as he went.[2]

And that was that. Oxford and Nero, together forever. The friendly human and the prickly cat. Somehow their partnership worked.

Since 1899, Lovelace had been thinking dark thoughts about Nero and his betrayal of the college. She had always thought of him as — well, not entirely a friend, but a workplace acquaintance with whom she shared a long history of mutual toleration. (*Enemies,* she kept hearing, as her thoughts returned to that party. *He called us his enemies. Not rivals or competitors.*) Oxford must feel the betrayal even more powerfully. He had certainly looked shocked when Fenella and Cressida told him Nero was an Anachronaut.

"Are you all right?" Lovelace asked Oxford now, nosing against his ankles.

Oxford picked her up, and placed her on the ledge of the window before him. One hand absently stroked her back. Lovelace preened under the attention.

"I know a lot of things I probably shouldn't," the tall man sighed. "Son of the Founders and all. I hear things. Secrets, behind the scenes... and I can't tell anyone."

Lovelace frowned. "What sort of things?"

"I didn't know about Nero and the Anachronauts," Oxford said, sounding wrecked. "That makes me wonder what else my mothers are keeping from me."

Lovelace butted his hand with her cheek. "You're not responsible for what the Anachronauts do. Even if Nero is your cat."

"Sure," said Oxford. "But how much of an idiot am I for not knowing?"

This wasn't the only thing that was bothering him; Lovelace could tell. But it wasn't her job to pry. She wasn't his cat.

"You know what would make you feel better?" she suggested.

Oxford huffed out a laugh. "Is it fried mackerel?"

"There's just *so much* fried mackerel in this palace!" she said with a little shimmy of delight. "How could you possibly stay sad with a belly full of fish?"

---

1. Technically Melusine from Admin made the official cat assignments every year, but she had long since learned to take 'dibs' from the cats into account, as long as they filled in the paperwork ahead of time.
2. "What about you?" Lovelace had asked Aesop after Nero was gone. "Any favourites?"

    Aesop, who was always a little shy around her, looked delighted to be asked. "I like the dark-haired one with the cheekbones," she admitted. "He's a bit of a nerd, but a decent sort. He won't give me any trouble."

thirty-five
1215 & 2034

"I can't remember what I had for lunch yesterday."

BOSWELL HAD A HEADACHE.

Cats were not supposed to get headaches, but then cats were not supposed to talk, for most of the history of the world.

When he closed his eyes, the headache grew worse. Flashes of memory took over, fragments of voices. Boswell did not like it at all. He was starting to think that some of those voices belonged to former colleagues he preferred not to think about right now. Colleagues like Nero. Colleagues like Aesop.

Boswell put off returning to the time aisle for as long as possible. The time aisles made the headaches worse. Something about that dry, scentless air set them off. His excuse, of course, was that he was waiting for his human.[1]

The marmalade tabby perched high on a steep metal staircase, observing the barge party and waiting for Ruthven to catch up. When the young man reached him, he looked a bit wild about the eyes. He was holding a full saucer of champagne he had managed somehow not to spill.

"After you," said Boswell grumpily.

Ruthven nodded, yanking at the cupboard door.

Inside, the bright whiteness of the time aisle was shocking

all over again, as was the calm quietude of the space and the entire lack of smell.

Boswell had half-expected this time aisle to be gone, and Cressida with it. But no, she was still here, sitting with her back to the flat white wall. Her golden Viking braids were dishevelled, as if kittens had been toying with them.

You couldn't see through her any more. Boswell's nose twitched. She still didn't smell right. But nothing felt right in this non-place. He could hear voices echoing in the back of his skull.

"We're never going back," said Aesop. *"No one can make us go back."*

"Welcome to Chronos College," said Nero. *"I suppose you'll do."*

"Just what I needed," said Cressida, taking the glass of champagne off Ruthven and drinking deeply. She looked expectantly at them both.

Boswell flexed his ears. "Am I mistaken, or did I see you chatting to Anne Boleyn back there?" he asked Ruthven. Saying her name made his headache a little stabbier, if that was possible.

"Not mistaken," mumbled the human. "We've met before."

"Made a lot of visits to the twenty-fourth century, has she?"

Something flashed through Boswell's head as he said it. *Has she?*

Ruthven looked annoyed, which was better than looking all wan and panicky. Boswell was at his most comfortable when surrounded by people who weren't fond of him. "The usual way travellers meet people from other periods of history," Ruthven said coldly.

Ah, yes. Of course, he had been Aesop's human. Ruthven and Aesop had worked together for two years, before they lost her. Plenty of time to go gadding about the sixteenth century, acquainting oneself with Tudor wives. Nothing to worry about.

"Do I get a cat?" demanded the woman in a sharp voice. "May I time travel? Are you ever going to consider me your equal? Or am I an artefact to be stored in a museum?"

"Boleyn," said Cressida dismissively. "That's no good, we already knew she was an Anachronaut. No one else?"

"I didn't know that," Ruthven said, surprised. "When did that happen?"

Cressida made a 'spin on' gesture. Boswell gave Ruthven a meaningful look. "Don't get distracted. Tell her who we saw."

"Melusine," admitted Ruthven. "Fleur Shropshire met with Melusine at the party."

"From Admin?" Cressida gasped. "She's a Founder! So this goes all the way to the top?"

"She's Oxford's mother," said Ruthven, as if that meant something.

"It's best if they remember as little as possible," said the tall woman with the aquiline nose. "Makes our job easier."

Boswell's head felt like he was being stabbed repeatedly with a tin opener. Two whole humans here, and neither of them were patting his fur. What was the point of them?

"Bloody hell," said Cressida. "Melusine from Admin. That confirms a theory I didn't want confirmed."

"Show your work, Church," sighed Boswell. The last thing he had patience for right now was cryptic messaging. It was all he could do to keep his head in the here-and-now instead of whatever was exploding at the back of his brain.

He was remembering things. Too many things. He didn't like what he was remembering.

They had to get out of this time aisle.

Cressida eyes brightened and she laughed. "Oh, Boz.

You've got the grumpy professor tone down. Are they all scared of you back home?"

"Terrified," said Ruthven, before Boswell could answer her ridiculous question.

Boswell huffed at them both. *Humans*. Why couldn't he have Lovelace here to back him up? "Let's hear your theory," he demanded.

Cressida took a deep breath. "We're all Anachronauts," she said.

A few minutes later, Boswell's paws landed on grass. It smelled medieval, but later than the tenth century. He didn't have Lovelace's knack for zeroing in on a specific time period by scent alone, but he knew the tenth century better than anyone who had ever lived there.

"This wasn't even a cupboard," complained Ruthven, not far behind him. "We crawled out of a box. Why is there a big box lying around on a field?"

"1215," said Cressida, looking around. "Damn it, I haven't been here before. I knew there had to be a conjunction connected to the signing of the Magna Carta. This year's been an Event for ages." She gasped suddenly. "Do we have time for me to steal a pen? Unless Monterey got that one already."

"*No pens*," said Boswell, catching his breath. Event Space was hard work, but it was better than the disorienting time aisles. His headache had subsided slightly. "Where next? Somewhere we can stay for more than two minutes."

"Quite quickly," urged Ruthven. "King John's soldiers are crossing that field towards us. There appears to be an airship above them with a big crown on it. And... a blimp behind that, covered in cartoon mice."

"Back in the box, back in the box!" said Cressida wildly.

"Can't we find somewhere comfortable?" complained Boswell. "If this is going to be a long conversation. Furniture. Food. By preference, I am an indoor cat."

"You say conversation," said Cressida, striding her way along yet another bright white time aisle. "I think you mean, potential napping spot."

"Ruthven looks tired," Boswell said pointedly.

"I'm fine, I'm awake," said Ruthven, his long legs keeping up with Cressida easily. "I want to hear more about this 'we're all Anachronauts' theory."

"Okay," said Cressida, still on the march. "We've always been told that the Anachronauts are anarchists. History saboteurs. But why would Time allow that unless she approved, somehow, of what they were doing? They have to be a feature, not a bug. Or they'd never have got this far."

"You sound like you admire them," said Boswell with disapproval.

"They are really well organised," said Cressida, not denying it. "Constantly recruiting. They've set up this whole network of time aisles within Event space, which is revolutionary when you think about it... and they're obsessed with historical parties, big dinners and elaborate cosplay. Who does that sound like?"

"Chronos College," Ruthven said heavily. "It sounds a lot like us. But... I mean, they were academics to start with, so..."

"They never stopped," insisted Cressida. "Aleister College never went rogue, they went *undercover*. The time aisle network and the behaviour of the Anachronauts is a separate research project, that's all. They've walled off whole years, whole decades, and they're messing them up, cramming rotary phones into Ancient Egypt and so on, do you really think they're not taking notes?"

Another headache stabbed through Boswell. Cressida's theory sounded correct. It sounded... like something he already knew.

"*You'll want to forget this, too,*" said Nero. "*It makes things easier.*"

"*So you say,*" said Aesop. "*I can't remember what I had for lunch yesterday. I didn't know I'd lose so much.*"

"Why?" Ruthven blurted. "Why all the secrecy? They can't exactly publish their research..."

"Neither can we," hissed Cressida, screeching to a stop just short of a particularly sharp-cornered turn in the time aisle. "Thanks to the Global Official Secrets Act, no one in the real world knows about us *or* the Anachronauts. Turn up at Cambridge or Harvard with your Masters of Time Travel thesis and your talking cat, and they'd laugh you off campus. Chronos College, Banksia College, Aleister College. We've always been a closed system. We have the same Founders. What exactly makes us different to them?"

"The difference," said Ruthven after a while, sounding brittle. "Is that they seem to know what the hell is going on. And no one ever bothered to tell us."

Or, thought Boswell. *They made the knowledge go away.* And then his head hurt too much for him to think much of anything else...

They stepped out of a cupboard to a landing above a staircase in a house that made Ruthven gasp in happy surprise.

"This is Fenthorp," the human said in a reverential tone, as they walked across polished floorboards that hurt Boswell's paws, into a room with bright green striped wallpaper, a wide window seat overlooking the gardens, and a bronze pineapple-shaped chandelier hanging from the ceiling. "We're inside the house. This is the freaking pineapple parlour. Lady Cradoc's Season 6 bedchamber is next door. Look at that chandelier! I think this is the same actual couch." He sat on it, and a small puff of dust burst forth from the green velvet cushions.

Boswell had no particular interest in that *Cramberleigh* show that the rest of the travellers got so het up about.[2] Cressida had loved it; he preferred to nap. However, now that he leaped up to the comfortable window seat, he did recognise the view from this house — the same rolling hills in the distance as that particular corner of 912 that he had long considered his personal nemesis. The forest and the Viking village were long gone, but he knew exactly where he was.

The headache had gone, but the sense of unease brought on by the flood of lost memories remained. Boswell was going to have to tell them the truth.

"Don't get too excited," said Cressida. "This is 2034, and that couch should never have been allowed to live this long. *Cramberleigh* filming is deep in the rear view mirror. No celeb-spotting for you today."

"Oh," said Ruthven, a little disappointed.

"I like this spot," Cressida added. "I come here for a kip sometimes. No one visits the upper floors much."

"Nice," said Ruthven, lifting his feet on to the couch and leaning back on a large cushion. He had been operating for too many hours without any rest. Boswell felt ashamed for not taking better care of him. Humans were so delicate.

"Did you say you come here often?" Boswell remarked.

"Oh, yes," said Cressida.

"This specific year?"

"This specific afternoon." She still stood at the window. "Right now, eight hopeful amateur bakers and four cranky celebrity chefs are being filmed in the historic kitchens downstairs, trying to prove they can bake a cake using a sixteenth century roasting jack.[3] Meanwhile, in that giant tent outside, the entire production crew are gathered to decide whether or not they tell the contestants that a rather significant political event has occurred since they went into filming lockdown."

"What political event?" murmured Ruthven, yawning on the couch.

"It's September 19th, 2038," said Cressida.

"Oh, the *war*."

Boswell had no idea to which war they were referring. He wasn't a history professor.

"You got it. They eventually inform the contestants, who lose their minds, and after a small cake riot everyone ends up fleeing the estate, leaving it utterly uninhabited for three glorious days."

"And you've been here before," Boswell said slowly. He knew he was repeating himself, but Cressida either didn't see what he was getting at, or she was being deliberately evasive.

"Eleven or twelve times. There's usually someone else popping in, on those other days — sooner or later every Anachronaut comes up with the same bright idea. But this afternoon is golden. No one ever interrupts."

"I would have thought if you're constantly coming in and out of this room," said Boswell in an acid voice. "Sooner later you would interrupt yourself."

"Crossover, you mean?" Cressida said, waving a hand airily. "Not in Event Space. It doesn't work that way."

"How does it work, then? Is it a different 2038 each time?"

"You're thinking about it too literally."

"How else am I supposed to think about it? You're defying all the rules of..." he stopped.

Cressida turned with her back to the window. She was silhouetted by the pale afternoon sun, but he could see the soft smile on her face. "There are no rules to time travel, Boz. Remember? She sorts herself out."

He sputtered quietly to himself. Certainly there were no

rules, but that didn't mean there were not... principles. Predictable, meaningful principles. Otherwise, what had he been doing all these years, lecturing students on Time Mechanics? It had to mean something.

"It's for the best," Aesop said sadly. "We can't know more than they do, Boswell. The humans won't forgive that."

"Doesn't bother me," said Nero. "You'll take my memory from my cold dead paws. But I can see that you two are going to be all wet about it."

"The anachronisms haven't broken through here yet," Cressida went on. "Not like poor old 912, with its skateboards and yo-yos. And sushi — you should have seen the faces of all those Viking merchants when sushi turned up! My favourite was introducing the tomato to Italians a millennium and a half early — I thought Cicero was going to cry over his first plate of spaghetti marinara."

"Church," Boswell said tiredly. "What aren't you telling me?"

She seemed so earnest, so real. But she felt less and less like she was the partner he had lost.

What secrets have I kept from you all these years, Church? What secrets have I kept from both of us?

Cressida was unaware of his inner turmoil. "I know it all sounds like nonsense, Boz. But I've been living this nonsense for a long time now. This place — this one afternoon. Sometimes Mikaela stabs Petey with a spoon, not a cake slice. And sometimes it's the sound guys who trash the set before the lighting guys. Sometimes one contestant makes it to the cars before the others... but no matter how many times I see it, this afternoon remains mostly the same. It's the closest thing I've found to a stable Event."

Boswell frowned. "This is an experiment to you."

"What do you think I am, an Anachronaut?" Cressida said lightly.

"You said we were all Anachronauts."

"It's the only thing that makes sense."

Boswell stretched his claws into the arm of the couch. "I suppose so," he grumbled. "Chronos College has always approved of the most ridiculous antics. What you lot — what *we* got up to wasn't exactly responsible. They keep sending young history nerds and talking cats off into history to gather data, and no one ever talks about what the data is for. Then there was the Boleyn Incident."

Anne Boleyn. She was the key to it, somehow. Those pieces of memories chasing Boswell around like a bad smell. If he could remember how he knew her, surely the rest of it would make sense.

Anne Boleyn. Aesop.

It was a bit rich, Boswell criticising how Chronos College operated. He was part of it, after all. He had been shaping young minds ever since he retired from the field. Seven years, and he hadn't asked nearly enough questions.

(Was he so busy mourning his partner, he didn't notice what else had been taken?)

Ruthven was asleep, curled up on the couch. Boswell wanted to lie on his warm stomach and sleep too. He used to do that with his Church, after a good mission. Or a bad mission. He trusted her so much.

"If it's true," Boswell muttered. "If Chronos College and the Anachronauts have always been in league with each other... what do we do about it? Who do we report this to? Do we try and stop it?"

"It's the coward's choice," said Nero. "But you'll be used to that."

"I don't know," said Cressida. "The Founders have to know about it already. Don't they? Maybe everyone knows except us."

Her voice fluttered, faded. When Boswell glanced up, he

saw that her whole body was also not quite here — utterly translucent. He could see the lines of the window frame through her Viking apron.

"I was never able to find my way out of Event Space," Cressida said, her eyes fixed on his as she dimmed. "It's too late for me — this me, anyway. But you, Boz. Cats can go anywhere. You can get Ruthven out. Old school time travel. Send a postcard. Tap the opal. Go home."

Boswell blinked, and Cressida was gone.

Again. He had lost her again. Even if she wasn't the real version, that only meant he'd failed her twice over. Boswell crawled down on to the couch and snuggled up against Ruthven's chest, listening to him breathe.

Wish you were here.

He craved oblivion. A good nap, to make it all better.

Instead, he got memories, more memories, piling in and around and on top of him.

Memories of Lovelace and Ptolemy. Of Nero and Banksia. Of *Aesop*.

Of Anne bloody Boleyn.

It was all starting to make sense, and Boswell didn't like it. Not one bit.

---

1. Boswell would never acknowledge that he could not actually open the door without Ruthven's assistance; whatever quirk of evolution allowed twenty-fourth century cats to speak in human language had not seen fit to provide them with opposable thumbs.
2. If Boswell was going to watch vintage television then it was Jeremy Brett's *Sherlock Holmes* or nothing; in truth he was a simple cat and far more likely to select that one channel that has a flickering hearth fire on eternal loop.
3. Cressida was referring to Season 7 of *Stately Baking*, also known as the Season Where Mikaela Tried To Stab Petey With A Cake Slice. This popular show always trod a careful line between feel-good cottagecore kindness in the kitchen, and deliberate psychological torment.

thirty-six
1526

further back than you might think

AESOP WAS TWITCHING WITH GLEE. The twitch began somewhere near the end of her fluffy black and orange tail and ended at her tiny pink nose. In the spaces between there was even more extraneous twitching.

"Castle, castle, castle," she chanted beneath her breath.

"Come on, Aes," Ruthven laughed. "You're an embarrassment right now."

She gave him a snooty look over her shoulder, and added about twelve twitches to her tail. She was going to strain something, at this rate. "Why aren't you more excited? This is our first castle, Ruthven. Our first sixteenth century hop. Our first... MOAT!"

She jerked back, just in time to stop her dainty paws from getting wet from what did in fact prove to be a large Tudor moat.

Ruthven scooped his cat up and hung her delicately over one shoulder, as he'd seen the other travellers do. He got a claw to the rib for his troubles, but Aesop balanced herself perfectly after a moment. "Hever Castle has two moats," he informed her.

"Well," said Aesop, recovering quickly. "That seems excessive, even for royalty."

"She's not royalty yet."

Aesop gently head-butted him on the side of the face as Ruthven escorted them both across the bridge. "I do hope you're not planning to waste this hop trolling for historical celebrities, my good man," she said archly. "We have a job to do. A vital, nay, essential task."

"I know," he muttered reluctantly. "I remember."

Hever Castle was spectacular. One of those traditional, boxy British motte-and-bailey castles with proper turrets, battlements and a gatehouse. The double moat gave the gardens a particularly grand look, sandwiched as they were between two opportunities for cats to fall into rectangular bodies of water.

Enticing as the castle was, Ruthven and Aesop were not supposed to go near it. The task as laid out for them was simply to count the box hedges in the gardens between the moat, and measure their heights. Get in, count, get out.[1]

"Shame about the maze," said Ruthven as they made their slow stroll through the various 'rooms' within the gardens, stopping to make notes here and there.

He was garbed in the authentic costume of a sixteenth century gardener, made from fabrics that were rather rough on the skin. Genuine burlap. He was going to need moisturiser, when he returned to the twenty-fourth century. Tunbridge laughed her arse off at him when she saw what he was wearing, and asked what he had done to offend Hogarth from Costume.[2]

"What maze?" asked Aesop now, leaping from Ruthven's shoulder to stroll prettily across the top of the nearest hedge. She was quite the loveliest calico cat imaginable, her black and orange tabby features set off by dramatic patches of white, not to mention her pale yellow eyes with rings of green. Well aware of how adorable she looked, Aesop had a tendency to preen when in especially flattering situations, such as direct sunlight.[3]

"There used to be a Tudor replica maze right about here," said Ruthven. "Uh. I mean, there will be. The gardens were radically overhauled in the Edwardian era, made to look like Tudor gardens. But actually they went way more elaborate than these Tudor gardens ever were, hundreds of years earlier right now."

"You're going to have to get better hold of your tenses," said Aesop, taking a step off the hedge into empty air, and promptly falling off.

Ruthven looked at the sky, and the moat, pretending he hadn't noticed. There were certain courtesies one learned to observe, when one was partnered with a cat.

A slightly rumpled Aesop leaped back up on the hedge and yawned pointedly. "I'm fine," she grumbled.

"Any reason you wouldn't be?" If Ruthven was acting any more innocent, there would have to be whistling involved.

"Shut up."

"Oh!"

Ruthven and Aesop both froze. That voice did not belong to either of them. Slowly, they turned to look over the hedge.

A young woman stood there before them. She wore an embroidered green gown that marked her out as a sixteenth-century Lady of Quality. Her hairline was plucked fashionably high, disappearing beneath a white linen cap and velvet headdress.

She carried a basket of flowers, in which was tucked several crumpled, much-read letters in tiny inked handwriting. Her gaze was wary. She wore a very familiar locket shaped like a 'B' which Ruthven had seen in a historical portrait, as well as the Famous Biographies section of his History exam.

"It's only bloody Anne Boleyn!" Aesop squealed in his ear.

"Be cool," Ruthven whispered back. Hever Castle. 1526. It would have been strange if this was not Anne Boleyn. Anne Boleyn in the grounds of her family home, at a crucial turning point in her life: Henry VIII had been courting her relentlessly, after she refused to become his mistress. Back in London, he was even now working on an annulment of his marriage to Queen Katherine of Aragon.

Anne Boleyn had a decade to live. She would marry the king twice over, give birth to his daughter, the future Elizabeth I, and ultimately be executed for treason and witchcraft.

Those letters in her basket might be missives from the king! Which month was it? Ruthven had forgotten the exact date. Staring into the face of history, he would be hard-pressed to remember his own name.

The lady regarded them both with a stoic attitude. "Pray, sir," she said. "How is it that you come to be in possession of a talking cat?"

"We're," said Ruthven, hoping inspiration would come to him, "...time travellers," he finished.

"Good save," said Aesop, smacking herself in the face with her own paw.

---

1. Traditionally, newly graduated travellers were given small, achievable tasks for their early hops, so as to warm up to more significant missions. Tasks like: 'count the box hedges of Hever Castle in 1526 and compare their heights to the same box hedges in 1557.' Restrictions like these rarely prevent travellers from tripping over someone famous, setting something on fire, or accidentally triggering an Event, but it means they are more likely to feel guilty afterwards.
2. The answer to the question "What did Ruthven do to offend Hogarth from Costume?" involves an awkward couple of drinks at the campus bar, which Ruthven realised belatedly was probably supposed to be a date.
3. Most cats preen when they find themselves looking especially good, but Ruthven was convinced Aesop did this twice as often as other cats.

thirty-seven
2034

"Before Monterey. Before Cressida."

RUTHVEN WOKE up to the warm heat of a cat curled against him. For a moment, just for a moment he allowed himself to imagine it was Aesop. She was here with him, and everything was all right.

He took a deep breath and opened his eyes.

Professor Boswell's light green irises stared back at him, startled. They had been snuggling together. Best not to mention it.

"Cressida disappeared," said Boswell gruffly. "I think perhaps she wasn't real in the first place."

"I'm sorry," breathed Ruthven. If it was Aesop sitting here on his stomach looking miserable, he would have reached out and scritched her behind the ear.

What the hell. He reached out and did it.

Boswell leaned into his hand for a moment, then pulled away.

It was odd, having it be just the two of them. Like real partners. "Tell me what you know about Anne Boleyn," said Ruthven.

Boswell responded with a long, flat stare. "What has she to do with anything?"

"Did you know she was an Anachronaut? Cressida did."

Boswell ducked his head, looking embarrassed. "I was around when they recruited Boleyn. She was the first human ever saved from her own time stream."

That... sounded like quite a story.

"Monterey must have really wanted to sleep with her," Ruthven said gravely.

Boswell laughed and then tried to pretend it was a sneeze halfway through. "Before Monterey. Before Cressida."

Ruthven was confused. "But Monterey and Cressida were in the first generation of trainees. The experimental workshops. There weren't any time travellers before you lot. Except Banksia and Burbage."

He'd never actually thought much about the timeline. Everyone knew that time travel had been invented by Professor Burbage (human) and Professor Banksia (cat) twenty years ago. But the experimental workshops — Lovelace and Monterey, Boswell and Cressida, the other early travellers... that all started nearly a decade later.

It had never occurred to Ruthven to wonder what happened in those intervening years. He had assumed it was mostly paperwork.

"Banksia and Burbage were the first travellers," Boswell said, scowling as if trying to keep it all straight in his head. Or possibly because he had resting scowl face. "There were more, long before the experimental workshops. Nine humans, and not enough cats to start with. But they soon trained us up."

Ruthven sat up straight on the uncomfortable couch, almost flinging Boswell off his legs. "Nine humans. Are you talking about the Founders?"

"You think a group of billionaires would fund time travel for the sake of humanity and not have a go at it themselves?" muttered Boswell. "They were all at it. Celeste and Melusine

Oxford, Kincaid, Dumas. The Pennyworths, all three of them. The Montereys — Jolyon and Vanessa."

"Why did they stop travelling?"

"No idea. Veil of secrecy all around. After Burbage and Banksia's disappearance, the Founders all retired from the field — poured all their energy into setting up the experimental workshops, and the colleges. Training up their kids as travellers while they pulled strings from behind the scenes. Soames Kincaid is still the Dean at Banksia, pushing his 'save the koalas' agenda. Celeste Oxford was the Dean at Aleister College before the Anachronauts took over. Dumas has been teaching under the name Professor Mycroft since Chronos College began... Vanessa Monterey used to have my old job in Time Mechanics. She went by Professor Valadon before she quit in a huff over that business with the Bonfire of the Vanities."

"You've known this all along?" Ruthven said, astonished. "Why does no one else know?"

Boswell gave him a canny look. "Do you think they don't? The history of Chronos College — and the other colleges, come to that — is somewhat redacted. But believe me. People know."

Ruthven felt sick. "Oxford and Monterey. They have to know all about it. If it's their parents. Right?" He couldn't wrap his head around it. The Founders and their secret history. Hiding out on campus as professors? Hiding the fact that they all used to time travel? It was so strange.

"Ah," said Boswell, scratching himself. "Well, the thing is, young man. Your friends may not know."

"What do you mean?"

Boswell looked miserable. He jumped off Ruthven's lap, and scrambled to the large window seat instead.

Ruthven joined him. The grounds of Fenthorp Manor looked messier now. The large pavilion tent had been abandoned. Bags and camera gear and what looked like giant cream cakes were haphazardly scattered here and there. Tyre tracks from several trucks and other vehicles disfigured the pretty green lawn.

Everyone had left in a hurry. It was 2034, and the contestants and crew of *Stately Baking* had been informed that the United Kingdom was at war.

"The thing is," said Boswell, leaning his fluffy face against the cool glass of the window. "Lovelace doesn't remember the Anne Boleyn incident. Twelve years ago, Abydos and Lancaster Pennyworth were working together, trying to prove they could rescue items from history if they plucked them out just before destruction. But the experiment went out of control. Next thing we knew, Anne Boleyn was standing in the twenty-fourth century, wearing the gown she had been executed in."

"That's not possible," said Ruthven, turning it over in his head. "How could someone take Anne Boleyn out of time without changing history? That year didn't become an Event until much later."

"That's what I'm telling you," Boswell said, his tail swishing in irritation. History remembers that Anne Boleyn died. The witnesses on the ground saw her die. Lovelace and I saw Boleyn in the twenty-fourth century, alive and well. We were in the meeting where it was decided what to do with her. And then we forgot all about it."

"The Founders are messing with people's memories? How long have you known this?" Ruthven didn't mean to sound accusing, but his tone got ahead of him.

"All this rampaging around time aisles has brought some old memories back into the light," said the marmalade tabby, sounding tired. He lowered his head, and pawed at the opal that hung from his collar. "It happened before, when I was searching the tenth century for Cressida. I felt the Event beginning in 912, and I almost didn't get out in time. The same thing happened in 913. 914. I got headaches, heard a ringing sound. I thought it was, well..." He pulled a face.

"Trauma?" Ruthven suggested.

"I suddenly recalled an old time hop. Early Imperial Rome. A palace courtyard, open to the sky. Augustus Caesar reaching out to pick a poisoned fig off a tree... My partner at my side. Not Cressida. *Dumas*."

"He's the one you said is really Professor Mycroft?" The affable professor, friendly with all the students. Particularly friendly with Monterey and Oxford, now Ruthven came to think of it.

"That bastard swans around the staff room grinning, like we're friends, knowing the memory of our travels was taken from me," Boswell said between gritted teeth. "My head was full of confusing memories that didn't match. Including the Anne Boleyn incident. I asked Lovelace, and she had no idea what I was talking about. I thought perhaps my opal had been damaged."

"You stopped travelling in time."

"I didn't want more memories to return. Cressida was lost, no getting her back. I didn't trust myself with anyone else." Boswell gave Ruthven a grudging sort of look. "Well done on not getting yourself killed yet, by the way."

"Cheers."

"And here we are again. Every minute I've spent in those bloody time aisles, in Event Space... it's dislodged whatever was holding back those memories. There are still gaps. But I have a clearer picture now."

"It's not a pretty picture," said Ruthven. "If Cressida was right, if the Anachronauts and Chronos College are all part of the same thing, then the Founders are behind it. We haven't been experimenting with time travel. We're the experiments. The test subjects."

"Running around mazes with peanut butter and bits of string," agreed Boswell morosely.

The two of them stared out at the destroyed lawn, the flapping walls of the tent.

"What do you think they'll do to us if they find out we know?" Ruthven asked finally.

"No idea," said Boswell. "I don't know about you, laddie, but I'm starting to think about life beyond Chronos College."

"Assuming we can get back to Basic Time at all," Ruthven reminded him. He was starting to feel a mad sort of yearning for the twenty-fourth century.

"There is that," said Boswell, butting him with his head. "Luckily for you, I'm a cat. I hear we're quite helpful when it comes to time travel."

thirty-eight
24th century paranoia

Anyone having memory issues? Concerns that they might have lost whole chunks of their personal history, including names of family members, childhood memories... the exact moment they found out that cats can talk?

Or is it just me?

> Zadie Kincaid, Various Unhinged
> Scribblings on the back of a toilet door
> near the Costume Department

thirty-nine
2034

"It's always about lost media for you, isn't it?"

"ACTIVATE YOUR OPAL," said Professor Boswell sternly.

"Opal has been activated all this time," Ruthven grumbled, but tapped the implant to turn it off and on again. "Opal activated."

"Write your postcard."

"Really?"

Of all the grumpy expressions Boswell had turned on him since this whole mess began, this was by far the grumpiest.

Ruthven pulled the postcard out from his satchel and wrote the words:

Wish you were here.

"You're making this up as you go along," he said under his breath as he wrote.

"That's time travel for you," said Boswell.

The two of them headed downstairs through the abandoned Fenthorp Manor 2034, through the kitchens with all the scattered lighting and camera equipment, and finally out into the back garden after a brief graze among the abandoned cakes.

Boswell licked whipped cream off his whiskers as he led the way.

The old greenhouse was still there, though the frame and the glasswork had both been replaced, by the looks of it, over years. So, not the same greenhouse at all, really.

The whole place still felt distinctly *Cramberleigh* to Ruthven, even if they were a long way from the 1960s. He didn't know much about this particular slice of the twenty-first century. Was this the decade with all the blogging? The one where everyone was obsessed with sourdough starters and/or the Spice Girls? The one where AI temporarily replaced all jobs and half the corporations in the world toppled into chaos and incoherent branding?

Clearly this was one of the decades with all the baking shows, but Ruthven had a vague idea that this described most of the twenty-first century, wars or no wars.

Without discussing it, both Ruthven and Boswell had decided that their attempt to break out of Event Space and into Basic Time should happen outside. As far away from time aisles and cupboard doors as possible.

Ruthven stared at the blank postcard — the words had already disappeared. "Should I write something else? Provide more information about where we are?"

"It never matters what you write," Boswell said impatiently.

"It feels like it matters."

"Go on, then. I'll sit here and lick myself while you come up with something profound."

Ruthven stood there, stylus hovering. Slowly, he wrote

Send Help Fenthorp Manor 2034.

He was overtaken by an impulse to cross it out and go with something more dramatic (possibly with a lot more swearing) but of course, there was no crossing out with postcards.

The letters glowed, and vanished.

"You mentioned the Pennyworths earlier," Ruthven murmured, eyes on the blank postcard as if it, not he, was about to deliver something profound. "I know the Dean, of course. But there are more of them?"

"Siblings," confirmed Boswell. "Florence, Daimler and Lancaster Pennyworth. Daimler's the Dean."

"I saw a doctor who was also called Pennyworth," Ruthven said quietly. "A psychologist. After Aesop…"

"That must have been Florence," said Boswell with a faraway look. "They suggested her to me, after Cressida. I told them cats don't do therapy. All we need are sunbeams and naps."

"I was having panic attacks," Ruthven admitted. He knew it wasn't shameful to ask for help when you needed it. That wasn't why he hesitated to share it now. He was looking back on his own history in light of this new information about the Founders and he did not like what he saw. "I couldn't remember how Aesop died. I still can't. I don't remember anything about that mission. The footage isn't in the Media Archives. Out of respect, they said."

"Humph."

"Do you think they did something to me? To hide what happened?" If there was a reason other than his own trauma that Ruthven could not remember what happened to his cat… what else couldn't he remember? How much of his memory had been tampered with?

Boswell stared at some geraniums as if they had all the answers. When he finally spoke, it wasn't to answer Ruthven's question — not directly, in any case. "Aesop was my trainer, you know. She was in the program from the beginning. Her, Nero, and Banksia."

That surprised Ruthven. "She always seemed such a young cat. I thought she was doing everything for the first time, like me." Had it been an act? He wasn't sure why that idea made him so uncomfortable.

"She changed," Boswell admitted. "Once they paired her with you. Flightier. Lighter. But when Lovelace and I were first brought in, Aesop had years of time travel under her collar already. She knew it all. She taught *us* how to partner with humans."

Ruthven didn't know how to deal with this revelation. He locked onto something else, something that had been bugging him. "If there was a whole generation of time travel we don't have in our records, where are those records? Not in the Media Archive, that's for sure."

Boswell snorted. "It's always about lost media for you, isn't it?"

Ruthven pressed on. "Surely they recorded all those early hops. We have footage of Banksia and Burbage in the Media Archive, but nothing to suggest other time travellers before you and Cressida, Monterey and Lovelace."

"They wiped your mind," Boswell grumbled. "And you're worried no one will ever get to watch Aesop and Kincaid meeting Blackbeard for the first time?"

Ruthven stared wildly at him. Boswell looked as if regretted the swipe.

"Was Soames Kincaid her partner? Before me." Ruthven felt weirdly jealous. Was this how Cressida had felt when she saw him working with Boswell? Was that why she kept pretending to forget his name?

"My memory isn't exactly reliable, lad," Boswell muttered, looking away. "I'm not sure what's true."

"Gah!" Ruthven leaned against the greenhouse. "It's so

frustrating. We're supposed to be documenting history, learning more about it. Preserving information about the past, not covering it up. How can we be trusted with the history of the world if we're not honest about our own history at Chronos College? What's the point of time travel?"

Boswell sat on Ruthven's foot. "I recommend we get out of here. Save our existential breakdowns for Basic Time."

"You're right. I know you're right." Ruthven took a deep breath. "Any sign of a hoop?"

Boswell sniffed the air. "Try the postcard again."

Ruthven checked. "Still blank. No, wait."

There was something there. So faint he could barely make it out, but it looked like writing.

"What does it say?" Boswell demanded.

Ruthven held the soft postcards to the sunlight. "I think... stand by. Or maybe... sandwich."

Boswell's ears twitched and he spun around in a circle, chasing his own tail "See that?"

A time hoop appeared in the air before them, gold and sparkling. It was faint, like a rainbow you had to keep your eye on so it wouldn't fade into the mist. Like Cressida had been, before she vanished.

"Should we chance it?" Ruthven asked. He didn't fancy the idea of a time hoop that was only halfway there. That seemed like a good way to end up with your leg in last Tuesday.

"Unless you want to spend the rest of your life in a year where no *Cramberleigh* episodes have yet been recovered," said Professor Boswell.

"Right, yes. Of course. Good point." Ruthven stared into the glittering, twisting, mirage of a time hoop. "On the count of three?"

forty
1969

"Don't tell me you don't have the jade pineapple either?"

BOSWELL CLUNG to Ruthven's jumper as they leapt into nothing, and landed... exactly where they had left.

The greenhouse shimmered before them. (Was it the same greenhouse? It looked both cleaner and dirtier at the same time.) Boswell leaped free of Ruthven's arms instantly (he wasn't Nero to be carried around all the time).

The pale shadow of a time hoop sputtered into non-existence.

Boswell blinked slowly at the greenhouse. Old or new? 2030s or 1960s? They were still here, regardless. Bloody Fenthorp Manor.

"It didn't work," said Ruthven. "Unless... what year is it?"

"I'm not Lovelace," Boswell grumped. "I don't pretend to be able to pick the difference between 1922 and 1923 by the scent of time-specific perfumes and petrochemicals."

He could smell ham somewhere nearby, which was promising. "It's lunch time."

"Got your priorities sorted, I see."

Ruthven headed off into the gardens, in a creeping manner bound to call more attention to himself than if he had walked normally. He was basically miming "I am a suspicious person who should be thrown off the property." Luckily for Boswell, no one was ever suspicious of a marmalade tabby.

Ruthven stopped sneaking around long enough to peer around a hedge in an exaggerated manner.

"You may as well wear a t-shirt proclaiming you're a member of the Catburglar's Union," Boswell complained.

"Shh. You were right about lunch." Ruthven crooked his finger.

Normally Boswell would not dignify that kind of outrageous gesture, but the ham smell was stronger now, and he wasn't used to missing meals. He trotted over, and wound around Ruthven's ankles before strutting out to see what lay beyond the hedge.

Film crew. Honking great big cameras on dollies, not all that light hand-held gear that had been scattered around in 2034.

The crew had set up a tent and a couple of ratty caravans to operate as trailers, because this was British telly and not Hollywood. A few actors wandered around in costume, drinking cups of tea and smoking behind the caravans. There were, Boswell noted with interest, abandoned ham sandwiches on a nearby table, along with cheese and onion crisps and a half-demolished sponge cake with jam and cream.

Those poor sandwiches. Someone had to put them out of their misery.

"It's 1969," Ruthven reported from somewhere above Boswell.

"Hmm? How do you know that?"

"Robson O'Sullivan's in uniform."[1]

"So you don't need me to dart out there and check the current shooting script to confirm the date?"

Ruthven sighed. "If you want a sandwich, go get a sandwich."

Three sandwiches later, after a near miss when several makeup artists spotted him and started squealing about how adorable he was, Boswell trotted to the greenhouse. "I would have thought you'd be more excited," he observed when he found Ruthven sitting on a bench, looking like the sad, brooding human he was. "*Cramberleigh* and all that."

"It's 1969," said Ruthven heavily.

"I'm aware."

"That's an Event. One of the Anachronaut-caused ones."

"Ah, yes," Boswell said wisely. He had spotted some of the telltale anachronisms of Event Space, including several iPods among the crew, and a flock of dodos careering across the manicured lawn. "I suppose that lot would be interested in partitioning off this particular year. Woodstock, after all."

Ruthven blinked at him. "The Moon landing, surely."

Boswell gave him a much slower blink. "I don't know if you've noticed, but the Anachronauts care more about famous parties than historical significance when creating their Events."

"So it's all about eating, drinking and making merry?" Ruthven looked even more depressed. "I'm surprised they haven't recruited Monterey."

Boswell leaped up to the bench and laid his head on Ruthven's knee. Not that he was hinting at anything at all. They weren't partners, merely workplace acquaintances. There was no need for Ruthven to... ahh, good lad. Boswell preened a bit as Ruthven stroked his fur. "Monterey had a theory, actually," he informed the human, turning this way and that so Ruthven could get full coverage with his pats. "He's always said the Anachronauts were trying to ruin his life by making sure he personally couldn't attend all those parties."

"And that's not true?" Ruthven hummed, continuing to pat.

Boswell rubbed against his hand. "I imagine ruining his life was a minor bonus," he purred. "My personal theory is that Anachronauts are arseholes."

"Sounds about right." Ruthven sighed. "It's hard to get excited about watching Edgar Wildegreen waved off to war when we're still stuck. The hop didn't work."

"It did not. I don't think that was a real time hoop," Boswell added. "It didn't smell right."

"So, we're trapped in Event Space forever?"

"It could be worse, dear boy. You could be trapped in Event Space without a cat."

Ruthven pulled together something like a smile and scratched Boswell behind the ears. "What now?"

Boswell twitched his nose. "Unless you fancy trying for a walk-on role in *Cramberleigh*, I suggest we take the offensive. Find some Anachronauts and ask them what the hell is going on."

"You don't think that might be dangerous?"

"What are they going to do, trap us in Event Space forever?"

"Good point. We don't have to trudge all the way to Woodstock to find them, do we? I'm pretty sure the groovy young things would make fun of my blazer."

Boswell smirked "Let's have a poke about in Cressida's time aisles, see what turns up."

"Huh," said Ruthven, looking up at the many windows of the manor house. "There was one just outside the pineapple parlour. Do you think if we go back in, it will drop us back down here?"

"Only one way to find out."

There were several libraries in Fenthorp Manor, which is how you knew it was a fancy house. Only one was ever used for *Cramberleigh*, because dragging all the big camera equipment into the wings of the house was more trouble than it was worth. The crew were currently filming in the Round Library, on the second floor: according to the shooting script that Ruthven had definitely stolen from downstairs, Sir Victor was about to pledge his troth to the future Lady Sophia Wildegreen.[2]

Ruthven might have been unmoved by the sight of Robson O'Sullivan, but he considered it an act of heroic restraint to creep past the doorway without asking Barbara Hill to sign his leg.[3]

Upstairs, Ruthven and Boswell got into a brief spat about whether the pineapple parlour was on the fourth or the fifth floor of the manor.

Ruthven flung open a cupboard door on the landing to prove his point that this definitely wasn't the right floor, even though he was proving his point to empty air, because Boswell had already grumbled off to the floor above.

Three brooms fell out at his feet, and Ruthven stared in horror into the eyes of...

Well, he wasn't sure who it was. Not a member of the 1969 cast and crew of *Cramberleigh*, that was for sure. An Anachronaut? Maybe.

She wore dark blue robes, which looked vaguely religious, with a hood to cover a shaven head. She looked younger than Ruthven, who himself often got mistaken for a student. She stared at him with the intensity of a thousand pissed-off cats.

"Don't tell me you don't have the jade pineapple either?" the woman demanded.

Ruthven backed up a step. He slammed the cupboard door closed, and used a broom handle to wedge it shut.

"What are you doing in here, I told you, this is the wrong floor," complained Boswell, strolling in.

"There's someone here," Ruthven said in a strangled voice.

"What sort of someone?"

The blue-robed woman stepped through the cupboard. Through it, like a ghost. She was translucent as Cressida had been translucent, and clearly saw no need to respect the rules of physics.[4]

"There!" Ruthven howled.

"I don't see anything!" Boswell said, alarmed. "Are you having some sort of fit?"

"I don't know what a jade pineapple is," Ruthven insisted, backing up to the window as the spooky woman in blue robes approached him. "Feel free to take the chandelier upstairs. Or maybe downstairs. I'm confused!"

Two cats came through the cupboard door. They were nothing like any cats Ruthven had seen outside a museum or Cleopatra's palace. They were the size of greyhounds, tall and stately, prowling with pointed ears pricked up. Their general shape was that of Egyptian Bast statues, though they had a glittery, purplish hue that was remarkably un-ancient and otherworldly.

Altogether, the most unconvincing cats he'd ever seen.

"Ruthven," snapped Boswell. "What in hellfire are you staring at?"

"Cats," sputtered Ruthven. "Giant purple cats. Blue robes..."

"Really," said the woman, sounding disappointed. "If you're not going to be helpful, we'll have to lock you up with the others."

"Please don't," Ruthven begged. His vision was already darkening around the edges, as if it had all got too much for him

The last thing he heard was Professor Boswell, shouting his name.

And then...

All he could see, all he could think, was *blue*.

---

1. Robson O'Sullivan played Sir Victor Wildegreen's dull son Edgar in *Cramberleigh* Seasons 1-4 before being sent off to war at the beginning of Season 5. When asked at a 1980s science fiction convention why the character's fate was never explained on screen (indeed, why Edgar was never mentioned again), Season 5 script editor Lindsey Gordon famously said "Fair cop, we forgot about him."
2. Sir Victor Wildegreen, lord of *Cramberleigh*, was played for eleven seasons by the legendary Christopher Seasalter (1922-2005). Known for his mesmerising combination of ghoulish melodrama and dry wit, Seasalter famously turned down roles in *Star Wars, Doctor Who, Blake's 7*, twelve different Hammer Horror productions, and *Midsomer Murders*. Indeed, after his stint on *Cramberleigh,* he returned to repertory theatre and remained there for the rest of his prodigious career. Seasalter's only film credit after 1975 is an appearance on Comic Relief in 1997: in this skit, twelve actors who have previously played the Ghost of Hamlet's Father find themselves in the same BBC lift, and engage in a violent duel to the death from which only Brian Blessed emerges alive. The conquered foes remain as ghosts haunting the lift. This obscure piece of media enjoyed a brief moment of viral pop culture acclaim thirty years later in an internet meme inspired by Seasalter's deadpan delivery of the line "We'll just wait here, then, Brian."
3. Lady Sophia, the third Lady Wildegreen, appeared in Seasons 5-6 of *Cramberleigh*, before dying of the Spanish flu. Played by Barbara Hill (1945-2022), best known for her long-running roles on soaps such as *Coronation Street* (Maggie Beardsley 1965-1968 & 1982-1993), *Emmerdale Farm* (Emma Bagshot 1976-1981), *EastEnders* (Shirley Magpie 1995-2012) and *Holby City* (Maggie Bagsley 2006, 2013-2018). Hill also had a starring role in *The Anne Hathaway Show* (1981), a short-lived sitcom based on the life of the wife of William Shakespeare in which the Bard never appears.
4. Unlike time travel, physics has rules.

forty-one
the answer

We're not academics.
    We're not students.
    We're not time travellers.
    We're not in control.
    We are the experiment.

> Zadie Kincaid, Thoroughly Unhinged about Time Travel, At the End of My Rope, Send Help, I think they're coming for me...

forty-two
1664

Party of the Delights

"FINALLY," Monterey announced to the group. "I'm enjoying time travel."

Lovelace, perched on his shoulder, snorted at him. "Because you've clearly been having a terrible time before now."

"I don't know why we didn't invent time aisles years ago," Monterey said, tapping her on her soft nose. "Much more civilised than that whole hoops business. And look at this! Marvellous. You don't get this at home."

'This' was a fabulously excessive garden party, held in the grounds of Versailles, France, 1664. Monterey had managed to pinch somebody's bright purple coat: he looked like he belonged here, as long as no one put up too much fuss about the turtleneck jumper being invented four centuries early.

That was unlikely to be a problem, given that this wasn't exactly the original Pleasures of the Enchanted Island garden party from the original 1664 that Monterey had Lovelace had visited the first time around.[1] Oh, there was Louis XV, the Sun-King himself, garbed all in red as the knight Roger from *Orlando Furioso*, mounted on a horse with a gemstone-encrusted harness.

There was a horse-drawn golden chariot, a giant carousel, and a stage all ready for a ballet performance. Every tree, every fountain, every spare inch of grass, was ornamented to make it look like the king's guests had fallen into a book of fairytales. There was the lovely Louise de Vallière, the king's mistress, more ornately dressed than his queen, Maria Theresa of Spain, or his mother — Anne of freaking Austria.[2]

Most of those things were the same. But this was in other regards, very much not the same party Monterey had attended the first time around.

The sky was an unsettling shade of purple, though it was supposed to be mid-afternoon. Since he had been standing here in his fabulous coat, Monterey had seen at least two jets fly over, and several helicopters.

Louise de Vallière was cosplaying Marilyn Monroe, who wouldn't be born for more than two hundred and fifty years. She had even found a steam vent to stand over, which was impressive for 1664.

Anne of Austria, who must be in her early sixties, was wearing comfy blue jeans and a Placebo t-shirt. Her hair was still elaborately styled for court, though someone had added the modern touch with a giant sunflower tucked into her beaded up-do.

The refreshments tables, along with the usual dainties, pastries and stuffed goose livers you might expect at a royal affair, displayed several crystal decanters filled with Skittles, and a pyramid of vodka cocktails in cans.

"It's getting worse," said Cressida, looking up at the sky. "Last time I came through this party, there weren't nearly as many anachronisms. Event Space has to be on the verge of collapse."

"You don't want me to enjoy this, do you?" Monterey complained, snatching up a platter of miniature hot dogs from a passing waiter on roller skates. "I've missed this century."

Lovelace coughed. "It's technically our fault you couldn't get back here before…"

"Not my point, darling!"

"Don't let me stop you fiddling while Rome burns," Cressida said sourly. "I can worry for both of us."

"I didn't say I wasn't worried," Monterey snarked back. "But this could be our last chance to nick a pen from Molière. I never managed it last time."

Cressida gave him an impatient look, then barked an unexpected laugh. "Don't you dare."

"Was that a dare I heard? If you insist…" Monterey liked it better when Cressida was laughing. It made him feel like all of time and space might not be ending right this minute.

Oxford, meanwhile, had a face like a wet weekend. Monterey had been far too busy chatting up Cleopatra in 48 BCE (Take that, bucket list!) to notice when Oxford's dour mood set in, but it was entrenched now.

Fenella had that wide-eyed, frantic look of the newbie traveller who wants to do everything at once but is terrified of getting it wrong. She still wore a white Ancient Greek peplos under a Napoleonic great-coat, now with the addition of a scarab necklace given to her by Cleopatra. It was a remarkably appropriate outfit for Event Space, where the electric scooters were piling up with all the abandoned skateboards, and the seventeenth century orchestra down by the stage was playing a cover of Rocket Man for the entertainment of the Sun King.

Monterey passed Fenella a mini hot dog, to keep her strength up.

"This is lovely," Fenella said. "But I'm not sure why we rushed out of Egypt so quickly. Cleopatra was quite willing to fend off Anachronauts with her taser army. We could have slept for more than ten minutes."

"You want food and sleep?" Cressida said, looking distracted. "What are you, a cat?"

Cressida, who had spent longer in Event Space than any of them, was starting to look worn around the edges. Her enormous Victorian bustle gown had lost its dramatic flounce, the tie-dye colours were not nearly as vibrant, and the hem dragged down with centuries of dust.

"I'm looking for someone," she said to Monterey in an undertone.

"An Anachronaut?" He didn't think they were likely to be all that friendly after what happened with the velociraptor back at Fenthorp Manor, 1899.

She shook her head. "I think we only need one cat to get us all back to Basic Time. But I don't have the theory in my head. Not all the pieces, anyway. I need to pull myself together, literally."

Monterey screwed his face up at her. "I understand nothing of what you just said. What does this person look like?"

"Me in a Viking helmet."

Monterey's eyes widened in response. Okay, then. Cressida was losing it. Maybe she'd already lost it.

She looked annoyed at his reaction. "Monterey. I've been scattered. Do you know what that means?"

"Of course," he said, offended. "It happened to a fellow I trained with. The basic definition was in our exams."

"The basic definition doesn't cover what happened to me."

"It's when your brain gets all scrambled from too much time travel. Risk is higher when you have a near miss with an Event. It's amazing Lovelace and I are sane, frankly." Monterey blew a kiss at his cat, who was helping herself to a sushi tray and ignored him. "Memory loss, hallucinations, and sometimes you think you're more than one person."

"Typical of Chronos College," Cressida said bitterly.

"Coming up with a fancy term to explain memory loss like it's natural, like it just happens."

"It does just happen. I told you, my mate Simeon forgot his parents. Completely forgot them. No explanation."

Nearby, Oxford choked on a mouthful of sparkling mineral water, and kept coughing for some moments.

Mixed emotions crossed Cressida's face: pity, panic, and then mild fury, like she wanted to smack Monterey over the head but not so much that she wanted to explain why.

"It's slightly different in my case," she said, finally.

Monterey was unconvinced. "Because you're special?"

"Because there are literally several of me. Monterey, *listen* for once."

A cat yowled out in pain.

Monterey spun on alert, his eyes going directly to Lovelace. She looked confused. Her head tipped to one side, listening for the source of the cry.

"Oh, hell," Monterey said, as his eyes fell on the revellers further down the slope from them. Louis XIV's glamorous, gilded party guests now included several female figures in very familiar blue cloaks. "The jade pineapple cult are back. Heading this way."

"There's a cat in trouble," Lovelace protested as he scooped her up.

"You, darling, *you're* the cat in trouble," Monterey babbled. "We have to get out of here."

"Stop them!" cried one of the bald women in blue: a clear sign something terrible was about to happen.

"Oxford, where's Fenella?" Cressida demanded.

Oxford flailed, his arm almost knocking over a waiter carrying a tray of Calippos. "She was here a minute ago."

"Did you lose my sister?"

"You were two feet away, I don't think this one's on me," he snapped back.

A time hoop sizzled into existence before their eyes. It wasn't like any time hoop Monterey had ever seen before. It was jagged and strange, like a tear rather than a hoop.

(As if a cat had drawn it in the air with a shaking claw.)

Oceanic light burst out of the tear, cresting, bubbling. A blur of orange smashed out through the rough shape, almost colliding with Monterey.

Professor Boswell rolled roughly on the grass, leaped to his feet, and hacked up a hairball.

"*Boz*," said Cressida, overwhelmed.

"They took him," Boswell snarled. "Ruthven. Didn't even show themselves to me, the cowards."

"Who took him?" asked Oxford in alarm. "It wasn't my mother, was it?"

"They're getting closer," Monterey noted. The women in blue marched steadily towards them as if they had all the time in the world. The lack of running away from his team had become a matter of concern.

"Blue robes," growled Boswell. "Purple cats. Something about a jade pineapple..."

"That's them!" blurted Monterey. "Literally right over there. Ladies in blue robes, looking terrifying. Can none of you see them?"

"I thought you were being dramatic," said Cressida, staring blankly in the direction of the advancing army of blue.

"I'm always dramatic, that doesn't make me wrong."

Damn it, Monterey was going to have to take a leadership position. He hated that. "Everyone follow me!" At least he could see what they were running away from.

He led his ragged group of friends up the slope, dodging serving staff and several giggling nobles in masks and costumes that at least looked like they belonged in the seventeenth century.

Boswell ran at his ankles, close enough to trip him up.

Monterey had to assume that Cressida and Oxford were on their heels. He clutched Lovelace tightly to his chest, not wanting to lose her again.

Monterey almost tripped over himself when he saw more blue robed women up ahead, walking slowly with what looked like large purple sphinxes at their side. "Purple cats," he whispered, not quite believing it.

"Steer clear of them," Boswell said sharply.

"Yes, furball, I'd worked out that much." Monterey hared off to the side, then back down the slope towards the golden stage, all set up for the fairy tale ballet.

The crowd were already taking their seats, though the ballet was not due to start until midnight. Louis XIV was the kind of host who assumed no one would ever want to sleep when he was in a party mood. Monterey appreciated that about the man.

"Up here!" yelled a voice.

Monterey stared around wildly. Too slow for Boswell, who leaped directly up on to the stage, winding around wooden tree silhouettes painted in gold, with jewelled fruits hanging from them.

Lovelace pushed away from Monterey's chest, her paws landing lightly on the high stage.

"What are they doing?" huffed Cressida beside him.

"Making a spectacle of themselves," Monterey said, scrambling up on to the stage himself. "You'd better come too. Protect me from homicidal ballerinas."

A time hoop hovered at the back of the stage. Monterey had almost missed it, because it looked like a giant golden mirror studded with rubies. But the roiling, oceanic light inside was familiar, as was tiny, big-eyed Fenella Church in her over-sized coat, standing on the other side of the hoop.

"Hurry up!" she called, reaching out a hand to beckon.

Boswell and Lovelace slowed, side by side, both of them tense.

Monterey felt Oxford and Cressida draw up on either side of him. "How did you open that without a cat?" Oxford called out sharply

Fenella took a step back, and they were able to see Nero, white and fluffy as ever, perched on Fenella's shoulders.

"She has a cat," said Nero, in a voice that dripped with at least 50% more than average arrogance. "I suggest you allow yourself to be rescued."

"Rescued," Cressida said scornfully. "You're an Anachronaut."

"I am indeed an Anachronaut," said Nero, radiating an aura that was pure 'cat who got the cream'.[3] "But what I am not is *them*."

Cats never need to point. They have expressive enough eyeballs to do the pointing for them.

Monterey glanced behind him. The seats for the audience were mostly filled with space nuns in blue cloaks, and purple cats. He saw a woman in a gold dress and mask suddenly shift, her features blurring, and then she, too, was bald and robed and gazing directly at him like she wanted to eat him for breakfast.

"These people really want to know where the jade pineapple is," Monterey said weakly.

"Is it you?" asked Cressida.

"Why would it be me? It's a *pineapple*."

"Sometimes things aren't what they say they are. I'm not a church."

The horde of blue cloaks shimmered, and multiplied. Monterey saw a blue-cloaked space nun ride up on the back of a horse that had recently been honoured by the royal buttocks of the Sun King.

He made a decision. "Humans, cats, all of you. Into the hoop."

Oxford, of all people, dragged his heels. "We can't trust Nero."

"Excellent, yes," agreed Monterey. "Good point. Let's continue not trusting him on the other side of that hoop."

"I'll bite his whiskers off if he tries anything," volunteered Lovelace.

"That, my dear, is why you are my favourite. Let's go!"

As the Pleasures of the Enchanted Island garden party of Versailles 1664 collapsed into an ocean of purple cats and blue space nuns, Monterey and his colleagues leaped through the time hoop.

Cresting, bubbling, gone.

---

1. For the life of him, Monterey could not remember what he and Lovelace had done to trigger 1664's Event… he drank a lot of champagne, and returned to the twenty-fourth century wearing a single boot with a bright red sole. The rest was a mystery.
2. Anne of Austria was also from Spain. She never visited Austria in her life, but the title was inherited from her father as part of his family name. Anne of Austria's father was also not from Austria.

    Let's face it, we're only mentioning her for the Musketeer fans at the back. You know who you are.
3. 'Cat who got the cream' was Nero's default expression. It can also be described as 'cat who shed all over your new black trousers.'

forty-three
basic time

LOVELACE HAD NEVER BEEN SO grateful in her life to feel the familiar cobblestones of the quad under her paws.

Then she breathed in. The scent was wrong. Oh, it was an artificial college campus on a space station, all right. But it wasn't her college. She darted several quick looks around the buildings, the gardens. The quad was almost identical to that of Chronos College, clearly built to exactly the same specifications. But everything was slightly off. The air had a minutely different quality. The trees and walls were slightly different shades.

She and Monterey had visited Banksia College before, for parties and the occasional academic conference (but mostly for parties) — their quad, she knew, was adorned with statuary of dodos, thylacines, and other saved-from extinction creatures. This must be Aleister College, home of the Anachronauts.

Still, it was Basic Time. Lovelace knew it in her heart. Basic Time, the twenty-fourth century. Home.

Standing in front of them, balancing on a stone pillar at the perfect height to be taller than every single one of them, was Nero. Fluffy, white, and dripping with arrogance.

"Excuse me," Lovelace said in polite tones worthy of tea with Miss Austen. "I intend to murder this cat."

She pounced. No one stopped her.

Monterey had never seen Lovelace in a fight before. (Swiping the occasional claw at someone attempting to arrest them did not count.) It was brutal. There was clawing, biting, scratching... Nero gave as good as he got, but Lovelace was burning with rage, and got in far more hits. They yowled, caterwauled and flew at each other. Fur literally flew.

"Do something," Fenella demanded, tugging at his sleeve.

Monterey glanced at Oxford. "Tenner says my cat beats your cat."

"No bet," replied Oxford calmly. "Your cat has moral outrage on her side. If she had a coat, I'd hold it for her."

"Bucket of cold water?" Cressida suggested.

"Let's not turn Lovelace's moral outrage on the rest of us," Monterey said quickly.

"*What is the meaning of this?*"

Lovelace and Nero broke apart, breathing hard. Lovelace's ear was torn slightly, and she had several scratches down one side. She had never looked more alive. Nero was missing whole chunks of fur, all over, and had bloodstains on his fluffy white tummy.

A small professor in a tweed suit was marching towards them. At least, Monterey assumed she was a professor, because this was a college campus, and she was wearing a tweed suit. She was on the mature side of age, but also had large, luminous eyes, and chestnut hair put up in a bun like a saucy librarian from an old movie. Her lapels were covered in floral brooches: roses, marigolds, sunflowers.

Monterey blinked, realising realised exactly where he knew

her from. It was Fleur Shropshire, TV and film star. She'd aged at least a decade since the moment of her death, possibly longer.

"We do not fight on campus," the professor said sternly to the two cats, who looked slightly ashamed of themselves. "Imagine if the students had seen you!"

"She started it, Professor Shelley," Nero mumbled.

Lovelace turned an expression on him so fiery, it was astounding that what remained of his fur did not combust.

"Boleyn and Claudius are waiting for us in the staff library," Fleur Shropshire/Professor Shelley went on, looking with distaste at the little crowd gathered on the quad. "While you've been gadding about rescuing your friends, Nero, every cat in our organisation has ditched us for the other side!"

Monterey coughed pointedly on the word 'friends.' Professor Shelley gave him an impatient look sharp enough to trim his nose hairs. Then her eye fell on Cressida, and she went pale. "Is that a copy? *Nero*. You brought a scattered copy out of Event Space?"

"It was an authorised rescue," Nero protested. "You said we couldn't let the blues and the purples collect any more witnesses."

"Never mind that," Shelley snapped. "The Founders are having a meeting right now, and they haven't invited us. Our cats, yes. But Boleyn, Marlowe, me... every Anachronaut human that isn't actually related to one of them was left off the guest list. You know what that means. We're expendable."

Lovelace arched her back, having found the next target of her ire. She leaped up to Monterey's shoulder; he steadied her automatically with a hand. "None of us know what any of this means," Lovelace said, hissing on the words. She was tense as if readying herself to go for Professor Shelley's throat. "I suggest you elaborate."

"It's a very long story," cut in Nero. "I could not begin to summarise the endnotes, let alone the main body of text. Don't worry, Professor Shelley," he added. "We have contingency plans in place for every eventuality."

"Nero," said Oxford in a strangled sort of voice. "Are you... associated with these people?"

Nero turned his piercing blue eyes on Oxford. Monterey had never looked especially closely at Nero's eyes before. Blue, yes, but this close they had a purple sort of sheen to them.

"We all keep secrets," said Nero evenly. "You've been keeping mine for years, Oxford. Covering up for your parents, all their secret plots. Why stop now?"

Oxford could not have looked more wounded if Nero had scratched him in the face. Wounded, and somewhat guilty. Monterey wondered what that meant.

A jangle of broadcast static filled the air around them.[1] A voice came over the sound system. "This is Boleyn speaking. They're here. The Grimalkins. They got Claudius. I haven't seen Marlowe — I think he got out through a hoop. The staff library is gone. If you can hear this, get out now."

"What are the Grimalkins?" Monterey asked.

Nero flicked a glance at him. "Large purple cats. Grim bald humans in blue."

"Oh. We've met."

Nero's eyes narrowed to slits. "They can't have found you very interesting, if they let you go. I doubt I'll be so lucky."

A flare of light, purple and blue, columned up from one of the outer buildings of the campus, then another, and another, like a wave of targeted fireworks.

Professor Shelley let out a small noise of helpless rage. "Control!" she said sharply, tapping her opal implant. "Can you hear me? Boleyn. Anyone?"

Nero leaped on to Oxford's shoulders. Oxford steadied him with one hand. Automatic reflexes.

"That's the staff library, residential halls, admin, and now the tech centre," said Nero. "Control is *gone*, Professor Shelley."

"We're trapped," said Fenella. "Nowhere to run."

Monterey scooped up Lovelace. She clung to him, claws out.

"Excellent rescue, Nero," said Cressida sarcastically. "Dragged directly into the frying pan." She glanced down at her hands, which were fading. Translucent. "I don't know if I have another frying pan in me."

"I'd offer a witty comeback," sighed Nero. "But you don't exist, so I shan't bother."

Another building near them flared with purple and blue light.

Media Archive, Monterey thought, something frantic building up in his chest. At least, it would be the Media Archive back on their own campus. It was probably the Party Planning building. "All this for a pineapple?" he said, voice wobbling a little.

Professor Shelley gave him the most exhausted, eye-rolling expression. If he had doubted she was a professor, that would have convinced him. "They're not *actually* looking for a pineapple."

Purple shapes shimmered before them, giant sphinx-style cats appearing in mid-prowl down the large stone steps, advancing across the quad. The statues were different, Monterey realised suddenly. Banksia College had statues dedicated to various ex-extinct animals. Chronos College had its lost heroes: Banksia and Burbage, Cressida Church, Ruthven's Aesop.

Aleister College had three statues of cats, arranged on the same large plinth, overlooking the quad. Monterey recognised all three of them. Banksia. Aesop. Nero. He had no idea why those three had been singled out, or how Nero of all cats had ended up on a plinth of honour.

His head was full of questions, but there was no time for answers.

The purple cats surrounded them, slow and steady, like they had all the time in the world.

Lovelace hid her face against Monterey's chest.

Professor Shelley backed up a step, as if there was anywhere to go. She bumped into Oxford, looked up at him as if she could not believe a person could be so tall, and used his arm to steady herself for a moment.

"Ah, well," said Nero. He spoke as if he was trying to be brave, and also as if he hoped someone was recording his final words for posterity. "Time to go out in a blaze of glory. The twenty-fourth century was fun while it lasted."

Blue light filled the quad. Blue and purple, and…

"Cressida!" cried Fenella, grasping at empty air. "Where did she go?"

"Don't worry about her," said Nero. "Worry about us."

Blue light spiralled around them all — waves of it, crests of it. Bubbling…

As Monterey's vision spun, sparkled and went dark, he thought he saw Nero leaping from Oxford's shoulders into empty air… but no, that wasn't Nero, at all. Nero wasn't purple…

Was he?

---

1. They used to have a public address system at Chronos College, back when Monterey was a student. The speakers fell mysteriously silent one day. The rumour was that the campus cats, tired of having their sensitive hearing disrupted by daily announcements, banded together to chew through every wire in the system. Clearly the cats of Aleister College were not so well-organised.

forty-four
elsewhere in the 24th century

TUNBRIDGE WOKE UP.

She hadn't been sleeping well. There was something wrong at Chronos College, and it felt like she was the only person who knew.

Well, her and Ptolemy. Her cat had been acting strange. Twitchy and irritable. When Ptolemy lost his chill, you knew there really was something to worry about.

It was the Rose Garden Incident, of course. Whatever went wrong that night went wrong so catastrophically that... well. The others hadn't come back, had they?

Oxford, Ruthven, Fenella, all missing. Boswell and Lovelace too. Nero had been around for a little while after the Rose Garden Incident: shown his face in the canteen, made a few snarky comments in a meeting. Then he, too, had made himself scarce. Tunbridge hadn't seen him in days.

All time travel was stopped. It had been seven days since the Rose Garden Incident. Melusine from Admin's tightly plotted travel schedule had been thrown out like the baby with the bathwater.

No hoops active. No one knew why.

Every traveller on staff was curious about what, exactly,

had happened. Tunbridge couldn't tell them. Not that she knew much more than she'd told Melusine and the investigation team.

Classes continued for the students, with various unemployed travellers subbed in for Professor Boswell in his Time Mechanics lectures and seminars. Tunbridge had done one, and found the whole thing excruciating. At least she insisted Ptolemy join her — he entertained the students cheerfully, allowing Tunbridge a whole extra hour in her day to bite her nails, and fret.

In short, everything was terrible and Tunbridge was so stressed her eyeballs were about to pop.

She woke up, in the middle of the night, to find five kilos of Russian Blue sitting on her chest.

"Ptolemy? Ugh, you're right on my ribs. Claws in."

"Sorry," said her cat, practically nose to nose with her. "Are you awake? I can pat your eyelids if that's helpful."

"That's never helpful," Tunbridge grumbled. "What do you want?"

"We've been summoned. Clandestine meeting in the Museum of Lost Things. Aren't you curious?"

"I'm not awake enough to be curious!"

Ptolemy paused for three seconds. "And now?"

"Yes, all right. Get off and I'll find some slippers."

Tunbridge got dressed. Being mysteriously summoned in the middle of the night is the sort of thing that can so easily lead to you having adventures in your pyjamas. Tunbridge read a lot of boarding school novels; she knew what tropes to avoid.

She pulled on a standard jumpsuit and warm boots with a cardigan over the top. She even grabbed her travel satchel, just in case.

"Humans collect so many things," Ptolemy complained as they made their way across the quad.

"Cats collect things too. They just make humans carry them," Tunbridge snapped.

The Museum of Lost Things was usually locked at this time of night, though everyone knew that Monterey regularly let himself in at all hours to deposit his latest stolen pen, and/or to host the occasional scavenger hunt.

Today, the door was propped open with a chair.

"We could just go back to bed," Tunbridge murmured.

"We were invited," Ptolemy insisted, winding his narrow silvery body around her ankles. "This doesn't count as rule-breaking."

"Chronos College has no rules," Tunbridge sighed. If only she had applied to a university with rules.

"Exactly."

"Fine."

The museum was dimly lit. Tunbridge made her way past the displays. Towards the back, she saw lights on in one of the glass-walled Reading Rooms, and a mixed gathering of humans holding large glasses of wine while shouting at each other.

Outside the Reading Room, two people slumped on a bench that didn't look particularly comfortable. An elegant black cat sat between them, straight-backed.

"Abydos?" said Ptolemy, darting forward. "Are you — what are you doing here?" He sounded both fond and suspicious at the same time.

Abydos. He was famous. One of the first Chronos College travellers who transferred to Aleister College and ran off with the Anachronauts, before Tunbridge even started as a student.

The black cat gave Ptolemy a long-suffering look. "I see you brought a plus-one."

"You too," said Ptolemy, a little chilly.

Tunbridge had been trying to work out which of the two humans was Abydos' equally famous partner Zephyr. Now, she gasped in horror. "Ptolemy. Was I not invited to this meeting? I changed out of my *pyjamas*."

Ptolemy gave her an exhausted look. "The exact message was that all cats were to come to the Museum of Lost Things for their own safety. Forgive me for wanting to ensure your safety, also. The Founders are all in there —" he nodded in the direction of the soundproof glass, "— so this is probably the safest place on campus."

"That's why our dad told Abydos to bring us along with the cats," said the taller of the two figures, an androgynous looking human with sleek hair and long eyelashes. "I'm Zephyr," they added. "This is my brother, Bellerophon Kincaid. He's a Banksia graduate, but don't hold that against him. He hardly ever brags about personally saving the honey buzzard from extinction, so I have to do it for him."

Bellerophon had dark hair, enormous eyes and a weirdly familiar face. He had the kind of muscled shoulders one might expect from a traveller who regularly carried koalas out of the burning bush.

"Have we met?" Tunbridge blurted.

Zephyr raised their eyebrows. "You're Lakshmi, aren't you? Our sister Zadie used to talk about you. She was your roommate during the first year of training."

"No, I…" Tunbridge felt unsteady for a moment. That was true, wasn't it? It felt true. She knew for a fact she hadn't had a roommate during training. The other students were so jealous she got a single every year…

And yet, when she thought about her first year as a student, an image of a room with two unmade single beds rose into her mind.

The name Zadie rang a bell. Wasn't there a Zadie Kincaid

who got into some kind of trouble publishing conspiracy theory zines across campus?

"Are you all right, Tunbridge?" Ptolemy asked in a warning sort of voice.

"I have a headache." She pressed her hands to her temple. "Who are all these people, anyway? What's going on? Why were the cats invited, and no one else?"

"Oh," said Bellerophon, rolling his eyes. "Secret Founders' meetings. They're always banging on about some terrible danger. Some of us would have rather not be dragged out of bed," he added sharply. "Especially if we're going to be parked out here all night."

"Speak for yourself," said Zephyr tiredly. "I do not want to be in that meeting."

"Founders," murmured Tunbridge, sneaking a peek back at the Reading Room. She'd never met any of the Founders, apart from Melusine. That tall woman with the aquiline nose had to be Oxford's other mother, she looked just like him except she also looked like she'd never smiled in her life...

But no, that couldn't be right. Tunbridge knew several of the people in that glass-walled Reading Room. Professor Mycroft was there, arguing furiously with Melusine from Admin, and Dean Pennyworth. That over there was Professor Valadon, who had left Chronos College years ago, after some kind of Bonfire-of-the-Vanities-related meltdown.

There were nine people in the Reading Room. Nine Founders. Many of whom, apparently, led secret lives right here at Chronos College.

"Where are the cats?" Tunbridge asked.

"Napping in the other Reading Room," said Abydos, waving a paw towards the other glass-walled room, which was quite dark. "They're not invited to the meeting either. We're all here in case things get bad out there."

"But," said Tunbridge. "Does 'out there' mean the rest of

the campus? There are a lot of humans on site. Travellers, support staff, students..."

Abydos scoffed. "Let's not pretend the Founders have ever cared about the wellbeing of students."

Ptolemy leaped up to the window of the darkened, cat-filled Reading Room. "My goodness," he said, peering in. "Look at them all. Not just our lot. I haven't seen some of these cats in years. Jocasta, Lumiere, Dingo, Bouncer, Cyrano..."

"Some are from the other campuses," said Bellerophon. "We came through the hoops with Socrates, Loki and Richelieu from Banksia College. Plus Dusty, my partner. The rest made their own way here."

"Some of these cats are Anachronauts!" announced Ptolemy, then turned around and saw Zephyr again. "Oh."

Zephyr gave a light wave. "I wouldn't overthink it. Apparently we're all on the same side again."

"Apparently we always were," said Abydos, who sounded slightly furious about it. "I'm going to kill Nero when I see him."

Tunbridge and Ptolemy exchanged uncomfortable looks. Nero. Who had somehow avoided joining the rescue mission for Cressida, whose own human had gone missing that night in the Rose Garden.

"Is Nero... an Anachronaut?" Tunbridge asked in a small voice.

Abydos laughed, and kept on laughing to the point where it seemed unhealthy.

After a minute or two, Zephyr patted Abydos hard on the back, and the cat finally subsided.

"Nero," he said after hawking up an ungainly hairball. "Has his paws in everything. All of it. The Violet Sunflower. The Basalt Sphinx. The Jade Pineapple. The secret history of the time colleges. Anne Bloody Boleyn."

"Technically," said Zephyr, nudging their cat. "Anne Boleyn was your fault, Abs."

"I'm sure I can blame Nero if I tell the story in enough detail," Abydos replied.

"I think I'm going to take this headache back to bed," Tunbridge murmured.

"No," said Ptolemy, eyes alight. His tail twitched, sticking right up over his head. "I want to hear this. This place has never made *sense*. Do you really know everything, Abydos? Are you really going to tell us?"

Abydos looked equally engaged, his amber eyes glowing brightly. "Why the hell not?" he said. "Everything's ending. Let's spill some milk on our way out."

part four
the future

forty-five
the anne boleyn incident

Transcript from the undisclosed surveillance recording outside the Second Reading Room, Museum of Lost Things, Chronos College.

ABYDOS: It all started with Anne Boleyn.
ZEPHYR: That's not where it started.
BELLEROPHON: That's where the story gets juicy, though.
ABYDOS: *I'm* starting the story with Anne Boleyn.
TUNBRIDGE: Don't mind me, I'll find a chair. Ptolemy, you good?
PTOLEMY: You are my chair.
ABYDOS: So, the Founders were the first time travellers.
TUNBRIDGE: *What*??
ABYDOS: Save your pearl clutching to the end. I travelled with Lancaster Pennyworth, mostly — that's him in there. The one who looks like the Dean's taller, better-looking brother.
ZEPHYR: I thought all humans look the same to you.
ABYDOS: Shhh, even a tree would notice how attractive Lancaster is. Anyway, we'd been working in pairs — Aesop with Florence, Lancaster with me. This was not long after

Banksia and Burbage huffed off into the sunset. About twelve years ago. We'd been travelling for a while, we were starting to figure out the rules...
TUNBRIDGE: Rules for time travel, you say?
PTOLEMY: Shhh.
ABYDOS: We knew you couldn't transport anything important out of its own time.
BELLEROPHON: 40,000 Australian marsupials beg to differ.
ZEPHYR: Don't be smug, Bello, we all know you're dashing and heroic.
TUNBRIDGE: Your face really is familiar, are you sure we haven't met?
BELLEROPHON: Zeph told you. You used to be roommates with my twin sister.
TUNBRIDGE: No, that's not it...
ABYDOS: *Anyway*. We were working on the theory that you could reclaim important or significant artefacts if you grabbed them in the moment before they were about to be destroyed, and Aesop had made this whole wishlist of suggestions, mostly from the Tudors. She's always been a bit funny about Anne Boleyn. I'm more of an Anne of Cleves cat myself..."
ZEPHYR: Catherine Parr.
TUNBRIDGE: Katherine of freaking Aragon, thank you very much.
ABYDOS: It wasn't exactly a rule, but Celeste and Melusine — this was before they divorced, and how messy did that get! Anyway, they kept trying to add rules to time travel. Everyone else voted them down. But they were trying an experimental guideline along the lines of — not sending travellers into time periods they were obsessively, outrageously fannish about.
TUNBRIDGE: That's such a mean rule.
PTOLEMY: Makes sense to me, after seeing your emotional meltdown when you saw Jane Austen at a distance.

TUNBRIDGE: You promised never to mention that! Clearly that particular rule didn't stick.

ABYDOS: It did not.

ZEPHYR: Turns out time travellers are capable of getting absurdly fannish about any time period they visit.

ABYDOS: Because Aesop was so dizzy about Anne Boleyn, she and Florence were sent off to rescue church artefacts from the Blitz, while Lancaster and I got the Anne Boleyn caper. We were looking for her necklace. The famous one with the 'B' on it, from the portraits. No one ever knew what happened to it after her execution. We spent weeks on the project, used up our six hop allotment, bribed Control to let us have some extra off the books...

BELLEROPHON: That's how Anachronauts are born.

ZEPHYR: Yeah, yeah. Don't knock it until you've tried it. Anachronauts throw the best parties.

BELLEROPHON: Don't mind us, we're just saving the world over at Banksia...

ABYDOS: Lancaster theorised that she must have worn it to her execution, or at least shortly before. We went along to see for ourselves. Not a fun day out. The necklace fell into the damned basket with her severed head. No way we were going to fish around in that. We went around again...

TUNBRIDGE: But that's so completely against... recommended behaviour when time travelling.

ABYDOS: Early days, my dear. This was before the Anachronauts. Before we knew about Events. We told Nero we couldn't find a way to grab the necklace without being seen by dozens of Tudor witnesses, and he suggested we use the Violet Sunflower.

ZEPHYR: So you stole it from my dad.

ABYDOS: It wasn't his! If it belonged to any of us, it was Nero. But, ah, yes. As it happened, the Violet Sunflower was at the time in the custody of Soames Kincaid, Dean of Banksia College.

TUNBRIDGE: You mentioned this sunflower before. Along with a pineapple and... a sphinx? What are they?

ABYDOS: They are the High Artefacts. The secrets of time travel.

TUNBRIDGE: And you stole one!

ABYDOS: Borrowed. With Nero's endorsement! It was the only way to adjust the memories of the witnesses to Anne Boleyn's death. Then it occurred to Lancaster in the moment that if we were erasing their memories anyway... we might as well, you know.

ZEPHYR: Rescue Anne Boleyn from her own execution.

BELLEROPHON: Scooped her up like a koala from a bushfire. Nice.

ABYDOS: It caused an Event, of course. We didn't know that at the time — we got out ahead of it. And there we were, standing in the middle of the quad with Anne Boleyn alive and well.

ZEPHYR: That was the beginning. The Anachronauts. All of it. Split the Founders, split the colleges. Everyone was arguing over it for weeks. Months. Bello and I overheard all sorts of things — you do, with a Founder for a parent.

TUNBRIDGE: I don't understand, Abydos. Were you expelled from Chronos College?

ZEPHYR: (Laughs indistinctly) Of course not. The Founders were delighted with the results of Abydos' experiment. They sent Anne Boleyn to Aleister College to teach history — Celeste Oxford was the Dean at the time, and she welcomed it all with open arms. Nero talked Celeste into providing more resources to *replicate* the experiment. They rescued more people from history — and the Events started racking up. Some of us thought it was all far more interesting than being here under the eye of Melusine and her schedule. So Abydos and I crossed over, to Aleister College. To the Anachronauts. We weren't the only ones who made that choice.

ABYDOS: They might be pure chaos over there, but at least they're honest about it. Plus, you get to hang out with Kit Marlowe.

ZEPHYR: He pours a mean cocktail.

ABYDOS: Chronos College has become such a bore over the years. For an institution that claims to have no rules, they have so many budget restrictions.

TUNBRIDGE: Ptolemy, you've been quiet. Did you know about this?

PTOLEMY: No, I did not. I'm wondering how many cats around here do. I also want to know more about this Violet Sunflower that can *erase memories*, apparently?

ABYDOS: Ah. That's...

ZEPHYR: That story's a lot less fun.

BELLEROPHON: Are you sure you don't remember our sister, Lakshmi?

TUNBRIDGE: I —

PTOLEMY: We want to know more. Right, Tunbridge?

TUNBRIDGE: Mostly, I want to know where my friends are.

ZEPHYR: Last I heard, Nero was off to rescue them.

PTOLEMY: And on a scale of one to fluffy evil genius, how trustworthy is Nero?

[awkward silence on the recording]

forty-six
cellmates

RUTHVEN OPENED HIS EYES. The walls were a dusky rose colour. It wasn't a time aisle. It didn't feel like Event Space either, but there was something entirely unfamiliar about the air.

"What now?" he asked himself. He was lying on a low bench in a pale pink cell that had no door, no windows.

"You think you've got problems," said a familiar voice behind him. "I just gained an uninvited roommate."

Ruthven jerked in surprise, fell off the bench, and felt something crunch. He hoped it wasn't him. It turned out to be his satchel, which had slightly broken his fall.

"Welcome to Chronos College," said a calico cat, sitting on the top of a brick wall and swishing her tail in the sun. "I'd come up with something more original to say, but there's no point in making an impression on you yet. Most students don't make the cut, and the failures will all be booted back to the real world with no memory of this weekend."

"What if I do make the cut?" Ruthven asked.

The calico cat smirked at him. At least, he thought it was a smirk. Possibly, she had something nasty caught in her teeth. "I'll impress you later. I don't imagine it will be hard."

"Joke's on you," he said. "I'm impressed already. I didn't know cats could talk."

"Oh, honey," said the calico cat. "This is only the beginning of things you don't know."

Raw pain stabbed through Ruthven's temples. "Aaargh."

"That will be the memories," said Cressida.

Of course it was Cressida. Who else would be waiting for him in a cell after he had been kidnapped by glowing purple cats? "For some reason, the effects of the Violet Sunflower start to fail if your body experiences enough time disruption. Travelling to the far future is one hell of a time disruption. Welcome to the Kidnapped By Purple Cats Club. I'm the president. You can be secretary. Any questions?"

Lovelace could feel every scratch and scrape from her fight with Nero. When she opened her eyes, he was the first thing she saw.

At least he looked more battered than she was. She was taking the win.

"Well," said another voice, grumpy and familiar. "Look what the cat dragged in."

"Boswell."

Lovelace trotted across the floor of a very small cell, and up on to the bench where her friend sat. She rubbed her nose against Boswell's for a moment, and leaned into the warmth of his fur.

"Sweet," said Nero. "No welcome for me?"

Lovelace narrowed her eyes at him. "Where's my Monterey?"

"Always about the humans for you two, isn't it?" said Nero. "So soft. As if time travel was all about them."

The cell was a pale yellow colour, and smelled faintly of sunflowers. The three cats were the only inhabitants.

Boswell rumbled a sound that vibrated against Lovelace's fur. "We need them. They need us."

"No!" Nero arched his back, eyes brighter blue than ever. They glittered coldly. "That's what the two of you will never understand. We don't need them. They're not going to stroll in and rescue us. Now, if you'll excuse me, I need to meditate on how fucked we are."

He swooshed his fur dramatically, turned his back on them and sulked.

"Any idea where we are?" Boswell asked Lovelace in a low purr.

The smell of sunflowers was distracting, but she refused to let it get the better of her. "Not a space station. Not a time period I recognise."

"Too far back?"

"Too far forward," she guessed.

"It's the thirtieth century," snorted Nero from his self-imposed exiled in the corner. "You can tell by the self-congratulatory boredom that seeps from the walls."

"How do you know?" Lovelace retorted. "How did this happen? We're not supposed to travel forward." Not a rule, but she'd assumed it was an impossibility.

Nero let out a short scream. "Why can't you let me brood in peace? I am, as it happens, extremely familiar with this century. Don't waste your time disbelieving me."

"We want answers," Boswell insisted. "What are you going to do otherwise, nap?"

"Chance would be a fine thing." Nero whirled back to face them, losing some tufts of fur along the way. His eyes blazed at them both — not quite as blue as they used to be. "I'm *from* here, you fools. Twenty years of freedom, over in an instant. Congratulations, you're stuck in the worst time period that ever existed. And I don't think I can escape it again."

"Cressida," breathed Ruthven, relieved to see her. At least he wasn't alone in this rose-coloured cell.

She had lost her Viking apron and operatic two-horned helmet, but it was clearly Cressida Church. She wore a soft jumpsuit in the same rich blue colour as those strange bald ladies in robes, and her hair was longer than he remembered. Longer than her statue, anyway.

Ruthven discreetly checked himself and realised he was also wearing the blue jumpsuit. Best not to worry too much about what had happened to his trousers, and who exactly had changed his clothes while he was unconscious.

"Have we met?" Cressida asked. "It's not always easy to be sure, as a time traveller. Memories have a nasty habit of disappearing."

"You and I travelled together recently," said Ruthven, confused. "We sort of share a cat."

Her eyes lit up. "You know Boz?"

"Boswell was my Professor at Chronos College. You wouldn't remember me from there, though. I was a first year when you, uh. Have you been here this whole time?"

"Heh. A professor, you say? Good old Boz." Cressida warmed up to him slightly, it seemed. "Sounds like you might have met one of my copies. Any version of me you met without a cat wasn't actually me. Hope I'm not breaking your heart."

Ruthven blinked slowly. "It wasn't you in Event Space? Viking Britain, the time aisles? Cleopatra?"

"Never spent any time in Event Space," said Cressida. "I heard about it from some Anachronauts, back when they were trying to recruit me. That bloody moggy Abydos tried to use the Violet Sunflower to force my hand, and Scattered me instead."

"You lost memory?" Ruthven had heard about some pretty nasty Scattering effects.

Cressida laughed bitterly. "Scattered can mean different things. Sometimes you lose memories. Sometimes different versions of yourself are literally scattered through history. I'm not the only one it happened to. Apparently there are like, twelve Fleur Shropshires out there causing havoc."

Even for a devoted fan of Fleur Shropshire, that seemed like too many.

"I ended up in 1964 with a doppelgänger who had no memories at all!" Cressida went on. "Had to pretend we were twins and she'd been in some kind of road accident."

"You're the one who set up the cry for help in the pilot episode of *Cramberleigh*!"

Cressida grinned. "Figured that out, did you? The hard part was getting my scatty 'twin' Bunty the job as production assistant. That job is like, 90% tea and messages and holding things for people. She got really into it. Hope she's doing okay. I wasn't there long — the Grimalkins pulled me out of the Sixties before I got to see how it all played out."

"We came to rescue you," Ruthven assured her. "At least, we tried. It all got a bit messy."

"That's time travel for you," said Cressida. "Look at me. I was the best, and I've been stuck in here for goodness knows how long. Days. Weeks? A whole bunch of futuristic cats reckon I have useful information for them about some bloody pineapple."

"Um," said Ruthven. He had so many questions. Futuristic cats? How far in the future? What the hell was going on?

"Hey," said Cressida softly. "Do you have a postcard? I still had mine when they stuck me in here. I wrote like, a hundred messages to Boswell. It shorted out in the end — and disappeared! Who knows when it ended up."

Ruthven dug through his satchel. He found the postcard and stylus easily enough, but the stylus didn't seem to work. Words did not appear on the soft surface when he tried to write.

"I think mine's broken," he said.

"Bugger," said Cressida cheerfully. "Keep waiting, I guess. See how many more expert witnesses they're pulling together for this shindig."

"Shindig," Ruthven repeated, his attention still on the postcard. For a moment it looked like someone was writing a message to him. Three dots appeared, and vanished. Appeared again, vanished.

"You know, the *trial*," said Cressida. "Didn't they tell you anything about where we are, and why we're here?"

Ruthven shook his head. "Who's on trial?"

"Us, I guess. Time travellers in general." Cressida shrugged, looking sheepish. "You know how Chronos College always said there are no rules for time travel? Turns out, there were a whole bunch of rules. And we've broken like, all of them."

Boswell could not recall when he first met Nero. The other cat was always there, from the beginning. He had an air about him, as if he had been at the college longer and knew more of its secrets than anyone else.

Boswell had always assumed that was just Nero being Nero. Pompous, egotistical, grandiose.

And yet, in his fragmented memories, the ones still clawing their way into his head, there was something else. Something he'd never paid any attention to before.

It was a single image of three cats. Banksia, before his disappearance. Aesop, before hers. Nero, proud and disdainful. Why was it, when Boswell thought hard about the past, he saw those three, always together before they were split apart?

What had he missed?

"Nero, you're not from the thirtieth century," Lovelace said scornfully. "That's absurd."

"I think you'll find, my dear," said Nero. "It is completely true. No one's ever tampered with my memory. I'm the only reliable witness left."

Lovelace narrowed her eyes. "What makes you so special?"

Nero smirked at her, and at Boswell. He yawned, and stretched...

And grew, before their eyes. Taller, larger than Boswell could ever have imagined. His hackles raised, Boswell took a defensive crouch and saw Lovelace do the same.

"What are you doing?"

"Showing you the truth," said Nero, now three times his usual size. "Hang on, I knew I was forgetting something..."

And his fur turned purple.

The cell was mint green. Light glowed from the walls, replacing the need for light fittings. Or doors and windows, apparently.

Monterey awoke on a very uncomfortable bench, lurching upwards as he realised he was (again!) without cat.

He saw a flailing movement on the far side of the cell. Oxford sat up, wild around the eyes, wearing a brilliant blue jumpsuit. "Nero!"

"Lovelace is gone too," Monterey said sourly. "Not to mention all those glowing purple jaguars."

"I thought they looked more like lynxes."

"No, they didn't have the tufty ears."

"My sister's gone," said Fenella, raising her voice to be heard over them. "Had you noticed?"

"Little bit more worried about my cat," Monterey snapped back. "If we've learned one thing over the last batshit couple of days, it's that your sister can take care of herself." He leaped to his feet, pacing around. "When did Chronos College get the funding for an army of — whatever those things were?"

"You think they were from the college?" Oxford said in disbelief. "You think my mum set up a glowing feline monster squad to round up truants and troublemakers?"

"I don't know," Monterey howled. "She's Melusine from Admin. I wouldn't put it past her! Maybe she got some kind of grant!"

"You're losing your mind."

"The purple cats were tracking the Anachronauts. And us. It has to be the college behind it. Who else would care?"

And what, oh what was a jade pineapple?

Oxford got to his own feet. "Anyone!" he raged. "We have been rampaging through time, causing all kinds of trouble, creating Events and answering to no one for decades. Maybe someone finally noticed."

"Someone? What someone?" Monterey swayed a little on his feet. Being unconscious was no substitute for proper sleep. "What do you know, Oxford?"

It was hard to face off against someone when they were so much taller than you.

Oxford didn't put up much of a fight. "None of this is my fault," he said quietly.

Monterey frowned. "I never said it was. But now I'm starting to wonder."

One of the walls sparked into life, rippling like the middle of a time hoop. The ripples coalesced into the image of a cat with metallic silver fur and little dark eyeglasses, like it had wandered in from a Sergeant Pepper memorial tribute disco.

"Detainees," said the disco cat. "The trial will begin in three hours. Prrrrepare your evidence."

The screen blinked back into a mint green wall.

"What was that about?" Fenella gasped. "Are we on trial? What crime did we commit?"

"What crime didn't we commit?" Oxford muttered.

"We're not Anachronauts," Monterey reminded him.

"We might as well be!"

"We haven't broken any rules," said Fenella.

Oxford laughed bitterly. "Chronos College doesn't have rules. We're allowed to go where we like, do what we like... as long as it's on my mother's schedule!"

"You know what," Monterey said explosively. "Time travel should fucking have rules."

They both looked at him like he had chopped his own head off.

"Are you feeling all right?" Oxford asked after a moment.

Monterey groaned, letting his head fall back against the mint green wall. "I have a headache. I want my cat. And we might be on trial."

"At least we're not in Event Space any more," ventured Fenella.

"Oh, yes," said Monterey. "This is so much better."

forty-seven
the matter of the jade pineapple

Transcript from the Trial of Nero, Banksia (in absentia) and Aesop (in absentia). Location: Theatre of Justice, 2912. Broadcast live across Mewtopia. Judicial Administrator Felicitas presiding.

JUDICIAL FELICITAS: Nero, you are charged with the theft of the Jade Pineapple, the Basalt Sphinx and the Violet Sunflower. How do you plead?
NERO: Unfairly maligned.
JUDICIAL FELICITAS: That's not one of the options.
NERO: I suppose I'll settle for not guilty if you're going to be boring about it.

JUDICIAL FELICITAS: Where's Banksia, Nero?
NERO: I haven't the least idea. She disappeared on a time hop over a decade ago with her special human. Lost in time. So tragic. Sadly missed.

JUDICIAL FELICITAS: Where's Aesop, Nero?
NERO: I believe that information is covered by the Global Official Secrets Act.
JUDICIAL FELICITAS: that Act was overturned in the twenty-fifth century.
NERO: Interesting. Well, I don't know. To be honest, I always assumed you lot grabbed her.
JUDICIAL FELICITAS: What can you tell us about the three High Artefacts that you and your friends stole from our government?
NERO: You'll have to be more specific.
JUDICIAL FELICITAS: The Jade Pineapple. The Basalt Sphinx. The Violet Sunflower.
NERO: Never heard of them. They sound like the ingredients for a lovely salad. Are we done? I'm due for a nap.

JUDICIAL FELICITAS: Please state your name and century of origin for the records.
FLEUR SHROPSHIRE: Since you don't appear to have my Wikipedia entry handy... My birth name was Flora Shelley. More recently, I've been going by Professor Shelley in the twenty-fourth century as the Professor of Celebrity Spotting and Major Talent over at Aleister College. But, of course, for a few decades in the twentieth century I was best known by the professional name of Fleur Shropshire. You may have seen some of my films.
JUDICIAL FELICITAS: All archives of twentieth century media were erased after the extinction of humanity, except for some television shows featuring cats.
FLEUR SHROPSHIRE: Oh. I did voice a rather darling cartoon cat for the Beeb...
JUDICIAL FELICITAS: *Jelly and Marmite*. An excellent

animated television experience. I shared it with my kittens to prove to them humanity did not completely waste their years on the planet.

FLEUR SHROPSHIRE: If you'd like me to sign something for your kittens... I'm sorry, did you say the extinction of humanity?

JUDICIAL FELICITAS: Yes.

FLEUR SHROPSHIRE: When was that?

JUDICIAL FELICITAS: The late twenty-eighth century. Approximately two hundred years ago.

FLEUR SHROPSHIRE: All humans were wiped out? What about those charming ladies you have working for you, with the bald heads and the signature blue hoods?

JUDICIAL FELICITAS: The Grimalkins are cats, using our natural shapeshifting abilities to blend in with humanity for the purposes of time travel.

FLEUR SHROPSHIRE: Gosh. Are the other animals all right? You didn't do anything to the dogs, did you?

JUDICIAL FELICITAS: The dogs were rounded up and sent to Australia. They're fine.

FLEUR SHROPSHIRE: What about the koalas?

JUDGE FELICITAS: They're not very happy about the dogs. May I continue?

FLEUR SHROPSHIRE: Carry on, darling, don't mind me.

JUDICIAL FELICITAS: I believe you are wearing the Violet Sunflower on your lapel.

FLEUR SHROPSHIRE: I don't think so, sweetie. I have a felt sunflower, and a topaz sunflower, and an opal marigold, and a gold marigold, and a mother of pearl rose, and I suppose this sunflower here looks a bit opal-ish, but, funny story...

JUDICIAL FELICITAS: The Violet Sunflower is a High Artefact. It is an extremely delicate and powerful piece of thirtieth century technology that should not be used to ornament a film star, however beloved she may be for voicing an adorable cartoon cat.

FLEUR SHROPSHIRE: You know what, I think I did have a Violet Sunflower, just here. See where there's a hole in the tweed? I suppose it must have fallen off.

JUDICIAL FELICITAS: Witness dismissed.

JUDICIAL FELICITAS: Please state your name and century of origin for the records.

ANNE BOLEYN: Anne Boleyn, sixteenth century.

JUDICIAL FELICITAS: Please explain why you were located in the twenty-fourth century when our operatives detained you.

ANNE BOLEYN: I was found guilty of high treason and executed by order of my husband, Henry VIII of England.

JUDICIAL FELICITAS: I'm so sorry to hear that, madam. It's that kind of behaviour that led to the extinction of humanity.

ANNE BOLEYN: I'm not the least surprised.

JUDICIAL FELICITAS: Are you aware of the three High Artefacts that were stolen from this century by the criminals Nero, Aesop and Banksia?

ANNE BOLEYN: That would be the Jade Pineapple, the Basalt Sphinx, and the Violet Sunflower.

JUDICIAL FELICITAS: You know their functions?

ANNE BOLEYN: I believe the Basalt Sphinx is used to enhance the intelligence, communicative skills and general higher powers of cats. Including talking like humans.

JUDICIAL FELICITAS: Actually, the origins of the Higher Feline Society date back as far as the twenty-fourth century. It's not known what evolutionary spark developed our superior powers, allowing our eventual conquest of the planet formerly run by humans.

ANNE BOLEYN: Cats are excellent at many things, but not record keeping, it seems.

JUDICIAL FELICITAS: Exactly!

ANNE BOLEYN: Who needs history? Just one more book to push off a table.

JUDICIAL FELICITAS: What was your function at Aleister College in the twenty-fourth century?

ANNE BOLEYN: Professor of History.

JUDICIAL FELICITAS: Fascinating. Did you personally have access to the Basalt Sphinx?

ANNE BOLEYN: No, Melusine from Admin kept it pretty close to her chest. She drank her morning coffee out of it.

[general hubbub in court, hissing of many cats in attendance]

JUDICIAL FELICITAS: She drank her coffee out of a High Artefact?

ANNE BOLEYN: It's shaped a bit like a mug, you see.

JUDICIAL FELICITAS: And what of the Jade Pineapple?

ANNE BOLEYN: That one contains the secrets of time travel technology, yes? The time hoops, the postcards, all of it.

JUDICIAL FELICITAS: [*hisses audibly*]

ANNE BOLEYN: I believe Banksia stole it.

JUDICIAL FELICITAS: This trial will determine whether Banksia, Aesop and Nero stole the Jade Pineapple!

ANNE BOLEYN: No, I mean Banksia stole it again. This was before I came to the twenty-fourth century. She and her pet human ran off with it, and no one has seen it since. The Colleges didn't need the Jade Pineapple to continue their work, of course, as they'd already built all the technology they needed to run the time travel program. But there were more glitches every year, and no one knew how to fix it. I imagine you have much the same issues yourselves.

JUDICIAL FELICITAS: Please do not speculate about our time travel glitches.

ANNE BOLEYN: It's all been a bit of a mess. Event Space spiralling towards self-destruction. Scattered copies of travellers, running around being all homicidal and difficult. It wasn't sustainable. We could see the writing on the wall. Not to mention your Grimalkin troops, bearing down upon us. That's why the Anachronauts ditched all their research projects to hold parties in their favourite travel spots. We were, oh, what's the phrase? Help me out, Nero.

NERO: Fiddling while Rome burns.

ANNE BOLEYN: That's the one.

JUDICIAL FELICITAS: What of the third High Artefact? The Violet Sunflower that was until recently resting upon the tweed lapel of your colleague, Professor Shelley?

ANNE BOLEYN: That's a really interesting one. The Violet Sunflower. Used to create the opal implants. Useful for communication and the like, but its true function is memory control. That's where the real power is, isn't it? Deciding what other people remember. Changing the past by literally rewriting memories. So convenient, in a bureaucratic society.

JUDICIAL FELICITAS: Cats have no use for bureaucracy.

ANNE BOLEYN: I wonder why you invented the Violet Sunflower, then.

JUDICIAL FELICITAS: Cats do like power.

ANNE BOLEYN: Queens are rather fond of it, too. Especially queens who once found themselves on the wrong end of a sword. If it wasn't for the Violet Sunflower, I would never have been rescued.

JUDICIAL FELICITAS: Are you saying you don't have the Violet Sunflower?

ANNE BOLEYN: I wish I did. If anyone in this courtroom was in possession of it, they probably could use it quite broadly. Is this trial being broadcast?

JUDICIAL FELICITAS: Every cat in Mewtopia is watching the trial from their homes. Unless they have any important sunbeams to nap in.

ANNE BOLEYN: I seem to recall that the Violet Sunflower doesn't have to be in the immediate proximity to be applied. Anyone holding the Violet Sunflower right now would be able to broadcast their commands to your whole city. Your whole world, perhaps? Isn't that clever.

JUDICIAL FELICITAS: The Violet Sunflower is an extremely powerful and sacred artefact, and should not be in the hands of criminals or humans.

ANNE BOLEYN: Someone holding that device could make you all forget about the trial altogether.

JUDICIAL FELICITAS: I hardly think...

ANNE BOLEYN: You'd forget about the trial, forget about all the prisoners brought here from the twenty-fourth century. Why, you might even forget about Nero, Banksia and Aesop stealing it in the first place. You might forget that the Jade Pineapple and the other High Artefacts were ever invented, let alone lost.

JUDICIAL FELICITAS: That would be a highly irregular use of such a device.

ANNE BOLEYN: Well, we wouldn't want to break any rules.

JUDICIAL FELICITAS: Where is the Violet Sunflower?

ANNE BOLEYN: I do hope it's in safe hands.

forty-eight
thirtieth century catastrophe

trial of the century

MEMORY WAS A PECULIAR THING.

Ruthven did not remember losing Aesop. He remembered the shock and the pain, and knowing she was gone, but he could never be certain exactly what had happened.

He hadn't been able to bring himself to look at the footage when he first buried himself in the Media Archive... and by the time he felt ready, there was no footage to be found. Records said that Ruthven and Aesop had been on a routine hop to investigate what kind of mushroom had been used for the Emperor Claudius' final meal.[1]

By then, 54 CE had become an Event thanks to an Anachronaut attack, so there was no way to investigate.

Of course, Ruthven could not investigate in person. He no longer had a cat.

What he did remember about that day was reporting to Melusine, who informed him with brutal efficiency that Aesop was dead, that he should probably have a psych evaluation, and that he now had a job in Media Archives. After that, Ruthven found his way to the Museum of Lost Things, collapsed in a corner with his legs stretched out in front of him, and waited for the misery to stop.

It did not. An hour or so later, Oxford found him and sat quietly at his side, keeping him company on the worst day of his life.

If Ruthven had not already known that Oxford was his favourite human, that would have done it for him.

Today was a day of revelations. Ruthven and Cressida were released from their pastel cell and transported by a floating perspex dome branded with the phrase Mewtopia Justice Division to the site of a trial.

They still did not know whether they were the ones on trial, but they did learn on their journey what kind of city might be created in a cat-dominated future utopia.

It was more whimsical than Ruthven had expected.

The city looked like a complex obstacle course designed for superheroes with a short attention span. Buildings were tall and curved, with outer platforms and jutting roof gardens so that the native cats of this century — large, powerful creatures of a size he associated with sheep, cows and even horses — could leap, climb and doze in the sunshine to their hearts' content.

The trial took place in an enormous outdoors stadium, with tiered seats and screens everywhere, like the Colosseum rebuilt in glass and steel.

"Welcome to the Theatre of Justice," chirruped their pod as its doors slid open, tipping them both on to a high tier of seating, separated by glass walls from other, equally high and precarious platforms.

Their platform was already occupied by an elderly male Anachronaut who introduced himself as Claudius Caesar, and promptly ignored them for the entire trial. He did not appear to recognise Ruthven, and this would be an awkward time to interview him about the fate of Aesop.

Two sleek purple cats, Ione and Igor, soon joined them on their seating platform, leaping easily across empty voids. At first they seemed quite friendly, asking curious questions about the twenty-fourth century and why the cats from there were so small and odd-coloured. Once the trial began, it became clear that Ione and Igor were guards, not random audience members. They leaned in and purred in a threatening manner whenever Ruthven or Cressida attempted to talk to each other.

(Claudius, who was crocheting a sock, took no notice of the terrifying future cats, and they were not nearly as growly in his general direction.)

As the trial got underway, Ruthven learned far more about Aesop than he had ever imagined. Mostly, that she was a thirtieth century criminal who had worked with Nero to steal time travel technology. To bring that technology — the High Artefacts with their eccentric names — to the twenty-fourth century.

It could all be lies, of course, but there had to be some truth in it. Especially considering that Nero was now twice the size he had been in the twenty-fourth century, and his fur was undeniably violet. Hard to argue with evidence like that.

(Ruthven tried to imagine Aesop huge and purple, and could not. She was a calico cat! Small, dainty... covered in black and orange spots. That was her whole thing.)

It was a lot. Almost too much. Ruthven could not have a nervous breakdown up here. Everyone would see him. Ione and Igor might bite his head off.

The judge — or rather, the Judicial Felicitas, an enormous cat whose purple fur was so dark it was nearly indigo — perched on a platform in the centre of the theatre, surrounded on all sides by these branching, tiered seats and deep chasms of empty air.

The interviews of the witnesses were thrown up on screens and broadcast through enormous speakers, so everyone could see despite the distances between them.

Ruthven could see many of his friends and colleagues — Boswell and Lovelace, Oxford and Monterey and Fenella, spread out on similar platforms to he and Cressida. They also had large purple cats close at hand, keeping an eye on them. He couldn't see how to reach them from here, not without some kind of trapeze.

He wasn't even sure he was allowed to move.

Nero continued to be purple. The trial had many shocks and surprises to come, but it was hard to beat that.

"Shapeshifting abilities," Cressida murmured at one point, during Fleur Shropshire's testimony. "That explains so much." Most of her attention was on Ruthven's postcard, with which she had been fiddling this whole time.

The rumbling in the throats of Ione and Igor was sufficiently threatening to quiet her.

After Fleur stepped down from the witness stand, Ruthven ventured: "Nero and the others could still be innocent."

Cressida didn't bother to reply, and the Emperor Claudius gave him a pitying look.

Ruthven couldn't wrap his head around Aesop being a criminal from a future of super-evolved power cats. Nero, sure. That didn't take a huge leap. He hadn't ever met Banksia, so couldn't make moral judgements in his general direction. But Aesop? His little Aesop?

The most concerning revelation was that of the Violet Sunflower — confirmation that Boswell's missing memories had been caused by Melusine and the other Founders.

That also suggested that Ruthven's loss of memory around

Aesop's death had nothing to do with trauma, and everything to do with *admin*.

Once Anne Boleyn's testimony began, Ruthven stopped wondering whether Nero and the others were innocent.

"You'd forget about the trial, forget about all the prisoners brought here from the twenty-fourth century. Why, you might even forget about Nero, Banksia and Aesop stealing it in the first place. You might forget that the Jade Pineapple and the other High Artefacts were ever invented, let alone lost."

Anne Boleyn, thirty seconds ago

The arena was in chaos. Someone had triggered some kind of emergency status for the Theatre of Justice. Glass staircases appeared out of nowhere, and vanished again. Automated pavements connected the platforms in wild, illogical patterns.

Cats everywhere were howling, caterwauling. Some fought each other, flipping back and forth in the air. Others cried out in confusion, or merely stared blankly into space.

"Can we run?" Ruthven asked Cressida.

"I think we'd better!"

Ione and Igor looked at Ruthven like they'd never seen him before... like they'd never seen humans before. Like they hadn't shared an in-depth conversation about twenty-fourth century feline habits a mere half an hour earlier.

A hissing automated pavement ran directly past their platform. Trying not to think about how high up they were, Ruthven leaped for it. Cressida came with him, her hand catching hold of his at the last moment.

Down, down, they leaped from platform to pavement and back again, making their way towards ground level.

The cats weren't trying to stop them. Mostly, they looked like they just wanted the pain in their heads to stop. The ones that did get in their way had creepy, glassy stares.

"Is this the Violet Sunflower at work?" Ruthven asked Cressida.

"Who knows?" she yelled back, squeezing his hand.

Assuming there was a High Artefact called the Violet Sunflower that had the capabilities Anne Boleyn had described, well...someone must have used it. How else to explain all this?

Ruthven and Cressida had lost track of the Emperor Claudius. In all fairness, they hadn't been trying to keep him.

"One of the Anachronauts must have done it," Cressida said breathlessly.

"Where are we running?" They were closer to ground level now, only a few tiers and leaps away from what felt like safety. And that meant they needed a plan.

"Away!" said Cressida.

Ruthven yanked on her arm, forcing her to stop for a moment. "What's the endgame? We're trapped in the far future. Can we use their time travel? Do they even have time hoops that work like ours?" What, he did not say aloud, if the only people in this century who understood how to send them home were the cats who had just had some kind of bomb go off in their memories?

"They have to have time travel!" Cressida yelled at him. "We stole it from them."

"I didn't steal anything! Don't shout at me!"

"You know what I mean!"

They stood helplessly together for a moment, teetering on a glass precipice.

Someone crashed into them. "Ruthven!"

"Oxford!"

It felt like a million years since they had been in the same space. In the same time period. It had, in fact, been six hundred years, give or take a few millennia. Ruthven stared up at his friend, realising all over again just how tall he was.

Oxford stared wildly back at him.

(Somewhere behind Ruthven, Cressida relinquished his hand and moved in to hug someone else.

"Still alive, Monterey?"

"Still making trouble, Cress?"

"I bet my escape plan's better than yours.")

The world was falling apart around them. Ruthven reached up, just as Oxford reached down and for a moment, they could not look away from each other.

"We're probably going to die in the next ten minutes," blurted Ruthven.

"Good point," said Oxford, and kissed him.

It was a good kiss. Good enough for Ruthven to forget, just for a second, that they were trapped in a future where humans were extinct, and they were surrounded by giant purple cats all going through some kind of horrific memory trauma.

He got about six seconds, in fact, of Oxford's mouth warm on his, and the pleasure of being held in his arms, before the noise and hubbub and general peril came rushing back with a vengeance.

"Jump," someone snarled in Ruthven's ear. It sounded a lot like Professor Boswell.

They jumped.

The next tier of glass platforms was a dizzying distance beneath them, far enough away to risk breaking limbs. But that didn't matter, because they didn't reach it.

The largest time hoop Ruthven had ever seen in his life opened up underneath him, and he fell into it feet-first. The only thing good about this truly terrifying course of events was that this time, it was Oxford holding his hand.

---

1. Mushrooms were infamously served to the emperor Claudius by his wife and niece Agrippina, shortly before his death from poisoning. The mushrooms were later declared innocent, and history has never proved otherwise...

forty-nine
the matter of the violet sunflower

CRESTING, swirling, bubbling... *drop*.

They landed hard on the rounded cobblestones of the quad, under a night sky. There were glowing street-lamps here and there about the place, illuminating the campus in a soft shade of peach.

"Everyone in one piece?" Boswell asked briskly.

Everyone included Ruthven and Oxford, Lovelace and Monterey, Fenella, Cressida, Boswell.

No Anachronauts. No *Nero*.

"Who brought us home?" Lovelace asked from her position, cradled against Monterey's chest.

Cressida waved the postcard she'd been fiddling with through the trial. "A couple of your Control kids made contact about thirty minutes ago. Quant and Khan? Took them a while to lock on to our location, even with all the opal implants we have between us. They're not used to looking forward in time. Good for them to develop new skills. This is a school, after all."

Ruthven dared a glance up at Oxford. He had *kissed* him. Like he meant it. Like it was something he had been thinking about doing for a long time.

What he saw now was not the pleased secret smile of someone who had finally kissed a boy he liked. Oxford looked wretched. When he saw Ruthven looking at him, the first thing he said was: "I'm sorry."

Now *Ruthven* felt wretched. He stepped back, feeling his face heat up with embarrassment. "For kissing me?"

"Not exactly. But you're going to hate me when I tell you the truth, so I shouldn't have done it."

The others were listening. Of course the others were listening.

"The truth about what, young Oxford?" Boswell asked in his sternest, most professorial voice.

Oxford relaxed his hand. Something gleamed there, a circle of purple glass.

"Is that a chronocle?" Ruthven demanded, then paused, catching up to his own thoughts. "Is that the Violet Sunflower?"

The Basalt Sphinx was a mug, according to Anne Boleyn. Why shouldn't the Violet Sunflower be another everyday object?

Oxford nodded slowly, looking ashamed of himself.

Lovelace hissed between her teeth. "You did that?" she demanded. "Set off that... mind bomb in the future."

"Settle, love," said Monterey. "Desperate times and all that. He got us out."

"Cressida and Control got us out," Lovelace snapped.

"Not *all* of us," Boswell added. "Nero may be an arsehole but he is one of us and no one rescued him."

"They're Anachronauts," said Cressida, not sounding especially bothered. "If they can't find their own escape route, I'll eat my two-horned Viking helmet."

Lovelace was still staring at Oxford. "Did you make a whole planet full of cats forget that we existed? That time travel existed? They were in pain, Oxford."

Oxford crumpled. He lowered himself to the nearby steps that ringed the quad, and put his head in his hands. "I didn't know it would be like that. I just tapped the glass and followed the instructions."

Ruthven felt frozen, not sure what to think or feel.

It was Boswell who went to Oxford, settling on the step nearest to him. "What was it supposed to be like?" the marmalade tabby asked.

"The Founders planned this," said Oxford, staring miserably at his knees. "Right from the start. They've always been concerned about keeping time travel secret. The Global Official Secrets Act. Containing their base to three colleges on three separate space stations. I don't know all the details, but they used the Jade Pineapple to shield the stations. It was never the government they were hiding from, or anyone else in the twenty-fourth century. It was the future. That future."

"So it's all true, what they said at the trial," murmured Ruthven. "Nero and Banksia and Aesop. They came from the thirtieth century?" Oxford had known about it. All along.

Hard not to feel like you'd swallowed a concrete block, with a revelation like that.

He saw Boswell shoot an uneasy look at Lovelace. She looked shocked, at least. Boswell looked tired.

Oxford stared into empty air. "Do you think Nero's okay? I thought they had more of a plan. Why did Professor Shelley pass the Violet Sunflower to me if the Anachronauts didn't have a plan to escape when I set it off?"

"Why don't you tell us?" said Lovelace. "Since you and Nero are such good friends with the Anachronauts."

Oxford gave her a startled look. "I honestly don't know much about them. Mum — Melusine didn't approve of how deep Mother was in with them. They both tried to keep me out of it."

"Celeste," said Boswell thoughtfully. "She's been involved with the Anachronauts all along, hasn't she?"

Oxford shrugged. "She was Dean of Aleister College, from the start. On paper she resigned when the Anachronauts took over, but... yeah. I don't think she ever really left them."

"The Founders approve of what the Anachronauts get up to?"

Oxford gave a dry laugh. "Nothing happens on this campus — at any of the colleges — without the Founders' approval."

Monterey lifted Lovelace down from his shoulders, setting her near Boswell on the step. Then he loomed over Oxford, looking about as gutted as Ruthven felt. "How do you know all this?" Monterey demanded. "The Founders. Our parents. How do you know so much about what they've been up to all these years?" *When I don't*, went unspoken.

Ruthven did not know why it was a relief that Monterey had not been lying to them all for years, even with the confirmation that Oxford had.

"I've always done whatever my parents told me," said Oxford, as if it was obvious.

"And I haven't?"

Oxford winced. "You rebelled, Monterey. You always rebel. You told them exactly what you thought of their plans, of their choices. And every time we talked about it, *you remembered less*. I was a coward. I didn't want that to happen to me. So I never said a word to question what they were doing, and they left me alone."

Monterey looked like he had been hit with a brick. "They took my memories?"

Oxford spun the circle of purple glass over and over in his fingers. "Mum had custody of the Basalt Sphinx. She oversees the cat development program. Banksia and Burbage hid the Jade Pineapple before they left, which is why we're all still hopping through twenty-year-old time hoops. But the Violet Sunflower — the Founders took turns with it. Some of the high-ranking Anachronauts, too. You never knew who was going to use it, and when."

"They gave it to you," said Lovelace, still glaring at him, even as she kneaded her claws against Monterey's arm. "Does that make you a high-ranking Anachronaut?"

Oxford shook his head. "I'm not anything. I don't know why Shelley pressed it on me, when we landed at Aleister College. I suppose she thought I'd give it to Nero — or that it was best in the hands of someone unimportant. They knew then, I think, that we'd be taken to the future. They installed a protocol to set off a mass wipe of the memories of the Grimalkins and the rest of the thirtieth century cats, if anyone got the opportunity. To erase the knowledge of time travel and humans. It was all set up, years ago. All I had to do was tap the thing, agree to the terms and conditions, and set it off."

"Do you think," said Ruthven, hating himself for saying it. "Someone else should hold on to it for now?"

Oxford met his gaze, looking sad. "Get it out of the wrong hands, eh? It is a lot of power. Who do you think we should trust?"

Not you. The thought came from nowhere. Ruthven wasn't sure if he felt judgement or pity over what Oxford had done. He held his hand out.

Oxford drew his hand back, keeping the Violet Sunflower out of Ruthven's reach. "I don't know much about how this works. But I do know that anyone who holds it for any length of time starts getting back all the memories that they lost. That's why the Founders and the Anachronauts passed it around between them, as a way of checking they still remembered everything they should."

Monterey stepped forward. "So if I — ow, bloody hell, Lovelace."

Lovelace had drawn blood through the sleeve of his blue jumpsuit. "*No*," she warned. "How much did they change? What if you're a whole different person when you get your memories back?"

Monterey froze in the act of reaching out for the chronocle. "I don't think you have too much to worry about, darling. According to Oxford, I was always a rebel."

Ruthven, aware that they were all crowding Oxford now, took his own step forward. "Am I going to learn more things about you that I don't like?" he asked. "If I get my memories back?"

Oxford gave him a wavering smile. "That's not even the reason you're going to hate me," he said. The circle of purple glass flipped back and forth in his fingers, as if Oxford was tempted to make this whole conversation go away. To make them forget what he had told them. He took a deep breath, and threw it away from himself.

The circle flipped, spun and bounced on the cobbles. It rolled along the uneven surface, finally coming to rest between the statues of Cressida, and of Aesop.

Cressida, following the glass with her gaze, was startled to see the statue of herself for the first time. "What the bloody hell is that monstrosity?"

"I told you about the statue," said Monterey quickly.

"You did not! Any conversations you had with me between 912 and now were with those other Cressidas, the scattered copies. Not me." Cressida backed away the statue, looking distressed. "They gave me that haircut for posterity?"

"You don't remember any of our conversations when you were running around in a tie-dyed bustle?" Monterey sounded crushed. "We bonded!"

"Never happened." Cressida gave him an awkward grin. "Text me a recap?"

"You're the worst," he said, shaking his head. "Fenella, back me up here. Tell Cressida she's the worst."

"You don't remember any of it?" Fenella asked Cressida in a small voice. "Fenthorp Manor, Fleur Shropshire's wake, Cleopatra? All our conversations?"

"You finally met Cleopatra?" Cressida crowed at Monterey, hugging him around the neck. "Nice one." She looked back at Fenella. "Sorry, we haven't met. You're one of the new kids, are you?"

Everyone stared at her.

"That's Fenella," said Ruthven. "Your sister."

"I don't have a sister," said Cressida. "Check my records. Only child. You think they pick people with *families* for this job? If you're not a Founders nepo baby, every candidate for time travel is vetted carefully. No one with emotional ties to the world outside gets admitted to the colleges. Otherwise we might notice they never let us leave."

A slow, horrible silence swept over the quad. As one, they all turned to look at Oxford. He winced.

"My memories are fake?" said Fenella. "They can do that? Not just take away... they give us new ones?" She pressed both her hands to her mouth.

"What they did to Monterey was bad," said Oxford quietly. "But, yeah. What they did to you was worse. I'm sorry, Fenella."

"Is that why they never issued me a cat? There's something wrong with me?"

"There's a whole lot wrong with this college," said Oxford. "Not with you."

"Stop talking," Lovelace invited in a hiss.

Fenella darted past Ruthven, past Cressida, heading for the statue. No one stopped her. She snatched up the fallen glass circle and held it tightly in her hand, turning back to face the group.

Her pale eyes glowed purple for a moment, as her fist tightened around the Violet Sunflower. She let out a breath, and turned her eyes on Oxford with an unflinching gaze. "At some point," she said calmly. "I'm going to hit you in the face, and you're going to let me. I'll stand on a box if I have to."

"That's fair," said Oxford. "Sorry, Zadie. I really am."

Not Fenella, after all. Not Cressida's sister. *Zadie.* Ruthven frowned. Why was that name familiar?

"Where are our parents?" demanded the angry young woman in a pixie-cut who was not Fenella Church. "The Founders. Where are they, right now, Oxford?"

"I assume they're in some kind of committee meeting, making decisions about our lives," said Oxford. "That's how it usually goes."

"No," said Zadie, rubbing her thumb over the surface of the Violet Sunflower. "They don't make decisions for us. Not anymore."

fifty
the museum of lost things

BOSWELL REMEMBERED ZADIE KINCAID.
Memories moved through his mind like someone had clawed open his brain, and dropped her inside.

Bright, sunny, big eyes, full of questions. *So many questions.*

Back then, he was a cat who had lost his partner, and the world felt like it was ending. He wanted to leave Chronos College — went to deliver his resignation in person to Dean Pennyworth.

Daimler Pennyworth was such a clothes horse, a primping and posing sort of man. Like what might happen if Monterey dropped every other personality trait, but doubled down on his vanity.

Boswell remembered quite clearly that the man had been wearing purple that day. A pin-striped suit, a cravat, shoes with red soles that looked like they'd been snatched directly from the wardrobe of Louis XIV... and a monocle, of all things. A lavender monocle, through which he peered at the marmalade tabby while assuring him that he was still valued. Chronos College could use him. Boswell had so much to offer.

Somehow, when he walked out of that office, Boswell had

not resigned. He had agreed to be the Professor of Time Mechanics instead.

Zadie was a second-year student in his classes. There was something about her spirit that reminded Boswell a little of Church — she was confident and smart, endlessly curious. Most of the human students chose time travel for the glamour of it, after childhood experiences of watching too many pirate movies, or some other history-related nerdery.

This one, however: she was genuinely interested in how time travel worked. The nuts and bolts. The more questions this daughter of a Founder asked, the more Boswell started to wonder how much he himself knew about what was going on behind the scenes at the college.

It was a dark time for Boswell, that first year of teaching. Learning how to be a cat without a human. It took him far too long to notice that Zadie was having a hard time, too. She stopped submitting assignments on time, skipped classes. When she was present, her questions became abrasive, challenging, cynical.

(Some of the staff gossiped about her, said she had some kind of blog on the college intranet that was stirring up trouble. When that got closed down, she was caught distributing hand-photocopied flyers to the younger students.)

Boswell's headache stabbed sharply. He remembered Fenella Church transferring over from Banksia the following year. She seemed cheerful and bright. Everyone said she was Cressida's sister, so he *kept his distance.*

Now, as the memories rolled back in on top of each other, he saw the truth. Zadie was Fenella. Fenella was Zadie. How many memories had the Founders tampered with, to hide their problem child so thoroughly?

How many other secrets had they hidden, over the years?

Boswell felt a hand scratching the back of his neck, in that particular spot which was so hard to reach on his own. He curled into the familiar scent...

His eyes snapped open. "Church." Real Church. His Church. He hadn't quite taken it in, what with the whirl of escaping the thirtieth century together. But he knew her with a certainty he hadn't felt before, with all those copies.

This was his maniac in trainers. Whole, alive, home.

"Boz," murmured his human. "You okay there, old man? You sort of toppled over."

"Memories," he grunted. "Apparently I've had a lot of work done recently."

"You remember me, though," Cressida said with confidence. "Right?"

Her scent was not exactly the same as it had been. But she smelled natural, and familiar. His.

Boswell leaned into her hand, rubbing his cheek against it. "Rings a bell."

"Only if I put a collar on you."

He wanted to bury himself in her lap and nap for a million years. Not yet. "Where did Zadie go?"

"The girl who was pretending to be my sister? She marched across campus to yell at some people."

Boswell leaped up, looking around the quad. The rest of them hovered nearby, awkward and unhelpful. Typical. "Did anyone go with her?"

"Oxford did," said Ruthven, sounding sour. "He seems to be the only one around here who knows what's actually going on."

"Well, then," said Boswell, pulling his haughty professorial persona on like a pair of tiny spectacles. "I suggest we join them. Unless you all wish to remain in ignorance?"

"Are you all right?" Lovelace asked in an undertone as they marched across campus, led by Boswell and Cressida.

"I don't want to talk about it," said Monterey. He smelled of misery and confusion.

She butted his shoulder with her head. "I'm still here. We're still here."

"I know, dear one," he said. "Stick close."

Tunbridge had been waiting outside the Reading Room in the Museum of Lost Things for hours. Whatever dire emergency had required the Founders to summon all the cats here in the middle of the night was clearly not as crucial as the nine of them pacing up and down, pouring more wine, and gesticulating wildly at each other behind sound-proofed glass.

Every time Tunbridge glanced around to check on the most dramatic committee meeting of all time, the Founders of the three colleges of time travel looked more and more unhinged.

Still, no one had attacked the campus. They were all safe, for now. Ptolemy was asleep on Tunbridge's lap.

Abydos was asleep too, sprawled across the lap of Zephyr Kincaid. Zephyr slumped against the shoulder of their younger brother Bellerophon, either asleep or close to it.

It was sweet that Ptolemy and Abydos had been so keen to extend their protection to their favourite humans, but surely this could have waited until morning.

The doors of the museum flung open. Fenella from Costume strode into the main hub of the museum like an opera singer about to launch into her big number. She wore an odd, baggy blue jumpsuit that looked like it had been printed on a machine — it had surely not been tailored by anyone human. Oxford, long-legged and miserable-looking, trailed after her as if he would rather be anywhere else.

Fenella stopped short, just in front of Tunbridge. A small woman, she bristled with fury. "Lakshmi," she said, her tongue hissing on the name. "Do you know me?"

Ptolemy sat up straight on Tunbridge's lap, ready to defend his human.

"Fenella?" Tunbridge said hesitantly. She stood up, pushing Ptolemy to the ground.

Clearly that was the wrong answer. Fenella's brows drew down in anger. She came striding forward and clasped Tunbridge's face in both hands as if she was about to kiss her, or maybe break her jaw.

Something cold and small and round hummed against Tunbridge's cheek. Reality blinked, for a moment, out of existence and back again. She could see purple lights at the back of her eyes... and oh, she had such a headache.

"Zadie," she breathed.

Everything went to hell, shortly after Zadie Kincaid marched into the Founders' meeting and let them have it: her father and his eight colleagues, at the mercy of one angry young woman holding a circle of glass.

Oxford had gone in there with her. Tunbridge was at her side, as were Zadie's siblings: one Anachronaut and one Banksia-affiliated traveller.

Monterey was in there too, hands in the air as he confronted his parents. Lovelace had nearly bitten Monterey's mother at least twice.

Oxford stood between both his mothers — Melusine from Admin and Celeste, the Dean of Aleister College.

It was chaos, pure and simple. And that was before the cats

woke up. Every cat from all three colleges had been napping in the other Reading Room. Now they were awake, they all had opinions about how much memory loss had been going around.

Ruthven could not keep track of any of it. He stayed well out of the way, drank half a glass of expensive red wine, and felt like death warmed over.

At one point he caught Oxford's eye, and motioned that he wanted to talk. Privately. Away from here. Surely Oxford wanted that too, even just to catch his breath...

But then a time hoop opened up in the middle of the museum, and Nero hopped through, followed by Fleur Shropshire, Anne Boleyn, Emperor Claudius, and every other Anachronaut who had been whisked off to the thirtieth century.

They had, after all, rescued themselves. And they had plenty to add to the committee meeting from hell.

There was a lot of screaming, and sarcasm, and emotional blackmail, and Ruthven was pretty sure it was all going to end with either Nero or Zadie Kincaid as Dean of the Colleges.

He felt like his head was about to explode.

So, he walked away.

The other end of the Museum of Lost Things was an oasis of calm. Ruthven made his way around the dusty glass cases, looking for somewhere quiet to have an emotional collapse.

He found Professor Boswell and Cressida by the Pens Nicked From Famous Authors Display, observing all the new additions to the collection from the last seven years. Cressida had snagged herself a large glass of wine, and an over-sized tweed jacket to layer over her baggy blue prison jumpsuit.

"I can't believe he got all three of the Bronte sisters," she was complaining as Ruthven approached. "That rogue has no sense of honour."

Boswell nodded in Ruthven's general direction. "Laddie."

Ruthven leaned against a case of old sweet wrappers with trivia facts written on them. "You didn't want to be in the middle of all that?"

Cressida and Boswell snorted in sync.

"I avoid committee meetings at the best of times," said Boswell.

"Oh, hey," said Cressida, pulling out a rather battered postcard from the pocket of her stolen jacket. "I should give this back to you, Ruthven. Saved our bacon. Maybe you should frame it."

Ruthven accepted it back. Whatever messages Cressida had passed to Control while they were in that trial, the postcard was now blank again.

"Thanks," he said.

Cressida gave him a warm smile. "Could have rescued myself a lot earlier if I'd had an extra one of those. But I hear the old man was in safe hands while I was gone."

"Oh, really." Ruthven twitched a smile of his own, looking over at the marmalade tabby. "Have you been saying nice things about me, Professor Boswell?"

Boswell glared at them both, and chose to pretend that cats could not talk.

Cressida and Ruthven, in a moment of complete shared understanding, scratched their cat behind his ears.

Ruthven walked aimlessly around the darkened campus for a while. Then he started panicking about what decisions might be made in that Reading Room. Then he decided that if he really wanted to know what decisions were being made, he should join the meeting.

He didn't want to be in that meeting. He didn't want to know any of it. He was feeling tired and fed up and betrayed.

So he went home.

The Media Archives were quiet, calm, and entirely lacking in angry people armed with glasses of red wine.

He was not even surprised to find Oxford there ahead of him, sprawled out on Ruthven's favourite chair in his tiny office with his long legs up on a crate full of old data discs.

"Thought you were in a meeting," said Ruthven.

Oxford jumped. The effect was like a startled spider, dangling from a web. He managed to stay in the chair. "Hey."

"Hey," Ruthven said automatically. This was awful. He had no idea how to *not* be friends with Oxford. He'd spent his entire time at Chronos College leaning towards him like a plant thirsting after sunshine.

"I have something to tell you," said Oxford, already wincing as if he knew his reception would not be warm.

"Really?" Ruthven blurted. "There's more?"

"Sorry."

"Is it worse than the last thing you told me?"

"It's related."

Ruthven wanted to laugh. He wanted to challenge Oxford to a duel. And also drop a piano on his head.

(He still wanted to kiss him.)

Ruthven spread his hands wide. "Go on, then. Hit me. What secrets do you have left boiling around in that head of yours? What's the one thing you can say that will make me regret our kiss?"

Oxford took a deep breath. "I know what happened to Aesop. I've known for a while."

Well. Yes. That would do it.

fifty-one
meet the professors

THEY TRAVELLED down to Earth's surface by flyer. Oxford had a *flyer*. Apparently, the favourite son of the Founders had been able to head planetside any time he liked.

"I didn't use it much," said Oxford apologetically. Everything that came out of his mouth was apologetic. He had 'forgive me?' stamped inside his bones, like in a stick of Blackpool rock.

"I didn't even realise," Ruthven said softly, his eyes on the blue and green of the sphere beneath them. "I didn't go home for the holidays. We never had *holidays*. I remembered that I didn't have living parents, but I didn't remember that I had nothing down there to go back to."

The latest update, by way of Tunbridge, was that Zadie was insisting everyone's memories be restored. Zadie, now she had her memory back, was making a great many demands. Ruthven was glad to get off campus before words like 'compulsory' were thrown around.

He wasn't sure he wanted to know what existed in the gaps between his memories of Chronos College. The only thing that tugged on him, the only absence that mattered was Aesop.

According to Oxford, he was now heading towards the answers he needed, with or without the support of the college administration. Ruthven did not care about the rest of it. Let the campuses burn down. Let the time hoops topple. Let the Anachronauts take over, and put David Bowie in charge.

"Thank you for trusting me with this," said Oxford, as they entered the Earth's atmosphere.

"I don't trust you," Ruthven said immediately.

"I deserve that."

"Yes, you bloody well do."

It would be easier to be angry if Oxford wasn't so sad. It was unfair. Ruthven deserved to be angry.

You don't betray someone for years and then hover around hoping they'll comfort you about it. Not that Oxford was asking for that. He hadn't asked for anything — except just enough patience for Ruthven to learn the last secret. To meet someone who would, apparently, explain everything.

Ruthven might be an idiot for getting in this flyer, for agreeing to leave Chronos College, in this particular company. He hadn't told Boswell, or Cressida, or anyone who might stop him.[1]

"I don't think Monterey's ever going to speak to me again," Oxford observed, an hour or so into the trip.

"He spent a weekend hanging out with *Lord Byron*," muttered Ruthven. "You'll be fine. He doesn't hold his friends to particularly high moral standards."

The latest news on Monterey was that he had holed himself up in his rooms with Lovelace and was getting very drunk. All attempts by Zadie Kincaid to bring him on board with her 'everyone gets their memories back' agenda had been met with shouting and hat-throwing.

Ruthven had never related to Monterey harder in his life.

"Where are we going?" he asked as the swirling continents of the planet threw up a familiar cluster of islands.

"East Anglia," said Oxford. "You'll know it when you see it."

Ruthven gave him a withering look. "You can't buy me off with a fannish pilgrimage to modern-day Fenthorp."

"Ha," said Oxford, with the first glimmer of his humour returning. "Shame. That was my entire nefarious plan."

Fenthorp Manor had survived to the twenty-fourth century.

Ruthven could not stave off the spark of excitement at seeing the building in real life. In his own century. He'd never thought to visit the site before.

Oxford landed the flyer with expert ease. The two of them climbed out, walking across the wide lawn towards the manor.

There was an expanded car park out the front with electrical charging units, and a holographic pillar detailing the historical significance of the site. Otherwise, the house looked much as it always had. A bit run down. No one had cleaned the mathematical tile in a couple of centuries, and the roof was in a shocking state of disrepair. Clearly it hadn't been the site of any film shoots lately.

Ruthven wondered if the greenhouse would still be there. And then he stopped wondering anything, because the front door of the house was opening...

He wasn't sure what he had expected. It was not this old man in an embroidered velvet jacket. He looked vaguely familiar, like when you meet the relative of someone you know well.

"Elliot Ruthven," said Oxford, at about 50% of his usual dramatic charm. He'd be radiating full charm in no time, at this rate. "This is my godfather. Professor Aleister Gordon Hepple-Burbage."

Ruthven heard himself mumble appropriately polite greetings, though it was hard to hear them over the loud screaming that had just erupted inside his head.

The Professor not only lived in Fenthorp Manor, but in the part of the house that was most recognisable from Cramberleigh filming. He led Oxford and Ruthven up to the second floor: the Round Library, where Sir Victor had proposed to Lady Sophia.

It was still a library, though most of the books on the shelves did not resemble the beautiful leather-bound editions from when it was filmed in the Sixties. The shelves were jammed wildly with vintage paperbacks, hardbacks in slipcovers, comic books, holozines and DVD cases, including something Ruthven instantly recognised as an ancient Alexandrian scroll-bucket.

There was no rhyme or reason to the collection. Flash Gordon sat alongside the Bronte sisters, Bridget Jones, Charles Dickens, *Grange Hill* novelisations and the Vorkosigan Saga.

There was a burning wood fire in the hearth, something that had been illegal on this planet for at least two centuries.

There was a cat curled up on the hearth rug.

It wasn't Aesop.

(Ruthven hated that, for a moment, he had thought it might be.)

This cat was grey, and sort of scraggy around the edges. A cat who had lived a long and interesting life. He was of no distinct breed, with pale green eyes, long ears and soft, thin fur that stuck out in all directions. He had a fluffy tail which twitched back and forth as if it had a life of its own. He resembled the heroic statue of Professor Banksia from the quad about as much as Cressida Church resembled hers.

The same could be said of Professor Burbage, who now

towed an entire tea trolley into the library, being the jovial sort of person who believed all guests should be greeted by proper refreshments. His statue was far younger, with a trim beard, tailored tweed suit, and shapely calves. This version of him involved grey hair, fluffy slippers and pyjama pants under the velvet jacket.

"You're Banksia," said Ruthven, staring at the cat on the hearth rug.

Professor Banksia arched his back and sniffed. "You're Elliot Ruthven, I imagine. Oxford's been on at us to invite you here." He gave a blushing Oxford a pointed look. "I suppose this means the cat is out of the bag?"

"You might say that," said Oxford.

"Oh dear," said Professor Burbage, pouring the tea. "Sounds messy. Has anyone asked about us?"

"Hard to say," said Oxford. "The Founders and the Anachronauts have been in Deep Committee for two days now, and the cats have formed their own group chat to talk about the humans behind their backs. You're probably not high on their agenda of things to yell at each other about."

"Until they remember that we know where the bodies are buried," said Banksia slyly.

Ruthven made a startled sort of hum.

"He didn't mean literal bodies," Oxford said quickly. "But the Lost Media Archives are here. All the footage of old missions, that you asked about. The classified stuff."

Ruthven let out a strangled noise, muffled only because his lips were welded shut. Violence was very much not his thing, but he did rather want to brain Oxford with a poker. Or, at least, a very heavy book.

"Not to mention us," said Banksia, rolling on to his back. "We're also classified."

"Everyone thinks you're dead," Ruthven blurted. "Well. Not everyone, I suppose." Lost Media Archives. All the answers he had been wanting. This meant more to him than getting back his actual memories. This was something solid.

Oxford had figured out that he needed this.

Professor Burbage pushed a cup of tea into Ruthven's hands, which helped a lot with the overwhelm coursing through his brain. "Sit down, young man. I expect you have questions."

"I don't know where to start!" Ruthven settled with his large cup and saucer on one end of a Chesterfield sofa. It was brightly floral, looking like it had been in this room since the twentieth century. "Oxford said your name is Hepple-Burbage. Are you a descendant of the Hepple family who have owned Fenthorp Manor for so many centuries?"

"That's right," Burbage said easily, settling into a chair that was clearly fitted to his own body after decades. "The last Hepple. I inherited the old pile from a great-uncle I'd never met, and planned to turn it into a research centre. Then one day, twenty years ago, a golden circle appeared on the chamomile lawn and three large purple cat-shaped creatures from the future fell through. My life plans shifted after that."

Ruthven looked at Banksia.

Banksia, scrappy little grey fluffball that he was, rolled his eyes. "Fine," he grumbled, and... changed.

His body swelled and expanded, muscles tensing like he was a small panther, not an average sized house cat. His grey, fluffy tail became sleek and whip-like. He glowed purple all over, his eyes gleaming with the same pale green...

Then he was Banksia again, a small grey cat preening his whiskers by the fire. "We learned to adapt," he said primly.

"He's like Nero," Ruthven said to Oxford.

"Apparently," said Oxford, looking twitchy.

"Have the two of you spoken at all, since he came back?"

"We're not here to talk about me and Nero."

Ruthven had so many questions crowding into his brain.

Aesop. Ask about Aesop. They have the footage here. Oxford said this was the only way to find out what happened to my cat.

He stared at the tea trolley instead. All very vintage and cozy. A large teapot on top, spare cups — Ruthven and Professor Burbage were the only ones currently drinking tea — and on the next shelf down, an enormous pineapple upside-down cake. Was that a joke? A reference to the Jade Pineapple? Ruthven was looking for patterns, desperate for it to all make sense.

"So," he said, clearing his throat. He managed to sip some tea without rattling the cup on the saucer. "They fell into your lap. Those cats from the future. Nero, Aesop, Banksia. With the High Artefacts?"

"Oh, yes," said Burbage. "The Jade Pineapple, the Violet Sunflower and the Basalt Sphinx. Each packed with secret knowledge that would allow us to travel in time. I called in a few friends from my university days who I thought would be interested — and might have enough money to sponsor such an endeavour. A few of them had been planning to found a school, but had never quite got it off the ground, so to speak. The whole thing developed quickly, once the Pennyworths got involved — their father was an orbital estate investor, and they were able to contribute the first derelict space station, ready for renovation. The Montereys took on that project, with the assistance of Dumas and Kincaid. Diana Melusine-Oxford managed the setting up of our early experiments, that woman is a demon with a schedule. And once we learned that cats were so essential to the safe time travelling process, well..."

"You needed more cats," Ruthven said in a low voice. "Intelligent, rational cats who could communicate."

Banksia yawned. "At first we only used the Basalt Sphinx to change our own appearances," he said. "So we could blend in. Took a while to realise we could do it the other way, to develop advanced abilities in ordinary cats. Soames Kincaid had bought a kitten for his eldest kid, and we, uh..."

"Experimented," said Ruthven. "Probably without any kind of ethics paperwork."

"Successfully!" Banksia insisted. "That was Abydos. He was our first new traveller."

"Such glorious days," said Professor Burbage, happy in his own bubble of nostalgia. "Wild experimentation, time travel without consequences, free academic playground, talking cats. No rules. We felt like kings."

"Gods," coughed Banksia. "We were gods of time."

"Well," said Ruthven. "I'm glad it didn't go to your heads."

Oxford coughed; hid a laugh.

"So what went wrong?" Ruthven went on. "You both disappeared thirteen years ago, before the college program was even properly underway. If it was so wonderful, why did you leave?"

Burbage and Banksia looked at each other uneasily.

"A difference of opinions," said Burbage. "We'd spotted a few anomalies during time travel, which made Banksia and the others suspect their people were hunting them, to retrieve the High Artefacts. The Founders got scared — next thing you knew they were building shields, retiring from the field, and training up their children instead. Meanwhile, they'd purchased two more space stations for college campuses. It seemed obvious that it was time to go public. Tell the world we had time travel. Bring in transparency with the application process, instead of scouring the world for orphans with a *Cramberleigh* fixation."

"The Founders felt otherwise," said Banksia. "Once public interest was invited, they would lose some measure of control. There were many meetings. Phrases like 'proprietary technology' were tossed around. 'Stockholder security.' Like *they* owned the Artefacts." He sniffed in disapproval, and his eyes glowed briefly purple.

"They allowed us to leave with our memories intact," said Burbage. They were not nearly as quick to use the Violet Sunflower, back then. I believe that came later."

"It did," Oxford said morosely.

"The Sunflower's ability to tamper with people's minds and memories was more powerful than we realised," Burbage went on. "Thirteen years ago, the Founders only were only using it to enforce their Global Official Secrets Act — to prevent anyone who signed the damned contract from discussing their secrets freely."

"*Their* Global Official Secrets Act?" Ruthven burst out, feeling outraged. "I thought it was a world government thing."

Oxford gave him a twisted smile. "The world government doesn't know about us," he admitted. The space stations are listed as private corporate real estate. No one knows about time travel who doesn't live and work at one of the colleges... or in this house."

"Ah yes," said Burbage. "We were allowed to be exiled from the program, as long as Banksia never leaves this property in his natural form." He glanced around his library. "It's not exactly a hardship, to live in exile. At least I got out before being a 'professor' of Chronos College meant marking essays and such. Though I do miss the adventure."

"You can always watch the old footage," said Banksia with a yawn. "They keep full backups of the Media Archives here, including all the secret files they don't want their current crop of travellers to hear about," he added to Ruthven. "Poor old Oxford here got the job of shipping new files to us, along with all the latest pompous memos from the Founders. Occasionally, he smuggles in some contraband like those amusing Zadie Kincaid pamphlets."

Ruthven met Oxford's eyes. "That's how you know what

happened to Aesop. You brought the footage here. You've seen it — the Ancient Rome mission that went wrong."

"It's a little more complicated than that," said Oxford, looking uncomfortable.

"You mean, you haven't seen the footage?"

"Have some pineapple upside-down cake," urged Burbage. "It's terribly good, we have a favourite patisserie in the village — well, not so much a village these days. Kettlewick is more of a residential hub with cake. But there's a charming little bowling green. I pop over there when Banksia gets sick of my company."

"Three pubs," Banksia mouthed.

"All the best villages have three pubs," replied Burbage.

Ruthven's eye was drawn back to the pineapple upside-down cake. "Were you expecting company?" That was a lot of cake for one professor… and one cat, if Banksia ate cake.

Aesop used to have such a sweet tooth, though she knew it was bad for her. She would lean over the sonic tooth cleaner for ages in the bathroom afterwards, complaining that it tickled her gums.

Another question rose on Ruthven's lips before they'd answered the first one. "Anne Boleyn said Banksia stole the Jade Pineapple. When you two disappeared. Is that true?"

"The truth," Burbage said, sounding a little sad. "Ah, well. Not stole as much as… removed it from the wrong hands. Insurance, you might say. To make sure they would allow us to stay away."

"We didn't think they'd be able to keep going without it," said Banksia, clawing a little at the hearthrug in his frustration. "But they already had so many time hoops, the postcards, the opals… they'd developed their own time technology based on what they learned from the Jade Pineapple. We gave it to a trusted friend to hide so that we could honestly say we had no idea where it was."

That might not be enough to keep you both safe now," Oxford said in concern. "Once the Founders and the Anachronauts wear themselves out with committee-based shouting matches, someone will come for you. If you're their only hope to get time travel back on track…"

"They can't seriously want to continue with it after everything!" said Ruthven.

Oxford gave him a long stare. "You don't know my mothers. All of the Founders. Controlling time travel, being part of a secret cabal with immense power. I don't know if they know how to give that up."

"They kept it all running so much longer than we expected," murmured Burbage. "Twenty years."

"I'd like to see Egypt again," Banksia said. "They were very nice to cats there. So many fish. And that Cleopatra was a jolly sort."

Ruthven rubbed his face. He still didn't have any answers about the one thing he had actually come here to find out. He looked helplessly over at Oxford.

Oxford nodded. "I know," he said. "I didn't think I'd have to explain this part."

"Why not?" And again, Ruthven's hopes warmed up. "Who was going to explain it?"

Professor Burbage gave Ruthven's arm a friendly pat. He leaned over the tea trolley to cut three wedges of cake. "You'll find her in the grounds," he said. "Be gentle, dear boy. She's been through a lot."

---

1. Ruthven had mentioned his unofficial getaway to Tunbridge, who was so distracted by the force of nature that was Zadie Kincaid on a rampage that she didn't have the energy to offer him more than a pitying look.

fifty-two
aesop

SOMEHOW RUTHVEN GOT himself down several flights of stairs, and all the way to the kitchen at the back of the ground floor before his body reacted to the news.

He let out a shuddering breath that was almost but not quite a sob, and reached out for Oxford, because he had not fully absorbed the idea that he couldn't trust him.

Oxford held him for a moment, his body warm and comforting, though it had no right to be.

"She's alive," muttered Ruthven. "And you *knew*."

Oxford said nothing. No justification. No excuses. No apology. He held on, and let Ruthven lean on him.

The greenhouse was long gone. Not even the frame of it remained. Instead, there was a series of white vegetation pods, humming along with power from a solar battery, growing veggies like everyone else did in the twenty-fourth century. They had similar food production pods up on Chronos College.

Otherwise, the grounds of Fenthorp were startling in their

familiarity. Grass hadn't changed in three hundred or more years; if anything, it was lusher than it had appeared in the 1960s and again in 2034. The hedges and trees had been tended carefully. They weren't exactly the same as they had looked when Ruthven visited here across the twentieth and twenty-first century, but it still felt *right*.

It was a sign of unbearable inherited wealth, so much land existing simply to look pretty, but preserving green space was one of the requirements of anyone over a certain tax bracket in this century. There were places like this all over England, all over the world. Groves of trees, chamomile lawns, hedge mazes, all created and maintained for tax incentives, since the Regreening Act of the 2040s.[1] Professor Burbage-Hepple must have enough socked away in the investment vaults that he didn't have to hire the place out to TV crews, anyway.

It occurred to Ruthven that he didn't know that much about his own century. His life at Chronos College had completely insulated him from what it was like to live in the world right now.

A long purple tail swished from within a small grove of silver birch trees.

She emerged from behind the trees, prowling. She looked like another one of those aetherial, glowing purple sphinxes that had lunged at Ruthven from out of a cupboard. Her eyes glowed yellow and green, and it was that — those familiar part-coloured irises, which confirmed for Ruthven that it really was her, beneath all the purple fur. Aesop. His tiny, adorable calico cat, transformed into something majestic.

No, not transformed. She had always been this. The tiny calico cat he thought he knew, *that* was the disguise.

Aesop blinked her eyes slowly at him, and then looked past Ruthven to his friend. "That's what I get for trusting an Oxford," she said in chilly tones.

Oxford was just as furious in reply. "You should never have

made me promise," he said. "Not about this. It wasn't fair. You don't do this to people you love, Aesop."

"Why not?" she snarled back. "You did."

"Aesop," Ruthven said, finally finding his voice.

The glowing purple feline turned back to him. "Ruthven," she said, and lowered her head. "I never wanted you to see me like this."

"I thought you were dead," he choked.

Aesop's eyes widened, the green rings darker against the yellow. "I missed you," she said in a very small voice.

Ruthven took an unsteady step forward. Aesop crouched, and leaped. He should have braced himself, but instead he went down in a cloud of fur and grass. The wind was knocked out of him, not leaving enough breath in his body to laugh for joy.

His cat — a beautiful, terrifying futuristic feline who was also, miraculously, his cat — repeatedly butted him gently in the face with her own. Her nose was still as cold and wet as ever, and he could feel the outline of her claws against his ribs.

"Do you look different?" he managed to say. "I hadn't noticed."

"I don't know how much you remember about our last trip to Ancient Rome," said Aesop, a short while later. Ruthven sat in the thick grass, his back against a birch tree, with a lap full of cat. So much more cat than he was used to. She spilled over his knees and on to the ground.

Oxford withdrew to the house, claiming he couldn't spend more time in real sunshine without a boater hat. Really, he was giving them privacy for their conversation.

Once again, Ruthven had too many questions to fit inside

his head. Most of them could be summed up as *how?* and *why?* and *when?*

"Very little," said Ruthven. "I know what was supposed to happen."

"Ha," Aesop said, her head nudging against his hand until he got the message and started to scritch behind her (now rather large) ears. "Standard mission, except that while we were looking for mushroom facts, there was an Anachronaut sabotage-and-extraction planned at the same time, to recruit the Emperor Claudius to their side. It's the only time in known history that Melusine's spreadsheet failed us. You and I were nearly out — I was a few seconds behind you, leaping into the time hoop — and in that moment, 54 CE became an Event."

"You were trapped?" Ruthven felt a wave of guilt, even if he couldn't remember any of it. Why hadn't he been carrying her? Why hadn't he checked she was keeping up?

Aesop blinked at him. Her eyelashes were even longer than they had been in her old body, and that was saying something. "You know about Event Space?"

"Spent some time there on my summer holidays. Not a fan."

"Understandable. I found myself stuck in 54 CE. In the palace where the Emperor had just disappeared into thin air."

"Wait, was he poisoned by mushrooms or a feather?"

Aesop rolled her eyes. "I don't know, Ruthven. In the timeline I witnessed, he was abducted before the entrees were served."

"Right, fair enough. How long were you stranded?"

"Fifteen," said Aesop grimly.

"Fifteen what?"

"Fifteen separate rounds of 54 CE. Believe me, by the end of it, I wanted to poison the Emperor Claudius myself. Not to mention, every other member of that wretched family. I only found my way out because I ran into a scattered version of Cressida, and she showed me how to use the time aisles."

"Viking hat Cressida, or tie-dyed Victorian bustle Cressida?"

"If we're talking purely costume, I'd go with Lancashire Witch Trials Cressida."

"Oh, that's new." Ruthven wondered how many other Cressidas were out there.

"I finally happened across one of those self-congratulatory dinner parties the Anachronauts love to throw for themselves, at Versailles."

"1664, Louis XIV's Party of the Delights of the Enchanted Island?" Ruthven asked. According to Boswell, Oxford and the others had spent some time at that particular party recently.

"1685, Reception of the Doge of Genoa," said Aesop. "Anachronauts are way too into the Sun King."

"They share a love of parties."

Aesop leaned her large purple head against his knee, closing her eyes. Ruthven continued to stroke her fur, wanting her to feel safe. "I was in a bit of a state by then," she said in a small voice. "Too long in Event Space. Too long in the time aisles. I got all my memories back and it was rough. I learned a lot about myself I didn't like very much. And... I'd lost my shape."

Her whole body scrunched up, as if in misery. Was this it? The reason she didn't want him to know she had survived?

"I think you're beautiful," he assured her.

"Not like I was. Not a real cat."

"You look real to me."

"I scared the hell out of Nero in 1685, anyway," Aesop said, rolling on to her back and lolling around so he could pat her belly. "He dragged me home to Basic Time, and made Oxford smuggle me here in his flyer so I could recover."

Ruthven's hand stopped moving. "Oxford brought you here? How long ago?"

Aesop gave a whole body shrug, her eyes still closed. "A few months."

"A few *months*? It's been three years for me."

"That's time travel," said Aesop, sounding a little sulky. "Oxford promised he wouldn't tell you until I was ready."

"Did you think this —" Ruthven scratched at her purple fur, "Would really matter to me?"

"Not the body," Aesop wailed. "Me. I was not a good cat, Ruthven. I was complicit in so much corruption. The Founders, and everything they did. We put that power in their hands, because their money made things easier, and time travel was fun. We thought no one was getting hurt. When Burbage and Banksia spoke up about ethics and accountability, I stayed silent."

"You agreed with them."

"They had some valid points. I wasn't brave enough to leave when they did. Worse: I wasn't unselfish enough."

Ruthven had a sudden thought. "Are you the friend who hid the Jade Pineapple for them?"

"Yes," Aesop said grumpily. "But I got nervous, being the only person who knew where it was. Nero was starting to suspect that I knew something about Burbage and Banksia's retreat. Then the Anne Boleyn Incident happened — Abydos and Lancaster's antics around her execution gave me the idea. I borrowed the Violet Sunflower, to delete the memory of where I put the Jade Pineapple, so no one would be able to force me to give it back. But I messed it up — completely blanked myself. They put me in with the kittens. Later, when the time aisles brought me a purple migraine from hell, I remembered everything I had done. Everything I was."

"You're not even complicit in the worst things the

Founders have done," Ruthven said. "That came later — the memory erasures, the manipulation."

"Don't let me off the hook," said Aesop. "We were irresponsible, right from the start. We treated Time like she was some kind of chew toy."

"I think you've been punished enough," said Ruthven, scratching her ears again. "Don't you?"

They ate the pineapple upside-down cake, all three slices between them, since Oxford had not returned.

"Brush your teeth later," Ruthven warned.

"You're not the boss of me," said Aesop, licking syrup off her whiskers.

"Why did you do it?" he blurted out.

Aesop gave him a steady look with those yellow-green eyes of hers. He was almost getting used to her purple panther-like appearance. "I wasn't going to leave you alone forever. I needed time to deal with having my memory back."

"No," he said. "Not that. Why did you steal the Artefacts and run away from your time in the first place?"

Something odd crossed her face. Embarrassment, he realised.

"Humans," admitted Aesop. "Banksia is full of scientific curiosity. Nero is desperate for everyone to think he's marvellous. I played on all that when I talked them into it. Just because I wanted to meet a human."

"We're really all gone, then?" Ruthven said, remembering the trial. Humans were due to go extinct in the late twenty-eighth century, according to the Judicial Felicitas. "What happened to us?"

Four centuries or so. That was less time than lay between Sappho and Catullus. Between Richard the Lionheart and

Elizabeth I. Between the 'death' of Anne Boleyn and the filming of *Cramberleigh*. Four centuries was *nothing*.

"No idea," said Aesop, having the grace to sound apologetic. "Mewtopia didn't care much about history, let alone the rise and fall of humanity."

That was... something that Ruthven needed to pack away to process when he was feeling more emotionally robust.

"How did you find out about us in the first place?" he asked. "What got you curious?"

"Oh, here we go." Aesop ducked her head, looking embarrassed. "Something I found deep in the archives. A show you might have heard of, actually."

"Not *Cramberleigh*?" Ruthven was both awed and horrified all at once. *Cramberleigh* had survived beyond humanity itself! "The cats had it archived?"

Aesop placed a comforting paw on his arm. "Only three episodes, I'm afraid."

"Three episodes." Awe gave way to a kind of numb shock. Somehow it was easier to deal with this tragedy than the loss of the human race. Three episodes of *Cramberleigh* to represent the entire history of the show? Which three? His brain immediately started spiralling. "Which three?" he demanded.[2]

Aesop patted him again. "4F."

"That Horrible Cat? That one's still lost."

"Clearly someone finds it between now and the thirtieth century."

Was it even a good episode? Ruthven didn't know. It was probably not a good idea to nip to the thirtieth century to grab it. "What else?"

"13G," said Aesop, making innocent eyes.

"Curiosity Killed the Cat," Ruthven completed automatically. His ability to match production codes to stories was his primary superpower. A suspicion crept up his spine. "Did they only save the episodes with 'cat' in the title? Tell me the last one wasn't Cat's Cradle?"

Cat's Cradle was one the worst *Return to Cramberleigh* episode of all-time. Only three episodes saved and that was one of them?

"I can't emphasise enough how little importance my people place on history that doesn't involve cats," said Aesop. "The same goes for pop culture."[3]

"But there are no actual cats in any of those episodes of *Cramberleigh*!" protested Ruthven. "Unless 4F has cats in it?"

"No. Just dumb squishy humans with their dumb squishy problems. But it was enough to get me curious about meeting my own dumb squishy humans."

"Questions like, can I steal precious time travel artefacts and run away to befriend an extinct species?"

Aesop looked approving. "That is one of my all-time favourite questions."

Ruthven shook his head. "*Cramberleigh* has a lot to answer for."

"Indeed."

Aesop was so big that Ruthven could lean his chin on her head and hug her entire body without squashing her. It was pretty great.

"Aesop... I liked rampaging irresponsibly through time with you," he said softly.

"Me too, my dear," said his cat. "Let's never do it again."

Ruthven and Oxford travelled in silence for the first hour or so of the flyer trip back up to the space station that they knew as Chronos College.

Ruthven had a lot to say, but couldn't bring himself to get started.

A few times, he saw Oxford twitch, then force himself to stay quiet.

"Okay," Ruthven said finally. "Go on. You first."

Oxford took a deep breath. "I know it's not fair to ask for forgiveness. I always knew that Monterey and Tunbridge and everyone would despise me when they found out how much I'd collaborated with the Founders and their bullshit. I should have resisted, I should have told you all what was happening, and I didn't. That's on me. I still can't stand the thought of you hating me."

"I don't hate you," said Ruthven honestly. "I have too much going on in my head right now to hold resentment about how you handled a horrible situation. Also I don't think *I'm* the one whose job it is to forgive you."

"I didn't tell you about Aesop."

"Yeah, and if it had been years, if it had been the whole time… but it wasn't. She wasn't ready. I get it." Ruthven nudged Oxford, wanting to get their easy friendship back, wanting to see him *smile*. "You're so dramatic."

"I wonder what's happening back home," Oxford muttered. "If Zadie still has control of the Violet Sunflower."

"If she has any sense, she'll destroy it," said Ruthven. "Of all the Artefacts, that's the most dangerous. All these secrets. It has to stop."

"My mothers always say that information is only power when you're the one who has it."

"You have been so messed up by your upbringing," Ruthven said flatly.

"Yeah," Oxford agreed. "But we got talking cats out of it."

"Indeed we did." Aesop was alive. She might not look the same, but Ruthven had her back. That made everything feel less hopeless than before. "There should be a better way," he said.

"To do time travel?" Oxford gave him a wild sort of look. "Time travel is over. It has to be. Right?"

"Chronos College is over," said Ruthven. "The Founders can't be trusted with this kind of power, not again. But surely it could be done safely, now we don't have to worry about the thirtieth century Feline Cops tracking us down."

Oxford gave him a wary look. "Safely, like with rules?"

"Absolutely with rules," said Ruthven. "With ethics statements, and open communication. No more secret experiments or Anachronauts running around behind everyone's backs. No deliberately creating Events."

Oxford blinked a few times. "Time travel without terrible consequences? Is that possible?"

"*With* consequences," Ruthven corrected. "Terrible or otherwise. And a new mission, a real mission, none of this bobbing around to measure hedges and meet historical celebrities. We only have four hundred years to save humanity."

Oxford was giving him an awed sort of look. "Do you think Time will allow us do that?"

Ruthven shrugged. "I think Nero and Banksia and Aesop probably couldn't be involved, because it would be changing their past. But I refuse to believe we don't have the power to change our future."

Oxford smiled in a way that Ruthven hadn't seen in a long time. It warmed him all the way through. "It's amazing, the lengths you'll go to make sure *Cramberleigh* survives a few extra centuries."

"Yes," said Ruthven, deadpan. "That is exactly why I want to save humanity."

Oxford's brows drew together as he thought about it. "How would it even work? I don't want to rain on your parade, but everything's such a mess up on campus. I don't think we can start time travel from scratch without the Jade Pineapple."

Ruthven smirked.

"No."

"Yep."

"You know where it is? Aesop erased that memory from her head!"

"True. But Banksia still remembers what it looked like. That was enough for me to figure out the location."

Oxford's hands twitched on the helm of the flyer. "I've never seen it. I don't think anyone has, except for the Founders..."

"And the cats who stole it in the first place. According to Banksia, it looks small and innocuous, like the other Artefacts were a mug and a chronocle. Aesop was able to hide it in plain sight."

"It's still on campus?"

"In the Museum of Lost Things."

"We have to go get it right now!" Oxford's eyes were bright. "What sort of something ordinary?" he asked after a moment. "Gum wrapper? Pocket lint."

Ruthven continued to smirk.

"Are seriously you not going to tell me?"

Ruthven settled back in the passenger seat of the flyer. "Now you know what it's like when people keep secrets."

"Too soon," Oxford growled, but his warm smile came back again, soon enough.

---

1. In the decade that followed the War of 2034, many sanctions were placed upon personal and corporate wealth. The environmental reparation responsibilities placed upon those of the highest tax bracket were so demanding that 50% of the billionaires gave up their fortunes voluntarily in a movement that went down in history as the Billionaire Badger Sanctuary Revolution.
2. Several months after this conversation, Ruthven finally decided which three *Cramberleigh* episodes he would personally choose to be preserved in the future, if someone put a gun to his head, and didn't

mind waiting several months for him to finalise his list. His choices were: 1F: Where Butlers Fear to Tread, 8D: Why Didn't The Petunias Eat Evans? and 14H: Knight and Dead, though he agonised over which of these he would definitely sacrifice in order to preserve "Full Moon Over Whitechapel, his favourite of the *Tales of Cramberleigh* tele-movies. Who was he kidding? He would walk over hot coals to save the entire Caligula West arc of Seasons 12-14, as well as (to his shame) the two appearances of that particular villain in *Return to Cramberleigh*. Three episodes? Impossible.

3. The archiving habits of cats also explains why the most recognised human science fiction author in the thirtieth century is C.J. Cherryh, and the only Shakespeare text Aesop had heard of before she began her career as a time traveller was the Bumper Book of Cat Quotes.

fifty-three
the end of time travel

Did ya miss me?

So much has happened since I've been gone. We have a whole new understanding of time, space, and the fucked-up personal history of this college.

Meanwhile, I've picked up a whole lot of costuming skills I never had before. Not to mention a Viking helmet with two horns which I am keeping, Cressida. Don't get lost in time if you want to hang on to your stuff.

Here are the headlines: the Founders are gone. Seriously gone. After a week of the most pointless committee meetings AKA screaming matches anyone at this university has ever suffered through, they packed their gold-plated luggage and shipped out. All of them.

Including my dad. We're not currently on speaking terms. Apparently Monterey's folks tried to drag him off with them but Lovelace threatened to bite their faces off, and they went without too much drama. Oxford's mothers assumed he would leave with them and it all got *very* chilly in the quad for about half an hour.

Was the Violet Sunflower involved in making them all

agree to leave so quietly? Of course not! That would be unethical.

Not a single cat went with the Founders. Nero and Boswell faced down Melusine in the quad and made her hand over the Basalt Sphinx into their custody.

Every cat who has ever been part of the time travel program formed a guard of honour to watch the Founders leave. Cheers to the solidarity and strength of all those cats refusing to be part of their bullshit for a moment longer.

(Solidarity! Unions work, y'all!)

No one's ever going to find the Violet Sunflower. I made sure of that, once I triple checked that everyone who wanted them had their memories back.

We've already had the notification that the termination of the lease for Satellite 12 is coming up. Chronos College is no more. Banksia College has put in a Global Government application to turn themselves into a nature sanctuary. Gotta put all those rescued koalas somewhere. (And I'm guessing the Global Government are pretty excited to find out that they saved a whole bunch of formerly extinct species already, talk about getting the most out of your funding.) Shout out to my bro Bell Kincaid who is leading the charge to keep the Banksia mission alive.

No one knows what's happening over at Aleister College, but my sib Zephyr heard a rumour that Claudius, Anne Boleyn, Christopher Marlowe and Fleur Shropshire haven't been seen in days. Mysterious...

You've probably been packing your bags, like the rest of us. I know that many of you are scared about what happens next. Most students, staff and travellers of Chronos College don't have anyone waiting for them planetside — and those of us whose parents dropped us in this mess aren't looking forward to seeing them any time soon.

This has been our home, our safe space, for as long as we

can remember. And yeah, I'm going to miss it. But it's for the best, I think, that we say goodbye to time travel.

Let it be a cool thing we did once, that no one will ever believe.

And if you think otherwise — if you wish we could give time travel one more go and get it right this time...

Well, go say hey to Ruthven in the Media Archive. He's distributing drives packed with travel highlights and extant *Cramberleigh* episodes (I recommend you pick up Monterey and Lovelace Greatest Hits, so hilarious). He also has a new project in the works that may or may not be time travel related, and he's looking for volunteers.

Don't tell him I sent you.

> Zadie Kincaid, a Love Letter to the End of Time Travel, final blog post before we shut down the Chronos College intranet once and for all. I'll be at the bar until they close us the hell down, come buy me a drink and tell me your story

fifty-four
a conversation in the office of professor boswell

"A PEN," said Boswell, smacking his face with his paw. "A fucking pen."

"More importantly," said Cressida. "Was it on the blue felt or the red felt? Either Monterey or I have just been disqualified from our little contest…"

"Keep dreaming, Cress," broke in Monterey. "The contest will never be over, even if we have to wait for new celebrities to be *born*."

Ruthven twirled the stylus — not even yellow and green, whoever named it the Jade Pineapple was seriously deluded — between his fingers.

The secret of time travel did not look all that impressive.

"Ruthven thinks we could start again," said Oxford, leaning against the door. He hadn't wanted to come — had insisted to Ruthven that they were more likely to listen to him if Oxford wasn't there. "Do it right this time around."

"Should we?" asked Tunbridge. "Can humans be trusted with time travel after the mess we made of it?"

"Can cats?" challenged Ptolemy, pressing his cold nose against the side of her neck.

"Do we make the sensible choice?" mused Monterey. "Or

the fabulous choice?" No one even slightly doubted that he was in.

"There have to be rules this time," insisted Tunbridge. "*Rules*."

"Guidelines, at least," said Lovelace. "Let's not go wild."

"We need a base of operations," said Cressida. "Not a college, right? And I'm assuming we don't have the budget for a space station."

"I have a place in mind," admitted Ruthven.

Boswell peered at him with amusement. "Does that make you Dean?"

Ruthven winced. "Please don't."

"I think," said Nero, and paused.

As usual he had found himself the high ground, atop a teetering pile of books that did not look structurally sound.

Boswell almost hadn't invited Nero to this meeting. He and Monterey had to sit on Lovelace for an hour beforehand, to make her promise not to start anything.

If they were going to move forward with this, they had to include everyone who wanted to be part of a more ethical, intelligent time travel program. Excluding any of the three original cats who had stolen the technology in the first place was a dangerous way to proceed.

Even if it meant making nice with Nero, who had not uttered a word of apology for all of his shady shenanigans. He had also not uttered a word of reproach about being abandoned in the future, and having to rescue himself.

He hadn't shipped out to Aleister College with the rest of his Anachronaut friends. Almost as if he was waiting for a better offer…

"Go on," said Lovelace, who sounded revolted by how polite she was being right now. "What do you think, Nero?"

"I think," said Nero in his familiar pompous tones. "If

we're going to do this, we have to be prepared to clean up our own mess along the way."

There was a moment of silence as everyone marvelled at his audacity.

"I agree," said Ruthven. "Let's get to work."

fifty-five
here's to the future

RUTHVEN WAS NOT a fan of genuine sunshine. He was still getting to grips with twenty-fourth century Earth, and all its natural processes. Rain. Pollen. Gusty winds that rattled the centuries-old roof.

Still, he couldn't shut himself away in the Fenthorp Manor cellar, new home of the Media Archive, every hour of the day. Especially not at this particular moment of the day, when the travellers were due to return.

Ruthven sat on a deckchair on the chamomile lawn behind the manor, sharing a tea table with Professor Boswell. To their left, Control provided tech support under the shade of a vintage gazebo. To their right, Aesop was gently chasing several students back and forth, her fur glowing bright purple in the afternoon sunlight.[1]

Six golden time hoops hung in the air above the grass, with the hillside view behind them. Every brick and pane of Fenthorp Manor vibrated as the portals hummed into life.

Windows were thrown open. Staff, students and other residents all stopped what they were doing to watch the spectacle: ovals brimming with oceanic light, cresting, bubbling...

Oxford came through first, in an outfit that made it very

clear he had been playing English cricket: layers of beige and cream, with the occasional grass stain. His hair was rumpled. Jocasta, Oxford's long-limbed tortoise-shell partner, slipped off his shoulder and proceeded in the direction of the kitchens.

She had learned to make herself scarce any time Oxford and Ruthven made eye contact, because that usually meant they were moving towards each other at great speed.

In this case, Oxford was loping forward, and Ruthven was calmly waiting from the comfort of his deckchair.

Humming. Cresting. Swirling. Bubbles.

Tunbridge came through next, whooping with triumph. She carried Ptolemy in one of two shopping bags, laden with books. Tunbridge was taking her mission to update the Fenthorp Manor libraries with long-lost publications very seriously. In her leisure time, she wore a t-shirt proclaiming ***Shhh! I'm a Time Librarian***.

Humming. Cresting. Swirling. Bubbles.

Zadie and Banksia strode through the hoop in mid-conversation. The conversation carried them all the way across the lawn and into the house without acknowledging the existence of anyone else. (At least their reports were always well-written and entertaining, when they got around to filing them.)

Humming. Cresting. Swirling. Bubbles.

Boleyn and Nero landed at a run, clearly pursued by someone or something. White fur floated in the air around them as they urged Control to close their hoop as a matter of great urgency.

Humming. Cresting. Swirling. Bubbles.

Cressida and Boswell fell through the hoop, wrestling over some kind of fried cake, that had clearly only been allowed to time travel because it already had bites taken out of it...

Humming. Cresting. Swirling. Bubbles.

Abydos and Zephyr stepped through with their usual dignity intact. Zephyr wore a full Roman toga, and Abydos dripped with more gold jewellery than a statue of Bast. Must have been quite the party...

Ruthven did not pay further attention to the returning travellers after that, because Oxford had reached him and was leaning over, blocking out the sun...

Humming. Cresting. Swirling. Bubbles.

"That's it," exploded Monterey, waving his hands in indignation as he stalked through the hoop, Lovelace clinging to his shoulder. "Event Space is cactus. That's the fourth formerly-Event year in as many hops that I can just stroll through without any resistance at all!"

"He's cranky because Cleopatra had no idea who he was," said Lovelace, biting his ear fondly.

"I am extremely memorable!" howled Monterey. "Ruthven, stop making out with your boyfriend while I am registering a complaint!"

Sunshine-warmed and thoroughly kissed, Ruthven drew back from Oxford and peered around his cream cricket jumper to make eye contact with Monterey. "I'll have that report in writing," he said firmly.

"But what are you going to do about it?" whined Monterey. "Cleopatra has completely forgotten that she wanted to be my best friend when we met in Event Space."

"I'm going to read your report with sympathy and compassion," Ruthven informed him. "And I think we should leave Cleopatra alone for a while, yes?"

"Authority does not suit you," declared Monterey, and strode away in high dudgeon.

"*Strong* disagree," said Oxford, dropping to the grass beside Ruthven's deckchair. "Any tea going?"

Professor Burbage poured the last from the pot, and passed it across.

"Good trip?" Ruthven asked.

Oxford took a deep swallow from his teacup. "I'll put that report in writing, shall I?"

"You do that."

"Brought you a present." Oxford leaned back on his elbows without spilling a drop. He gave Ruthven a lazy grin. "Guess what it is?"

"*Cramberleigh* Episode 4F: That Horrible Cat," Ruthven said immediately.

His boyfriend closed his eyes and shook his head. "It's never 4F. You know it's never 4F."

"Someday, it will be 4F. How else will 4F end up in the archives of the terrifying future ruled by giant purple cats?"

"Maybe that will never happen. Since we're changing the future."

Not yet. They weren't changing the future *yet*. Ruthven felt it was the sort of thing you should work up to. Couldn't risk stuffing it up. They might only get one chance... even with the secrets of time travel at their fingertips.

If not them, who?

"Humanity has to find 4F," he said now. "Or Aesop will never see it in the future, and never convince her friends to steal time travel and run away. That would be a paradox."

"No such thing as a paradox," said Oxford in unison with the half-dozing Professor Burbage.

"No such thing as your face," Ruthven grumped.

"I like your face," Oxford informed him, and kissed him again.

Lovelace found Boswell in one of the upper rooms — he'd taken a fancy to it, though it didn't seem like anything special to her. The pineapple chandelier was still an eyesore, and the carpet didn't look like it had been replaced since the twenty-second century. "Come on," she said, hopping up to join him on the window seat. "You'll miss the party. They're screening the new episode of *Cramberleigh* that Oxford found. Quant and Khan are making their famous chilli."

"I can take or leave *Cramberleigh*," murmured the marmalade tabby.

"Liar. It's from Season 3."

"Season 3?" Boswell's ears pricked up. "No one in this century has ever seen an episode from Season 3."

"They think it might include the first ever speaking line for Evans the footman," Lovelace continued, to tantalise him.

"Fine," Boswell said in an exaggerated sigh. "I suppose I'll show up."

Lovelace nudged the side of his face with her nose. "They're silly, our humans. But I'm quite fond."

Boswell made an unintelligible grumble sound that in no way endorsed her sentiment. Lovelace wasn't going to call him on it.

Neither of them budged from their comfy spot.

"Do you think they can do it?" she murmured. "Save humanity from whatever makes them extinct? Prevent the future from falling into the hands of glowing purple cats?"

"Not without our help," said Boswell.

"Obviously not without our help."

"I think it's possible," he conceded. "I wouldn't bet against them."

Lovelace nodded sagely. "I don't really care about humanity," she admitted in a whisper. "Only our humans. But if this is what they want..."

"They never seem to appreciate finding dead mice on their doorsteps," agreed Boswell in a satisfied purr.[2] I suppose we have to find some other way to make them happy."

"You old softy," said Lovelace, leaning into his warmth. After a few moments, she began purring too.

THE END

1. The Fenthorp Project's curriculum remained rather ad hoc for now, and they had failed to include any kind of physical activity in the initial program draft. It was Monterey's idea that the cats take turns to jump out at students to test their reflexes when startled. Aesop promptly turned this into the most epic, week-long game of tag and no one had complained yet. It was good to see the students having fun in between the long lectures about history, ethics and survival.
2. An endless supply of mice was the one of the many things thing that made Fenthorp Manor superior to Chronos College, in Boswell's opinion. He also enjoyed the lack of essays to mark, and the excellent kitchen staff with their ready supply of beef tea and raw mince. He'd never admit to the humans, of course, how content he was with this new life they had built together. If he left enough dead mice on their doorsteps, they'd figure it out eventually.

historical events and those responsible

An incomplete, unreliable list of known Events up until the collapse of Chronos College.

This list is imperfect, based on information known to Chronos College Admin, and does not include details that have been redacted due to the Global Official Secrets Act or for any other reason. Chronos College has historically ascribed all Events with an unknown source to the Anachronauts regardless of evidence or lack thereof.

- 776 BCE (The Anachronauts, traditional first date of the Olympics)
- 551-479 BCE (The Anachronauts, the life of Confucius)
- 431 BCE (Cressida, Boswell & the staging of Euripides' *Medea*)
- 323 BCE (The Anachronauts, Death of Alexander)
- 69-30 BCE (The Anachronauts, the life of Cleopatra)

Historical Events and Those Responsible

- 48 BCE (Monterey & Lovelace, the burning of the Library of Alexandria, preceding the life of Cleopatra Incident)
- 54 CE (The Anachronauts and/or Ruthven and Aesop, Death of Emperor Claudius)
- 911-915 (Boswell and others, due to the failed recovery of Cressida) *disputed*
- 1215 (The Anachronauts, signing of the Magna Carta)
- 1520 (Monterey and Lovelace, Henry VIII & Francis I, Field of the Cloth of Gold)
- 1533-1535 (The Anachronauts, most of the marriage of Anne Boleyn and Henry VIII)
- 1536 (Abydos and Lancaster Pennyworth, the execution of Anne Boleyn... credit later redacted)
- 1537 (Combined Effort; The Medici Raid, Bonfire of the Vanities, arrest of most Anachronauts)
- 1664 (Monterey and Lovelace, Louis XIV's Party of the Delights of the Enchanted Island)
- 1668 (The Anachronauts, Louis XIV's Grand Entertainment)
- 1685 (The Anachronauts, Louis XIV's Reception of the Doge of Genua)
- 1694 (The Anachronauts, Admiral Russell's Punch party)
- 1836 (The Anachronauts, Andrew Jackson's Cheese Party)
- 1888 (The Anachronauts, the year the bustle went out of fashion)
- 1899 (The Anachronauts, reasons unknown)
- 1923 (The Anachronauts, Opening Night of Les Noches)
- 1936 (Banksia College, failed attempt to rescue the last Thylacine to die in captivity)

Historical Events and Those Responsible

- 1945 (The Anachronauts, VE Day)
- 1963 (uncredited, but let's face it, probably the JFK thing)
- 1964 (The Anachronauts, first pilot episode of *Cramberleigh* shot on location at Fenthorp Manor)
- 1969 (The Anachronauts, Moon Landing/Woodstock but probably Woodstock)
- 1978 CE (The Anachronauts, the tragic death of Fleur Shropshire/Freddie Mercury's Halloween party)
- 1989 CE (The Anachronauts, the wiping of *Cramberleigh*)
- 2012 CE (Banksia College, successful attempt to rescue Lonesome George, the last Pinta Giant Tortoise in the Galapagos)
- 2034 CE (The Anachronauts, the war)
- 2049 CE (The Anachronauts, the Last Met Gala)

cramberleigh: production guide

Cast and Characters

Gladioli — a maid (Seasons 1-11), a receptionist and occasional secret agent (Seasons 12-14), a maid again (*Tales of Cramberleigh*), and a cook/housekeeper (*Return to Cramberleigh*). Regularly haunted. Has an uncanny affinity with roses and other plants which is later retconned to be paranormal. Annually wins a prize for her raspberry blancmange at the Cramberleigh Fair, except for the year when the prize was taken out by a time-travelling Boudicca who had a surprising talent for handling gelatine. Played by **Joanna Wetland**, co-creator & writer of *Cramberleigh*.

Sir Victor Wildegreen — lord of the manor (Seasons 1-11) and occasional mad scientist (Seasons 8-11). A widower who marries young socialite Ann because she looks so much like his first wife, Lady Lavinia. Ditto his third wife Sophia. Father of Edgar, Lucy and Abigail. Stepfather of Rosamund, Rudolf and Ichabod. Killed in the Cramberleigh Explosion (1975) Played by **Christopher Seasalter**, renowned theatre actor with a surprisingly short IMDB page.

Lady Ann Wildegreen — lady of the manor (Seasons 1-4) and Gothic heroine. Died on the Titanic. Played by the iconic **Fleur Shropshire**.

Lady Sophia Wildegreen — lady of the house in Seasons 5-6. Died of Spanish flu. Mother of Rosamund, Rudolf and Ichabod. Stepmother of Lucy and Abigail. Played by **Barbara Hill**.

Edgar Wildegreen — Sir Victor and the late Lady Lavinia's eldest son. Famously dull. Was 'sent off to war' in Season 5 and never mentioned again. Played by **Robson O'Sullivan**.

Lucy Wildegreen-Waugh — Sir Victor and the late Lady Lavinia's daughter. Young Lucy (Seasons 1-2) was played by child actor **Millie Stubbs**. She was then recast, returning from boarding school as a glamorous blonde played by **Carol Gleeson** (Seasons 4-13) Lucy had a tumultuous marriage with artist-poet Aubrey Waugh. She finally demanded a divorce, only to be widowed in the Season 11 explosion. Thrown forward into the 1970s, Lucy joined the new C Squad, becoming a secret agent. She was written out of Season 14 with no explanation provided on screen for Lucy's absence. Carol Gleeson did not return for either of the 1980s reboots, though Young Lucy as a child appeared in flashback footage in the clip show "Blast From the Past."

Aubrey Waugh (Seasons 6-11) — Lucy's disreputable, unreliable Bohemian husband. He cheated on her multiple times, with several actresses, lady scientists, time-displaced travellers, vampires and on one memorable occasion: a talking rosebush. Played by Leslie Bluff.

Dr Abigail Wildegreen — Sir Victor & Lady Sophia's daughter, born during episode 6A. Played between Seasons 6-10 by a variety of convenient babies, small creepy child actors and for two episodes, a china doll in Lady Cradoc's collection. Did not appear in Season 11 despite never being formally written out of the show. Was later retconned to have been "at boarding school" when the Season 11 explosion took place. Abigail returned as a recurring character after the time jump (Seasons 12-14), now a cranky archaeologist in her 50s played by **Beatrix Smythe**. Abigail was revealed to be Agent A, the secret boss of Cramberleigh Central in the final episode. She returned once more in *Tales of Cramberleigh*: The Curse of Auntie's Mummy. Smyth was asked back for *Return to Cramberleigh*, but had a schedule conflict with her regular role in *All Creatures Great and Small*.

Lady Cradoc/Aunt Phyllida — recurring character (Seasons 1-7), main character (Seasons 8-12), recurring character (Seasons 13-14). A character once described as "if all the aunts in the PG Wodehouse novels ganged up on you over tea." Played by the legendary **Joan Buckingham**, who also played Daphne Cradoc and X-C-5 the Android in *Return to Cramberleigh*.

Henry Cradoc — main character Seasons 2-4, played by **Rupert More**. Son of Lady Cradoc. Constantly falling in love with showgirls and otherwise getting into alarming scrapes. Source of the 'Cousin Henry's Terrible Fate' meme of the early 2020s.

Mayfair the butler — Seasons 1-5. Played with great butlerish charm by **Winchester Sinden**, who went on to play fifteen further iconic butlers during his long career. He just had that sort of face.

Bones the butler/Alfie Bones — Seasons 6-14 & *Return to Cramberleigh*. Played by **Angus Thames**. Transformed into a vampire in Season 10. Survived the Season 11 Explosion because of being a vampire. His talents include discretion, biting and espionage.

Evans — Seasons 3-13, played by **Brian Henley Leech**. A young footman with a Welsh accent, regularly on hand for scrapes and shenanigans, often getting in trouble with Mayfair the butler. Was constantly falling in love with ladies above his station, while never noticing that every scullery maid ever hired was swooning at his feet. Promoted to chauffeur in Season 9 with the family purchase of a new Rolls Royce. Survivor of the Season 11 explosion, Evans benefited from the Seventies Spy reboot of the show, serving as the 'wheels' for C Squad. Confessed his romantic feelings for Lucy Wildegreen-Waugh in the penultimate episode of Season 13, only to be kidnapped by a Russian submarine, thus failing to show up at their first date.

Rosamund Radcliffe-Swythe — Seasons 5-9, played by Jackie Eliot (credited as **Jacqueline Eliot**). Daughter of Lady Sophia, stepdaughter of Sir Victor, sister of Ichabod and Rudolf, stepsister of Lucy, half sister of Abigail. Rosamund was written out after her wedding, the implication being that she and her new husband Dr Swythe moved to a base on Mars after successfully saving Cramberleigh from several attempted alien invasions.

Ichabod Radcliffe — Seasons 5-10, played by **Val Munro**. Son of Lady Sophia, stepson of Sir Victor, brother of Rosamund and Rudolf, stepsister of Lucy, half-brother of Abigail. Excellent on horseback. Val Munro insisted on doing his own stunts, which led to no less than three major injuries during his time on the show. Ichabod left Cramberleigh with the Von Mont family at the end of season 10, after falling in love with Scarlet Von Mont (or, as speculated wildly by fans, with Carmillo Von Mont). It was left open as to whether Ichabod had been turned as a vampire, but no one develops a widow's peak and a taste for velvet jackets over a weekend without supernatural intervention.

Rudolf Radcliffe — Seasons 5-11, played by **Barnaby Hadoke**. Son of Lady Sophia, stepson of Sir Victor, brother of Rosamund and Ichabod, stepbrother of Lucy, half brother of Abigail. The elder and least interesting of Lady Sophia's children, Rudolf was often a bit of a bully, and famous for saying the wrong thing at dinner parties. He was killed with many other family members in the explosion at the end of Season 11.

Mrs Merryday the cook — Seasons 7-10, played by Dame Irene Porter. Co-creator of *Cramberleigh*, Porter collaborated on the original pilot script with her friend and colleague Joanna Wetland, but was unavailable to play Lady Ann as originally intended. She later joined the cast as Mrs Merryday, a minor supporting character with five different food-related catchphrases. Like Joan Buckingham with Lady Cradoc, Porter played the character 'aged up' as she was only thirty when she began the role.

Dr Bernard Swythe — Season 9, played by **Dirk Sparrow**. A Scientist from the Ministry sent to Cramberleigh to investigate a series of suspicious events leading up to the Invasion from Mars. Marries Rosamund in the final episode of the season.

Carmillo Von Mont — Season 10, played by the later Hammer Horror star **Giles Omerod**. This mysterious gentleman buys Farrington Farm, builds a castle on the grounds, and along with his two sisters Mrs Grey and Miss Scarlet Von Mont, starts biting all the neighbours. Half of the popular Carmillo/Ichabod slash fandom, often referred to as Calmbod.

Sheena Swythe — Seasons 12-14 and *Return to Cramberleigh*, played by **Jackie Eliot**. Grand-daughter of Rosamund, this secret agent is assigned to Cramberleigh Central and C Squad. She befriends Mrs Waugh (technically her step-great-aunt) and Evans in particular. Her role in Season 12 is often to explain the quirks of the 1970s to these hapless time-displaced Edwardians. Always gets the best outfits.

Mr Knight — a gentlemanly secret agent (recurring Seasons 12-13, main cast Season 14). Played by **Bartlett Mayhew**, who also made guest appearances as Captain Antony Knight of the Bow Street Runners in Full Moon Over Whitechapel (1982) and Agent K in three episodes of *Return to Cramberleigh* (1985). Iconic for wearing a bowler hat, and for forming part of three out of the five most popular fandom pairings: KnightWaugh, DeadKnight and DeadKnightWest.

Dead Desmond — a secret agent with the ability to return from the dead. Played by **Garfield Morse**. Desmond was introduced in Season 14 as a recurring character, and later became a series regular in *Return to Cramberleigh* along with his grandson Colin, played by the same actor. In the final episode, R3M Swan Song, Colin falls down the grand staircase and is killed, only to discover he has his grandfather's talent. Morse also plays Sgt Darwin Deadly of the Bow Street Runners in Full Moon Over Whitechapel (1982)

Caligula West — recurring popular villain (Seasons 12-14), played by **Gareth Kerr**. This charming, sinister politician and scientist is the leader of the Romedroids, a robotic army of creepy doppelgängers. His motive is always to bring about the return of the fallen Republic of Rome, and also make long and intense eye contact with anyone who tries to thwart him. A proposed spin-off was mooted and failed to be picked up in 1983, to the dismay of all fans who were certain it would have been a better show than *Return to Cramberleigh*. Gareth Kerr returned to play the character alongside Agent K for 3 episodes of *Return to Cramberleigh* in 1985, but despite the promo teaser suggesting otherwise, did not appear in R3K "Romedroids Forever" (1986) — in a surprise twist, Caligula West's daughter Drusilla (played by Juliet Knyves) took over his criminal empire. Gareth Kerr wrote a novel about the backstory of his character, *The Rise and Fall of Caligula West* (Random House, 1992). It is incredibly hard to find a copy, but if you stumble across one in a second hand bookshop, it will almost certainly be signed.

Episode Guide

XX - Unaired Pilot (1964) 1 episode

Sir Victor brings a bride home to Cramberleigh, and Lady Cradoc is doing something mysterious in the library. Shot on location.

Season 1 (1965) 13 episodes

1903-1905: Sir Victor Wildegreen brings his second wife Lady Ann home to Cramberleigh as a new bride — she must compete with his quirky family and strange servants, especially Aunt Phyllida who disapproves of Ann and everyone else around her.

1A The New Lady Wildegreen

This episode was a revised version of the unaired pilot, restructured for sound stages rather than location shooting. The greenhouse scenes were cut short, with some of the dialogue reused elsewhere. Also lost: the courting scenes set in "London" (originally filmed in Nottingham) where Sir Victor convinced Ann to become his bride. The maid Gladioli's part was substantially rewritten over the entirety of Season 1 to "add an air of Gothic mystery" that the new story editor, Aldis Whitby, was keen to bring in.

1B Halcyon Days
1C Governess in the Attic
1D A Maid For All Seasons
1E In Pursuit of Happiness
1F Where Butlers Fear To Tread
1G Summer 1904
1H The Crimson Pimpernel
1I A Picnic in the Parlour
1J Your Obedient Servant
1K A Surfeit of Aunts
1L The Lady Swoons
1M Green Baize

Season 2 (1966) 13 episodes

1906-7

2A Oh No, Cousin Henry!
2B Dinner at Marigold's
2C A Bit of a Scrape
2D What the Tweeny Heard
2E The Oncoming Storm

2F The Flag of Rebellion
2G Courage Calls to Courage
2H A Bear For Lucy
2I Aunt Phyllida Regrets
2J Kitchen Scraps
2K Best in Show
2L A Suitable Baron
2M The New Maid

Season 3 (1967) 13 episodes

1908-1910

3A Afternoon At The Races
3B The Fortunes of Phyllida
3C All The Fun of the Fair
3D A Valet's Hand — *first speaking lines for Evans the footman*
3E Masterpiece
3F The Marchioness and the Mademoiselle
3G Flight of Fancy
3H Nemesis
3I A Discreet Affair
3J Votes for Women
3K Over the Hills and Far Away
3L Life and Art
3M End of an Era — *the household reacts to the news of the death of King Edward*

Season 4 (1968) 13 episodes

1910-1912: Lucy (18) returns from boarding school with a new face; Lady Ann is written out

4A Kensington Square — *Lady Ann tries to solve the mystery of Sir Victor's visits to London*

4B Field of War — *the household is divided and everyone takes sides*

4C Gift of the Gab — *a charming professor turns the eye of Lady Ann*

4D Sunday Dinner

4E No Regular Occupation — *after being unfairly dismissed, Gladioli investigates other employment options in London and is kidnapped by a fortune teller who hints at the existence of black magic*

4F That Horrible Cat [still missing]

4G Working Together

4H A Friendly Policeman — *Gladioli is restored to Cramberleigh, her name cleared after the arrest of Madame Blanc*

4I Woolworth Pearls — *Cousin Henry falls in love with an unsuitable girl again*

4J A Loud Crash — *Lucy Wildegreen, now 18 years old, returns home to Cramberleigh from her boarding school and causes all sorts of chaos in the household*

4K Like a Hurricane

4L Leave it At That — *finally done with her unhappy marriage, Lady Ann makes plans to travel abroad, and offers to take Gladioli with her. At the last minute, Gladioli chooses Cramberleigh over her mistress. Only after Lady Ann has left is it revealed to the TV audience that the ship she booked passage on was the Titanic. (final appearance of Fleur Shropshire as Lady Ann Wildegreen)*

4M Nothing At All To Be Done — *Sir Victor gets a telegram about the fate of Lady Ann. The household reacts to the terrible news.*

Season 5 (1969) 13 episodes

1914-1918 The War Years: Edgar goes to war, Lucy drives an ambulance. Sir Victor marries Sophia, who looks remarkably similar to his 2 previous wives. Gains 2 stepsons: Rudolf and Ichabod Radcliffe, and a stepdaughter, Rosamund Radcliffe

Now shot on film and making regular use of locations, this is famously the season that introduced "the real" Cramberleigh, AKA Fenthorp, a manor house near the town of Kettlewick, which had previously featured in the opening and closing credits of the show, though many of the set designs were based on early visits to the house.

Final season to be produced by the iconic Valerie Forsyte, a groundbreaking and glass-ceiling-smashing female producer who had helmed *Cramberleigh* since its early days.

5A Edgar goes to War
5B The Next Lady Wildegreen
5C Patriotic Fellows
5D Lucy's War
5E Meet the ANZACs
5F The Batman
5G To Whom It May Concern
5H The Telegram
5I Wounded Officers' Tea Party
5J The Proposal
5K Hospital Corners
5L Fit For Heroes
5M Armistice

Season 6 (1970) 13 episodes

1919-20: The first season in colour! Birth of Abigail Wildegreen. Lady Sophia dies of Spanish flu. Lucy's wedding to Aubrey Waugh.

6A Birth of A Wildegreen
6B Nanny Knows Best
6C Fevered Brow — *Spanish flu hits Cramberleigh, and Lady Sophia falls gravely ill*

6D To Let — *after the death of Lady Sophia, Sir Victor plans to shut up the house and move to the seaside. The servants are all given 4 weeks' notice*
6E Victory Parade
6F In Pursuit of a Poet — *Lucy meets Aubrey Waugh*
6G My Man Bones
6H A Charming Argument
6I Ruin
6J In Chancery
6K Be Civil To The Girls
6L Maid of Honour — *Lucy's wedding part I*
6M To Have and To Hold — *Lucy's wedding part II*

Season 7 (1971) 13 episodes

1921: The last season that is considered 'pure historical' though a question mark is placed over the final episode.
7A Who Spoiled The Party
7B Sawn In Half
7C Mr Churchill's Peaches — *the Winston Churchill episode*
7D Black Friday
7E Raspberries for Gladioli
7F A Mysterious Affair At Cramberleigh — *the Agatha Christie episode*
7G Jolly Holiday
7H Discretion
7I Sunk
7J Rain Stops Play — *the cricket episode*
7K Despondency
7L A Mere Flirtation
7M The Widower — *Lucy and Ichabod become obsessed with finding out whether or not Sir Victor is courting a new bride after catching him with a mysterious dark-haired lady*

who resembles their respective mothers. This episode implies that he is in regular communication with the ghosts of his three late wives.

Season 8 (1972) 13 episodes

1922: "The Season With The Carnivorous Plants." Sir Victor conducts strange experiments in the greenhouse with surprising results.
    8A Whatever Happened to Abigail
    8B A Potting Shed With A View
    8C This Island Greenhouse
    8D Why Didn't The Petunias Eat Evans?
    8E Tree Vs Butler
    8F Lady Cradoc's Shrubbery
    8G A Gladioli By Any Other Name
    8H Knock Twice For Yes
    8I But What Do They Eat?
    8J Great Birnam Wood
    8K One Footman Short
    8L Vegetative State
    8M Best Garden in the Village

Season 9 (1973) 13 episodes

1923: "The Season With The Invasion From Mars." Dr Swythe visits from the Ministry to investigate strange happenings at Cramberleigh, and is romanced by Rosamund. Sir Victor's science experiments continue. Martians invade.
    9A Cramberleigh Revisited
    9B The Wildegreen Experiment
    9C Dr Swythe, I Presume
    9D A New Rolls
    9E Bright Young Aliens

9F The Day Cramberleigh Stood Still
9G Invasion of the Aunt-Snatchers
9H Creature From the Attic
9I Forbidden Village
9J War of the Drawing Rooms
9K The Invisible Butler
9L My Favourite Rosamund
9M Married on Mars

Season 10 (1974) 13 episodes

1924: "The Season With The Vampires." The sinister and attractive Von Mont family move into the area, building a gothic castle on a nearby farm.

10A Mrs Merryday's Meringues
10B A Vampire of Property
10C We Do Not Drink... Port
10D That Von Mont Woman
10E A Taste of The Good Life
10F Good Fences Make Good Neighbours
10G Dead Men's Table Manners
10H Nosferatu
10I Unexpected Death
10J A Lovely Neck
10K Turbot Soup
10L Sleep By Day

10M Bat Among the Pigeons — *The Wildegreen family are relieved when the Von Monts finally vacate the nearby farm. Sir Victor is alarmed to realise his stepson Ichabod went with them. He and Evans the chauffeur speed to London to stop Ichabod marrying Miss Scarlet, but they are too late. Gladioli discovers that Bones the butler is the vampire responsible for many of the recent murders! She agrees to keep his secret...*

Season 11 (1975) 13 episodes

1925: "The Season With The Time Travellers."

11A Boudicca's Berry Blancmange — *the legendary Queen of the Iceni (guest star: Britt Manning) appears in the grounds of Cramberleigh and befriends Gladioli the maid on the eve of the local village fair. Whose blancmange will win first prize?*

11B Rasputin in Residence — *another surprise time traveller arrives at Cramberleigh*

11C The Wrong Viking

11D An Unexpected Guest

11E The Tables Turned

11F Time of the Traveller

11G Hons and Vandals

11H The Man in the White Toga

11I Timepiece

11J A Passage To Somewhere — *the concept of time aisles is introduced*

11K When We Were Very Late

11L Wildegreens at Waugh — *Lucy demands a divorce*

11M Who Invited Guy Fawkes? — *The episode concludes with an explosion in the drawing room.*

KILLED: Sir Victor Wildegreen, Rudolf Radcliffe, Aubrey Waugh, assorted other members of the household including family and servants.

SURVIVORS: Gladioli the maid, Evans the chauffeur, Lucy ("Mrs Waugh"), Lady Cradoc. Mr Bones the Butler is later revealed to have survived the explosion due to his vampire nature.

Absent family members such as Rosamund Radcliffe-Swythe, Ichabod Radcliffe and Abigail Wildegreen were later revealed to be still alive in 1977, though Rosamund only appears offscreen in phone calls to her granddaughter Sheena.)

Season 12 (1976) 13 episodes

Thrown forward fifty years in time, four survivors of the explosion find themselves in 1976. Cramberleigh is now the secret base of C Squad, British Intelligence.

12A A House Called Central — *After going their separate ways and trying to start new lives in 1976, Gladioli, Evans and Lucy are eventually drawn back to Cramberleigh, and accept jobs in the secret service. Gladioli replaces the receptionist, working on behalf of their unseen boss, Agent A. Lady Cradoc, who refused to leave Cramberleigh in the first place, barricades herself in the pineapple parlour.*

12B Four Spies and An Archaeologist — *Lucy Waugh meets her step-great-niece Sheena Swythe, the secret agent assigned to train the new recruits in C Squad. Sheena and the mysterious Mr Knight take Lucy and Evans on an intensive on-the-job training weekend, where they uncover a sphinx-themed secret society, a sarcophagus-smuggling operation, and a cranky archaeologist in her 50s named Dr Abigail Wildegreen.*

12C Hot Ice — *Evans and his driving skills are put to the test as C Squad deal with a series of diamond heists around the Home Counties.*

12D The Secret Silver Service — *Lucy is assigned to assist Mr Knight on a top secret job, only to discover that Bones, her family's former butler, is alive and well and working as a double agent. ("Alive" is an overstatement, he's still a vampire.)*

12E Sheena's Day Out

12F M is For Mousetrap — *the Tabitha Gristie episode*

12G Hound of the Wildegreens

12H Who Stole the Pyramids? — *Dr Abigail Wildegreen returns in this Egyptology themed adventure.*

12I School For Spies — *Lady Cradoc decides she wants to join C Squad and is highly offended when she is sent on a training course for beginners. She uncovers a conspiracy at the heart of British Intelligence.*

12J Gladioli Galore — *Gladioli's plant-based supernatural abilities are useful to British Intelligence when Kew Gardens is taken hostage by a gang of evil Latvian botanists. She goes undercover and falls for a dreamy secret agent who is licensed to weed-kill.*

12K Et Tu, Bones? — *Mr Bones the former butler is seconded to C-Squad along with Dr Abigail Wildegreen to deal with a series of mysterious deaths caused by androids that look like Ancient Romans. First appearance of Gareth Kerr as Caligula West.*

12L The Scene of the Crime

12M I Spy

Season 13 (1977) 13 episodes

Once voted best vintage action spy TV season of all time by *Cult!Watch!Now!A!Holozine!* in 2058.

13A Return of the Romedroids — *featuring Gareth Kerr as Caligula West.*

13B Lobster Waltz

13C The Spy That Never Was

13D Red Herring

13E Too Much Mistletoe

13F Mission: Unknowable

13G Curiosity Killed the Cat

13H Revenge of the Romedroids

13I The Aunt from D.A.N.G.E.R

13J From Gladioli With Love

13K Death on the Cards

13L Mrs Waugh Regrets — *Evans finally confesses his feelings for Lucy, who agrees to a first date. He fails to appear after being kidnapped by a Russian submarine*

13M Triskaidekaphobia — *Trapped in a nightmarish*

replica of Cramberleigh, and taunted by clues to their past, as well as the number 13, Lucy and her great-aunt Lady Cradoc must rely on their wits to escape the trap set up by a former foe... (final appearance of Carol Gleeson as Lucy Wildegreen-Waugh)

Season 14 (1978) 13 episodes

The new C Squad: Lady Cradoc, Sheena Swythe, Evans the Wheels and Mr Bones are now permanently joined by the mysterious Mr Knight. Gladioli continues as receptionist at Cramberleigh Central, with an ongoing subplot of trying to uncover the true identity of her boss, Agent A, whom she only communicates with through a speaker on her desk.

This season also experiments with longer storylines over double episodes. The unexplained absence of Mrs Waugh/Lucy is a subject of great and furious debate across Cramberry fan forums for centuries to come.

14A Agent A Needs You
14B A Knight to Remember (Part 1)
14C A Lady Never Forgets (Part 2)
14D Rise and Fall... (Part 1) — *featuring Gareth Kerr as Caligula West.*
14E ... of the Romedroid Empire (Part 2) — *featuring Gareth Kerr as Caligula West.*
14F Swift Death
14G They Keep Killing Desmond (Part 1)
14H Knight and Dead (Part 2)
14I The Hidden Paw
14J Avenging Angel
14K Remembrance of the Romedroids
14L A Crime's Discovered (Part 1)
14M Agent A Uncovered? (Part 2)

Tales From Cramberleigh (1982) 3 movie length episodes
1. Full Moon Over Whitechapel
2. Curse of Auntie's Mummy
3. Boudicca 2025

Return to Cramberleigh (1984-1986)

Main Cast: Lady Cradoc, Bones the butler, Sheena Swythe, Dead Desmond — also Daphne Cradoc, Colin Drake, Tulip and Tempany Swythe, and Alfie Bones, played by the same actors as the main ensemble. Gladioli appears as a cook/housekeeper in most episodes, often without dialogue.

This unpopular reboot of the show is generally regarded as 'pants.' *Cramberleigh* fans credit the loss of quality to the reduced involvement by original creators Joanna Wetland and Irene Porter, who were busy creating the new and highly successful *Pantheon Place*, an American glamour soap featuring characters of Greek Myth.

Season 1 (1984) 13 episodes
R1A Timequake
R1B Ghostwatch
R1C Deadlock
R1D Kill Switch
R1E Family Tree
R1F Trojan Horse
R1G Ghosts in the Attic
R1H Pineapples for Phyllida
R1I Dead Butler Walking
R1J Ring O' Roses
R1K Flashpoint
R1L Dangerous Aunts

R1M Destiny

Season 2 (1985) 13 episodes

R2A Deliverance
R2B Under Pressure
R2C Diamond
R2D Voice From The Future
R2E Hostage Situation
R2F Blast From The Past (1985) — *a clip show using footage from the unaired pilot (1964).*
R2G Dead Again
R2H Terminate
R2I All That Glitters
R2J Grit
R2K Cellar at the Edge of Yesterday — *Agent K (formerly known as Mr Knight) contacts Dead Desmond to reactivate him as a field agent. Their mission: to finally bring an end to Caligula West, creator of the Romedroids*
R2L Evil — *Guest Appearances: Bartlett Mayhew as Agent K, Gareth Kerr as Caligula West*
R2M Power — *Guest Appearances: Bartlett Mayhew as Agent K, Gareth Kerr as Caligula West*

Season 3 (1986) 13 episodes

R3A Before Times
R3B Under Siege
R3C Ghostlit
R3D Jaded
R3E Crash Land
R3F Cat's Cradle
R3G The Truth About Opals
R3H Death Trap
R3I Generation Cramberleigh
R3J The Last Sphinx

R3K Romedroids Forever
R3L Master Plan
R3M Swan Song — *Daphne and Alfie take the plunge, the Swythe twins embrace their past, Colin takes a tumble, and Gladioli stops to smell the roses.*

All episodes of Cramberleigh were wiped from record in 1989 in an act of 'time terrorism' perpetuated by the mysterious group known as The Anachronauts. Thank goodness for all the time travellers who have worked hard to rebuild the archive!

Tune into the Cramberry forums this week to vote on your favourite episodes. Which missing episode do you wish they'd find next? Do you believe the Fleur Shropshire conspiracy theory?

Gareth Kerr GIFs & fic links are always welcome.

bonus kickstarter thank you page

in honour of my earliest backers
and their beloved cats

With Thanks To

- Socrates (Soccy), Herodotus (Roddy), Aristotle (Harry) and Thucydides (Theucles). Also Brie, Tum, Kesh, Abydos, Pendle & Broom, Kheldar, Kassia (Kass), Sirrka Velvet Sparrow and Loki.
- Jack Gulick, Lightning, Thunder, and Storm.
- Olivia Atwater, Dinah, and Pumpkin.
- Debbie Y. Lee and Zephyr, Ginger, Panda, Caspian, Aral, and Archie.
- Urs Stafford, Becca, Billy, Meg, and Jazz.
- Amber, Wraith (Floof), and Kestrel.
- Tehani, Lady Cordelia and Lord Miles (Marley).
- L.C.
- Tsana Dolichva, Murka, Ghost, Sonia & Basil.
- Paul, Nakimi, Smudge and Miss Chief.
- Elanor Matton-Johnson and Tiger, Missy, Belle, Mika, Paws and Puma.
- Nicola Norton and Moux, Oberon & Caspian.
- Badger and Possum.

- Karen S. and Lacey.
- Barb, Benvolio, Lilly, Smoky, BanditNO, Ninja, Tessa, Tikka, Erin, Sammie, Bozo, Tigger, Chicken and Lucy.
- Jacq and Fenn.
- Thoraiya, (RIP) Cliffy, Aerin, Satin, Sammy, and all my feline patients past and present, especially the ones who left scars.
- Cathy Green.
- Alisa Maas and her mischievous sidekicks, Fred and George.
- Dominique Soutière and Luna.
- Jerrie the filkferengi and Bummy, Abish, Esmeralda, Dixie, Dolly, Piper, Bast, Reese, Kiwi.
- E.L. Winberry and Kelly, Domino, Kelly, Aloha, Delenn, Aonghus, Murdock, Calcifer, and Oni.
- The parade - Expo&Homer, Kitayn, Mad Max, and Jupiter&Shadow. Love to you all! Pam R.
- Marie, Jam and Toast.
- Sarah Swanson, Scooby, Tiger Blossom & Black Lotus.
- Karen Healey and Tiger-Flick.
- TJ and Sabriel & Tiana.
- Nikki & Suzy.
- Beth, Davida, Callie, Bea, & Doh.
- Danny, Helen, Ski and Fancy.
- Belle McQuattie, Addie & Charlie.
- GhostCat, Skunky, Twoki, Himalay, Snuggles, Magic, Gizmo, Precious, Junior, Andy, Havs now Cali, and Tommy.
- Jean Sitkei and Carnation, Diana, Puff, Smokey, Rusty, Jessie, Tyler, Abby, Max, Brittany, Lucy & Jack.

Bonus Kickstarter Thank You Page

- Cara and Bogie, Letty, Simba, Palomides, Mocha, Lego, Petey, and Nala (and Alice, an honorary member).
- Grace Spengler & Furrytoes.
- Hyperion, Star and Ember.
- Julia Rios and Mrowsera, Desdemona, Ophelia, Lady Clarissa Blacktail, Miss Letitia Geraldine Fluffington (Baker by Appointment to the Crown), Hellinda, Harley, Sybil, Dinah Bell, Misho, Spats, and Bo Kitty.
- Rebecca Buchanan and Dice.
- Mindy and Garfunkel, Persephone, Aphrodite, Attila, Seffy 2, Jasmine, Chilly, Archie, Nefertiti, Bartholomeow, Calliope and Julius.
- MelissaB and Ariel.
- Sarah Swarbrick.
- Amy R and Spot.
- Eve Proper, Oreo, and Smoky.
- Emma Robins.
- Sarah and Jasper, Nellie & Pippin.
- Bentley, CJ, and Cody.
- Fatima and Khadija & Rello and Sven.
- Catriona MacAuslan.
- Lauren Messenger and Tabitha.
- Ailene and Twisty.
- Alexandra Pierce.
- Natalie Charest and Balou, Esme, Oshie, and Nacho.
- Dennine Dudley and Mico (always), Rocky (who time travels), Clytie (who's here), and The Adored Horde.
- Anna and Mocha.
- Narrelle M. Harris, in memory of Petra.
- Tali and Percy Foster.

- Ju Landéesse and Meryl.
- J's godkitties Lilly, Fay, Findus, and Kimba.
- Alys, Dinah, Ben, and Anya.
- Khafra and Maahes (and Tamlyn).
- Mieneke van der Salm and Elmo, Mara, Stitch, Patch, and Solo.
- Konstanze Tants.
- Spacecat Lore, with furbabies Lord Fluffens and Commander Ambrose.
- Heather M Magee and Samantha, Leela & Spike.
- Stephanie Gunn, Cookie, Jilly, Crystal, Sumi, Puss Puss and Woofy.
- Robin Hill and Smokey, Scampi, Tigger & Cheetah.
- Sadie Slater, Orange Cat, Smol Cat, Not Our Cat and the Cat Who Sits Over There.
- Stephanie Burgis and Pebbles.
- Andrew, Ozzie, Jenni Craig & Sir Samuel Thomas (Tom) Finch.
- Miriam Faye and Tiddles, Jonathan Aragorn, James Fëanor, Samantha Tinúviel, Jack Sparrow, Matilda Ekaterin, Jarvis Galeni, Sebastian Aral and Kaylee Aeryn.
- Adrian Smith and Mimi, Mini, Micro & Rusty.
- Michael Bernardi.
- Mr Bingley and Mr Darcy.
- Cheryl Morgan and Augustus.
- Stas and all the lovable strays.
- Mark Webb.
- Jayne Scott and Nox.
- NaomiL and Jaxx.
- Charlotte E. English and Jane, Emma and Peeps.
- Rob&Leece and Kimba, Patch, Squirty, Milo, Gus, Corky, Toodles and Vince.

- Trevor McCarthy.
- iamnotalibrarian.
- Katharine (thiefofcamorr) and Misha.
- Dana Statton Thompson, Mittens, and Little Mouse.
- Naticia, Apollo & Autumn.
- Zandra & Sarah with Merry & Pippin, and in memory of Shadow, Tipsy, Spook, Hamlet, Ophelia, Kitty, Maimi, Nigel, Midge, Pete, and the barn crew.
- Anna Hepworth and the late Chairman Miao.
- June Budworth, Sandy, Julian, Freckle, & Millie.
- Orca, Eris, and in memory of Syrinx, Porkchop and Chinky.
- Stephen Webb, Mistah Paige, Nolstergeist, & Magical Mr. Murphstoffolees.
- Eva Jayet Alaminos, Nova and Cosmos.
- Erika Ensign and all the alumni of Kitten Academy.
- Joris Meijer and Willem, Karel, Hera, Julius, Clarence, Balou, Lola, Zappa, Toots.
- Robert Tienken and Clara.
- Alicia Long and Katie, Thomas, Teddy, Peeper, Paint, Chase, Little Cat, Zoe & Stella.
- Andrew Hatchell and Jake & Mimi.
- Jasmine S. and Nico & Rand.
- Andreas & Regina, Lilly, Lucifer, Mephisto, Merlin, Nero, Plüschi and Queenie.
- E.D. Pearlman, Maui, Molokai, Alani, and Leo
- Dave Versace, in fond memory of Grymalkin, Manson and Printy
- Meredith, Kaylee, Ruby, Xander, Indigo, Lucy, Darcie, and Merlin Mahoney

- Brian Quirt and the von Underfoot Clowder: Victoria Shatori Quirt-Gates Princess Bat Bat von Underfoot, Hypatia Marie Quirt-Gates Prodigal Princess von Underfoot, Pixel Pixiecat Quirt-Gates Court Jester von Underfoot, Grande Dame Tabitha Madeline Quirt-Gates Duchess Purrington von Underfoot.
- Rebecca Dominguez and Eve, Pewter, Muesli, Spectre and Jet.
- L Riggle Miller with cats Chloe, Lily, and Jake.
- Tania and Robin, with Sweet Pea, Pippi, Porchie, Stumpy, Jimbo, Little Jim, Cocoa and Grampa's Arnold and Boy Cat, Tim, Ginger Jim, Jamie, and Pebbles.
- Chris Kemp-Philp and dedicated to all my beloved cats, both past and present. >^..^< Thomas, Purdy, Nibbles, Boo, Heidi, Tia, Tyger, Pollyanna, Prince & Dobby. >^..^<
- Scott Casey and Neva, Grizzy & Baby Girl.
- Jarney Stamos, Indiosa, Mousemeat, Chairman Meow, Mr. Meowgi, Cody, Marykat Olsen, Gandalf, Smeags.
- Ziri Vier, Casper, Coal , & Scamp.
- Pinky and Courtney, Shadow, Davy, Leokadia & Robi
- Clarissa Gosling, in memory of Pluto.
- Fred Langridge.
- Lilly, Gili & Paz.
- Houman Sadri, Ciggy and Emil.
- Natalie Haigh and Fancy, Kochanski "Ski", Kaylee, Missy, Persie and Timmy.
- Leonie Eileen Duane.
- Serena Dawn Jenkins & Sheba, Comfort, Baby/Angel, Solo, Tiger & the many, many cats

who have loved and lived with the Jenkins family throughout time.
- Charlie, Tinker, Jordan and Tabby.
- Alicia, JB, Davey, and Lexie.
- Viktoria Glasmachers and Timmy
- Jenni Hughes.
- Ares, Artemis, Nyx and Theia.
- Fred, Ginger, Friskie, Nipper, and Edward.
- TrishVK.
- Jamie Dockendorff, Nyx, Pan, & Dragon.
- Sally and Tiger, Grani, Sugieh and Sheelba.
- Samanda S. and Nimbus, Toffee, D'Artagnan, Bandito & Itsy-Bitsy. Plus honorary cats Amigo & Pi.
- Amanda Taylor-Chaisson, Julie, and Cali.
- Kizzia M and Moppet, Mittens & Plié.
- Kit Stubbs, Ph.D., and Charlie, Rosie, Millie & Momo.
- Lolita.
- Mally.
- Alex Coles and Zoe.
- Ryan C, Chase & Nim.
- Catherine Brown and Caesar, Tess, Barney, Cleopatra, Seymour, and Percy.
- Jean Weber and Minou.
- Lianne, Bailey and Kahlua.
- Lauren E. Mitchell, Toby, Pippin, and all the cats who have been, will be, and are.

isn't everyone obsessed with lost media?

a Kickstarter-Exclusive Afterword, mostly about the joy of the published Programme Guide in an age before Wikipedia

by Tansy Rayner Roberts

I was raised on *Upstairs Downstairs, Doctor Who, All Creatures Great and Small, Allo Allo, Blackadder, EastEnders*, and just about every film that ever came out of Pinewood or Ealing Studios.

My mum migrated from Lancashire, England to Tasmania, Australia, in the late 1960s. She embraced many things about Australia, but local TV was not one of them. Thanks to our household's early adoption of VHS technology, I grew up surrounded by videos of British sitcoms, science fiction, costume drama and cheap & cheerful comedy movies, mostly recorded off the ABC late at night.

(I did watch Australian and even US shows, but rarely in company with Mum, who to this day complains about how much shouting occurs in American TV, the same argument she made back then. TV in Other Accents was for after school and Saturday mornings. No wonder I grew up with something that wasn't quite an English accent... but wasn't entirely Australian either.)

Imagine an eccentric uncle who fills his house with arcane collections of antique stamps, or butterflies pinned to felt, or cursed Egyptian coins. Our house was like that, but with every piece of media involving Dirk Bogarde.

Of course, there was *Doctor Who*. From an early age, I was staring at stray black and white episodes of The Space Pirates, or The Tenth Planet. *Doctor Who* was actually a pretty normal thing to be into, when I was a kid in 80s Australia — we had constantly running repeats of Pertwee and Tom Baker on our national broadcaster. Everyone knew what a Dalek was.

(But in my house, thanks to all those dodgy bootlegged tapes my mother traded from the local fan club, we didn't QUITE like *Doctor Who* the way everyone else did. There was nothing casual about the way we did anything.)

To date, I know more random facts about Barbara Windsor from the *Carry On* movies than I know about any modern actor. And I regret nothing.

I've always had collector's brain. It's rough to be a completionist, when you're introduced to *Doctor Who* at a young age. Thanks to the mass destruction/discarding of crucial film canisters in the late 70s, there are so many gaps in the catalogue. Every now and then a new episode gets found! Just enough to whet our hopes for the rest, out there in the world, unwatched.

(Sure, they keep making more of the show, but what about the lost episodes from 1966? Are we supposed to just give up on them?)

I grew up reading Target novelisations of lost stories, and inhaling *Doctor Who Magazine* with all its behind the scenes features. Most of all, I grew up reading the *Doctor Who Programme Guide*, cover to cover. I often read about particular Doctor Who stories before I got to see or hear them, which led to some rather warped first viewing experiences. I've never particularly cared about spoilers — when you're obsessed with a show that lost half its back catalogue before you were born, spoilers are sometimes a best case scenario.

I've met plenty of completionist Classic *Who* fans over the years, especially since the internet rose up to bring us all together. My years in the podcast salt mines of the twenty-first century have allowed me to find many sympathetic ears as we collectively rage about never getting to see all of The Myth Makers, or The Daleks' Master Plan.

The thing that listeners of the *Verity!* podcast might not entirely realise, is that it wasn't just Doctor Who for me. I watched all TV like that. Obsessed with episodes I'd missed, trying desperately to catch the history of seasons that aired before I came along.

(That one time I had a sleepover at my cousin's house and discovered *Days of our Lives* REALLY messed me up in that regard, do you know how much history there is in that show? Then there was *Neighbours*, which didn't start screening in southern Tasmania until they had several seasons of lore under their belt. At least I got to watch *Home and Away* from the beginning — and thanks to repeats when we were living in England, I did it twice.)

I was at least as obsessed with *Grange Hill* as I was with Doctor Who, between the ages of 9 and 15 (cough, possibly and also 45, let's not pretend I ever let go). It was harder, because I didn't know anyone who cared. In any given 80s Australian playground, you could throw a rock and hit a kid who cared about Daleks. But where were the kids who also cared about the epic, awkward never-quite-made-it romance between Ziggy Hargreaves and Georgina Hayes?

Grange Hill, a perfectly normal (but brilliant!) British school show, was first broadcast in 1978, the year I was born. I properly discovered it with Season 8 (1985): introducing Calley, Gonch, Hollo, Ronnie and the iconic Mr Bronson.

There were already 7 seasons I had missed. No way to catch up, of course. No VHS releases in the late 1980s (or as my children always refer to it, the Late-ies). Not even a Wikipedia page to look up old info. As with *Doctor Who*, I found *Grange Hill* novelisations in libraries and second-hand book shops which introduced me to earlier characters and storylines. (Frustratingly, most of the books were actually cool bonus stories, not covering stories from actual episodes. How dare they.)

I managed to stumble across at least one season of the *Grange Hill* spin off, *Tucker's Luck*, featuring the first main character of the show, a rumpled not-quite-bad-boy played by Todd Carty. By the time the tenth anniversary of the show rolled around, I struck gold: a glorious Behind the Scenes anniversary book that provided me with photos, cast info and a production guide. Oh, that production guide.

I can't tell you how many times I re-read that book. Assume at least once or twice a year until Wikipedia was invented. And a few times after that, quite possibly.

Loving *Grange Hill* in the Late-ies required wiles and strategy. In Australia, it always aired in different places, and different times. It might be the sensible 5:30pm time slot after school. Or, if the broadcast gods were being particularly sinister, it might air daily in three episode blocks over a school holiday. Catch it if you can!

Thanks to the release, decades later, of early seasons in DVD box sets, plus that one summer in VERY recent memory when I sat down and watched all the seasons I'd missed on YouTube… I've caught up, finally, with *Grange Hill*.

(In writing this essay, I did literally just learn there is a DVD release of Season 7 that didn't exist last time I was looking… oh no, now I own it…)

Reader, it wasn't just *Grange Hill*.

There was *Upstairs Downstairs*, a show I watched avidly with my mum, though its glorious 5 seasons were over by 1975, and I wasn't born for another 3 years after that. In my memory, it was always on television, there was always a new season, and it lasted for my entire childhood, which can't be correct. (Looking back, the first season was packed with adult content which I definitely absorbed about age 6 or 7. It's all maids hanging themselves, young masters seducing unsuitable women, and suffragettes being force-fed.)

I never realised *Upstairs Downstairs* wasn't a current show — we were well used to getting TV shows many years after they screened in England — but it's entirely possible it was a repeat. In any case, you know the drill by now. I hoarded the novelisations (I still have them!), obsessed over the main characters, and imprinted deeply on the idea of a town house in London full of masters, mistresses, butlers and maids. (See my new gaslamp fantasy series Sparks & Philtres — *House Perilous* in particular wears a coat that is distinctly influenced by 165 Eaton Place.)

I got hold of a DVD box set of *UpDown* a decade or two ago and learned for the first time that I had watched an edited version of the show — Sarah the saucy maid didn't actually leave at the end of the first episode at all! The first 6 episodes had been filmed in black and white due to an ITV strike, and they later went back and remade the first episode from scratch so as to have it in colour. They then filmed 2 alternate endings, to be switched in depending on whether the viewers would be allowed to see the black and white episodes, or skipping ahead.

Yes, I'm still a bit mad about this particular revelation. You might have noticed that the re-filming of a pilot (something often done for a variety of TV production reasons) has wormed its way into this book. Other *UpDown* references in

Time of the Cat include Lady Marjorie's shocking death (off screen) on the Titanic, an idea that came full circle in recent years with the first episode of *Downton Abbey*, sexy stepchild to the long-lamented *UpDown*. I'm assuming it was deliberate homage. Julian Fellowes has the look of a fellow who owns the *UpDown* box set, and has watched all of the black and white episodes.

Cramberleigh, the fictional TV show at the heart of *Time of the Cat*, is an unholy Frankenstein's monster of *UpDown*, *The Forsyte Saga*, *Downton* and many other posh house stories, alongside my more science fictional and spy hijinks loves of the 1960s-70s.

With Gladioli and her creator/performer Joanna Wetland, I intended the most gracious of nods to Jean Marsh, my personal heroine, an icon of British and international screens who not only played three of the all-time best wicked witches of all time (Mombi, Bavmorda and Morgaine) but was also co-creator and writer of both *Upstairs Downstairs* and another period drama that owns real estate inside my head: *The House of Eliot*.

You can't discuss lost media without talking about the physical side of it. As we lurch into a world that is increasingly about the digital and the virtual, it's not all rosy. Whole swathes of quite recent media have been buried at the whim of their networks, never released in physical formats, and sometimes never released as all, shoved into a vault (or burned on a pyre, who can tell) for tax purposes.

So now we have THAT to worry about.

Whenever there's a news story about the precarious nature of digital content, I see friends on Facebook talking with great relief about the massive physical collections they have, of DVDs and Blu-Rays — and even old VHS tapes. Vinyl made a massive comeback over the last decade, and even the trusty cassette walkman has found new fans to devote themselves to the art of fixing a dodgy tape with a pencil.

I still own VHS tapes with which I will not part — I've dumped many over the years, especially once I was able to upgrade my collections of *Buffy*, *Xena* and yes, *Doctor Who*. But even though we don't currently own a VHS player there are some tapes I'm not willing to let go of, despite having more up-to-date versions.

(In case you're wondering how my mother adapted to the digital age, she got heavily into exploring the history of rock music when David Bowie died, and now at age 80 owns an extraordinary physical media collection of... let's just say more DVDs and CDs than one should comfortably fit into a very small cottage. I don't know how she does it. There's only so much 'being clever with cupboard space' that makes sense. Clearly she does have a TARDIS somewhere.)

They say the golden age of science fiction is twelve, and the science fiction I discovered at age 12 was *Blake's 7*. I adored this grim, sarcastic dystopia, though my early introduction was fragmented. At first I was only able to watch the episodes my friend Erika had in her parents' collection — the telemovie edits of Season 1, and the nearly complete Season 4 recorded from TV on Betamax.

I fell hard. I was obsessed. Soon, I had my own source — a babysitting gig with one of my mum's old *Doctor Who* fan club friends, who had every episode of *Blake's 7* on their shelves. To this day it's the best job I've ever had. I arrived after the children were asleep, and got to stay for 3-4 hours, watching anything I wanted. The only bad part was agonising over which episodes to choose!

VHS releases for *Blake's 7* did emerge around that time, and I purchased many them (I think that's where the babysitting money went) but oh, I *still* resent how expensive they were. $30, I swear they were $30 each (in 1990!!), and every tape only contained TWO episodes. I picked and chose carefully, based on my trusty Programme Guide. Yes, I had a *Blake's 7* Programme Guide too. And yes, I still own it. You don't throw things like that away. What if the internet goes down and we fall into our own grim dystopia? How will I be able to check which Season 2 episode featured John Leeson wearing a chandelier on his head?[1]

I still own those tapes. I will never throw them away, even though I no longer have anything to play them on. You've heard of the sunk cost fallacy? Bury my ashes with Children of Auron/Rumours of Death, still bearing their price tag.

I was a uni student when I fell in love with *The Forsyte Saga*. It was on TV in the early 00's, and I liked it so much that I read the book. I then liked the book so much that one of my officemates, upon inheriting random boxes of vintage books from a relative, presented me with a leather-bound set on the grounds that no one would appreciate them more.

(More than fair.)

It wasn't quite enough. I'm a completionist, after all. While I'd seen the whole show, and read the books (which go further than the show, all the way past the characters I actually cared about, and beyond the lives of their children), there was still one version waiting for me, and I wouldn't rest until I had watched it.

The original version of *The Forsyte Saga* was kind of

famous, in the history of British television. Filmed in 1967, it had substantial overlap with many of the old shows I loved, though it had clearly avoided me by not being prominently repeated on the ABC during the Eighties.

The 26 episode run of *The Forsyte Saga*, when repeated on BBC1 in 1968, was one of the most popular TV serials of all time. Sunday nights came to a standstill over it. It was one of the last major drama serials to be made in England in black and white.

That kind of popularity doesn't exist any more. The world's population has risen dramatically since 1968, but the idea of a country rolling to a standstill to all watch the same TV show at exactly the same time... short of a coronation, the Olympics or a major news disaster, it really doesn't happen.

The closest equivalent is when a hugely popular show drops a new season on a streaming network — but for every diehard fan who binges the whole of Season 4 of *Sex Education* or Season 1 of *The Sandman* on drop day, there's another who has to wait for the weekend, another who can only manage to watch one episode a week, and another who has to wait until their partner or kids are in the mood before they even start... not to mention all the viewers who aren't currently subscribed to the relevant streaming network, and won't switch over until they've finished their Farscape marathon on Prime.

Anyway, I watched the 60s version of *The Forsyte Saga* from the university library, all 26 episodes of rather slow and stilted but excellent steamy family drama in black and white.[2] (No slower than Tomb of the Cybermen, despite all the long dresses and front parlours.)

Later, when I saw my opportunity, I bought my own copy on DVD just in case I need to watch it again. And last Christmas, despite the fact that Wikipedia exists, I bought myself a small press edition of the Programme Guide of *The Forsyte Saga*.

When the end times come upon us, and the digital content all disappears along with the Wi-fi, we survivors will be hanging out our shingle as to what resources we can offer to our neighbours and friends, in trade for survival.

You heard it here first. I'm the one with all the Programme Guides of TV shows you won't be able to watch.

So, there's a little insight into the inside of my brain, and my relationship with media. Honestly, writing it all down like this is a little confronting. But the end result is a brain that seems to be able to produce books, so I won't worry about it too much.

I didn't study Media at university. That would work well for the narrative or this essay, wouldn't it? Instead, I fell a tiny bit too deep into the Classics Department (oh no, Tansy got obsessed with something niche, how out of character!) and ended up with a doctorate.

Historical research was, of course, what I'd been doing all along. Collecting old *Grange Hill* novelisations in the hopes of finding out more about the inner thoughts of Tricia Yates isn't that different from poking at old coins to try to figure out what people thought about Roman empresses while they were alive.

History, especially the history of anyone who wasn't a big name, wealthy white male aristocrat, is mostly about blank spaces. It's about the absence of information, occasionally scattered with tiny, unreliable crumbs.

It's also full of questions, and biases, and assumptions, and mistakes.

Isn't Everyone Obsessed with Lost Media?

History is a messy road, scattered with examples of lost media.

Queen Victoria's youngest daughter destroyed piles of her letters and journal entries. No one ever found Agrippina the Younger's memoir/family history, which isn't all that surprising considering her son had her murdered. Medieval monks left us with nothing but fragments of Sappho's beautiful, bisexual love poetry. 70% of all silent movies ever made are lost, and that percentage is much higher outside English-speaking countries. The Yongle Encyclopedia of the Ming Dynasty was the largest known general encyclopaedia in the world before Wikipedia surpassed it… but most of it was lost or destroyed in the late nineteenth century.

Sometimes we know what's missing, thanks to sources discussing them, and the spaces they leave behind. Sometimes we're not sure — we only think they *might* exist, and they take on a mythic status.

Were *The Iliad* and *The Odyssey* part of a larger myth cycle?

Does anyone really know what was in the Library of Alexandria, and what was destroyed (which time) with it?

Julius Caesar's early love poetry: do we think it was likely awesome or awful? (Would anyone have told him if it was bad??)

Did Ovid ever intend to cover the other half of the calendar in *Fasti 2: Saturnalia Booglaloo?*

I didn't mean to write another time travel book. Short of being asked to write a *Doctor Who* tie-in novel (and no one's ever asked me!) I never thought I'd want to. Time travel has always been a bit too sciencey for me — I love reading the stories, but writing them? There'd be so much planning. So much admin. **So many rules.**

I did it once with *Liquid Gold*, my second ever novel, before I knew better. And I hit so many of my favourite tropes then: going back to see deceased parents in their youth, looking forward to get spoilers about future relationships & children, and Guess Which Character Becomes a Futuristic Despot? I didn't need to do it again.

Then I tripped and fell into a cat wearing a Viking hat with two horns...

With *Time of the Cat* I have been inspired by many things, not only the TV shows I obsessed about in my youth. Connie Willis' *To Say Nothing of the Dog* had a huge impact on me, as did Kage Baker's Company novels and stories. Both of them looked at the idea that time travel could be used by historians or archaeologists: to preserve and learn about the past, to save lost treasures. I've never liked the idea of time travel as something that is scary, or dangerous, or about changing history. *Doctor Who* taught me that time travel was for wild, shameless adventuring and tourism... but Connie Willis and Kage Baker taught me that it could be a world inhabited by batty professors, cranky research assistants and book nerds.

While not exactly time travel, I also want to give a shout out to Kim Newman's *Diogenes Club* books, which delighted me with their pastiche of various favourite kinds of media, while presenting the twentieth century as a far more stylish version of itself than witnesses might suppose.

Everything I do is in some way informed by the sheer amount of *Doctor Who* et. al trivia that lodged itself in my brain at an early age. All that British telly, all those old movies, all those actors. I recently started rewatching a bunch of movies I remembered from my childhood — farce comedies, for the most part, all boobs and innuendo and comedy old men's trousers falling off slowly while Ronnie Corbett looks panicked. I'd resisted the urge for so long, expecting to find such a wall of institutionalised sexism that I wouldn't be able to get through it. (I still have not embarked upon the epic *Carry On* rewatch I've been tempted by for over a decade, mostly because part of my brain tells me it should be a podcast, and I don't think I want anyone to witness what I find in those archives!)

What I loved about rewatching these old movies, was the actors. It was recognising the faces of Valerie Leon and Margaret Nolan. Watching Beryl Reid at her pinnacle of 'interfering matriarch' performances. Admiring the comic timing of Katy Manning and Joanna Lumley. Recognising Ian Ogilvy from somewhere, assuming he MUST have been in *Doctor Who*, only to figure out he was instead a stray husband in *UpDown*. Spotting young Donald Sinden in the *Doctor* movies, and remembering how the first time I saw him perform was as an old man in a sitcom, alongside Windsor Davies.

Watching old TV and movies is the closest we actually get to time travel. It may well be my favourite method.

I'm 45 and I don't have a memory as sharp as I did when I was 10. I struggle to remember names of actors and even acquaintances these days. Archiving their details in the old grey matter doesn't come as easily as it used to.

But you show me Joan Sims, I know she's Joan Sims. I still connect 1960s actors to the roles they've played up and down the Home Counties, even when they turn up in a 90s sitcom, or as the surprise voice of the Sorting Hat.

I used to know every tramp, butler and minor Time Lord by name.

Mark Williams isn't Father Brown to me, or even Mr

Weasley... he's Petersen from *Red Dwarf*. Julie Walters I remember from a film called *She'll Be Wearing Pink Pyjamas*. Pauline Collins will always be Sarah from *UpDown* with a side order of Shirley Valentine — it was decades before I got to see her 1960s turn in *Doctor Who* as the 'not-quite-but almost-companion' Samantha Briggs. When I spotted her as Queen Victoria in New Who... it was Sarah I thought of first.

I love creating imaginary media. My *Belladonna U* series is about fannish magical students, and I took great love and care in creating TV shows, RPGs and other media for them to obsess over. What counts as geeky when you're living in a fantasy world already?

When it came to *Cramberleigh*, I didn't just create three decades of lore about a lost TV show (though, I did — see the Programme Guide in this volume). I also created the fandom. One of my favourite things about getting older is seeing younger generations fall in love with old media, just like I did as a kid.[3] (Even if it's a little confronting to see what counts as "old" media these days...) Old shows get rediscovered, thanks to streaming access, or availability on YouTube. Fandoms grow.

Is it unlikely that, two centuries in the future, a university campus full of enthusiastic young time travellers would become obsessed with a TV show they've never actually seen before thanks to it being erased in the late 80s? That they would devote a huge part of their professional and leisure time to tracking and reclaiming those episodes?

If anything, that's the least unlikely element of *Time of the Cat*. The history of *Doctor Who* fandom — sixty years, I'm writing this a month before the anniversary — is packed with wild and unlikely obsessives, a chaotic creative force of fans who didn't just admire their favourite show, or create art in its honour… they set out to reclaim it, rebuild it, to keep it alive whenever it seemed to be gasping for air, or on the verge of extinction.

It's about loving a TV show so much, it's not enough to sit there and watch it. You want to capture it, record it, pin it to a wall. You want to learn all about what makes it tick. And if it disappears… you want to make more of it yourself, or literally set out to track down the pieces of what was lost.

Time of the Cat is a book about love. It's about an obsessive, mildly unhealthy but basically wholesome love affair between a university and a lost TV show.

It may be one of the most niche novels I've ever or will ever write.

Many authors say that they write for themselves, not an audience. I've often considered that to be true for myself. But I've never done it quite so… shamelessly before. So indulgently.

When I taught creative writing, I used to encourage students to create a List of Awesome which I referred to as their cultural stash. Those things you love without reservation. Your obsessions, your faves, your "guilty" pleasures. If you fill your stories with items from your list, I told my students, you'll not only stay engaged enough to write all the way to the end… your passion will excite readers, no matter what form that passion takes.

So. That's what I've done.

And I added talking cats.[4]

Tansy Rayner Roberts,
October 2023

1. I don't need to check. It was *Gambit*.
2. Many references to this particular adaptation of *Forsyte* have wormed their way into *Time of the Cat*, of course, including the naming of several characters. I'm particularly proud of the Fleur Shropshire reference, but there's also an Irene, a Soames and Jolyon kicking about. More than anything, *The Forsyte Saga* is the story of a house that means different things to different generations, in quite a different but overlapping way to the houses centred in *UpDown* and *Downton*.
3. My kids don't love the things that I loved in the same way — and when they do, it's rarely because of my influence, but more often because my mum showed them a VHS tape of *Red Dwarf* or *Maid Marian and Her Merry Men*...
4. This afterword is to be included exclusively in the Kickstarter editions of *Time of the Cat*. You possibly didn't expect it to include nearly 4000 words of rambling about *Grange Hill* and *Upstairs Downstairs*, but... it's me. What else could you possibly have expected?

about the author

Tansy Rayner Roberts is an award-winning Australian science fiction and fantasy author. She has been a co-host of the epic all-female Doctor Who podcast *Verity!* for more than a decade. Tansy would 100% use time travel to rescue Agrippina's family memoir, the unedited letters of Queen Victoria, and all the missing episodes of The Daleks' Master Plan. She lives with her family in Tasmania.

- Listen to Tansy on Sheep Might Fly, a podcast where she reads aloud her stories as audio serials.
- Read Tansy's stories before anyone else when you pledge to her Patreon.
- What tea is Tansy drinking? Find out when you subscribe to her excellent newsletter: tinyurl.com/tansyrr
- Follow Tansy on Bookbub so you never miss a release.

facebook.com/TansyRRoberts
instagram.com/tansyrr
patreon.com/tansyrr
bookbub.com/authors/tansy-rayner-roberts

also by tansy rayner roberts

TEACUP MAGIC

Tea & Sympathetic Magic

The Frost Fair Affair

Spellcracker's Honeymoon

Lady Liesl's Seaside Surprise

Have Spirit, Will Duchess

BELLADONNA U

Unreal Alchemy

Holiday Brew

Practical Witching

SPARKS & PHILTRES

Gate Sinister

House Perilous

THE CREATURE COURT

Power & Majesty

The Shattered City

Reign of Beasts

Cabaret of Monsters

MUSKETEER SPACE

Musketeer Space

Joyeux

Castle Charming

Castle Ever After

Gorgons Deserve Nice Things

Love & Romanpunk

Girl Reporter

Merry Happy Valkyrie

Splashdance Silver

Liquid Gold

Ink Black Magic

NON-FICTION & ESSAYS

Pratchett's Women: Unauthorised Essays

From Baby Brain to Writer Brain: Writing Through A World Of Parenting Distractions

It's Raining Musketeers

AS EDITOR

Mother of Invention (with Rivqa Rafael)

Cranky Ladies of History (with Tehani Croft)

Adventures Across Space and Time: A Doctor Who Reader (with Paul Booth, Matt Hills & Joy Piedmont)